someday

also by david levithan

someday

david levithan

alfred a. knopf
new york

THIS IS A BORZOI BOOK PUBLISHED BY ALFRED A. KNOPF

All rights reserved. Published in the United States by Alfred A. Knopf, an imprint of Random House Children's Books, a division of Penguin Random House LLC, New York.

Knopf, Borzoi Books, and the colophon are registered trademarks of Penguin Random House LLC.

Visit us on the Web! GetUnderlined.com

Educators and librarians, for a variety of teaching tools, visit us at RHTeachersLibrarians.com

Library of Congress Cataloging-in-Publication Data is available upon request. ISBN 978-0-399-55305-9 (trade) — ISBN 978-0-399-55306-6 (lib. bdg.) — ISBN 978-0-399-55307-3 (ebook)

Composite jacket art used under license from Shutterstock.com

The text of this book is set in 11.35-point Goudy Old Style MT Std.

Printed in the United States of America
October 2018
10 9 8 7 6 5 4 3 2 1

First Edition

For Hailey
(May you find happiness every day)

RHIANNON

Every time the doorbell rings, I think it might be A. Every time someone looks at me for a beat too long. Every time a message arrives in my inbox. Every time the phone displays a number I don't know. For a second or two, I fool myself into believing.

It's hard to remember someone when you don't know what they look like. Because A changes from day to day, it's impossible to choose a memory and have it mean more than that single day. No matter how I picture A, it's not going to be what A looks like now. I remember A as a boy and as a girl, as tall and short, skin and hair all different colors. A blur. But the blur takes the shape of how A made me feel, and that may be the most accurate shape of all.

A has been gone a month. I should be used to it. But how can there be any separation when A is in so many of my thoughts? Isn't that as close as you can get to another person, to have them constantly inside your head?

As I'm thinking all these things, feeling all these things, I can't let any of them show. Look at me and you will see: A girl who has finally buried the remains of her last bad relationship. A girl with a great new boyfriend. A girl with friends who support her and a family that isn't more annoying than any other family. You will not see anything missing—you will not sense the part of her that's been left inside someone else. Maybe if you look into her eyes long enough and know what

1

to look for. But the point is: The person who knew how to look at me like that is gone.

My boyfriend, Alexander, knows there's something I'm not telling him, but he's not the kind of guy who wants to know everything. He gives me space. He tells me it's fine to take things slow. I can tell that he's fallen for me, that he really wants this to work. I want it to work, too.

But I also want A.

Even if we can't be together. Even if we're no longer near each other. Even if all I get is a *hello*, and not even a *how are you?*—I want to know where A is, and that A thinks of me at least some of the time. Even if it means nothing now, I want to know it meant something once.

The doorbell rings. I am the only one home. My thoughts race to A—I allow myself to picture the stranger at the door who isn't really a stranger. I imagine the light in his eyes, or maybe her eyes. I imagine A saying a solution has been found, a way has been devised to stay in the same body for longer than a single day without hurting anyone.

"Coming!" I yell out. I'm stupidly nervous as I get to the door and throw it open.

The boy I find there is familiar, but at first I don't recognize him.

"Are you Rhiannon?" he asks.

As I nod, I'm realizing who he is.

"Nathan?" I say.

Now he's surprised, too.

"I know you, don't I?" he asks.

I answer honestly. "It depends on what you remember."

I know this is dangerous ground. Nathan is not supposed to remember the day that A was in his body, borrowing his life. He is not supposed to remember the way he and I danced in a basement, or anything that happened after.

"It was your name," he says. "I kept thinking your name. Like when you wake up from a dream and there's only one part you can remember? That's what your name was. So I went online and checked out all the Rhiannons who live near me. When I saw your picture . . . I felt like I'd seen you before. But I couldn't remember where or when." His hands are starting to shake. "What happened? If you have any idea what I'm talking about, can you *please* tell me what happened? I only have pieces. . . ."

What kind of rational person would ever believe the truth? Who wouldn't laugh when someone tells them it's possible to move from one body to another? That's how I reacted at first.

The only reason I stopped being rational was because something irrational happened to me. And I knew it.

I can see that Nathan knows it, too. Still, I warn him, "You're not going to believe me."

"You'd be amazed at what I can believe at this point," he replies.

I know I need to be careful. I know there's no going back once the story is out. I know he might not be trustworthy.

But A is gone. A can't be hurt by this. And I . . . I need to tell someone. I need to share this with someone who at least partly deserves to hear it.

So I let Nathan in. I sit him down.

I tell him as much of the truth as I can.

NATHAN

By my calculations, if you live to be eighty years old, you end up being alive for 29,220 days. And you're likely to live much longer than those 29,220 days.

So one day shouldn't matter.

Especially if it's a day you can't remember. I mean, I have plenty of days I can't remember. Most days are days I can't remember, once I get a month or two away from them.

What was I up to on October 29th? Or September 7th? Well, I guess I woke up at home. I went to school. I saw my friends. I imagine I ate breakfast, lunch, and dinner, though I couldn't tell you any of the more intimate details.

Most of our memory is based on educated guesswork. And our memory loses days all the time.

But it's weirder and scarier if it's a day you lose *as it's happening*. A day when you wake up the next morning and have no idea where you've been or what you've done. A day that's a total blank.

When you have a day like that, it's a hole in your life, and as much as you're trying to pretend it's not there, you can't help but poke it, probe it. Because even though it's empty, you can still feel something when you touch its sides.

I woke up on the side of the road.

Passed out, the police said.

Drunk, they thought. Then they tested and saw I wasn't.

Out too late, they said. When they brought me home, they told my parents I needed to watch myself.

But I don't drink. I don't stay out late.

It didn't make any sense.

It was like I'd been possessed. And soon that was the story. *The devil made me do it.*

Only in this case, the devil had an email address. And when I emailed him, he swore he wasn't the devil.

It got really weird. This reverend got involved. Talked to my parents about killing my demons. I wanted to believe him, because it's easier to believe that an empty space is an evil space. We don't want to be helpless, so we create things to fight. Only my fight never got started. I stopped believing the reverend after he began to act like *he* was the evil one, luring this girl to my house and attacking her. He didn't even explain himself after I helped her escape. He said he'd needed to talk to her. Then he was gone.

Meanwhile, the person who'd taken my life for a day— they said they bounced from body to body, day after day. I didn't know how to believe that. I had more questions.

But then that person was gone, too. And I was left with this blank space where a day of my life used to be.

But blank is never really blank. Take a blank sheet of paper. Yeah, there's no writing on it. Nothing for you to read. But then hold it really close. Stare at it for a long time. You'll start to see patterns there. You'll start to see shapes and gradations and distortions. Hold it up to the light and you'll see even more. You'll see a whole topography within the blankness. And sometimes, if you look really carefully, you'll start to see a word.

For me, that word was *Rhiannon.*

I had no idea what it meant. I had no idea why I was remembering it. But it was there in the depth of the blank space.

The next part was easy. There were only three Rhiannons within a fifty-mile radius. One of them was near my age. And she looked familiar, though I couldn't have explained why.

The hard part was figuring out what to do with this information. I had no idea what I would say to her. *I remember you but I don't understand why.* That sounded weird. And I was tired of having everyone look at me like I was weird.

But now here I am. I've come over to her house, because not going over to her house was killing me. I ring her doorbell. And from the minute she sees me, she knows exactly who I am.

I'm not prepared for that.

I'm also not prepared for everything she tells me, and how easily she says it. It's almost like she's grateful to tell me what she knows, like I'm the one doing her the favor. But I'm just as grateful. All along, we've been partners at the jigsaw, and it's only now that we're realizing how some of the pieces fit. She's telling me the person who talked to me, the person who took that day from me and lived my life before leaving me at the side of the road, is named A. I tell her that, yeah, I met A two days in a row, when he/she was calling himself/herself Andrew and was in the bodies of two different girls, two days in a row. Rhiannon doesn't seem surprised. But I'm damn surprised to be talking to someone who hears what I have to say and believes all of it. Rhiannon tells me A was really sorry about what happened with me—and from the way she apologizes on A's behalf, I realize that, whoa, she is *totally in love* with this person who goes from body to body. The hole A's left in her life is even bigger than the one in mine. I lost a day. She's lost more than that.

"You must think I'm crazy," she says to me when she's done.

How can I convey to her that I've had the same thought about a million times over the past couple months? How can I get across that when weird things—when *really* weird things— happen to you, it suddenly opens you up into believing all these other really weird things could be true?

"I think what happened to us is crazy," I tell her. "But that's not us."

I fill her in on the parts I know—about how Reverend Poole said I'd been possessed by the devil, and that there were other people who'd had the same thing happen to them all around the world. He told me I wasn't alone, which was the thing I most wanted to hear. The whole time, though, he was using me—and when I finally figured that out, he turned on me. He said I had no idea what I was involved in. He told me I'd ruined my only chance of knowing what was wrong with me. I'd have no future, because part of me would always be stuck in the past.

I'm sixteen years old. Having an adult yell these things at me was hard, even as I also felt it was, you know, *wrong*. He was the only person who'd believed me, and because of that, I'd believed him in return. But now I couldn't. Because what he was doing was cursing me.

I didn't know what to say. I guess I thought I'd have an- other chance, that he'd come back and we'd talk it over. I thought he was getting something out of helping me. But as I said, he was just using me. Once he was gone, that was it.

I tell all this to Rhiannon as we sit at her kitchen table.

"You haven't heard from him at all?" she asks.

I shake my head, then ask back, "And you haven't heard from A?"

I can see how much it hurts her to say no. I'll be honest— I've never had a girlfriend, and I've definitely never been in love. But I've been around enough people in love to know what one of them looks like. A's disappeared, but her love hasn't.

"A has to be out there somewhere," I say.

"I'm sick of waiting," she responds.

"Then let's look," I tell her.

There has to be a way.

X

To stay in a body, you must take that body over.

To take a body over, you must kill the person inside.

It is not an easy thing to do, to assert your own self over the self that exists in the body, to smother it until it is no longer there. But it can be done.

I stare down at the body in the bed. It is rare for me to have done so much damage, so I'm fascinated by the result. The regular response to a dead body is to close its eyes, but I prefer them open. That way I can study what's missing.

Here is the face I have seen in the mirror for the past few months. Anderson Poole, age fifty-eight. When I look into his eyes, they are only eyes, no more expressive than his dead fingers or his dead nose. The first time this happened, I thought there would be an aftercurrent of life—some element to enable the feeble and the desperate to believe that the spirit that had once been inside was now somewhere else, instead of completely annihilated. But all I see is utter emptiness.

There is no reason for me to be here. At any moment, the hotel management will overrule the DO NOT DISTURB sign and come in to find the reverend in a state far beyond disturbance. *He died of natural causes,* the inquest will conclude. *His mind failed. The rest of the body followed.*

Nobody will know I was here. Nobody will know that the mind failed because I cut the wires.

9

It was time to move on. I was getting bored. Anderson Poole was no longer useful.

I am in a younger body now. A college student who will not be attending class much longer. I feel stronger in this body. More attractive. I like that. Nobody ever looked at Anderson Poole as he walked down the street. It was his position as a reverend that they revered. That was the reason they listened to him.

"You came so close," I say to him, my new hand closing his left eye, then opening it again. "You almost had him. But you scared him away."

Poole does not respond; I am not expecting him to.

The phone rings. No doubt the front desk, giving him one last chance.

I have to go soon. I cannot be here when the maid finds him. Screams. Prays. Calls the police.

Nobody will mourn him. He has no family left. He had a few friends, but as I choked off his memories and made his decisions for him, the friends fell away. His death will cause no great disruption in anyone else's life. I knew this from the start. I am not heartless, after all.

It is important for me to come back and see the body. I don't have to, and sometimes I can't. But I try. It's not to pay respects. The body can't accept any respects—it's dead. By seeing what a body looks like without a life inside, I get a sense of what I am, what I bring.

I would like to compare notes on this with someone else like me. I want to sit down with him and discuss the act of being a life without being a body. I want to make my brethren understand the power we have, and how we can use that power. I want my history recorded in someone else's thoughts.

Poor Anderson Poole. When I started with him, I learned everything there was to know about him. I used that. Then I dismantled it bit by bit. He no longer had his own memories—just the memories I had *about* him. Now that we are separate, I will make no effort to retain those memories. His life, for all practical purposes, will vanish.

Were I to thank him now, it would be for being so weak, so pliable. I take one last look in his eyes, witness their useless stare.

How vulnerable it makes you, to depend on a body.

How much better to never rely on any single one.

A

Day 6065

Life is harder when you have someone to miss.

I wake up in a suburb of Denver and feel like I am living in a suburb of my own life. The alarm goes off and I want to sleep.

But I have a responsibility. An obligation. So I get out of bed. I figure I am in the body and the life of a girl named Danielle. I get dressed. I try to avoid imagining what Rhiannon is doing. Two hours' time difference. Two hours and a world away.

I have proven myself right, but in the wrong way. I always knew that connection was dangerous, that connection would drag me down, because connection is impossible for me in a lasting way. Yes, a line can be drawn between any two points . . . but not if one of the points disappears every day.

My only consolation is that it would have been worse if the connection had been given more time to take hold. It would have hurt more. I have to hope she's happy, because if she's happy, then my own unhappiness is worth it.

I never wanted to have these kinds of thoughts. I never wanted to look back in this way. Before, I was able to move on. Before, I did not feel that any part of me was left behind when the day was done. Before, I did not think of my life as being anywhere other than where I was at that given moment.

I try to focus on the lives I am in, the lives I am borrowing

12

for a day. I try to lose myself in their to-do lists, their home-work, their squabbles, their sleep.

It doesn't work.

Danielle is taciturn today. She barely responds when her mother asks her questions on the way to school. She nods along to her friends, but if they were to stop and ask her what they'd just said, she'd be in trouble. Her best friend giggles when a certain boy passes, but Danielle (I) doesn't (don't) even bother to recall his name.

I walk through the halls. I try not to pay too much atten-tion, try not to read the stories unfolding on the faces of the people around me, the poetry of their gestures and balladry of those who walk alone. It's not that I find them boring. No, it's the opposite—everyone is too interesting to me now, be-cause I know more about how they feel, what it's like to care about the life you're in and the other people around you.

Two days ago, I stayed home and played a video game for most of the day. After about six hours, I had gotten to the top level. Once I reached the end of the game, I felt a momentary exhilaration. Then . . . a sadness. Because it was done now. I could go back to the start and try again. I could find things I'd missed the first time around. But it would still come to an end. I would still reach the point where I couldn't go any further.

That is my life now. Replaying a game I feel I've already won, without any sense that it means anything anymore to get to the next levels. Killing time, so all I'm left with is time that's dead.

I know Danielle does not deserve this. I am constantly apologizing to her as she stumbles through school, barely pay-ing attention to what the teachers are saying. I rally in English class, when there's a quiz on chapters seven through ten of *Jane Eyre*. I don't want her to fail.

It's hardest when I'm by a computer. Such a brutal portal. I know, if I wanted to, I could see Rhiannon at any time. I could *reach* Rhiannon at any time. Maybe not instantly, but eventually. I know the comfort I would take from her. But I also know that after a certain point, after I took and took and took, she wouldn't have any comfort left. Any promise I made to her would be worthless, no matter how much of my own worth I put into it. Any attention she gave me would be a distraction from the reality of her life, not a reality in itself.

I can't do that to her. I can't string her along with hope. I will always change. I will always be impossible to love.

It's not like there's anyone I can talk to about this. It's not like I can pull aside Danielle's best friend—Hy, short for Hyacinth—and say, *I'm not myself today . . . and this is why.* I can't pull back the curtain, because in terms of Danielle's life, I *am* the curtain, the thing that is getting in the way.

I never used to wonder if I was the only one who lived like this. I never thought to look for others. *I am just like you,* Poole intimated. But I knew that even if he also moved from body to body, life to life, what he did within those bodies was *not* like what I chose to do. He wanted to draw me close, to tell me secrets. But I didn't want to hear them, not if they led to dereliction and damage.

That's why I ran. To end things before I could ruin them.

I've been running ever since. Not in a geographical sense—I have stayed near Denver for almost a month. But I am always seeing myself in relation to the place I'm getting away from, not in relation to anywhere I'm going toward.

I am not going toward anything.

I just live.

After school, Danielle and her friends go downtown to shop. They're not looking for anything in particular. It's just something to do.

I follow along. If I'm asked my opinion, I give it, but in as noncommittal a way as possible. I tell Hy I'm sleepy. She says we should go to City of Saints, the local coffee shop. I have no way to tell her that I don't particularly want to wake up right now.

When Rhiannon was in my life, everything was a rush. I think about driving to get coffee with her, driving to see her again, how scared I was that each day would be the last day she'd like me, and how excited I was when this didn't prove to be true. I picture her kissing me hello, the welcome in her eyes.

I hear the scream as a hand grabs on to my shoulder and violently pulls me back. I realize that the scream was Danielle's name, and the hand belongs to Hy, and the truck I was about to step in front of is honking as it pushes past. Hy is saying "Oh my God" over and over and one of Danielle's other friends is saying "That was close" and a third friend is saying "Wow, I guess you really *do* need that coffee"—making a joke that nobody's finding funny. Danielle's heart is now, after the fact, pounding with fear.

"I'm so sorry," I say. "I am so, so sorry."

Hy tells me it's alright, because she thinks I'm apologizing to her. But I'm not. I'm apologizing to Danielle once again.

I wasn't paying attention.

I must always pay attention.

The other friends are calling Hy a hero. The light changes, and we cross the street. I'm still a little shaky. Hy puts her arm around me, tells me it's okay. Everything's fine.

"I'm buying your coffee," I tell her.

She doesn't argue with that.

The rest of the day, I stay present.

This is enough. Danielle's friends and family don't mind if she's quiet, as long as they can feel she's there. I listen to what they have to say. I try to store it away, and hope I'm storing it where Danielle will be able to find it. Hy thinks her crush on someone named France is getting out of control. Chaundra is inclined to agree. Holly is worried about her brother. Danielle's mother is worried that her boss is on the way out. Danielle's father is worried that the Broncos are going to screw up their season. Danielle's sister is working on a project about lizards.

These people think Danielle is here. They think she is the one who is listening. I used to get satisfaction from playing my part well, never letting anyone realize I was, in fact, an actor. It didn't occur to me that I would ever let anyone see beneath the act, that there would ever be someone who saw me as a me. Nobody did. Nobody until Rhiannon. Nobody since Rhiannon.

I am lost in here.

I am lost, and I can't ignore the most dangerous question of all:

What if I want to be found?

A

Day 6076

I am woken one Saturday morning by a text:

On my way. You better be up.

I imagine that even when you sleep in the same bed night after night, in familiar sheets surrounded by familiar walls, there is still a profound dislocation at the moment of waking. You grasp first to figure out where you are, then reach for who you are. With me, this becomes confused. Where I am and who I am are essentially the same thing.

This morning I am Marco. I use his muscle memory to unlock his phone even as I'm figuring out his name. I am typing *Just getting up. How long 'til you're here?* before I can figure out who Manny, the person I'm texting, is.

10 min. Didn't you set your alarm? I told you to set your alarm!

Marco did not set his alarm. I never sleep through alarms.

Stop texting, I reply. *Drive.*

Shut up. At a light. Be ready in 9.

I try to wash away the mental fog in the shower, but I only get a partial clearing. Manny is Marco's best friend. I can access memories of him from when he was tiny, so they must be lifelong friends. Today's a big day for them—somehow I know it's important to get up and get ready. But I'm not entirely sure why.

It's 9:04—not that early. I can't tell whether there are other people in the house, still asleep, or whether I'm the only one

17

around. I don't have time to check—I can see Manny's car pulling up to the curb. He doesn't honk. He just waits.

I wave through the window, find my wallet, and head out of my room, out the front door.

Manny laughs when I get in the car.

"What?" I ask.

"I swear to God, if you didn't have me as your alarm, you'd miss your entire life. You got the money?"

Even though Marco's wallet is in my pocket, I have a feeling the answer's no. The mind is weird this way: Without knowing how much money is actually in the wallet, I know it's not the amount Manny's talking about.

"Shit," I say.

Manny shakes his head. "I'm gonna start charging your parents for babysitting, you dumbass. Let's try this again."

"One sec," I promise. Then I'm out of the car and back through the front door, which I forgot to lock behind me. When I get to Marco's room, I'm momentarily stymied.

Where's the money? I ask him.

And just like that, I know to look for the shoebox under the bed, where there's a wad of cash waiting for me.

What's this for? I ask again.

But this time, nada. Some personal facts are closer to the surface than others.

When I get back to the car, Manny pretends he's been napping.

"I haven't been gone that long," I tell him.

"You, my friend, are lucky I worked an extra fifteen minutes of fuck-up time into the schedule. We've been waiting for months for this, man. Leave your dumbassery in the backyard, okay?"

Somehow Manny makes *dumbassery* a term of affection; he's amused by my delays, not angered.

18

"So what have you been up to since the last time I saw you?" I ask. This is one of the many Careful Questions I have in my arsenal.

"Well, it's been a fucking lonely ten hours, but somehow I made it through," Manny replies. "I'm so excited for you to meet Heller after all the hype. The guy's shit is for real, you know? I still can't believe he's doing us."

"Unreal," I say. "Completely unreal."

"Ric's gonna be floored. I mean, his cobra is the bomb, but what Heller's gonna do to us is going to make that cobra look like a *worm*, amiright?"

"So right."

I really need to get in the game here. Best friends are like family members when they talk—the shared-history shorthand is a beast for me to decode. I latch on where I can—in this case, I know Ric is Manny's brother. And it isn't much of a jump from there to recall the cobra tattoo on his arm, to know that's what Manny is talking about. Which means, as I clue in, that Heller must be a tattoo artist. And Marco and Manny must be going for tattoos. Their first tattoos.

Now I understand why Manny is so excited. This *is* a big day for them.

I can see the narcotic effect the expectation is having on Manny; he's smiling at what's going to happen a short while from now, buzzing on the trajectory that leads from now to then.

"Have you decided which one yet?" he asks. Then he doesn't give Marco any time to answer, saying, "No—wait 'til we get there. Surprise me."

"That's easy enough to do," I tell him.

"Just DON'T WUSS OUT!" He punches me on the arm playfully. "I swear, the pain is going to be worth it. And I'll be there the whole time. Whatever you do, stay in the chair, right?"

Is he saying this because he senses my own hesitation, or because of a history of hesitation on Marco's part? I suspect it's because of Marco, but I worry it's because of me.

Manny talks some more about when Ric got his tattoo, and how he kept taking the bandage off to show it to everyone, and how it came so damn close to getting infected. In trying to get Marco to remember this, I see all kinds of other memories instead. Ric and Manny bringing me to the beach, Manny's bathing suit a junior version of Ric's. Me and Manny sitting on his front porch, waiting for his mom to get home, setting our Pokémon cards out, swapping the doubles. More recently: Manny kissing a girl at a party while another girl talked to me and tried to get my attention. Manny throwing chicken nuggets at me and me throwing them back, the same birthday lunch we've had for as long as Marco can remember. Whichever of us is the birthday boy always gets a Happy Meal.

I get caught up in the times they've had together, and Manny lets me get caught. I'm not sure how long we drive before we pull up to a house and Manny says, "This is it."

I've never gotten a tattoo before. I was expecting the tattoo place to be a storefront in a strip mall, neon letters spelling out T-A-T-T-O-O. But this looks like a house where a family of five could live, complete with a side door, like one belonging to a dentist or a doctor with a home office. That's where we're headed.

"If anyone asks, you're eighteen," Manny tells me. "But no one's going to ask."

This only makes me more nervous. Manny knocks on the office door, and it's opened by a guy who's probably thirty and is covered by more than thirty tattoos—all these different people in weird poses being devoured by the landscape. He sees me staring at them and says, "Garden of Earthly Delights."

"Heller, man, thanks for fitting us in," Manny says, shaking his hand. "The wait list is, what, three months now?"

"Megan would know, not me," Heller says.

He leads us from the waiting room into what was clearly once a dentist's office. There are still a few advertisements for invisible braces and teeth whiteners up on the counters. But the rest of the office is covered by photographs of tattoos, each one so detailed that it looks like an illuminated manuscript has been taken from its spine and splayed across the walls. It's a transcription of creatures we've never seen but still imagine or fear, kaleidoscopic castles and canyons brought to the size of a human heart. All on the same landscape of skin, though each body has its own tint, its own surface and shape.

I have always thought of the body as something that is written from the inside. I don't need Rhiannon's name on my skin, because it is already indelible in my thoughts. But looking at Heller's conjurings, I suddenly understand the desire for such visible permanence, such open reminding. I, who have no body, can be sure that I take my life with me wherever I go, because it's all I have. But I see that if you only have one body, there is an intimation to memorialize your life upon that body, to take something that could be decoration and turn it into commemoration, to choose something that's beneath and let it rise to the top so it can become part of the way you are first seen.

The scary part, I think, is not the pain but the permanence. Heller operates beyond erasers, beyond delete keys. His art will only last as long as a life . . . but it will last as long as a life.

I want to fake sickness. I want to plead faintness. I want to back off, far away. I should not be inside a body when something irreversible is done to it.

But I can tell that Manny isn't going to let me off the hook. Heller is handing him a piece of paper and Manny's showing

21

it to me—a dragon with wings unfurled, the serpentine grace of Ric's tattoo with the added element of flight. It is not meant to be an icon or a symbol—no, it is meant to live and breathe on Manny's skin, to be his own dragon spirit manifest, to captivate and compel in ways that a simple human form cannot.

"Now you," Heller says. Instead of giving me a single piece of paper, he gives me three.

The first is a phoenix transcending the flames underneath it, clear-eyed and calm as it transforms.

The second is a kraken, its arms clovered into a web, its eyes darker and more distant than those of the phoenix, as if it knows its own majesty and doesn't want the spell to break.

The third is a tree, its trunk as solid as time and its leaves as fleeting as time. It would not stand out in a forest of its peers, but on its own it possesses a simple magnificence, the consciousness of a creature that feeds on light.

So . . . phoenix, kraken, tree. Fire, water, earth. Each demonstrating its own artistry, each as real in its own logic as a vision is to an eye.

"So the moment of truth has arrived," Manny says. "At long last, after all these years of us talking about it—what's it going to be?"

This is an important decision. Marco should have some memory stored away of which choice he was planning to make. It should be something I'm able to find.

I focus. Even though I know it means a noticeable lapse inward, I look. I ask. But there isn't any answer. Maybe when Marco went to sleep last night, he still hadn't made up his mind.

But now's the time for the answer. Whether he's here or not.

Manny sees me wavering and gets instantly distressed.

"This is it, man," he says. "Don't skip out on me now. They're all amazing choices. Which is it going to be?"

The phoenix calls to me. It looks me in the eye and knows who I am. It knows that we each can be more than just one thing. It knows that we live in a perpetual state of beginning and a perpetual state of ending. I would wear that on my skin, were I ever given skin of my own. I would let it send its wordless message to everyone I meet, as a way for them to get to know me a little more, to understand my flight path a little better.

That is my choice.

But it's *my* choice, not Marco's.

"I'm right here with you," Manny says. "Believe me, I wouldn't let your dumbass self do anything you'd regret."

There is an out here. There are words I can say that would lead to me leaving, would lead to us both getting away from Heller without any ink being led to the needle.

But there's another factor. I see it in Manny's eyes. I hear it in his voice. I sense it in all the history that Marco is sharing with me. If I leave now, Manny will never forget it. There will always be this moment and all that was leading up to it . . . then the disappointment when it fell apart. Will Manny forgive Marco if I make us leave? For sure. But will it be worse instead of better between them, and is Manny the most important person in Marco's life? Yes. And yes.

So I don't say the words I should probably say. I ignore the escape route.

"I can go first if you want more time," Manny offers.

"No," I say. "I've got it."

Phoenix, kraken, or tree?

Fire, water, or earth?

Who are you, Marco?

Which are you?

I don't know.

Then I realize I don't have to be the one to decide. I don't know Marco well, but there's someone else in the room who does.

"You choose," I tell Manny. "You know me best."

Manny is not expecting this at all. "Are you sure? Really?"

"Really."

"You like all of them?"

"I do. But which is the most like me?"

For all of his surprise, Manny doesn't hesitate. He points right at the tree.

"No question," he says.

If he'd picked either the phoenix or the kraken, I might have worried he was only doing it to match his dragon. But because he picks the tree, I know it must be true.

"There's your answer," I tell Heller.

"Alrighty, then. Take a seat and we'll get things started."

I get into the dentist's chair as Heller calls out to Megan, his girlfriend/assistant. They run a tight ship, and explain everything to me as they go—how they're sterilizing the instruments in the autoclave, how they're going to need to shave and clean my arm before sketching onto it.

"He's really afraid of needles," Manny volunteers. "So be careful—he'll probably flinch."

Usually I'd try to act true to Marco's personality. But I decide Marco's going to be braver than usual today, and not so afraid of needles.

After everything is clean and ready, Heller draws the tree on me, outlining all the paths the needle and ink will take. It's a weird sensation, to have him sketching on my skin—but it's even weirder when the needle leaves the first drop of color underneath. The pain is like a sharp burn. I expected it to be a more liquid feeling, but instead it stings.

24

"How are you doing?" Heller asks.

"Fine!" I say, trying to sound cheery.

But Manny sees my body tense. He sees me squeezing my eyes shut and opening them.

"It's going to be so cool," he tells me. "You're going to love it."

I think it will get easier, but the pain is consistent, the skin having something to say each time it's interrupted. I of all people should be able to step away from the body, to vacate myself in thought. But the presence of the pain means I can't be anywhere but present. I wonder whether this pain is now mine, or whether it's actually Marco's. Does the body remember pain, or is it only the mind? I am doing something human beings want to do all the time for the people they love— experience the pain on their behalf. But I am doing it for a stranger, someone who will never know it, and thus will never be able to recognize and appreciate it.

I do not watch what Heller is doing. I watch Manny stealing glances, see his reaction to the ink and the blood and the tree taking shape. It's so clear he cares about how it goes, because he cares so much about Marco. I imagine Rhiannon here with me. Holding my hand. Trying to divert some of the pain.

Then I try to stop myself from thinking that. It doesn't help.

The needle persists. Heller hums snatches of the song falling from the speakers. Even though the pain is the same no matter what the color, no matter where the shading, I imagine I can feel the picture taking shape. It's hard not to think of the tree sinking in, taking root. It's also hard not to think that no matter how deep the roots go, they'll never reach me. Only Marco.

It takes hours, and even then, Heller isn't done. He needs the colors to set before he can bless the tattoo with some of its finer details. He asks me if I want to look, but when I do, all I see is a bloody, carved mess.

"Don't worry," Heller assures me. "Blood passes. Ink stays."

Megan bandages me up, and then it's Manny's turn in the chair.

"Dragon, come to me!" he incants.

"You are such a dork," I say, since I think that's what Marco would say.

Manny laughs. "Takes one to know one, dumbass."

It feels so comfortable, right then. I almost forget it's not really me he's talking to. I almost think he sees me inside, and knows I'm the one along for this ride.

But of course it's Marco who stays by his side. It's Marco who doesn't give him a hard time when he ends up being the one who flinches and screams despite his attempts at self-control. It's Marco who stands like a tree while he writhes like a dragon.

When we're through, it takes the whole wad of cash to pay Heller. He tells us when we can come back for the finishing touches—and reminds us to let the healing happen before we start showing off to the world.

The pain has already passed. For Marco, it may never have been there. I have absorbed it. And because I've absorbed it, I know what it's like, in a way he never will.

But he will be left with a tree. As Manny and I get pizza, drive around, and see a movie, I keep touching the bandage on my arm, as if I can feel the lines underneath. It occurs to me that unlike most people I inhabit for a day, Marco will have a lasting mark of my presence, even if he never knows it. I am grateful that the mark is his, not mine—the tree, not the phoenix. The tree hides me better. The only person who'd ever see me in its branches would be me, if I were ever to see

Marco again. But that almost never happens. Marco will see it every day. I will have to remember it—which I know I will not. Just as the pain dissipates, so, too, will the lines of the memory unravel. I may recall the fact of the tree, but not its shape.

I hide my melancholy as Manny drops me off, just as I hide the bandage from my parents when I get inside. As far as Manny is concerned, he's just had one of the very best days ever, with his very best friend.

That night, alone in Marco's room, I unfold Heller's drawing of the tree and try to memorize it. I try to turn my thoughts into a tattoo, but the thoughts resist the ink. I don't want this to make me feel less real, but it does. I cannot help but feel impermanent. I cannot help but feel I am destined to fade.

X

It helps if the person is weak.

If I want less of a challenge, I stay with someone who is already on his way to giving up. Living is a fight, and I can pick out the ones who've stopped fighting, who are stuck in their own loneliness and/or confusion and/or pain. The fewer connections, the better. The more despair, the better. Some people guard their selves like a fortress. But others leave the doors unlocked and the windows open. They welcome the burglary.

I have not done well this time. My vanity thought it would be good to be young, to be the object of attention. But after a day, I can feel his self *wanting*, can feel it trying to reject me in the same way a body will reject an organ that brings the wrong blood to its system. His family attachments are strong. There is a home he misses. There are things he wants to do. I can feel him pushing against me. Resisting. I could separate him from this body, tamp him down, but it would take time and energy. Better to roll the dice and see what I get next.

In the meantime, there's fun to be had in our remaining hours together.

The young, handsome white guys are always fun. They're the ones who are naturally given things, who find that gates swing open before they touch them. These guys take advantage. Sometimes they don't know they're doing it. Most of the time they do. They are harder to erase because they like their lives. But I stay in there anyway, because I like their lives, too.

This guy's six feet tall, maybe six one. Swimmer's build. Eighteen years old. College freshman. Already knows which frat he's going to pledge. Attractive enough that I could get sex if I wanted to get sex, and strong enough that I could cause other people harm if I wanted to cause other people harm.

But I'd much rather mess with his life and leave him to clean it up. Take away as much of that advantage as I can. If I can't use it, there's no reason for him to have it when I'm gone.

It's easy enough to do. His girlfriend has been texting non-stop. Apparently, while I was getting a late breakfast, this guy was supposed to be walking her to class. At first she's mad that he stood her up. She thinks he's asleep. Then the day goes on and she's starting to get concerned. The interesting part is that she's more concerned about him being truthful with her than she is about whether he's alright. She thinks her position is precarious.

I need a vehicle for their undoing, and with this guy's body, it's not hard to find one. Leigh is working behind the counter at one of those coffee shops that exist just so Starbucks can kick it in the teeth. The Better Maryland Bean. Whatever. Leigh's there, and she's bored. Until I walk in—then she's not so bored anymore.

I've got this.

Start with a smile. Tell her I just moved here for school. Ask about her tattoo. Make sure she sees my eyes linger as she pulls up her sleeve to show me the whole thing. There aren't any other customers in line; we have all the time in the world. I ask a question to make it clear I'm really asking if she has a boyfriend. Get the answer I want.

Next I lean closer. Ask if I can get her number. Then, when she says yes, take the marker from the counter, the one she uses to write names on the cups, and ask her to write her number on my arm. Big.

"That way," I say, "I won't forget it."

She's game. She's charmed. Writes her name and her phone number from my wrist to my elbow. Even adds a winking smiley face at the end.

Now it's time to find this guy's girlfriend.

Leigh says the cold brew is on the house, but I tell her no way, and make sure I'm generous with the tip jar. It's not my money, so I can afford to be generous. This particular teenager drives a BMW; Mommy and Daddy give him a pretty good allowance.

The Girlfriend texts again. Every time she texts, I want to punish her more.

I don't let her know I'm on my way.

I make a mockery of the speed limit and run red lights when there aren't any cars coming. I'm a young, privileged white boy—if I get pulled over, the worst thing that will happen is I'll be a few minutes late to somewhere I don't need to be. If I were a young, privileged white *girl*, I wouldn't even get a ticket, if my smile was effective enough. But I'm not worried about this guy paying for a ticket. Plus, he listens to Maroon 5. He deserves a ticket.

Lucky for him, there aren't any police around to oblige. I find his campus parking spot, then head over to Girlfriend's dorm. A swipe of my ID gets me in. Her room is on the ground floor. I don't text ahead—I just pound on the door. When she opens it, she doesn't look happy to see me. She looks pissed.

"Where the fuck have you been?" Girlfriend says.

I force myself to remember her name. "Gemma," I say,

"it's so good to see you." I grin, and she's completely thrown off guard.

She doesn't ask me in, but I push my way in anyway.

She goes back to wanting a fight. Says it's not that she needs to know where I am all the time, but promises are promises.

I stand there grinning. For all I know, this guy really loves Gemma. For all I know, he's fine with his dating life being a surveillance state. For all I know, he's the kind of guy who'd never cheat.

Too bad.

I hold my arms out in a what-can-you-do? pose. I start counting. It takes her six seconds to notice.

"What's that?" she asks, pointing to my right arm. "What *the fuck* is that?"

I don't say a word. Just keep grinning.

She comes over and grabs my wrist. Turns my arm so she can read it.

"Who the fuck is Leigh?"

I stop grinning. I look her dead in the eye and say, "That's none of your business."

I think I'm the only one in the room enjoying this. She's angry as hell and starting to cry now, which makes her angrier, that she's crying in front of this guy. She wants to yell, but when she lets out, "What do you mean, it's none of my business?" it's more like a plea. I'm sure if he were here, it would break his heart wide open.

"You need to calm down," I tell her.

As expected, this only makes her madder.

"*Calm down?*" she yells, shoving this guy in the chest. "Don't you fucking tell me to *calm down.*"

I start laughing, because really, it's all so predictable. She doesn't like me laughing (also predictable) and launches herself at me.

31

Dumb move. I am taller than her. Bigger than her. I could beat the shit out of her. I could smash her face in. I could break her arm in three places. I could put my hands around her throat and strangle her right here and that would be that. She is entirely at my mercy because there is nothing to hold me accountable. She has no idea what kind of stupid danger she's in as she swats at me and screams. If I weren't finding it so funny, I could start hitting back. I could take the lamp off her desk and bash it down. I could knock out her teeth or crack her skull. She has no idea. She thinks her boyfriend is here. She thinks her boyfriend would never do that. But if I wanted to, I could do it. I have all the power here.

She swings at me and I catch her arm. I yank it behind her back. Her anger turns to terror. This guy's never come close to crossing this line.

She wriggles in my grip. I lean into her ear and whisper, "You text too much."

She starts to really scream. "GET OUT! GET OUT!" I let her break free. She screams it again. "GET OUT!"

I know how this plays out. In a minute, maybe less, there will be a knock at the door, a friend or floormate asking if everything's okay. Worst-case scenario, I'm face to face with a campus cop.

Or at least that's the worst-case scenario for me. For Girlfriend, there are even worse options.

But I'm tired now. There's always a point in a joke like this when it stops being funny enough to merit the mental energy it's taking. She's shaking and crying now, looking at him in horror. I try to take it in as much as I can, so when he wakes up tomorrow, he'll feel the echo of his own horror, vaguely remembering what happened but having no idea why he did what he did. It'll probably drive him crazy. She'll never forgive him.

I guess that's enough for me.

"See ya," I say. There's a teddy bear on her bed, clearly beloved. I grab it and take it with me, for effect.

In the hall, there are three people who've been listening in, debating what to do. When I pass them, I say hey, and one of them says hey back to me.

Girlfriend needs a better support system. But that's not really my problem.

I can't go back to this guy's room now, just in case there's going to be some immediate follow-up to what just happened. It's better to keep him out of the way until he's himself again and has to deal with it.

I leave the car behind. I walk awhile. When I have to pee, I pee, shocking a pair of elderly women out for an afternoon stroll. I consider peeing on them, but even the elderly carry phones nowadays, and I'm not in the mood to be in the back of a patrol car. I think for a moment about leaving this guy with a broken leg or spine—maybe if he's in traction, Girlfriend will somehow feel like it's her fault, which would be an interesting twist. But it's too hard to time it so I wouldn't have to deal with the pain and mess. Better to make a clean departure. Lucky boy.

I get him a hotel room. Let him wonder tomorrow how he got there and what the phone number on his arm means. Let the rest dawn on him. His life is about to get very ugly.

When sleep comes, I'm sure to let go fully—I bring his memories to the front of his mind, and give up on my presence entirely.

The next morning, I wake up inside someone else, and within a few minutes I know I've done well. A divorced divorce lawyer. Rich and miserable. His kids no longer speak to him. His hypochondria is acute. His hair is greasy; his shirts all have small splattered-soup stains that only a person who doesn't care could ignore. There's no one around to tell him to take his shirts to the cleaners, no one around to take out the trash when he's worried he'll throw out his back. It's almost like he welcomes me when I arrive. The less time he has to spend in his own life, the better.

I can use that.

NATHAN

It's not that we hit dead ends. There aren't even roads to turn onto.

I can tell Rhiannon's boyfriend, Alexander, is a little confused by my sudden presence in her life. He can't put his finger on what connects us . . . and who can blame him for that? She told him we met at a party—technically true. But there's no way to tell him the reason I'm so attentive isn't because I want to sleep with her or date her. I'm attentive because she's the only one besides me who knows the most unknowable thing about my life.

A lot of the couples in my school are glued together emotionally, but Alexander is all about them having their own lives—which is great for me, because it means he doesn't get all weird when he comes over and finds me and Rhiannon on her computer, searching the Internet for news of body snatchings.

"Watching more Lorraine Hines videos?" he asks. This is a pretty good guess, since it feels like everyone's been watching them lately.

"Just searching for the elusive truth," Rhiannon replies. Which could be taken to mean we were trying to get the elusive truth from a Lorraine Hines video. But I know A's location is the real truth that eludes her.

I don't know how Rhiannon does it. It's clear that she likes Alexander. It's clear that he treats her well, and that Rhiannon is still getting used to the thought of being treated well. I also notice that she never lies to him, if only because he doesn't know the right questions to ask. And even if he did, even if she told him everything . . . the strange part is that he might actually believe her. Us. But I can see how it's easier not to risk that.

We search and search the Internet for some trace of A. We read about other people's experiences of being taken over, and wonder whether they're like us, or whether they're just crackpots, making it up in a way we're not making it up.

Finally I ask her the question that's been nagging at me the most. We're in her room, looking at the same "strange phenomena" websites for the twelfth time.

"We're looking for a sign of him, right?" I say.

Rhiannon nods.

I press on. "What about leaving him a sign? Why not let him know you're looking?"

"How?" she says. She sounds defensive.

"There's this thing called social media? And you have a pretty distinctive name?"

"What am I supposed to say? *Status update: Missing you, A.* Alexander will see that and say, *Hey, babe, I'm right here.*"

"He wouldn't actually say *babe*, would he? Ew."

"No. But anything I post, everyone sees. Not just A."

"You don't need to write him a message. Just give him a sign."

"Like what?"

I think about it for a second. "Do you guys have, like, a song?"

She looks at me strangely.

"What?" I ask.

She shakes her head slightly. "Nothing. I mean, it's just that—you were there for it. When A and I talked about it, A was you. In your body. It's stupid, really. Just a song."

36

"What's the song?"

She tells me the name of the song, and I feel the echo of a memory—that's the only way I can describe it. I don't actually remember talking to her about the song. But the fact that she and I talked about it once makes sense to me.

"Watch," I say.

I go on YouTube and find the video for the song. Then I copy and paste the link into her status box. In front of it, I type: *Listening to this on repeat.*

"Okay," Rhiannon says. I hit return. Then I go back to YouTube and type *I miss* into the search box. Among other things, I get an old Johnny Cash song, "I Still Miss Someone." I copy the link for that, then go to the comments section under the original song, type *This one, too,* and add the link.

"Not very subtle," Rhiannon tells me.

"Maybe to you. And to me. And to A. To everyone else— *totally* subtle."

I hit return.

RHIANNON

It feels wrong.
  It feels like I'm pleading.
  It feels like I'm saying I'm unhappy with my life.
  It feels like I'm saying I'm unhappy with Alexander.
  It feels exposed.
  It feels like I'm shouting into the wilderness.
  It feels like I'm setting myself up for disappointment.
  It feels like I'm setting myself up for silence.
  It feels like I'm breaking a promise I never really made.
  It feels desperate.
  It feels like I haven't thought it through.
  It feels like I'm giving something that was ours away to the world.
  It feels like I don't have enough things that were ours to afford to give one away to the world.
  It feels treacherous.
  It feels like I don't really have a choice.

Posted by M at 10:34 p.m.

I don't think I can do this any longer. And by "this" I mean "life." The pain is out of control—and I am not talking about the kind of pain where you can get medication to make it go away. I am talking about a pain I carry with me everywhere, a pain that has nothing to do with biology or chemistry. The pain started because of who I am. Now it is all I am. There is no way to treat it. No way to calm it down. No way to get it to stop clawing. A thousand times a day I try to think of a way to destroy myself without hurting someone else. A thousand times a day I fail. My pain is the feeling of that failure. My pain is louder to me because it is inaudible to others. I don't expect anyone to be able to help me. The world around me does not exist. I am alone in this, and if I could find a way to die alone, I would.

A

Day 6082

I used to think nobody could see me. The body I was in was impenetrable from the outside—no one else would ever expect I was there, and therefore even when I slipped up, it would be written off as the action of the person whose life I was borrowing. No one is entirely predictable—we all have surprising bursts. I hid behind that.

I got better at hiding over time, once I figured out what was going on. As a kid, I was a poor mimic, but because kids produce surprising burst after surprising burst, nothing I did ever seemed so out of character that any parent, teacher, or friend suspected the truth. Around ten or eleven, I better understood the ways to disappear, even if I still didn't understand why I was so different from everyone else. The past couple of years, I treated it like a test I was passing. I stopped wondering what I sounded like, because the sound of my thoughts was enough. I stopped wondering what I looked like, because whatever I looked like that day was enough. I stopped wanting people to see me, because to have them see me would be the ultimate failure of the test.

I took the roles I played to heart because I didn't have a heart of my own. I only showed anger when I thought I was meant to show anger. I only showed affection when I felt it was my obligation to show affection. I didn't know what most of these emotions actually felt like, because I never got to express them purely. Only sorrow appeared unfiltered, because what made me cry was often the same as what would have made anyone else cry. Joy, though, was the opposite, because my joy was always edged by the fact that it wasn't really mine.

Only with Rhiannon did I get to be directly myself. Now, after, I fear a part of the impulse has lingered. I fear I am beginning to show through.

On Monday, my (temporary, one-day-only) best friend tells me she senses there's something I'm not saying, something I want to say. I tell her no, I'm just a little tired, a little lost in my own mind. I don't think she believes me, and for a second, I have the desire to tell her everything, to tell her about Rhiannon and ask her what I should do.

On Tuesday, two guys in class give me a hard time because they were expecting me to agree that America is better off with closed borders, and that most of the problems facing America today can be traced to immigration. *You're totally reversing your opinion*, they tell me, disgusted. I know I should not be deviating from what he would normally say. But I can't force myself to repeat something I know isn't true.

On Wednesday, my (not really *my*) girlfriend must use the same shampoo as Rhiannon, because every time she comes close to me, it's like a trapdoor. When she kisses me, I trick myself into being in the past, imagining it can be the present. I must put a lot into it, because when she pulls back, she says, *Well, Tara, that was enthusiastic.* And I tell her, *I love the way you smell.* She says, *I don't smell like anything.* I want to say, *You smell like Rhiannon.* But what I say is, *You smell like ~~Rhiannon~~ you.*

On Thursday, I'm on crutches that I barely know how to use. After first period, a friend takes my backpack from me and says, *You need to let me help you.* I have a feeling the boy I'm in has turned down her help before. But this time, I welcome it.

41

When Friday comes, I wake up in the body of a girl named Whitney Jones. She gets up at 5:32 a.m. for swim practice, and I force myself to go, even though I know her performance is going to be off. It takes me about two periods in school to realize she's one of the only black girls in class—a point brought home in third-period history, when both the teacher and other students keep looking at her when they're talking about Selma, as if her skin color makes her an expert on something that happened decades before she was born. I would guess they don't even realize they're doing it—when people are thinking about a difference, their eyes will usually wander to someone they think embodies that difference. It always makes me feel strange, because I'm not nearly as used to it as the people I'm in are. I try to take the scrutiny on the surface level on which it's intended—they're looking at Whitney while they talk about John Lewis because their minds are thinking, *Black people.* But now, paranoid, I wonder if they also see me, a different kind of different one, underneath.

Whitney's best friend is named Didi, and they have plans to hang out after school at Didi's apartment. It soon becomes obvious that Didi is obsessed with a popular series of online videos on a site called Truth Serum, created by a woman named Lorraine Hines, whose catchphrase (it's all over the site) is *Truth IS the Serum.* Each video on the site is like a public confessional, only *confession* isn't really the right word for all of them. Some of the truths are more political—a woman telling how she really feels about being ogled on the subway, a man talking about trying to explain the concept of race to his biracial children. Most of the truths are very, very personal—people not just admitting affairs, but explaining why they think the affairs happened, or people confronting the pain of their childhoods, including (sometimes) their own culpability, or (more often) the culpability of the people they trusted and loved. There's no narrative imposed, no set structure. The truth unfolds into whatever shape it takes when it's exposed to the air.

Some videos are five minutes long and reduce me to tears. Others are ten minutes long and make me laugh at how true they are. Didi and I watch five, then ten of them. Sometimes, when Lorraine Hines thinks the person needs to be talking to someone in order to release the truth, she'll ask some questions. But most of the time, she's off camera, and the only person you see is the person telling the truth.

"I swear, I could watch this all day," Didi says after we've watched a sixty-year-old man talk about how he's never been interested in sex, and feels like he's had a completely full life without it. "Although afterwards I'm always torn between wanting everyone to be truthful like this in real life and thinking that it would be a bad, bad idea. Because it's one thing to watch people do it, and another to have people do it to your face, right?"

I nod.

She continues. "Like, how long do you think we could make it, only telling the truth?"

"Two minutes?" I say. This may or may not be the truth.

"Let's try it!" she says energetically, as if she just suggested we sneak some chocolate from the kitchen.

I laugh.

"What?" she asks. "Nervous?"

There's no way to tell her that no, that's not why I'm laughing. I'm laughing because for a second I was thinking I could actually play the truth game—that any answer Whitney gave could be truthful when I'm doing the speaking.

"You go first," I say.

"Do a starter question. Like . . . how was your day?"

"Okay. How was your day?"

"It doesn't have to be— Oh, okay. It's so funny, because even though I know we're doing truth serum, my first impulse was to say that my day was fine. And that's not a lie, really. But I guess there's more to it than that. I was looking forward to this part all day, because I knew it would be the best part. When I'm in class, I'm paying attention, right? But I'm also kinda not there. Not in the way I'm here, hanging out. I don't *enjoy* school. I think you do, at least some of the time. I think when you get an answer right or get an A on a paper, you get a kick out of that. But I think of it as something that means a lot to other people, not to me. You know what I mean? Like, if I get an A, that means a lot to my parents and it will mean a lot to whoever looks at my college applications. But to me? It's not what matters. How about you? How was *your* day?"

I think I can answer this one, since it's the part of Whitney's life I know best. "I'm still tired from swim practice, which seems designed to ruin you for the whole day. It's a lift during, but then the buzz wears off and it's like, shit, there are still thirteen more waking hours to go. I had the usual Token Black Girl experience in history class. I know my life is completely informed by this country's racial history, but that doesn't mean everyone has to talk to me like I am the class's representative of that racial history—as if every white kid in there hasn't been molded by the very same things! That's *exhausting.* And then even at lunch, I have to wonder whether people notice me because of me or because of the way I look. *Exhausting.* So I guess, coming from another direction, I agree with you: This right now is definitely the best part of the day. I think some of the people on those videos are doing it because they like the sound of their own voices, but I think others genuinely seem to have no idea why they're telling the truth to a world of strangers—and that is, to me at least, much more truthful. When you're telling the truth, you should look terrified and exhilarated at the same time, because telling the truth is navigating both of those feelings at the same exact time." I stop. "Is that truthful enough for you?"

Didi looks like she needs to catch her breath. "I mean— yes. That was great. But what do you mean, *Token Black Girl?* That's not how I see you at all. You're just . . . Whitney."

It occurs to me that Didi might have been in my history class. I might not have noticed her there, since we hadn't had lunch together yet, so I hadn't identified her as my best friend.

"Not you," I say. Not because I know it's true, but because it makes the moment easier. "More Mr. Snyder."

"Snerder."

"Didn't I say Snerder?"

"No, you said Snyder."

She's looking at me like I just spit some truth serum out on her floor instead of swallowing it.

"Are you okay?" she asks.

In response, I give her the same words I've given so many other people, without any of them ever understanding what I really mean.

"I'm not myself today."

This defuses the situation somewhat.

"I think watching too much Lorraine Hines will do that," Didi says. "You probably said Snerder. And he can be a total dick. No matter what color you are."

I must remember that I am Whitney. I must remember that Didi is her friend. I must remember that if Whitney wants to call Didi on her assumptions, that's Whitney's decision, not mine. So instead of telling her what I really think, I say, "All this truth serum's made me hungry. Do you have any popcorn in the kitchen?"

"Let's check," she says, leaving the conversation as fast as she can leave the room.

45

For the rest of the afternoon, until I can plead a dinner excuse, I go through the motions.

Meaning: I could be anyone.

Also meaning: I am no one at all.

Later that night, alone in Whitney's room, I try not to think about Didi, and wonder some more about the people in the videos. I head to the Truth Serum website, which is arranged to look like a truth-themed lifestyle magazine, with Lorraine Hines front and center. It's a little off-putting, how thrilled she seems by other people laying themselves bare. But when you filter her out and focus on the truth tellers themselves, there is something magnetic about the bareness, and the bravery of the ones who wear the terror and exhilaration so clearly.

I watch some more videos. A pastor questioning God. A teenager describing his suicide attempt and why he's grateful his stomach was pumped in time. A grandmother whose big truth is that she has been happy with her life, and how she feels that in a culture of complaint, it is frowned upon to talk about a life that's gone well.

The more I hear these truths, the more I can feel my own growing restless. Why do these people get to lay it all out while I have to remain silent? Why can't I be with the only person who took my truth seriously? If I went on this site and posted a video, there would be two options, both of them bad:

People wouldn't believe me. Or they would.

People would treat me as a lunatic. Or they would take me at my word—and hunt me down to understand how I came to be how I am.

Also, if I made a video, it wouldn't be me they saw. And whoever's life I borrowed would have to bear the stigma of my presence for the rest of their future.

So . . . definitely not an option.

I go back to the Truth Serum home page and see a button labeled Anonymous Truth. I click on it and Lorraine Hines appears.

"For many of us, the truth can only be said if there's someone listening. But often the truth becomes harder if the person listening is someone we know. We here at Truth Serum want to provide a safe forum for you to share your truth with someone you don't know. Just click the link below and you will be paired at random with a person who will witness your truth without judgment."

I don't know that I believe anyone can ever listen without judgment—but still I click on the link. There's no risk that I can see. I will be elsewhere in the morning.

I am put in a chat box with someone who goes by the initials WL. I am reminded before WL comes into the chat that our conversation will be anonymous. I enter the initials AA.

I feel the skittish foolishness that comes from relying on my own anonymity, even though WL can't see me, complicated by the fact that I already feel I'm hiding behind Whitney's body.

WL: Hello. I am WL (not my real initials) and I will be your truth listener today. Please, tell me your truth.

I'm disappointed by how rote this is. I'm probably talking to some cut-rate artificial intelligence—artificial semi-intelligence. I almost log off. But then I decide, no, I might as well acknowledge my reaction, in the spirit of telling the truth.

AA: That seems abrupt. And vague.

I figure this is the part when it will become obvious if it's a computer I'm talking to.

47

WL: It is. But that's how this works.

AA: But what do you mean by "your truth"? Don't we have many? I mean, I'm wearing a red shirt right now. That's a truth.

WL: That isn't the truth you came here to talk about, though, is it?

AA: No. It isn't.

WL: So tell me that truth. The one that brought you here.

Why *am* I here? Maybe to be forced into this question. Because that's the thing about my life—nobody asks me anything. And if nobody's asking, it's easy to keep all the answers on the shelf, gathering dust. I can forget they exist. I can avoid them.

The reason I'm here isn't because of what happens to me every day. The reason I'm here is . . .

AA: I am in love with someone I can't be with.

I exhale. It is an effort to admit this, even to a stranger. It is an effort to admit it to myself.

WL: Why not?

AA: Because she isn't here.

WL: Where is she?

AA: 1500 miles away. I left her. I had to.

WL has no idea how old I am. WL has no idea what I look like. WL has no idea where I am.

48

In many ways, WL knows me better than anyone in front of me ever does.

WL: Why did you have to leave?

AA: Because there was no way for me to stay.

WL: Why?

AA: Because I have a condition that prevents me from being able to stay with her.

This is the closest I can come to explaining it. I know it isn't entirely truthful. But even with WL, I have to draw a line. I can only trust so far. I can only expect understanding to a certain degree.

WL: A medical condition? A psychological condition?

Same thing, I want to tell WL.

AA: A medical condition.

But this doesn't feel like the truth. I keep typing.

AA: No, that's not right. It's who I am. Neither medical nor psychological. Or even spiritual. It's just . . . the way my life is.

WL: What about your life is preventing you from being with her?

AA: I just can't be with her.

WL: Fear of commitment?

49

"No," I say to the screen. It's not fear of commitment. It's a knowledge that commitment is impossible. I don't fear it at all.

AA: No. I travel a lot. I mean, I have to travel a lot. There's no way out of it.

WL: So you can't be home for her?

AA: I would love to be. But I can't.

WL: And have you talked this over with her?

AA: Yes.

WL: And she agrees that it cannot work?

Be truthful, I tell myself.

AA: I think so.

WL: You think so?

AA: She knows about my condition. I think she would try to love me anyway. But because I'm the one who's lived with it my whole life, I know better than her that it will never work.

WL: Is that true?

AA: Yes. Of course it's true.

WL: Are you sure? You are meant to be telling your truth here.

AA: I know that it's true.

WL: "Know" is a strong word. You believe. You suspect. But can you really know?

Calmly, I type:

AA: By any rational measure, she and I cannot be together.

WL: What does your heart say?

AA: My heart wants it to be possible. But the universe isn't governed by wants. Or even needs. Some things don't work, no matter how much you want them to.

WL: That is not truth. That's theory. What do you want?

AA: To be able to be with her.

It hurts to say that. *Fool fool fool.*

WL: What does she want?

AA: I don't know. I'm not her.

WL: Why don't you ask?

AA: Because she's there, and I'm here, and it's better for us not to torture one another.

WL: Did she tell you it's better?

I didn't give her a chance. I didn't want it to be a prolonged argument. I didn't want the ending to ruin everything that came before. I wanted to leave her in the arms of someone who might love her for who she is—and who could love her day after day.

AA: No. I left before she could.

WL: That is an interesting truth.

I feel my listener doesn't like what they're hearing. I try to trick myself into thinking that it's WL's disapproval I'm concerned with, and not the nagging disapproval in my own thoughts.

AA: There are other factors.

WL: What are they?

AA: I can't tell you.

I expect WL to fight this, but instead I get:

WL: I respect that. Have you told her?

AA: About the other factors? Yes.

WL: All of it?

AA: Yes.

WL: And what was her reaction?

AA: She didn't believe me. And then she did.

WL: And how did that feel?

AA: Beautiful.

WL: Why would you stop, then?

AA: Because it can't work.

WL: But even if you're not together, you can still talk. Why did you stop?

AA: Because I didn't want to hurt her. Because I don't want to be hurt. Because I'm afraid. Because wanting to change the things you can't change—that is so devastating.

WL: But still—you want to talk to her.

AA: Of course.

WL: There's your truth.

I am formulating my response to that when another message appears.

WL has logged out.

The chat box doesn't close. As if I may still want a transcript of my truths. As if I won't remember where this has led me.

I push back from the desk, and it's only when I do this that I remember I am Whitney right now. I am in Whitney's body. For a moment there, I completely forgot. I became the bodiless self I imagine everyone becomes when they're engaged entirely in thought and words.

I should turn off the computer. But there's a part of me

53

that doesn't want to put the answers back on the shelf, that doesn't want to walk away.

I pull myself back to the keys. Before I can stop myself, I go on Facebook, type in her name. It's an immediate gut punch to see her picture, to have her exist in a form other than memory.

I have to see more.

I click on her name and her page comes up. The profile picture is bigger now—her alone, smiling in front of a movie theater. The photo is recent, from a week ago. I know I should stop myself, that no good can come of this, but I click on the photos tab. I want to see more.

And there he is. Alexander. Who got to stay. Who got to be with Rhiannon.

My instincts must have been right, because the two of them look happy.

Even if he's not in the profile photo, he must be the person she's smiling at.

I jump back out to the overall photo page, the mosaic of the photographic past. The first few rows are mostly them as a couple. Then there are pictures of her alone. Some with family. Some with friends. I don't remember the friends' names. I don't recognize most of them. Justin, her evil ex, is nowhere to be found. Which is a relief.

Her recent life is laid out in front of my eyes. *But it's not life,* I tell myself. *It's only a representation of life.* I am telling myself this, but the sadness is gripping me. I am telling myself this is not real, but the weight of it is real. The truth. The hard truth.

There are no pictures of us.

Not because she deleted them.

There were never any pictures of us.

Never any record.

We were never a part of the shareable present, so we are not a part of the shareable past.

This hurts. This hurts so much that the feeling transfers to Whitney's body, because my sorrow, my anger, my helplessness are more than just the mind can hold.

I go back to Rhiannon's home page. I am staying wide of the message button. I am not going to message her.

I suppose I should be grateful. Years ago, there would have been no way to do this. I would have been a submarine without a periscope. *Leaving* would have meant *leaving completely behind*. Out of sight, out of reach.

But now she is within reach—and I can feel myself reaching. There is the illusion that she can feel me doing this.

She cannot feel me doing this. She cannot sense me seeing her. She cannot know. Because I cannot be seen like she can be seen.

I start to scroll down. Most of the posts are ones she's been tagged in—now that I see the friends' names, I remember them. Preston likes to share cat videos. Rebecca comments about how much she doesn't like cat videos. Alexander posts artwork he likes—Hockney mountains and Sugimoto horizons.

And Rhiannon . . .

Rhiannon posts a song.

At first I gloss over it. Then I realize what it is. What it means. No—what it *could* mean.

I am back in the car, singing along at the top of my lungs.

No, not my lungs. Justin's lungs.

It doesn't matter. Once Rhiannon knows I am there, I am there. I am singing with her. And again in that basement. As Nathan.

I am so happy, thinking about it. And sad.

We were so happy then. And sad.

There's no way this is an accident. There's no way this wasn't intended. I scroll down and see, in the comments section, another song. Not our song. But still—irrefutable.

"I Still Miss Someone."

Is it meant for me to see? Or is it just how she was feeling, her own in-joke to herself?

The message button is calling to me.

But it is a siren. I know it is a siren.

The lines between *I cannot do this* and *I should not do this* and *I will not do this* are all confused. I almost wish the window with WL were still open, so I could ask WL what to do. To which WL would no doubt ask back: *Which of the three above statements is the truth?*

And I would respond: *They are all the truth.*

Then: *None of them are the truth.*

I don't know if I'm looking for a barrier, but I find one. I am, of course, using Whitney's account. Right now, I cannot message Rhiannon. Only Whitney can. Rhiannon would know it was me. But that would still leave Whitney. I could hijack her account—change her password, message from it secretly until Whitney took it back. But what kind of person would I be if I did that to her? Not one worthy of Rhiannon.

It will have to be enough to know she is there.

For now.

Before I can spend too much time scrutinizing photos that were never meant to be scrutinized . . . before I can spend too much time debating the words I won't allow myself to type . . . I log out. Clear history. Shut everything down.

I know it's wrong for me to think it, but Rhiannon feels closer now.

. . . failure. My pain is louder to me because it is inaudible to others. I don't expect anyone to be able to help me. The world around me does not exist. I am alone in this, and if I could find a way to die alone, I would.

Comment from MoBetter:
You need to talk to someone. Get some help. There is always a way to treat pain. If there's no one near you to talk to, the National Suicide Prevention Lifeline is 1-800-273-8255. Good luck.

Comment from AnarchyUKGo:
Just do it. Kill as many people as you want. Take all the stupid ones with you.

Comment from 1derWomanFierce:
Get out of your own head. It helps.

Comment from PurpleCrayon12:
I've had these thoughts, too. I think of it as the eclipse state. I found writing about it very helpful. Don't keep it inside—express it. And MoBetter is right . . . you have to talk to someone. The fact that you're posting about it is a good step. It shows you want to share the burden. And there are many loving and kind people out there who will willingly take some of the weight. Don't think you're alone.

Comment from M:
None of you understand.

RHIANNON

I don't know what I was thinking. Or, worse, I do know what I was thinking. I imagined the minute—no, the second—I posted that song, A would know I'd done it. I'd get an instant response. Because everything felt so instant when A was here.

Stop. I know I have to stop. Listen to myself. Wonder: Was it really A I loved, or was it the intensity, the feeling that our orbit had grown so tight that it could fit into an atom—and would cause an explosion if we were to separate? How can Alexander compete with that? Why am I even thinking of it as a competition?

Alexander is here. He wins.

But I'm not sure that Alexander feels like he's winning. Or that I'm much of a prize.

It's Saturday and we're on our way to Will's house for a picnic in his backyard. I should probably think of it as Will and Preston's house, because ever since they started dating, Preston has been spending most of his time there. Alexander and I are bringing a fruit salad, which meant we had to go to the grocery store ("our first-date grocery store") and buy about twenty-five dollars' worth of fruit to chop up and put in a bowl.

I'm driving and Alexander is looking at his phone, scrolling down his Facebook. I don't even notice until he says, "Hey, why'd you put this song up?" He holds out his phone so I can see the link.

"It's just a song I like," I tell him. "It was stuck in my head, so I decided to inflict it on other people."

"Oh? Cool."

He goes back to scrolling, not even checking the comments section to find the second song. And the stupid thing is that I am suddenly mad at him for not reading more into it . . . which is *extra* stupid because getting mad is exactly what Justin would have done. Justin would have taken it as an attack, even if he didn't know what it meant. He would have attacked back.

Maybe we inherit bad traits from our exes, just like we inherit bad traits from our parents, because out of the blue I find myself picking a fight with Alexander, saying, "*Oh, cool*—what does that even mean?"

He doesn't look up from his phone. "It means that I didn't know you liked that song, but I'm perfectly happy that you do."

"I didn't put it up there for your approval."

"I never said that you did."

I know I'm being the unreasonable one, and Alexander's tone makes it clear that he knows it, too.

I should say I'm sorry. A would say sorry. Justin would not say sorry. Alexander would say sorry. But I'm still angry. Not at Alexander. At the universe. Alexander just happens to be here to bear the brunt of it. Which might be my passive-aggressive way of getting him to hate the unfair universe, too. Which is pretty messed up.

"Have you heard from Steve or Stephanie?" Alexander asks. Safer ground.

"Yes. The war continues. Nobody wants to pick a side, so we didn't invite either of them. It's weird, but Rebecca says that's the only way to do it, when we're all together."

"Makes sense," Alexander says, even though he's only met

Steve and Stephanie once, and they spent most of the time pulling each other aside to fight.

"Couples are weird," I say.

He smiles at that. "Yeah, they are. Single people, too."

I can't be mad at him for long. But I don't think that's enough to call it love.

Will has built a fire to make his backyard warm enough for a picnic. We sit on a blanket covered with too much food. Will says, "Peel me a grape!" to Preston, and as Will, Rebecca, Ben, and Alexander laugh, Preston does exactly that. Then he holds the sad grape skin in one hand and the gelatinous pulp in the other hand and asks which part, exactly, Will was wanting. Will says, "Really, it's just that I've always wanted a boy who'd peel a grape for me. Thank you."

"Peel me a blueberry!" Rebecca commands Ben.

"No," he says. "That's messy."

Rebecca is leaning on Ben. Will plays a little with Preston's hair. Alexander offers me more tea from the thermos, and I shake my head. I am surrounded by my best friends. I am sitting next to a boyfriend who treats me well. We are gathered around an afternoon campfire, its warmth creating a comfortable space in the wide air. I should be happy. But instead I feel like I am standing outside my own happiness. When I was with A, I was inside it. I could touch it freely, could recognize it. But now I have no idea how to get to it. I have no idea what it really is.

I don't understand how it's possible to know you have a good life, but still be missing out on it. I don't understand why I won't let myself give in to what I have. It's good. What I have is good.

"Anything you'd like peeled?" Alexander asks me.

I shiver.

He doesn't say, "What?" But it's there in the way he's looking at me. The way Rebecca, who knows me even better, is looking at me.

"It's nothing," I tell Alexander, tell them all. "I just thought about how freaked out I would get when my dad would say *keep your eyes peeled* when I was a kid—I thought that meant there was a way your eyelids could be peeled like a banana."

"That always freaked me out, too!" Preston says. "Or—oh God—when people say *bless you* when you sneeze? I know it's polite. But when I was a kid, I was like, *WHAT IS SO BAD ABOUT A SNEEZE THAT YOU NEED TO BLESS ME?!?* I mean, if you skin your knee and are bleeding all over, no one says *bless you*. If you puke up your guts, no one says *bless you*. So I couldn't help but wonder how a sneeze was, like, *worse*."

The rest of them start talking about other things that freaked them out as kids. I eat strawberries and leave the tops in a circle on my plate. I don't think any of my friends notice that I'm not really there.

Not until we're cleaning up. Not until Rebecca holds back and waits until everyone else is inside to ask me if something's wrong.

"I'm fine," I say. "Everything's fine."

She gives me a level glance. "Any time you have to say that twice, it's at least half-untrue. Is there something wrong with you and Alexander?"

I shake my head. "Nothing wrong. It's just that . . . isn't it okay if there are some days that aren't wrong but aren't really right, either? He hasn't done anything wrong. I'm the one who isn't feeling right. Do you know what I mean?"

"All too well. There are days when I look at Ben and think, *Why am I even bothering—we're only going to break up when we go to college. I think my time could be better used elsewhere.*

Like, learning Russian. Or watching every BBC mystery that I can find on Netflix. But then he does something stupid and endearing like texting me to see how my day went, and I'm like, *Oh yeah. That's why I do this.*" She hands me some plates to take back to the kitchen. "Look—with Justin, you were always so desperate for him to love you that you never really got to experience what it's like when the two of you are balanced. It's different when you're balanced. Let yourself get used to it instead of assuming you know how it works."

This is typical Rebecca: a little bit wise, a little bit condescending. What I want to ask her—what I can't ask her—is if it always feels like you're pretending, if part of being in a relationship is feeling like you are going through the motions of being in a relationship. Will and Preston have been together for about the same amount of time that Alexander and I have been together, and they seem to be genuinely happy and genuinely in love.

But I guess neither of them is wondering about someone else.

"Come on," Rebecca says. "Let's go inside. You don't need to commit to forever, or even to tomorrow. But commit to right now. We all want you to be here."

She's right. When I get back into the kitchen, Preston gives me a hug and Will turns the music up a little louder and asks me to dance, even though his signature dance move is the pogo. Alexander pours me some pink lemonade. Ben asks Rebecca to dance and she swats him away. The night begins, and goes on. I manage to step into my happiness. But I am always looking back, checking where I came from.

Comment from M:
None of you understand.

Comment from PurpleCrayon12:
Why do you say that? (I don't ask this to dispute what you're saying. I want to know why you feel we don't understand.)

Comment from M:
I don't belong in this body. I have nothing to do with this body. I am trapped in this body. I exist separate from this body. But I can't die, because I am afraid I will take this body with me.

Comment from PurpleCrayon12:
There are times I wish I could separate from my body.

Comment from M:
The fact that you can say that shows how little you understand.

Comment from PurpleCrayon12:
You don't know anything about me.

Comment from M:
This is pointless.

Comment from Someone:
I understand.

X

It is easy to find the boy, because he has not moved. His life does not change.

It is easy to follow him, because he has never seen this body before. He has no idea I am here. He has no idea I have returned.

I made a mistake. When I contacted Nathan, when I told him what he wanted to hear—that he had been possessed by the devil for a day, that his actions had not been his own—I felt I had power over him. I knew I could not take his body—for whatever reason, once a body has been occupied, it develops a resistance to being occupied again. But I thought his mind would be a minor challenge at most. A teenage boy discovered by the side of the road, having no idea how he'd gotten there or what he'd done—his uncertainty was my great weapon, and his desire for certainty was my great leverage. Then, when the other body traveler contacted the boy, I thought, *At last, here is a line.* It is worthless to have a hook if you don't also have a line. So I manipulated the boy, set up the confrontation. The body traveler walked into this boy's house, was right in front of me. I recognized her for what she was, and she recognized me for what I was. She was afraid, as I knew she should be. Man should tremble when faced with the manipulations of that which is greater than Man. I had the lure set, the hook within reach. But then she struggled, and the boy surprised me by interfering, giving the girl a chance to flee. I was angry. At the boy, certainly—but also at myself.

I wonder if Nathan knows that the reverend is dead.

Probably not. I doubt anyone noticed. And if nobody notices a death, it is very hard to find out about it.

This body is a different form of anonymity. When I am in a new body, I have the power of unknowability. To those I am watching, I am a complete stranger. I am scenery. And the whole time, I am taking in their moves, their fears, their faults. It is nearly impossible to run from me.

I could be the man next to you in the grocery store.

I could be the man handing you your change.

I could be the man in the window across the street.

I could be the man who gets on the bus two people after you.

I could be the man hitting on you.

The man bumping your shoulder.

The man in your blind spot.

The man right in front of you.

If that doesn't confer power, I don't know what does.

Nathan doesn't see me in my car across the street as he heads to school. He does not understand that, after school, I am the man walking behind him, into a café. He doesn't think it's strange that I sit next to him. Because I have a book and am turning the pages at regular intervals, he doesn't understand that he is my focus.

A girl comes in to meet him. They exchange pleasantries. He says she looks tired. She mentions a bad conversation she had with her boyfriend. I am about to start reading the pages in front of me, so fruitless is this exchange. But then he asks if there's been any word from someone named A. I am paying attention now, even though the answer is no. They talk about tracking A down. They do not call A *he* or *she.* They do not understand that I am taking in every word.

I understand many things at once:

This girl met Nathan on the night he was possessed.

A was the person who possessed him.

A is now gone.

But she still cares about A. Deeply.

I picture A as the frightened, ignorant girl I met in Nathan's house. It is stupid to leave a trail, and that is exactly what A has done. I don't know whether it would be better to educate her or kill her. Her existence, like the existence of any other body traveler, threatens my own existence. To know the truth about one of us is to know at least a partial truth about all of us. If people begin to look, they will find us. They will fight. Thus, we must remain unknowable.

A clearly does not know this. And because of this, A has been a fool. She may have run away from me, and from these people. But if she can make a mistake once, she can make it again and again.

Nathan and the girl, whose name he does not say, keep talking about other things. Boring things. I leave, because it's better to leave than to become familiar. I do not want them to remember me. My work here is not yet done, just as it is not yet defined.

Teach or kill?

Fix or destroy?

I am bothered by the whole A thing. I am hoping this means she did not trust other people with her name. I am hoping it was just a disguise for when she felt it convenient to "confide."

I gave myself a name, chosen because the first letter does not do what you think it will do. I knew early on that I was

66

male. Even when I was punished with a female body, I knew to act and think like a man. I would not get far otherwise.

This is what I would teach another body traveler: Look around you. See the person who is considered the strongest, then become that person. No matter what body you're inside, be that person. And when you learn how to stay, when you get more choice—be that person even more. Society is biased and ugly. Use that bias and ugliness to your advantage. Most everyone else does, if they have any power at all.

Even the sad sack of skin and bones that I'm in now has more power than most. I can use that. Having money gives you an advantage, especially if you use it. And being white. And being a man.

Nobody is expecting this man to steal, because he doesn't *need* to steal. So I take whatever I want.

I go to a restaurant, have an expensive dinner, then walk out before the check comes. I go to a drugstore and pocket some Advil. Then, just for fun, I find an item that will set off the alarm—an electric razor, on the pricier side for CVS—and I put it in a teenager's backpack as he searches through deodorants. His fault for leaving his backpack around like that.

I know this is all child's play, but isn't child's play how most of us fill the days? Isn't it how our leaders have chosen to lead? I fit right in.

I am already getting tired of this body. I appreciate the lack of resistance it offers, but I miss being desirable. I had a long enough time in Poole's body; I would like to go back to being the object of some carnal attention.

Before I leave this man's body, I must drain his bank account. This is remarkably easy to do. All I have to do is visit his bank, speak in an even, calm manner about needing funds for a new business venture, then transfer the majority of the money to the accounts I set up for myself years ago. His children will be left with practically nothing, but if they deserved more than nothing, I imagine they would have called or written at some point. If they're relying on getting their daddy's money when he's gone—well, it's mine now.

I will have to wait a few days for the transfer to go through. It will be worth my while to do so.

In the meantime, there's more damage to be done.

There's always more damage to be done.

A

Day 6088

I check her Facebook all the time, waiting for something to happen. Some other message. I check every hour. Every ten minutes. Five minutes. I worry that there's something I'm not seeing because we're not friends.

When I wake up, I check the phone first. I see she was out with her boyfriend. I take a shower and think about her picture, about whether she looked happy or was just pretending to look happy. I feel ashamed that I want her to be pretending, then tell myself I don't *really* want that. I check for another update after I get dressed, mindlessly pulling things from the drawers. Not thinking about the day at all. Just thinking about her.

Then it hits me: I have been awake for almost an hour and I haven't even thought about who I am today, haven't even learned this person's name. With a few touches on the phone, I am looking at Moses Cheng's Facebook profile. He only has forty friends. His sister tags him in family photos, but he doesn't post anything himself. I'm not sure if this means he doesn't have many friends or if it just means he doesn't like Facebook. Then I search around a little in his mind and realize the answer's both.

Moses's sister is waiting for him in the kitchen. "Here," she says, throwing him a granola bar. "No time to waste. We've got to go."

"I need my bag," I tell her. She groans and tells me to go get it.

I'm hoping that Moses doesn't need anything in his backpack today that he didn't have there yesterday. I hope he put his homework in, because I don't have time to look for it. His sister is already calling up for him to hurry. I don't think she's being impatient—I think I'm late. Because I got lost thinking of Rhiannon.

In the car, Moses's sister reminds him she can't drive him home—she has band practice.

"Are you going to be okay?" she asks him.

I'm sure I'll be able to find my way. I tell her I'll be fine. And then I resist checking Rhiannon's page on Moses's phone, because his sister is keeping an eye out. Because of the time difference, Rhiannon's been up for hours now. I don't understand why she hasn't posted anything.

I tell myself to stop.

I don't listen to myself.

Moses is on the shorter side and the slighter side—usually this is helpful when it comes time to be invisible. But for whatever reason, people keep seeing him and shoving him. It's like a reverse game of pinball, where the pinball stays on a straight course and it's the bumpers that move toward him.

It's a little better out of the hallways. But not much. In math class, the guy behind me keeps poking my back with his pencil. The first time he does it, I startle—which he thinks is hysterical. It doesn't take me long to find that the guy's name is Carl and this is a regular occurrence. I don't find any memory of Moses fighting back. So I just sit there and take it. I look around for some sympathetic looks, but no one seems to care. Moses is not the only one who's used to it.

At the end of class, the teacher asks for homework to be passed up to the front of the room, and I can't find Moses's

70

in his backpack. Meanwhile, Carl is shoving his paper in my face, telling me to pass it up. I want to rip it into shreds. I want to shower the shreds over his head. And at the same time, I want to know why I'm letting him get to me. It's like my navigation through the day has been stripped of any possibility of autopilot. I need autopilot.

The bell rings and Carl takes a bottle of Gatorade out of his bag, opens the cap, and pours the contents into my backpack. I don't even see it happening at first, I'm so mad at myself about the homework. Then I see him dropping the empty bottle into my bag, and I remember that Moses's phone is in there. Even though I know I should not engage, I take the bottle out of my backpack and hold it by its neck and swing it at Carl's laughing face. It's a plastic bottle, and the damage I do is minimal, but his surprise is immense. *Now* people are paying attention, and are yelling that it's a fight. But I don't want to fight, I just want to save the phone, so I go for my backpack, which gives Carl the opening he needs to throw me to the ground. I can feel myself being lifted, just for a second, and then I'm falling and I'm hitting and he's yelling that he's going to hurt me. The teacher's coming over now, and Carl is claiming self-defense. School security comes and is only slightly less belligerent than Carl. I am marched to the vice principal's office, and the whole time I'm trying to dry off the phone—I'm actually asking if there's any way to get a bag of rice from the cafeteria, because I've heard that rice can help, but the security guard is completely ignoring anything I say. I look behind me, assuming I'll see Carl marched in the same formation. But apparently I'm the only one being corralled. It's the time between class periods now, so the halls are full. People look confused to see me being pulled along by security. I can see a few asking their friends who I am.

The phone won't turn on. My backpack is leaking a trail

on the linoleum floor of the hallway. The security guard is yelling at me to put the phone away, asking me what the hell I'm doing, as if having a dead phone out is an admission of guilt in all things.

I am shown into the vice principal's office. He's on the phone, and when he hangs up, I realize the call was about me, because straight off he says, "So . . . you hit a fellow student with a bottle."

"It was plastic," I tell him.

This is the wrong thing to say.

"I don't care if it was made of feathers," the vice principal fumes. "This school has zero tolerance for violence. Zero."

"Please," I say. "Let me give you some context."

I know there's a twisted code of honor about never tattling on another student, never speaking up against someone who's done you wrong. I know I will only make it worse by breaking this code. But the code of honor was written by bullies for the protection of bullies, and I don't want to follow it.

I tell the vice principal what happened. I tell him about all the abuses Moses has put up with from Carl and his friends— every single one I can find in Moses's memory, leading up to today. When I tell the vice principal how the bottle came to be in my hand, I see him look at my bag and the pool of Gatorade gathering underneath it.

"I apologize for snapping," I tell him. "I know that was wrong. But I couldn't take it anymore. I had to protect myself."

"Carl Richards says *he* was protecting himself," the vice principal points out.

"Yeah," I say, gesturing to my body. "Because I'm so threatening."

The vice principal snort-laughs at that, then collects himself, picks up his phone again, and says, "Please find out what classroom Carl Richards is in now and have him sent to see me in five minutes. Thank you." When he hangs up, he looks at me for a hard few seconds before saying, "Alright. I want you to go see Ms. Tate in the guidance office. Tell her everything you told me, and anything else you might come to remember. Then wait there until the end of school. I'll talk to Mr. Richards and hear his 'context,' and then Ms. Tate and I will discuss our next steps. This is a very serious matter, and I am taking it very seriously."

"Thank you, sir."

I pick up my dripping bag and start to head out.

"You also have permission to go to the men's room to dry that off. The guidance suite has carpeting."

"Understood, sir."

I know I have to get out quick, because I don't want to run into Carl again. Which is cowardly of me, because Moses will have to face him eventually—and since I'm the one who messed up, I should shoulder the initial, inevitable blowback. But I dodge, because I can.

The bathroom is empty. I use about forty paper towels to dry everything off. Some of the books have pages stained orange, and anything that was sitting at the bottom of the backpack—a small notebook, a pack of gum, another granola bar—is now the consistency of pulp.

I try turning on the phone again. Nothing.

I want to go to the library, to use the computer to check Facebook.

Then I remember, no—I have to get to the "guidance suite."

The minute I walk into Ms. Tate's office, she says, "Moses, this isn't like you. This isn't like you *at all*." I am not surprised that she would say this, but I am surprised that she knows him enough to make the distinction. They've clearly

73

talked before, but never about the real problems. Now I have to tell her what I've already told the vice principal—and as I do, she looks more and more concerned. I don't have time to verify it, but I imagine that Moses has only gone to the guidance counselor before to talk about grades and colleges.

"I see, I see," she says when I'm done. Then she closes her eyes for the slightest of moments, breathes in, and resumes. "Look. You are a smart boy, Moses. And you did a stupid thing. But part of being smart is doing stupid things and learning from them. We do have a zero-tolerance policy at this school about violence. And we also have a zero-tolerance policy about bullying. When those two policies collide— well, it calls for a little tolerance on our part. But whatever happens—and it's truly out of my hands—you must never attack anyone else here ever again. Period. Is that clear?"

I nod.

"Good. Now give me your phone. I'm going to see if Mary in the cafeteria can spare some rice. I hear that's the best shot you have. Sucks up the moisture. You'd have to ask Mr. Prue in chemistry for the specifics."

She leaves, and I sit there alone for a few minutes. Her computer is on, and I wonder if there's time to check Facebook and then erase the history. It feels like too much of a risk. A ridiculous risk. In fact, I can't believe I'm thinking about myself at a time like this. Whatever the vice principal decides, I have made Moses's life worse than it was before I came into it. If I'd been focusing on him and not on myself, I would have had the homework, and my backpack probably would have been zipped. I would have thought for a second about its placement and I would have been sure to keep it out of Carl's reach.

Ms. Tate returns with a bag full of rice, and assures me that my phone is somewhere in the middle of it. She says to let it sit like that overnight. There's only a half hour left in school now, and she tells me to read in the corner until the bell rings. I pull out one of my books, and she sees the wet warp and orange taint of the pages.

"Oh dear," she says. "Can you still read it?"

"It's mostly on the edges," I tell her. The pages are hard to turn, and I'm not really registering any of the words, but I make sure to act like I'm reading so I don't have to talk to her anymore. Eventually she seems to forget I'm there, even when she calls the vice principal to ask what's to be done now. I don't hear his answer.

I wonder if Moses's parents will be called. From his memories, they seem like reasonable people. But this is not a reasonable thing their son has done, so there's no precedent.

When the bell rings, Ms. Tate tells me, "Be here before homeroom tomorrow—let's say seven-fifteen. We'll discuss next steps then. I would advise you not to take the trouble you're in lightly, and to think long and hard about what you've done. This is not to excuse Carl from anything that *he* did— but there have to be methods of dealing with him that do not involve fighting in school."

I don't challenge this point. But the question lingers, and I think both Ms. Tate and I feel it: What would those methods be? How do you stop someone like Carl, short of taking him down?

My guess is that the fight was not spectacular enough to merit school-wide gossip, because I make it to my locker unimpeded. I feel that if word had spread, Moses's sister would have tried to get in touch with him. Although for all I know, she's texted repeatedly.

It's not that far of a walk home—fifteen minutes tops. I can't map it or anything, so I rely on Moses's memory. As people board buses and get rides, I try to make myself unremarkable. A lot of people are walking in the direction of Taco Bell and McDonald's, so I veer down a side alley. I'm eager to get back to Moses's computer, behind the closed door of Moses's room. I am trying not to think about what it will be like for him when he wakes up tomorrow morning and realizes he has to get to school early to see Ms. Tate for the verdict on whether he'll be suspended or expelled.

I hear a car coming and step to the side so it can pass. But instead of passing, it pulls up beside me. I turn and see someone who looks a lot like Carl—his brother?—in the driver's seat, and then Carl in the passenger seat and some other guys in the back. The car turns into me, blocking my way, and stops. I turn around to run, but they're already jumping out of the car.

I am so, so stupid.

"Hey, Cheng!" Carl's brother calls out, slamming his door. "Think you're tough, crying all over Petty's office? Think it's okay to attack someone in class, do you?"

He's at least nine inches taller than me and might weigh twice as much. There's no way this is fair.

"Fucking Cheng," Carl snarls.

I don't like the way they're using my last name.

"Ready to fight now?" Carl's brother taunts. "Gonna break out your karate moves?"

I want to leave my body, which isn't even my body. I want to be able to leave while what's about to happen is happening. Flight and fight aren't really options. That leaves fright.

Protect your head.

I have no idea where I learned this. But when the first blow comes—Carl's brother steps aside and makes Carl do it—I don't try to strike back. I don't open myself up by lashing out. No, I roll up and protect my head. I try to use the wall next to me to cover as much as possible. They start to kick me then, in the side. It hurts. A lot. But I am protecting my head. *Moses's* head.

I hear shouting. The kicking stops. There's more shouting. I can feel them moving away from me. Something soft comes and presses against me. The car doors open and slam. The engine starts. I open my eyes. It's a dog—there's a dog next to me. "Are you okay?" a woman is asking. She has her phone in her hand. I think it's to call the police, but instead she says, "I got the whole thing. I got pictures of all those guys." I'm trying to sit up, but it really hurts. I wipe my forehead and there's blood.

"Okay, okay," the woman says. "Don't move. I'm calling an ambulance."

I start crying. Because I'm hurting, yes. But also because I've done this to him. I've done this.

More people are gathering now, asking what happened. One of them says he's a doctor and heard the shouting from his office. He checks me out and gets me to stand. We go to his office and he stops the bleeding, explaining that it's just a cut, that I'm going to be okay. It looks worse than it is.

Then he checks my side and tells me I may have broken a few ribs. Tells me to lie down. Asks me for my parents' number.

I try. But I don't know it.

I explain about my phone, and I probably seem incoherent at first, answering *What's your parents' phone number?* with something about rice. But eventually the bag of rice is retrieved from my backpack. They take the phone out—too soon. It doesn't work.

I tell them to call the school. To ask for Ms. Tate.

When they think I can't hear, the doctor and his assistant

say they can't believe that kids today don't know any phone numbers. I want to go to sleep. But I force myself to stay awake.

The ambulance arrives and I'm taken to the hospital for X-rays and for treatment. About ten minutes later, Ms. Tate comes in and says my parents are on their way. I look behind her and see my sister in the hall, crying. I wonder if she's going to blame herself, for letting me walk home alone even though I told her it was going to be okay.

When my parents arrive, my sister stays in the hall. My mother is focused on how I'm feeling and what the doctors have said. My father is seething, and tells me that the boys who attacked me are being arrested as we speak. Apparently the video caught all their faces.

I should be comforted by this. But there is nothing that feels like comfort to be experienced. There's only pain and guilt and sadness and monumental remorse.

I used to think I was good at this.

I am not good at this.

I am dangerous to anyone I'm in.

Moses's mother studies his face. The next time the doctor comes in, she asks her if it's okay for me to sleep.

"There's no sign of a concussion," the doctor says. "Let's just finish here, then you can take him home and he can sleep."

So at least I protected my head.

No, not my head.

Moses's head.

They give me painkillers. I take them. As soon as I get into bed and my mother turns out the lights, I crash.

I wake up in fits and starts over the next few hours. Either my father or mother is watching over me. My sister has expressed sympathy but has kept her distance.

I don't have the energy to say anything, or even the energy to figure out if there is anything I could possibly say. Sleep pulls me under soon enough.

This body is done with me for today.

A

Day 6089

It feels unfair to wake up the next morning as someone else.

Gwen has type 1 diabetes and an insulin pump, so I know I will have to be extra attentive—what's second nature to her is not going to be second nature to me. I feel like I'm betraying Moses by not thinking about him, about what might be happening to him, but I know it's more important to pay attention to Gwen and what she's going to need for the day. Staying in bed and feeling awful is not an option. I will have to get out of bed, be social, monitor my blood sugar, and feel awful.

There's a knock on the door.

"Are you up?" a voice—Gwen's mother—asks. Then she adds, "We're all waiting for you downstairs."

She says it sweetly, so I know I'm not in trouble. I feel I *should* be in trouble.

But not Gwen, I remind myself. *She didn't do anything to Moses. You did.*

I pull a robe over my pajamas and open the door. There are excited noises coming from downstairs. *The kitchen,* Gwen's memory tells me.

I swing open the door and there's a cheer of "Happy birthday!" Gwen's parents are there, as well as four younger kids who don't share any family resemblance in their features but deeply resemble a family in the way they exist with each other.

There are cookies on the kitchen table that spell out H-A-P-P-Y B-I-R-T-H-D-A-Y.

"Cookies for breakfast!" one of the kids shouts out. Santiago, age seven. He's only lived here three months, so this must be his first birthday celebration here. Cookies for breakfast is this family's thing. "We made special ones for you!"

Santiago reaches for a cookie, but Alicia (age nine) stops him.

"Not yet," she scolds. "We have to sing first."

A spirited rendition of "Happy Birthday to You" follows.

Gwen (age seventeen) smiles. Because I make sure she smiles. Because I know she should smile.

But I feel more awful than ever. Why this, of all days? Why should I get to usurp a happy day, especially after I just caused an unhappy day for someone else? How is that fair?

And why am I expecting fairness?

Gwen's family is so joyously excited for her. They love her so much. I try to allow that to take me in, to welcome me into my own expression of joy, because sometimes the only thing you have to pull you to a better place is the sheer force of invitation from the people who love you dearly. I know the fairest thing I can do for Gwen—other than leaving, which I can't—is to try to give back to her family the affection that they are providing to her now, having no idea whatsoever that she's not really here.

There's no candle to blow out—I'm told there will be a big cake tonight. Now there are hugs and presents, until it's time to go to school. Ozzie (age ten) wants me to wear an IT'S MY BIRTHDAY button on my shirt. Alicia tells him that buttons like that aren't cool when you're a *teenager*, which, she emphasizes, is something he should *already know.*

I almost put on the button to take Ozzie's side. But I'm afraid of what the kids on the bus will say.

I head back upstairs to shower and change. In the shower, it all comes back to me—Moses in the hospital bed, the look of hate on Carl's face.

It wasn't your fault, I tell myself. *It was Carl's fault. And his brother's. And all those guys.*

I believe this. But I also believe that Moses would have been safe if he'd been navigating himself through the day.

After I'm dressed, I go online to make sure I know how Gwen's insulin pump works. It's the same kind I've had before, but I double-check. I also make sure to confirm the right levels from Gwen's memory. At some point, I'm going to need to take a run, which is what Gwen does to make sure she gets the physical activity she needs. After school, usually.

I don't go anywhere near Facebook. There's no time. And I don't deserve to see anything Rhiannon may have left me.

I figure I'll have some time to think on the bus, but Gwen's best friend, Connor, is saving her a seat. He throws little streamers in the air when she sits down, and the people in the seats around us wish Gwen a happy birthday. I realize I could have worn the button.

"I'm so excited for tonight!" Connor says. "It's going to be such a great party! Your parents are *the best.*"

I don't argue. Instead I think of Moses's parents at his bedside. What they must be waking up to today. The conversations they must be having. His mother's worry. His father's anger.

We get to school and are soon joined by Candace and Lizette, Gwen's other best friends. And Emily, Gwen's *other* other best friend. Candace, Lizette, and Emily have decorated Gwen's locker like it's the biggest booth at a birthday convention—Gwen must love panda bears, because there are panda bears everywhere. And for presents, Candace, Lizette, Emily, and Connor have all gotten her picture books featuring pandas. ("Mine also features donuts," Emily says as she hands hers over.)

Gwen says thank you. Gwen is blown away. Gwen tells her best friends how happy she is.

I am pretending. I am a fraud.

School is still school, and class is still class, but people are nicer when they have a chance to be nicer. Everyone seems to know it's my birthday.

"Have you checked your Facebook yet?" Candace asks after Spanish class. "I left you the cutest panda pic."

I take out my phone and check. There are so many birthday greetings. I could spend the whole day going into Gwen's memory to figure out who all these people are.

"Isn't that the cutest?" Candace asks.

I look at the photo—it's a panda from the National Zoo cuddling a baby panda. They look like the happiest pandas I've ever seen.

"That's adorable," I say. Then Candace gives me a hug and heads to a classroom that isn't mine. I have about a minute before I have to be in physics. I type Rhiannon's name into the search field. But before I can click, Lizette is at my side, asking me if I saw the photo Candace left me, then asking me if we did the cookie thing this morning at home.

I use the minute I have to talk to her. Then I put away my phone.

Moses must still be in pain.

Moses must be wondering what happened.

Moses must be afraid to go back to school.

Everyone must be talking about what happened to Moses.

Maybe they've seen the video.

What will that do to him?

Emily blindfolds me on the way to lunch. She leads me, and I trust her. We don't go to the cafeteria, but to a corner of the library. There, Emily leads my friends in what can only be called a choral birthday medley, with the Beatles' "Birthday" song featured prominently. There's an apple with a candle in it, surrounded by other apples. ("We know you'll be getting enough cake later.") My friends toast me with apples. Then we go to the cafeteria and get real lunch. They don't let me pay for mine.

I want to get my phone. I want to go on Facebook and look for Moses Cheng. Even though I know he's not going to post anything.

And Rhiannon. Even though I feel farther away from her than ever.

"Oh no," Connor says. "She wouldn't dare."

I look up from our table and see a girl walking over. Before I can figure out who she is, she's in front of me, holding out a blue box tied with a yellow ribbon.

"Here," she says sweetly. "Happy birthday."

Lizette puts out a hand to stop me from taking it.

"Uh-uh," she says. "Dee, you are *not* invited to this party."

"What?" Dee snaps back, all sweetness gone. "I'm not allowed to give her a present?"

Lizette stares her down. "The only present she ever wanted from you was some love and honesty. But you gave that present to *Be-lin-da* instead, and we do *not* allow regifting at this particular table."

Dee pulls the box back. "Okay, fine." Then she looks right at me. "You can't say I never tried. This is me trying. And look at how well *that* goes."

She heads off, and even before she's out of earshot, Lizette, Emily, Candace, and Connor are all asking me if I'm okay, in a way that makes it clear that they are expecting Gwen to be a wreck.

"I'm fine," I assure them. "I'm great."

Which is true, because I still don't know who Dee is.

Lizette high-fives me. "That's my girl," she says.

The mood turns even more celebratory, as if I've just vanquished a dragon.

They'll all be so disappointed when it goes back to normal tomorrow.

Unless . . .

I get out of my seat.

"Where is she?" I ask, scanning the cafeteria.

Connor points to a corner. "There. Why?"

"I need to tell her myself. To never do that again."

My friends look surprised, but they also look happy—and they aren't stopping me.

I walk right over to Dee's table. She's already laughing with her friends, probably about me. When she finally sees me there, it's her turn to look surprised. I notice the present is nowhere in sight.

"What?" she says. "You let them talk to me like that and then you come over here? What's that about?"

"It's about this," I tell her. "It's about me not needing them to tell you off. It's about me telling you off firsthand, and telling you to never pull that shit again. I am done. Completely done. And I wanted you to hear it from me."

I don't give her time to respond. Partly because I've started shaking. Like my body is trying to tell me something.

As I'm walking back to my table, I can already see my friends cheering. They think I've done the right thing. I thought I was doing the right thing. But who was I doing it for? Gwen? Me? Moses? In the pit of my stomach, I'm wondering: *What if she really loves Dee?* But I don't let myself check. What's done can't be undone.

"That was beautiful," Lizette says as soon as I'm back in my seat.

"Best birthday resolution ever," Emily chimes in.

"Best start of a birthday year ever," Candace agrees.

And it's Connor who asks it again: "Are you okay?"

I tell them again that I'm great.

But this time it feels more hollow than before. And I'm not even sure why.

Gwen has a lot of friends. They are there in the halls and in her classes. They are there on her Facebook page. And they are all there at her house for the party that night.

Everyone in the family and many of my friends have chipped in with decorations, so it's like every age I've already been is represented—construction paper cutouts and crayon drawings alongside a supercut of the past year playing in a loop on the TV screen. Friends laughing. Friends in costumes. Friends singing. Gwen at the center of it all.

I work hard to keep track of who's who, but I can barely keep up. April (age four) hangs by my side and provides a good diversion, especially because a lot of my friends have to introduce themselves to her and explain who they are.

Then the moment comes when the lights are turned off and a cake is carried in, its eighteen candles ("One for good luck!") flickering to show me all the friendly faces who've gathered to celebrate with me. "Make a wish!" Gwen's mother calls out, and I want to wish for word from Rhiannon and I know I should wish for Moses's speedy recovery, and I get tangled between the two and debate in my head for too long, to the point where they can all see me deliberating and they find it funny. I wish for Moses's speedy recovery, and then the minute the candles are blown out, my belief in wishes is also extinguished, and I feel ridiculous for being so anguished and feel disgusting for taking Gwen's wish and using it for myself.

As the cake is cut, I go to the bathroom, ostensibly to check my insulin (which is fine, even though I didn't get a chance to run with everything going on, so I'm a little bit off). Really, I'm doing it to take myself out of this scene for a moment. Because it's not my scene. When I was a kid, I could trick myself into thinking that the birthdays were really my own birthdays, that there was a direct, to-the-day correspondence between the age I was and the ages of the bodies I was in. Then, when I was twelve, it happened: two birthdays in the same week. And suddenly I realized that what was happening to me was neither precise nor predictable. The birthdays had never been mine.

A birthday—a real birthday—is yet another thing I will never have.

I tried to pick a day for myself. August 5th. That lasted for a couple of years. But ultimately it felt arbitrary, a lie I was telling myself to feel better. And the moment I saw the lie for what it was, it was hard to believe it.

So I taught myself not to miss it. To know I was different, and to accept that.

That worked better. But it's not working anymore.

The sounds of a birthday party through a closed door are unmistakable: the colorful bubbles of conversation, the heartfelt laughter, the feet of small children running around the people acting like larger, older children. I recognize these sounds and know their chaotic delight, but only through a door.

I know Gwen has to return to the party. I know she'll be missed if she's gone for too long. Once upon a time, I didn't know what that was like, to be missed. Now I do, and I understand why I can't avoid the love being sent Gwen's way.

I must dive back into the festivities. I must swim within the conversations, swim from gift to gift, wish to wish. Some people swim to get somewhere. Others swim to stay in shape, or to get faster. Right now, I'm going to swim so I won't drown.

Comment from M:
This is pointless.

Comment from Someone:
I understand.

Comment from M:
Not possible.

Comment from Someone:
Listen to me first. I have depersonalization/derealization disorder. You might not even know what that is. I didn't, until I found out I had it.

Like you, I have periods when I feel completely separate from my body and from the world around me. It's a hard thing to put into words. The best I've been able to come up with is that it's like everything you see is part of this video game. Only with a video game, you know you're holding the control. But my DPD/DRD is like I'm watching the video game but I don't have the controller. I am convinced that I'm an avatar, not a person. I am convinced that the divide between the massive number of thoughts in my head and the actions around me is too wide to be crossed. I'm not just isolated from the world; I'm isolated WITHIN MYSELF. My thoughts are the only active things that I can believe. And that can be very frustrating and very confusing and very painful.

For a while, I thought I was going crazy. It was only when I found out that what I was experiencing had a name and that I wasn't the only one who had it (2% of the population has DPD in some form) that I could start to actually take action against it. It's not possible to make it go away, but knowing what it is and how it works means I can contain it a little more—contain it by naming it, both to myself and to other people.

I am not saying you have DPD and/or DRD. But I am saying that whatever it is you're facing, the odds are nearly 100% that there's someone else who is also facing it. Acknowledging it and naming it and understanding it as much as it can be understood are the most important things you can do. You say you want to die. I felt that way, too. But you also don't want to kill the body you're in. That means you want to live. The fact that you're talking about it—even with strangers—is a good step. You are on your way to acknowledgment.

Comment from PurpleCrayon12:
Thank you for sharing that, Someone.

Comment from M:
I appreciate what you're saying. I do. But with me, it's different.

Comment from Someone:
How?

Comment from M:
You experience separation from your own body. I am in a different body every day.

NATHAN

It's not that I'm completely antisocial—I just don't go out of my way to talk to people. At school, sure. I talk to friends. I talk to teachers when I have to. I talk to the guidance counselor when she "checks in" on me, even though what I really want to tell her is that in a high school where kids are dealing drugs and getting pregnant and beating the crap out of each other in the hallways, her attention would probably be better spent on other kids, not me.

Once school is done, I've usually run out of social energy. If my mother has asked me to go on some errands, I'll do them. But otherwise, it's straight home.

I'm walking home on Wednesday when a car pulls up beside me and a woman rolls down the passenger window.

"Excuse me!" she calls out. And honestly, my first reaction is to wish she'd try someone else. But there isn't anyone else around, so I stop. I don't say hello or anything, but she smiles and acts like I have.

"I'm a little lost," she says. "I was hoping you could help?"

"Sure," I tell her. Though now I'm thinking, *Can't you just use your phone?*

Before I can ask where she needs to go, she gawps at me and says, "Hey, aren't you that kid who was possessed by the devil?"

Now I totally regret stopping, because this woman has to be in her fifties or sixties, and she must have better things to remember than a news story from three months ago.

"I don't know what you're talking about," I tell her.

"Of course you do! You were picked up at the side of the road. Said the devil got you drunk or something like that. It was hysterical!"

"I'm gonna go," I mumble. Because something always stops me from being fully rude, I end up in this awkward state of halfway rude.

"Oh, don't worry about it!" the woman calls out. "*Vigilabo ego sum vobis!*"

"Excuse me?"

"I'm sorry. I won't bother you too much longer. Can you just give me directions?"

I want to get the hell out of there, but still: only halfway rude. So I say, "Sure. Where are you going?"

"Twenty Maple Lane," she says, a glint in her eye.

That's my address.

"What?" I say.

"As I told you, *vigilabo ego sum vobis.*"

What the hell? "I don't know what that means!" I tell her.

"You will!" she chirps out. Then she guns the motor and drives away.

At the end of the road, she turns in the direction away from my house. But I'm still nervous as I keep going. I almost call my mother, but I can imagine what her reaction would be if I told her she needed to come pick me up because some old woman gave me a taste of stranger danger. My credibility has already been shot. Even if I cry puppy, they act like I'm crying wolf.

So I walk home with my phone camera looking behind me so I can see if the car returns. When I get home, I'm there alone, so I lock all the doors.

Nothing happens.

I start to wonder if I misheard her. Maybe it was Maple

91

Drive and not Maple Lane—our town has both, even though I don't think either has a single maple tree.

I try to forget it.

Three days later, my mother takes me shopping for new pants.

I tell her I don't need new pants. She points to the frayed bottoms of the khakis I'm wearing and tells me they are—her exact word—*unacceptable.* The way she says it, you'd think it's a miracle that people don't throw stones at me as I walk down the street. Underneath the tirade, I can hear the true sentiment: *You've embarrassed us enough this year, haven't you? Must you keep doing it?* Of course, there's no way she can erase what happened when A took over my life. But she *can* buy me new pants.

We go to the Gap. I find the same exact pants I'm wearing, in the same exact size. I imagine we're done—but no. She says I have to try them on.

So there I am, peeling off my khakis so I can put on their better-loved twin. A pair of ankles and shoes appears below the changing room door—I figure it's the salesperson asking me if everything's fitting, even though I haven't had enough time to put anything on. But instead, a young voice says, "Hey, Nathan . . . *vigilabo ego sum vobis.*"

I am literally caught with my pants down. I quickly yank them up and pull open the door. There's nobody there, so I run back into the store. The only person I find is my mother, who is asking me where the new pants are. I push past her and try to find the woman from the other day. But there's nobody anywhere close to her description—and it wasn't her voice.

"Nathan, I'm talking to you!" my mother is saying. I'm still looking around the store. One woman meets my gaze for a second, then looks away. I don't even remember what kind of shoes they were, under the door. I wasn't paying attention. There are a few other people looking anxious, but everybody looks anxious nowadays. It's just a part of who we are, especially in public.

"Did they fit?" my mother asks.

"Of course they fit!" I yell, which causes her to give me her best you-are-the-least-grateful-son-in-the-history-of-sons expression.

"Well, where are they?" she asks.

I go back to the changing room and someone has already removed and probably refolded the khakis. So my mother and I go through this dance one more time. This time I'm not disturbed. But in the relative quiet of the changing room, I do take out my phone and type *vigilabo ego sum vobis* into Google Translate.

It's Latin.

I'm watching you.

I could tell Rhiannon about this, I think. But I still feel like I'm this random boy who's invited himself into her life because of this strange thing that happened to both of us. I don't know if our friendship is strong enough for me to start freaking her out on a regular basis.

So I keep my mouth shut. I go on with life. I turn on the news and try to let that be my cause of stress and outrage, instead of something more personal. Except the news feels like a personal attack against anyone with a shred of intelligence and decency, which doesn't make me feel much better. I try to think of ways my mind could be playing with me . . . but that's a stretch and a strain.

Especially when it continues.

This time it's my inbox that's stalked. The emails start

and they don't stop. Dozens of them, sent at uneven intervals from an email address I've never seen before.

The subject line is always *Vigilabo ego sum vobis.*

The messages are all blank.

I send one message back:

A?

The only reply? More *Vigilabo ego sum vobis.*

In the middle of the night, the doorbell rings. I hear my father get out of bed to answer it. I hear him come back and tell my mother nobody was there.

"Just a prank," he says. "Probably some kids."

"Probably picking on Nathan," my mother says needlessly. "I wish they'd leave us alone."

It's unclear whether I'm a part of that *us.*

The next day, I am home alone after school.

The doorbell rings.

I don't answer it.

It rings again.

And again.

It's not like I can call the police and report that someone's ringing my doorbell. The police are already in the Nathan-is-a-wolf-crier camp.

The fifteenth time, I go down to the door. "GO AWAY!" I yell. But I can't see anyone through the peephole. I go to the front window, pull the curtain aside, and peek out.

There's a car across the street. Not the woman from before. Not a woman at all. A man, probably my dad's age. He's been waiting for me to pull back that curtain. He mimes a pistol with his hand and shoots at me. Then he mouths words that can only be *vigilabo ego sum vobis*. I think he'll drive off then. But he doesn't. I let the curtain drop and head back to my room.

I call Rhiann'on. I don't tell her what's happening, because I don't know that there's anything she can do about it. I just need to talk to someone, to have someone on the line if the guy across the street tries anything.

I don't even know what he'd try.

Eventually I take another look outside, and the car is gone.

I don't want to be home alone anymore. I go to the public library after school. I sit at the computers, surrounded by other people at the computers, and I feel at least temporarily safe. I don't understand why this is happening to me. I don't know what I've done that makes me deserve to have these things go wrong.

A girl from school, Alexandra Berkman, sits down next to me. We're in some classes together, and we talk about French for a few minutes. Then she asks if I can watch her stuff while she goes to the washroom. I say sure, and when she comes back, I ask her if she'll do the same for me.

It's a one-person bathroom deal, and someone must have jumped right in after Alexandra left, since the door's locked and I have to wait a few minutes to get in. Eventually a seven-year-old boy emerges, without a parent. I am not optimistic about what the condition of the toilet seat is going to be. But I go in anyway.

I'm just about to lock the door when it's pushed hard from the outside. "Hey!" I cry out, figuring it's someone trying to get in who didn't see me go in first. But then a harder push comes and I'm knocked back. A guy comes storming in—big guy, about ten years older than me. "I'm in here!" I protest, and in response he punches me in the gut. I fall back onto the toilet seat, and he locks the door behind him and goes for my throat. I kick out and try to slide out from under him, but his grip is tightening and I can't get enough air to scream. He knocks my head back onto the toilet tank and it hurts like hell.

Then, with a grin, he asks, "Did you miss me, Nathan?"

I don't know what he means—until I look into his eyes and know exactly what he means. I just don't know how it's possible.

"Not so heroic now, are you?" the guy taunts. "Not so disagreeable. We had an agreement, didn't we, Nathan? And you broke that agreement. Well, *ego vigilabo fuerit vobis*. Except that there comes a time when watching isn't enough. It's time you played your part. And this time, you won't mess it up."

I try to play dumb. "Who are you?" I gasp. "What do you mean?"

He lifts me up by the throat. This guy is strong. Much stronger than Reverend Poole.

I am terrified.

"We did not come here for you to talk," the guy who used to be Poole says way too calmly. "It's my turn to talk—and I strongly recommend that you listen."

"I'm all ears," I squeak.

"Unless I remove one," he says, not really joking. "You see, Nathan, I can do whatever I want to you, whenever I want. You will never see me coming, because I could be anyone. That much should be clear to you now."

I try to nod, but he's still got me by the throat.

"Got it," I croak out.

"Good," he says, lowering me but not letting me go. "You must find the person you lost last time. You will not get another chance—and you do not have much time. If you don't get her back to me in the next week, I will start to dismantle your life piece by piece, until there is nothing left."

"But we don't know where she is! Honestly, we don't."

"Well, then—you'd better find her."

It's strange to think of A as a her. It's also wrong that I used the word *we*.

I wait too long to reply. He switches hands and pushes me by the back of my neck toward the sink. I thrust my hands down and push against the basin so he can't slam my face into it.

He lets go.

"Good," he says. "You have some fight in you. Use it. But don't try to fight me. That would be irresponsible to your well-being. And don't tell anyone else about this—not even A's girlfriend."

"How do you know about A?" I blurt.

But he's not going to tell me.

"I'll be in touch," he says.

When he opens the door, there's a line of people waiting outside. They seem surprised to see two of us inside the bathroom.

"We were having sex," Poole explains to the woman at the front of the line.

"WHAT?" she yells. Luckily for me, she seems to be a hundred years old.

Poole strides out of the library, leaving me to be the target of the angry, curious, and/or disgusted looks.

It's only when I get back to Alexandra that I realize I didn't even use the bathroom, and I still have to go.

"Are you okay?" she asks as I grab my bag.

"There's just . . . stuff I need to do," I get out. She gives me a look to let me know she doesn't particularly care to hear the details.

Nobody will. Not really. Rhiannon, possibly. But I feel that telling her will only bring her more trouble, especially if Poole somehow knows she exists. (Who else could A's girlfriend be?)

I am on my own on this one. And, oh yeah, completely screwed.

I have no idea how to escape this.

X

It takes a few days before I am the right type of person to do what I want to do. There's nothing like the disappointment of waking up in an old woman's body—good for invisibility and very little else. They can be receptacles of affection, but I have no need for affection. Fear is much more effective.

I have tried to master the path from person to person. I have tried to force my intentionality into the equation. But the metaphysical mathematics elude me; I have learned how to stay in a body by killing the host, but I still am left to the whims of the gods when it comes to traveling to my next body. There used to be some correspondence in age, but that appears to have become untethered. I can end up as anyone from day to day.

Naturally, I have preferences.

Just as this body is strong, its former owner is ashamed. He has desires that are not the right desires—they are not *acceptable* desires in the community in which he lives. He does not want to be who he is, so I can easily come in and take his place.

After scaring the pathetically susceptible Nathan Daldry in the bathroom of his local library, I head to the gym. Even if this man is a mess in his head, his body is a well-tuned vehicle. I spend time conditioning, then lifting. I have missed this rush, the feeling of force, the glorious pain of exertion. There is sweat and there is the acceleration of the heart and a struggle to maintain a steady supply of breath. But most of all, there is strength. I can revel in his strength. Even as I feel the weights press against me, I experience my own counterbalance, my own push against. This is the body I was meant to have. This is the only kind of body that allows me to feel my promise is manifest.

I push myself to the body's limit. Then comes the slow-down, the shower, and the unwind. But I'm still wound, even as I leave. I don't want to go home. I want sex. I want to use this body that way. To take pleasure. To be desired, and then to take advantage of that desire.

It doesn't matter what this guy was into before. So he goes onto an app, and it takes about twenty minutes for me to find what *I'm* into. A "date" in name. But really a hookup. One and done.

We meet at a bar. She gets tipsy and I get voracious. We all know where it goes from there. I even let her stay over. Not out of any generosity of spirit, but because I know his shame will only push deeper if she's around. If he can sense at all what's happened, he probably doesn't want to come back.

Which is, right now, fine by me.

She actually looks touched when I ask her to spend the night. Grateful. It makes me want to laugh at her.

One and done.

Fun and stun.

Done and run.

I hold my tongue all night so I can get more from her. The next morning, though, when I'm still in his body and she's still in my bed, I shake her off mercilessly. Tell her it was no good, and that I only asked her to stay out of pity. She gets angry, and I yawn. After she storms out, I take a nap. Then I head back to the gym.

A couple of his friends text him. I don't reply, and they don't try again.

100

I call in sick to work. Then I check his bank accounts and decide that tomorrow he'll quit his job. He had no idea, but he's already served his last day.

When you're given a Ferrari, you don't trade it in for a Camry.

This body is mine now.

RHIANNON

Alexander's parents are out of town a lot. Something involving their jobs and needing to travel. They don't see each other that much, and they don't see Alexander much. At first I thought it was cool that they were never around—I could spend as many hours as I wanted at his house, doing homework on the lime-green couch in his room, curling up next to him for study breaks. He'd read me poems or tell me stories, and we'd never have to worry about a knock on the door.

But now, even though I enjoy the freedom their absence gives us, I think it's a little sad that they leave Alexander alone so much. His room makes much more sense—the way he creates all these intricate distractions, all these creative ways of having conversations with art and color and light when there aren't any real conversations to be had with other people.

I'm thinking about this after school on Monday, when I'm back on the lime-green couch, supposedly doing biology homework but really wondering about how our lives work.

"Do you miss them?" I ask Alexander. He's on the bed, supposedly reading *Robinson Crusoe*. "Your parents, I mean."

He doesn't ask me why I'm asking the question at this particular moment. Instead he says, "Yeah. I do."

"Couldn't they arrange it so they didn't leave at the same time?"

"They used to do that. When I was little. But it was always Mom who had to stay back—not because she's a mom,

102

but because her job was a little more flexible. Unfortunately, that didn't last. The traveling's a part of what they do, and if they want to keep their jobs, they go where they have to go. It sucks, but it pays the bills." He stops for a second, then starts again. "No. That makes it sound worse than it is. The honest truth is that they like what they do, and they're good at it, and even though it sucks that they're gone, it would suck even more if they were miserable."

"That makes sense," I say.

The honest truth is something Alexander says a lot. It's something he believes in. He's always telling me that one of the best parts of our relationship is how natural it feels to be truthful with one another—the last people he dated weren't as truthful, and the relationships skidded because of that.

I know he's right. And I know I am much more truthful with him than I ever could have been with Justin. I am discovering that the best possible relationship is one where you can say whatever is on your mind—no matter how random, no matter how hard, no matter how silly—and the other person will always be open to hear it. I have never had that before. With A, it felt that way, but we didn't have the time to do it. We were always too caught up in figuring out how our relationship would work, or how it wouldn't work. With Alexander, I can ask about his parents, or I can ask about dinner, or I can tell him about a cartoon I watched when I was six, or I can read a sentence from my biology book to him in a Kermit the Frog voice—I can say whatever I want, ask whatever I want. He is open to whatever words I send his way. I don't have to worry anymore about saying the wrong thing. About landing on the certain words, or certain thoughts, that turn out to be emotional land mines. I know he's not going to shout at me or tear me down for saying something stupid. It is incredible to have that pressure lifted.

He can do the same with me, of course. He can say anything, ask anything. But that was never a problem with Justin. The problem always came when I opened my mouth.

The problem with Alexander is different. The problem with him is that he gives me the honest truth, and I give him the dishonest truth in return.

Or maybe it isn't a problem. I don't know. Because it *is* still the truth. I don't lie to him. It's just that the truth I give him has sentences missing.

I told him about Justin. That was hard. Not because I thought he'd take Justin's side or think less of me or decide that any girl who'd stay with an asshole like that wasn't worth being with. If I hadn't really known Alexander, I would have been afraid of all of those things. But because I knew Alexander, the thing that made it hardest to talk about was my own embarrassment. It didn't bother me that Alexander would hear what I had to say—it was that *I* had to hear it. I had to sit there in his arms and listen to how I'd narrowed my vision so that all I could see was Justin, all I could care about was Justin. He didn't treat me well, and it rarely occurred to me that I could be treated better. Neither of us really knew what we were doing, but we didn't recognize that. We thought it was love.

Now I know: Love isn't so straightforward. It's never a matter of telling yourself to do it and doing it. It's never a matter of someone else telling you to do it and doing it. It can't exist between two people if they can't also feel it exist outside of them, too. It can involve hurt, but it shouldn't make you hurt all the time. Then it's not love. It's a trap disguised as love.

Alexander knows I fell into the trap. He knows I didn't set it, but he also knows I laid my own traps, too. I told him all of this partly to be honest and partly to warn him. I knew he wouldn't be scared away.

104

He said Justin wasn't a threat to him or to me anymore. He also said the girl I was when I was in love with Justin wasn't a threat, either, because she was gone now. I told him I appreciated him saying that, but the old me will never be gone. She'll always be alive in me somewhere. I just have to make sure she's never in charge again, no matter how loud she gets, demanding to have her way.

I said all this, and still he wasn't scared away.

Now he goes back to reading *Robinson Crusoe* and I supposedly return to biology. Every now and then, he hums the song that's playing in his head, and doesn't even realize he's doing it. It could be annoying, but I think it's sweet.

He's told me about his exes, the ones who weren't truthful with him. One moved away, and he hasn't bothered to stay in touch with her. One kept lying even after they broke up, telling everyone that it had been Alexander's fault, that he hadn't even tried to make it work. They're not in touch, either. But the most recent was this girl Cara, and the two of them have stayed friends. We've even hung out with her, in a bigger group. I felt a little weird about it, but Alexander told me that it was all good, that he and Cara knew they were bad for each other as boyfriend-girlfriend but okay for each other once they took the *boy-* and *girl-* off and just made it friend-friend.

Thinking about Cara makes me wonder why I can't be friends with A.

I know it's not the same. I know we didn't break up because we stopped feeling like we should be together. We knew we should be together, or at least try—but we also knew we *couldn't*. Which isn't the same thing.

But still, there's nothing saying we can't be in touch.

The twisted thing is I'm thinking that I'm wanting it as much for Alexander as for me. Because until I can get this straightened out, my truth is always going to be dishonest.

And if the stumbling block is that I'm missing A, then I should at least get through the silence, because the silence is the worst part.

It's not about getting A back.

It's not about being with A again.

It's about knowing where A is and what A's doing.

It's about having A in my life in whatever way can actually work.

So I take out my phone. I check my email. I try not to think about it too much. I just do it. I put A's email in the TO: spot, and a simple *Hello* in the subject line.

I keep the message simple.

A,

I know you thought it would be easier if you disappeared. It isn't. Even if we can't be together, I still want to talk to you.

R

I am about to hit send, but then I read it over and decide to change a word.

A,

I know you thought it would be easier if you disappeared. It isn't. Even though we can't be together, I still want to talk to you.

R

Without reading it again, I hit send.

The response is instant.

There's an email in my inbox, telling me my message is undeliverable. The mailbox no longer exists.

106

I check the address. I resend the message. The same thing happens.

"Ugh," I say out loud.

"What?" Alexander asks from his perch.

"Nothing," I say. Then I decide to get closer to an honest truth. "I was just trying to email a friend of mine who moved away. But the mailbox is full or deleted or something. My email didn't go through. I wish they'd tell you that before you spend the time writing the email instead of after."

"Ugh," Alexander says.

"Exactly!"

He goes back to work, humming happily. I can't go back to work—now that the idea of talking to A again has taken hold, it won't let go.

But there isn't any other way.

I think about the post I left on Facebook. The songs. If A saw them, why didn't A respond?

Maybe I wasn't clear enough.

Even though I can't be too clear when I'm someplace other people can see.

Dishonest truth.

Or maybe just dishonest.

But I have to try again.

I go on to my Facebook. I think of another song to post. I go on YouTube and find one called "Say Something."

But how will A know why I'm posting it? How will A know it's ours?

And how can I post it without anyone else knowing it's ours?

I look at Alexander on the bed. Now I'm definitely being dishonest. Because I realize how I can do it.

I attach the link for "Say Something"—and for the caption, I write:

A— *You can interrupt me any time.*

I post it. Exhale. Go back to my biology.

About ten minutes later, Alexander says, "Something!"

I look at him and find him smiling. His phone is in his hand.

"Now, did you want me to interrupt you, or was this just a way to see if I was checking my Facebook when I should be reading this terminally boring book?"

"Both, I imagine."

Still smiling, he puts down *Robinson Crusoe* and sails on over to the couch. I move my legs to make a space for him.

"So now that you have my undivided attention . . . ," he says.

Once he sits down, I put my legs back where they were, only now they're on his lap.

"Do you want to do my bio homework for me?" I ask.

He playfully, emphatically shakes his head.

"Do you want to read me the sexy passages from *Robinson Crusoe?*"

Another head shake.

"Do you want to kiss awhile and then get something to eat?"

This gets a nod.

A very enthusiastic nod.

He is the first person I've been with who has been so enthusiastic. No doubts. No regrets. No conflict. Just . . . happiness to be here with me.

I still feel dishonest. But the honest truth is that I want to kiss him, and mean it.

So I do.

A

Day 6099

Say something.

I don't see the message until the day is almost done. And it's awkward because my father is hovering behind me—not exactly looking at what I'm checking out, but watching the clock closely, to make sure I don't spend more than my allotted half hour on the computer.

Turns out, I'm on probation.

Or, more to the point, Lilah White is on probation.

Her phone's been taken away. She has to come home directly after school.

She is not, under any circumstances, to talk to Jeff James.

Her boyfriend. Or her ex-boyfriend. It depends on who you ask. Or it depends on who she's talking to, because it seems like there are at least a half-dozen different versions out there.

The facts, as I can figure them out, are:

(1)   Lilah and Jeff had been going out for a year.

(2)   Shortly after their anniversary, Jeff decided it was going to be their last anniversary, and broke up with her.

(2a)   Or, I should say, attempted to break up with her.

(3)   Lilah did not take it well.

(4)   Lilah tried to get him back.

(5)   This failed.

(6)   So Lilah decided to forward all the naked photos Jeff had sent her to any friend she had in her phone.

(6a) Some of these photos had other people in them.

(7)   In retaliation, Jeff sent out the nudes Lilah had sent *him*.

(7a) Some of these photos had other people in them.

(8)   Some of the boyfriends and girlfriends of the other people mentioned in (6a) and (7a) were not happy about this, and retaliated with more nude photos.

(9)   It did not take long for someone at their school to realize that the student body was suddenly awash in photos of student bodies.

(9a) The chain was traced back to Lilah.

(10) She was put on probation, and her phone was taken away.

(11) She was also forbidden from seeing Jeff, who was also put on probation and, I assumed, forbidden from seeing her.

(12) According to what Lilah has said to some friends, Jeff felt so bad about everything and was so impressed by how upset his breakup had made her that he took her back and they're now together.

(12a) But considering what some of Lilah's other friends had to say to her about Jeff today (*asshole, user, jerk, so glad that's over*, etc.), there's certainly a contingent that thinks they're still broken up.

There's no way for me to ask Lilah for clarification—it was unhelpful enough to skim through her memories of Jeff. I learned much more about him anatomically than I did about him emotionally.

All of the drama happened last week, so I made it through the day by remaining pretty silent; there were so many people talking *to* her and *about* her that she herself didn't have to contribute much more than a nod or two every now and then.

I am grateful that I wasn't stuck in her body the day they discovered all the photos. The blowback a week later is still strong enough to feel. Her father can't look her in the eye (although I can't say for sure that he looked her in the eye before the photos got out there). But even with his eyes pointed toward the floor or ten feet over her head, he can still lay down the law. Which is how I'm forced to process Rhiannon's post with his breath somewhere in the vicinity of my neck.

Say something.

A— You can interrupt me any time.

The first time I see it, my heart skips seven beats, then lands on all seven beats in quick succession.

She is writing to me.

Talking to me.

Telling me something.

I read it again. And again.

I play the song. Lilah's father is now at the refrigerator, across from me. He pauses for a moment when the song comes on, looking confused. But he'd rather ignore his curiosity than have to engage with his daughter.

Give me a siiiiiiign, the singer pleads.

I read the post again. And again.

A— You can interrupt me any time.

I look at the comments and the first one is from Alexander.

I will be interrupting you in exactly three seconds.

Then a comment from her.

Thank you for the interruption. Though my statement is still open.

Lilah's father notices something on my face, and comes to see what I'm looking at. I quickly click to Lilah's home page. Unfortunately, the first comment there is from a girl calling her a *shameless slut.*

"Report her," Lilah's father says, reading over my shoulder. He even leans over and clicks on the box that brings up the Report Post link.

"No," I say instinctively. "That'll only make it worse."

He keeps his eyes on the screen as he says, "Well, you should have thought about that before, no?" Then he reports her. Only it's Lilah reporting her, since it's Lilah who's signed in.

The comment disappears.

I'm sure Lilah would say I hate you! now, or something to that effect. But I don't see the point. And after what happened to Moses, I'm wary of opening my mouth when I shouldn't.

The one thing I know is that I'm not going to be able to respond to Rhiannon tonight. Not from this computer.

I go to erase the history of what I've looked at. But Lilah's dad sees me and stops me with a fierce "What are you doing?"

"Nothing," I say. "Habit."

"I think your half hour is done early tonight," he replies, turning off the screen. "If you need the computer for your homework, let me know, and we can resume. Social time is over."

"C'mon, Dad!" I protest . . . but only because he'll be suspicious if I don't.

"Go to your room," he says. His words don't have the force of a command. It sounds like he's sick of having to say them. And it's only been a week.

I manage to complete Lilah's homework without the computer. And late at night, I sneak out of my room and erase the history so Lilah will never have any connection to Rhiannon. I have to do it quickly, before her father catches me. I tell myself that's why I don't respond to Rhiannon immediately. But the truth is that I still don't know what to say.

Comment from M:
You experience separation from your own body. I am in a different body every day.

Comment from Someone:
It's not unusual to feel alienated by your own body, to feel that you don't know it at all.

Comment from M:
I'm telling you—it's impossible for you to understand. I am not talking in metaphors here.

Comment from AnarchyUKGo:
This shit is CRAZY! Keep going, man.

Comment from Someone:
Private message me?

Comment from M:
Okay. But there's really no way you can help. I've tried everything. The only thing left is to try to erase myself.

Comment from PurpleCrayon12:
Often the moment we want to erase ourselves is the moment we most need to spell ourselves out.

Comment from AnarchyUKGo:
Spell this: D-I-E

AnarchyUKGo has been blocked by moderator

Comment from PurpleCrayon12:
Don't listen to that asshole. He (and I'm sure it's a he) has no idea.

Comment from PurpleCrayon12:
Are you still here?

Comment from PurpleCrayon12:
I guess you guys left.

Comment from PurpleCrayon12:
Good luck.

Comment from PurpleCrayon12:
I'm still here if you want to talk.

A

Day 6100

I wake up in the body of Alvin Ruiz, and it's like the body is happy to see me. I don't have to drag it out of bed—it's ready to leap out. My senses have a vibrancy that they rarely have at 6:49 a.m. I try to get a sense of his past, but I keep getting bounced into the present, because the present is calling, *NO-TICE ME NOTICE ME NOTICE ME*. There are so many things to notice. So many things to do. The body is telling me to do them all. I want to do them all. I am capable of doing everything and today I will do everything.

Wait, I tell myself. But I say it in a small voice. The body has a bigger voice today.

I know I should get on the computer and respond to Rhiannon. But first I want to clean my room. No—I want to redecorate my room. I'm going to start by moving the bed into the middle of the room. And then maybe I can make everything in the room orbit around the bed. That would be pretty cool. Except I need to get breakfast. It is the most important meal of the day, and I am one of the most important people in the world, according to the body. And the body would know.

I wish my parents and my two sisters a good morning and they're tired when they look back at me. I can't figure out which cereal to have, so I pour half a bowl of Frosted Flakes and then another bowl half-full of Raisin Bran, and I decide I will alternate spoonfuls of each. My mother asks me what time I went to bed; she says she heard me up late. I can't remember what time I went to bed. It's not important. Why waste time sleeping when there's so much to do when you're awake?

I finish my cereal and see that one of the cupboard doors is off its hinges and I tell my parents I can fix that, and they tell me it's time to go to school so I figure I'll just fix it when I get home and then when I get back to my room I see that I haven't done enough with my redecoration yet, but really I need to be messaging Rhiannon so I open the computer and try to ignore my sister telling me it's time to go, but then I understand it's time to go and figure I can just email Rhiannon from school.

My older sister is driving us and she's annoyed because I keep switching the radio looking for the perfect song—like, one I would sound really good singing along to—and every now and then I think I find that song and I sing along a little but it's not good enough so I change it, and she tells me to stop but I start telling her how I'm looking for the perfect song and she's like, "It's too early for this," but I consider that to be *unfortunate thinking* because why would you give away hours of your day just because they're "early" and there's so much to do and you can't give any hours away. I'm thinking this but I'm also saying this at the same time and my sister in the back seat has headphones on so she's not a part of it, but my sister who's driving is listening and maybe I'm getting through and making her life better even if I can't find the perfect song.

When I get to school, I see my friend Greg and I tell him I have to remember to message Rhiannon and he's like, "Who's Rhiannon?" and it's like my mind pushes against the body a little then because I know that I need to shut up about Rhiannon, so instead I tell him about how I'm redecorating

116

my room and how once people see what I've done, everyone is going to want to put their beds in the middle of their bedrooms. He says I'm in overdrive today, aren't I? And I'm like, why be slow? Because there's so much I can do. In fact, I offer to come over and redecorate Greg's room after school, but he says it's cool and his room isn't big enough to have the bed in the middle. I tell him that's *small thinking* and start telling him how *small thinking* leads to *small lives*, but then the bell rings and I have to get to first period, but when I'm in first period I'm restless to get out of first period, because school is just a way of imposing slowness on otherwise fast people, and I could be writing to Rhiannon right now but instead I'm having to listen to something about Oliver Cromwell, and with all due respect to Oliver Cromwell, Rhiannon seems a little more important to me, which the teacher doesn't seem to recognize. I am tempted to take out my phone but I think I've gotten in trouble a lot for taking my phone out in this class before so I don't do it though I really want to do it because Steve Jobs knew that an iPhone could be a device to break out of slowness and smallness, and I wonder if there's a way for me to make an app that helps everyone else get over the slowness and smallness that things like school and work impose on us, and I'm thinking this is a really good idea and I'm dying to tell someone about it, but all anyone here wants to talk about is *Oliver Cromwell* and I can't stand it, and I tell myself A, *focus*, because I can't just message Rhiannon, I have to think of a way to do it without it being Alvin who does it, because there's no point if she's only going to respond to Alvin and not me, because I'm not going to be Alvin forever, even though maybe it would be a good thing to be Alvin forever, because the body is definitely telling me that Alvin is a great place to be and that other bodies don't get to experience 10% of what Alvin gets to experience, and I have to say, it's *really convincing* because even if Oliver Cromwell won't recognize it, there's a lot of shit that needs to be done, and it's not the small or slow people who will do it. No, it's people like Steve Jobs and me who will do it.

Second period is better because it's *Jane Eyre*—it's always *Jane Eyre* or *To Kill a Mockingbird* or *Romeo and Juliet*—and there's class participation, so I raise my hand when the teacher asks about themes so far, and I'm saying it's about how we all have secrets locked up that we don't let the people we love see, because we know those secrets will scare them away, and I talk all about what Rochester's keeping in the attic, and the teacher interrupts me to say we're not up to that part yet in class reading, and I keep talking because you can't really talk about the themes of *Jane Eyre* without talking about what's in the attic, and then I'm talking about *Wide Sargasso Sea*, which I know this teacher hasn't assigned—that was in another school—but the whole point of *Wide Sargasso Sea* is to engage in the themes of *Jane Eyre*, and I think maybe the teacher's never thought about this because she's looking helpless and I'm thinking I might as well be teaching this class, and I can see my classmates getting really into it, except maybe Greg and my friend Isabella, who seems to be signaling me to stop, but now I've totally forgotten what my point was going to be because I had to look at Isabella, and I conclude by saying really we should be reading *Wide Sargasso Sea*, too, to appreci-ate all the implicit colonialism in Rochester's world, and the teacher is thanking me for my contribution and then she's calling on Rick Myers, who I bet hasn't even read the whole book yet, because he's talking about Jane Eyre—the charac-ter, not the book—as a paradigm of innocence, and I'm say-ing, no, you're not innocent if you're part of the colonialist system, and the teacher is telling me it's not my turn, which strikes me as a very colonial thing for her to say, but I don't think anyone but me is appreciating the irony.

I try to explain this irony to Greg and Isabella between classes but they seem annoyed, and I get a sense that I'm wearing them down, which is a good reminder that sometimes my friends are slower and smaller than I am, and maybe I need to act with friends like I acted with the songs this morning, and if I keep flipping through them, I'll find the perfect one. But in the meantime, it's fine if they can't sing along to what I'm saying. I can't expect them to understand everything I know, because empirically I know more than they do. Or at least that's what the body is telling me, that's the sense that I get, although I'm also trying to think as myself and I'm thinking the thoughts are way too fast and furious right now, like the body isn't regulating how many my mind can take, so it's sending more and more and more of them and one of the reasons I can't be slow or small is because if I'm small or slow there's no way I'll be able to get to all of these thoughts that I really need to address in order to have any chance of doing anything at all.

I'm still thinking of other things I could've said in English class and as a result I miss most of Spanish literature, which is an advanced class I'm taking because I have been surrounded by Spanish for most of my life, and suddenly I'm thinking the app I was thinking about before could be bilingual, too, and it's making me sad a little because already I'm thinking there's no way I'm going to be able to build an app all by myself, and there's no way I'm going to be able to say the right thing to Rhiannon, and what if the reason I liked *Wide Sargasso Sea* so much is because *I'm* the one locked in the attic. And that thought could be very depressing, but then I'm thinking what if the attic is actually reality, and it's everyone outside of it who isn't real? What if I'm the truth and they're just pretending to be the truth? What if I'm not hidden—what if I'm *hiding* instead?

I ask Isabella this during fourth-period study hall and she tells me there's nothing about me that's hidden or hiding, which I decide to take as a compliment. She also tells me I'm being manic, and I think she's jealous because I am clearly getting so much more done than she is, and understanding much more, and I am *enjoying* it, whereas she doesn't seem to be enjoying anything. There's a small part of me—the part that, hey!, is A, not Alvin—who understands what she's saying, but the body doesn't care about that. If anything, it greases the tubes so even more thoughts crash right into my head, and I can handle them, really I can, but not if I keep being interrupted by people or myself. There are also computers in study hall, so I tell Isabella I have something to do, and I go to the library computers and guess what? THEY HAVE BLOCKED FACEBOOK. So I have to use my phone under the table, and I'm getting to Rhiannon's page when one of the librarians tells me to put my phone away, and I tell her that if her computers allowed me to go on Facebook, then I wouldn't have to take out my phone—and I'm sure to say it nicely, not combative at all, because I'm thinking maybe I can persuade her to unblock Facebook, but she says that this is a study hall and that whenever a teacher assigns Facebook as worthy of study, she'll unblock it. So I start to tell her that there are hundreds of social scientists who are poring over our use of social media to write the story of our times, and she politely tells me that I am not one of those social scientists, and I ask her how I'll ever become one if my educational system does not appreciate the scientific value of analyzing what is inarguably the strongest social force of our time, and she says she's not disputing that, but I interrupt and tell her that's *exactly*

120

what she's doing when she blocks students from analyzing Facebook, and now she's telling me I'm speaking too loud for the library, and I'm telling her I am perfectly happy to whisper my dissent as long as she is willing to listen to it. She smiles at that, then tells me I should put my powers of articulation to better uses, and I start to outline my attempts and how they involve Facebook and apps—and I guess she stops believing in my powers of articulation, because she excuses herself to go check out a book to a student, so I turn to Geraldo, the guy sitting next to me, but he just stares ahead at the computer he's using, and I see he's on Wikipedia and I can't believe that the library approves of WIKIPEDIA but not Facebook, and I want to point this out to Geraldo but I know the subtlety of this distinction will be lost on him, so instead I give in and go on Wikipedia and try to learn more about Oliver Cromwell because apparently he's very important.

It's in this pause that I try to step away from the body, try to be more of myself. But it's hard. The chemistry is spelling itself out in distractions and enthusiasms. I'm on a high that has nothing to do with me, and it's high in the sense that the steering wheel is largely out of my reach.

The thoughts keep coming. The thoughts of Rhiannon, of "Say Something," are there, but every time I get close to them, another thought gets in the way. The best I can do is try to keep my private things private. Because Alvin is not as discerning. I have so much to say, so I try to say it all. I have so much to feel, so I try to feel it all at once. I have so much to do, so I must try to do it.

I talk all through lunch, and want to talk all through earth science. In art class I practically explode. We are supposed to be doing still life, but it's like I object to the entire concept of a still life. Let my classmates try to sketch apples. I am trying to draw the person locked in the apple, the person in the apple attic, the way that attic must look from the inside. Charcoal isn't enough to convey this. So I'm grabbing colored pencils and magic markers out of drawers, wondering why markers are considered *magic* while colored pencils aren't. The teacher asks me what I'm doing, but as far as I'm concerned, anyone who would force an artist to draw an apple is the enemy. I am creating in a frenzy; I am taking all of those thoughts in their greased tubes and I am detouring them straight to the page. It's brilliant. I can see the truth coming to life right in front of me. I am doing something only extraordinary artists can do: I am taking the shimmers and the unseen depths and I am making them tangible. I want the whole class to crowd around me and see how it's done, and at the same time I want them all to go away, to leave me alone to perform this art-class miracle. I am on the precipice of something great—I am about to take the leap—and then the teacher *interrupts me,* actually puts his hand in front of my face because apparently he's been talking to me and I haven't been hearing him, and now I don't have any choice but to hear him and it's like all my inspiration vanishes and I can't believe this supposed art teacher just did that to me, and of course he doesn't understand what I'm doing, of course he's freaking out because what I've drawn *does not resemble an apple,* and I tell him he has to step aside before it's gone, and he clearly does not like being told to step aside, because now he's telling me we *had an agreement* and he's invoking the name of Mrs. Schaffer, and he's telling me Mrs. Schaffer was the broker of *the agreement* and he's suggesting that maybe I need to go talk to Mrs. Schaffer *right now* and when I hesitate, he takes my art away from me, which really upsets me, because I haven't even signed my name yet, and I can totally imagine him signing his own name on it and saying it's his because even though he says it does not resemble an apple, he also must understand what I've just done and now he's going to claim it as his own, so I do what I have every right to do, which is ask him to give it back, and he says he'll put it in his desk for safekeeping—AS IF I CAN TRUST THAT—and he's asking if he has to call Mrs. Schaffer, and it's only then that I check and see that Mrs. Schaffer is some school psychologist, and I realize the only way out of this is to tell him, sure, I'll go see her. I leave the classroom and then go somewhere else where I can use my phone until the bell rings. The part of me that isn't Alvin knows it's probably a good idea to see Mrs. Schaffer, but the body doesn't like that thought at all, so it sends even more thoughts and—tricky!—I start to think about Rhiannon, and how it's hours later back in Maryland, and now she's gone almost twenty-four hours without a response from me, and if that isn't a reason to give up, then what is? So I go to the men's room and make myself comfortable in a stall and check Facebook and see Rhiannon's post again. I want to listen to the song and sing along, because when it's from Rhiannon it IS the perfect song, but there are guys using some of the other toilets and if I start singing they won't get it, so I let it play softly and then I hit *Like* and then I think, *No, don't do that,* and I hit it again to unlike it and then I get worried Rhiannon will think I'm unliking her, but the odds she saw it are very slim because I did it within a second, maybe two seconds, and I guess the only thing to do is to make a new profile, but I'm not sure how to do that on a phone. I'd have to log Alvin off and I'm not sure I'm in the right state to talk to Rhiannon yet and there are about a hundred ways I could make Facebook's interface a much more user-friendly interface, and some guy is yelling, "Who's playing music?" and I want to get my art back from the art teacher but if I go back there now he'll know I wasn't with Mrs. Schaffer, and I really think Alvin should talk to Mrs. Schaffer, but I don't know where she is and his body isn't going to tell me easily. I know the answer must be there somewhere . . . it's getting up the energy to find it that's the problem.

And there's also gym class to attend. Basketball. I totally get into the game. I am on fire. I am seeing superhuman angles. I am understanding the ball's trajectory like no one else on the court. People are passing to me because they can see I know exactly what to do. Sometimes I get distracted by what someone on the bench is wearing, or the color of their sneakers, because it makes me think about what kind of sneakers would look best on my feet, but most of the shots I take end up in the basket. As we're walking back to the locker room, Alex Nevens, who's actually on the basketball team, tells me I was on fire. I don't disagree.

I can't believe I haven't written to Rhiannon yet, and I'm really wishing I hadn't killed my email account as a way of killing the temptation to get back in touch with her. Then I realize it would be much easier to make a new email account than a new Facebook page, but I'm in math class and the same draconian phone rule applies, so I try to give my mind over to trigonometry, only my mind is bigger than that, and about halfway through the class a woman comes into the doorway and asks for me and I know immediately that this is Mrs. Schaffer and that even though there are only about twenty minutes left in the school day, I am going to be spending them with her.

I go willingly. She asks me how I'm doing, and I see she has my piece from art class in her hand. I tell her the truth, which is that I'm doing great great great great great. Which is maybe too many *greats*, because I can tell she doesn't believe me, and she seems super interested when we get to her office in how super interested I am in how the framed posters are all a little bit askew, like she's testing all the kids with psychological problems to see if they think the frames are crooked or if it's just their perception that's off. I know my perception's not off, so I share my theory with her, and I have to say that for a second Mrs. Schaffer actually seems a little bit embarrassed, because clearly she had no idea all her frames were crooked, but now that I've pointed it out she sees it, but she can't go and fix them with me watching, because she is very conscious about power dynamics and that would make my power a little more dynamic, as it were.

She asks me how much I slept last night, which seems to be a very popular question. I tell her I'm not sure, since I slept through it. But then I tell her three hours. Maybe four. She asks me if I could rate my energy level right now on a scale of one to ten, what would it be? And I tell her it's normal. Which is a nine. Because a ten should be reserved for people like soldiers and astronauts.

I am trying to do the best I can, even though Alvin's eyes can't help but be drawn to the frames, and finally I can't take it anymore and very reasonably I say to Mrs. Schaffer, "Excuse me for a moment," and then I straighten every single one of them. You'd think I had a level or something, they're so even. Then I sit back down.

Mrs. Schaffer says she's concerned about me and that she is going to recommend to my parents that I get "an outside opinion." I love that phrase because isn't any opinion that's not mine an outside opinion? I'm the only one inside. I'm the only one who knows. Even though I am pushing to remember that I am not actually the *I* here. As someone who's supposed to be separate, who's supposed to be an observer, I'm thinking, *Yes, Mrs. S. Get Alvin some help.* Because the inside opinion here doesn't even recognize it's an opinion. It thinks it's the truth. And it's wrong.

I want to tell her this, but she's dialing my parents now—she didn't even ask me for the number; she already had it on her desk. And I'm getting mad not only because she's tattling on me but because I feel she asked me a question and then cut me off before I could answer it. So as soon as she hangs up and tells me they're on their way, I start to talk to her about what happened in English class, including the injustice of both the teacher's behavior and the system that keeps people locked in attics. Mrs. Schaffer finds this interesting but doesn't seem to have much to contribute, and then it's like I blink and my parents are there, and I'm a little annoyed because I don't think I've gotten to the point yet, and then I'm resentful because Mrs. Schaffer thinks she can introduce a totally different point of her own into the conversation, and then she's asking my parents all these questions about me *as if I'm not actually in the same room with them*, and she says casually that my friends are concerned, and I wonder who the traitors are. But no. I am not going to let this get in my way. I'm not going to let their failure of perception affect the things I can do. I am excited to get back to my room and redecorate. My dad is saying the word *committed* and Mrs. Schaffer is saying that's not what she's talking about, that's not the first step, and I want to tell them, yes, I am very committed to a lot of things, like my room, and people stuck in attics, and Rhiannon, and the thought of Rhiannon kicks me back into my own head a little more, and even though Alvin and his body do NOT want my input here, I am thinking I am going to go along with whatever Alvin's parents want to do, and my body actually shivers at that thought, which I try to hide, but all the adults in the room see it and I can see them all filing it away, another symptom for them to Google tonight, because somewhere along the way we opened Pandora's box and found all this technology in there, and were all, *HOORAY! THINGS!* And then we realized or maybe only semi-realized—like, *very occasionally* realized—that the gods only left us this box because they wanted us to fragment ourselves, both as a society and individually, so now we're all slaves to the fragmentation and some of us take it better than others and it's not our fault that our bodies had all these circuits waiting to be blown, because it wasn't until the box was opened that the circuits became vulnerable, and I just want to take Steve Jobs's face and push it into some mud, although that's not really fair because he was only giving us what we wanted, over and over and over again.

Mrs. Schaffer makes another call and my parents stare at me and Mrs. Schaffer says she can get me in for an evaluation tomorrow at ten a.m., and I feel it's probably not the right time to point out I'll probably be up way before that. My parents agree to ten a.m. and herd me away like it's the end of the first day of kindergarten. School's been over for almost an hour now but there are still kids around, and when Isabella sees us, she comes over and is real friendly and I find myself despising her. I'm not going to say anything, but then I say, "Et tu, Judas?" And at first I don't think she hears me. But then she says, "This isn't what you're like, Alvin. This isn't you, and all we're doing is trying to get you back." I understand what she means, but I laugh because she's wrong, because what's more me than my extremes? Or at least that's what the body wants me to think as it drenches me in chemistry. I really have to get out of here.

It hurts that Rhiannon asked me to say something and here I am, saying nothing. I feel this so intensely that Alvin's body relents a little—or maybe it just pours its chemistry into my own extreme thoughts. I realize I don't have the right vocabulary to articulate what it feels like to be inside this body, because on the car ride home, Mr. and Mrs. Ruiz are asking me, and I don't have anything to tell them except "There are just a lot of thoughts, all at once, all the time."

"I know, I know," Mr. Ruiz mutters, but doesn't say any more than that.

When we get home, I go for the computer, but they're right there in my room with me, watching what I do, so I go back down to the TV room and switch channels until dinner. At dinner, they ask me how my day was in school, and I tell them all about how my drawing was stolen and what the point of *Jane Eyre* is and why Oliver Cromwell isn't as important as everyone says he is, and I only stop because I think I'm scaring my sisters and I can't expect them to be able to keep up with me, not like this.

I finally get to the computer after dinner, and there's a short time when my parents are in the kitchen talking, their voices drowned out by the dishwasher, when I can actually get some privacy. I go to create a new email account, then spend about a half hour trying to think of the right name, because some of them, like AMissesRhiannon, are a little too obvious and might be weird if Alexander sees them in her inbox, because boyfriends always look at what's in the inbox even if they say they don't, and other names are just too random, like when I type in A it suggests A798009043, which would be impossible to remember, and I wonder how many A's it would take to get a screen name, but AAAAAAAAAA is taken and so is AAAAAAAAAAA and at a certain point it says I have an invalid address, and finally I settle on AforR7777 because 7 is a lucky number, and that works.

Now, what do I say?

My mother comes in and tells me I should get some sleep, and I look at my clock and somehow it's eleven, which can't possibly be right. And I guess that maybe I worked on redecorating my room in between thinking of the perfect email address, because all the drawers and shelves are pulled away from the walls, so I can have a path AROUND my room if I

128

want to walk around all the furniture. I tell my mom that I'm not tired, but in my mind—my own mind—I know I have to be asleep by midnight, because if I'm not, what happens isn't any fun. The question is whether I email Rhiannon first. I'm all ready to do it, but it's one in the morning back on the East Coast, so it's not like she's awake to get it, and the A part of me—wait, the A part is all of me, not just a part—isn't sure it can write clearly right now.

It's ridiculous, but I run around that room with all the energy I've got. If something trips me up, I make the path wider. I am convinced this is a whole new way of decorating a room. I feel like a genius for inventing it. Also, I'm wearing myself out. I'm getting pretty tired. Ordinarily, I'd go get some coffee now. But I abstain. Because my parents are definitely still up, later than they usually are. But also because I know I have to be in bed by midnight.

I brush my teeth so hard the gums bleed. I use at least three cups of mouthwash before the blood is gone. I don't want to sleep with a bloody mouth. Then I get into my pajamas and make my way into bed, and while the list of things I've done today is far longer than most people's, I'm also aware of all the things I haven't done, like write to Rhiannon, which was the only thing I wanted to do, really, but sometimes the body is just too tricky and it knows how to get to the mind, more so now than at any point in history, and I am angry at my body even as it prepares itself for my departure, as it shows the most mercy it's shown all day by letting me sleep, letting me sleep, letting me sleep.

Someone: Hello

M: Hi

Someone: So what do you mean, that you're in different bodies?

M: I mean exactly that.

X

I wonder at what point human beings will stop needing bodies in order to live. I wonder if historians of the future will look back on this time as the period of the great divorce. Pity the people of mere decades ago, who needed to go to the bank for their money, the grocery store for their food, the shady theater for their titillation, the bar for a conversation. Now all you need is a finger, a brain, and a computer—and even the finger is arguable. I can satisfy all my needs and urges without venturing outside. My identity walks the wires for me, all around the world. The body is now the afterthought. The birthplace, not the home.

The fact that I know this gives me an advantage. The people who are nostalgic for their bodies, who think their bodies can save them from the anonymity that is being thrust upon them—

They have already lost, and they don't even know it.

A

Day 6101

I'm on the floor, but I have a blanket and a pillow. I've wrapped the blanket around me like it's a sleeping bag. But it's not a sleeping bag.

I am at the foot of the bed. I sit up and look in the bed and see a man, a woman, and two boys younger than me. My parents and my brothers, still sleeping. By the lamplight coming in around the room's single shade, I can tell we're in a motel. The furniture is shabby, the rug worn. I can hear a faucet dripping in the bathroom. There are five trash bags in a line by the door, as if they're waiting to go outside. But quickly I realize it's not garbage inside. It's everything we have.

It's six in the morning and I'm not supposed to be up yet. My head itches.

I try to go back to sleep.

I'm woken about a half hour later by a hand that reaches down from the bed and shakes my shoulder. I'm not entirely sure whether I'm asleep or awake—I've drifted away from life, but not into anywhere else.

It's my mother waking me, and she's hurrying me because I get first shower and have to be quick. When I turn the light on in the bathroom, I swear I hear the insects scatter. The water pressure is an ungenerous trickle, and when I quickly

132

get out, both of the towels are still damp from the day before. As I pat myself as dry as I can get, I discover that my name is Joe and my family's lived here for over two months after getting kicked out of our apartment. I also realize that I was supposed to bring new clothes from my garbage bag into the bathroom with me. When I walk out in a towel, my brothers think it's the funniest thing they've ever seen. One of them jumps into the bathroom and locks the door while I'm still digging for underwear, so I have to change in the hall that isn't really a hall. The hall is what's outside.

Joe might be used to this, but I'm not. I have no idea if Joe feels sorry for himself, but I feel sorry that he has to live like this.

Even though I'm just out of the shower, my head still itches. As one brother bolts out of the bathroom and the next one bolts in, I can see my mom noticing my scratching. I try to stop doing it. But the more I think about not doing it, the more I have to do it. It feels like something's crawling in there. I scrape against my scalp and expect something to come back on my fingers.

"Stop that," my mother says. She opens her trash bag, reaches in, and fishes out a red knit cap with hearts all over it. "Here," she tells me, handing it over. "Wear this."

I don't understand how a hat's going to make me stop itching. And I must look confused, because she says, "Just keep it on, okay? And don't itch. If you're itching, they'll send you home. And you know I can't be home today. I'll see if Renee has any of that shampoo. It'll be fine. But don't get sent home. If you keep the hat on, no one will know."

Now I'm sure I have lice, and my hair is full of phantom crawling. I'm not sure the hat will keep that in.

My mother knocks on the bathroom door, and my second brother opens it, wet-headed but dressed.

"Don't miss the bus," she tells us all. Then, when our backpacks have been retrieved from under the bed, she tells each of us she loves us, and wishes us a good day.

As the oldest, I figure I'm the leader. My brothers, Jesse and Jarid, think the hat is hysterical, but I ignore them. I access the location of the bus stop and start heading there, until Jarid stops me and says, "Hey, what about Jasmine?" I don't even have time to ask who that is, because a voice from across the parking lot says, "Yeah, what about me?" I see a girl about my age coming our way. She looks right at my head and says, "I do not want to know what that's about." Then she leads us to the bus stop, like Wendy commandeering the Lost Boys.

It's only when we're waiting for the bus that I think of Rhiannon. I feel for my phone in my pocket, but of course there isn't any phone in my pocket, and I doubt there will be one in my backpack. Hopefully there will be a computer at school. I remember I set up a new email—but then I can't recall what it was. I can remember the barrage of thoughts I had, but none of them are particularly distinct. I remember running in circles around my room. I remember the look on the guidance counselor's face as I straightened her frames. But I can't remember what was in those frames. I can't remember the furniture I was running around.

"Come on, Joe," Jasmine says. I look up and it's a city bus, not a school bus, that's here. Jasmine takes out a bus pass, and I find one in my pocket, too. My brothers follow.

We don't talk on the bus. We just look tiredly out at the buildings we pass, stare at the other people on the bus until we realize we're staring. Jasmine closes her eyes, and for a second I think she's asleep. But when she opens them up again, I can tell she was closing her eyes in order to think.

When she rings the bell to make the bus stop, I stand to go. When we're off the bus, I follow her to school. My brothers go to one building and Jasmine and I go to another. When we get inside, I start to head for my locker, but stop when Jasmine chastises me and tells me I need to get breakfast.

I follow her to the cafeteria, where eggs are being scooped from a vat and garnished with a slice of white toast. At the end of the line, there's a bowl of fruit; Jasmine takes an apple and hands me an orange. Then we sit down to eat, and as we do, she stares at my face so long that I'm worried there are bugs crawling down from my hair.

"What?" I say.

"Nothing," she tells me.

The cafeteria isn't like a lunchtime cafeteria—there can't be more than two dozen of us here, and everyone's keeping to themselves . . . or at least they are until two guys come to our table. Theo and Stace. Stace has already eaten half his allotment of eggs, and they're in the middle of an argument as they sit down.

"I'm telling you," Stace says, "there's cheese in there. They definitely put cheese in. These are cheesy eggs, man."

"There's no cheese in here. There's barely eggs."

Stace takes another big forkful. "Don't be a hater. This shit's good. *Cheesy* good."

"No cheese. None."

"Fuck you. There is."

Theo looks to Jasmine for help. "Will you please tell this fool that there isn't any cheese in these eggs?"

"There could be," she says. "Who knows?"

I'm taking a bite now, and I think maybe there's cheese. But then I take another bite and I'm not that sure.

"You taste it, right?" Stace asks me.

And because for some reason I'm liking Stace more than Theo, I say, "Yeah, I taste it. It's almost like a gouda."

Stace, Theo, and Jasmine all look at me then.

135

"What the fuck are you talking about—a *gouda?*" Theo says.

"Are you making fun of me?" Stace adds, hurt.

"I don't think he is," Jasmine says. Then she looks at me and says, "You're full of surprises, aren't you?"

I can barely concentrate in class. Now my head isn't just itchy, it's starting to sweat hard. It gets to the point that I have to sit on my hands to prevent myself from scratching myself into an obvious frenzy. The worst is when I imagine the lice march-ing down my neck, down my back, jumping onto the ground, walking up everyone else's legs.

Only one teacher, my English teacher, asks me to take off the hat.

"Ma'am, I can't," I say. "Please."

I'm pleading, and she hears it. She lets me keep it on.

I plan to go to the library to use the computers at lunch. But there aren't any computers. There isn't even a library.

"When did they get rid of the library?" I ask Jasmine over our pizza squares at lunch.

"When people stopped caring about us" is all she'll answer.

I scratch my scalp then, through the hat. She sees me doing it, but doesn't say anything.

She reminds me of Rhiannon, even though she doesn't look anything like Rhiannon. I am seeing right inside, and that's what looks like Rhiannon. I wonder if Joe sees her like this, too. At the end of lunch, she makes sure that all the homework she has to hand in is at the front of her bag, and she makes me do the same thing, possibly to make sure I've done it. At the end, I thank her, and she doesn't look like it's too out of the ordinary for him to thank her. Which gives me hope that Joe might, in fact, recognize what's going on.

* * *

By seventh period, my head is unbearable. I reach under the hat to scratch, and come back with a small black bug pressed under my fingernail. I know I should go to the school nurse, but I heed my mother's warning about being sent home. I wait until the end of the day, when being sent home won't be a big deal—but then I worry that they'll say I can't come back tomorrow. Also, I figure I have to pick up Jesse and Jarid.

I find Jasmine after school and figure she'll be coming back with us, but she reminds me she has a newspaper to "put to bed," and while I think of a few stupid things I could say about putting a newspaper to bed, I don't say any of them, because it's clear that she's stressed by the deadline and is taking whatever she has to do very seriously. I also don't say I'm going to miss her, because I'm guessing that's not something Joe would say, because he's so used to seeing her every day. But I *do* miss her as Jesse, Jarid, and I make our way back home. When we get to the motel room, our mother still isn't home and our father looks like he's in the same position we left him in, asleep. Only his clothes are different, which might mean he left the room and worked, or might mean he got up intending to leave but then decided against it. Whatever the case, my brothers stay silent around him, not wanting to wake the bear.

It's only three in the afternoon, and I can't imagine spending the remaining waking hours still in this claustrophobic room and its claustrophobic silence.

"Come on," I tell Jesse and Jarid. "Let's go somewhere. Bring your homework."

When we're back out in front of the motel, I ask them if there's a park nearby. From their reaction, you'd think I'd asked them for a stairway to the moon. I ask them where the

137

nearest library is, and this time they shrug. I try to find one in my memories, but only get a blank. I look into the motel office, but there's no one behind the counter, and I'm also worried about calling too much attention to us, especially with the hat on. I'm sure Jasmine would know, but Jasmine's not here. I start us walking, and instead of finding a library, I find a Burger King. I don't have any money, so food isn't exactly an option, but I sit us down in a booth anyway and figure if we're doing homework, no one will ask us to leave. This ends up being true, but it's hard for me to keep Jesse and Jarid focused, especially when there are so many people eating hamburgers and fries around them. The breaking point comes when someone leaves their tray on a table near us, with a handful of fries still on it. Jarid spies this, and without missing a beat, goes over and retrieves the tray. Jesse cheers and I decide I'm not going to stop them. Instead of shoving the fries down with abandon, they treat each fry like a separate delicacy. It's like they're tasting each grain of salt before they swallow.

I'm amused by this, but then someone who looks perilously like a manager comes over to us, decidedly unamused.

"I'm afraid you can't do that," he scolds, reaching for the tray. Jarid clamps down to keep it.

"Let go of that," the manager orders. And there's something about the way he's talking to a ten-year-old that makes me snap.

"*You* need to let go of that," I tell him. "My brother hasn't done anything wrong, and if you don't stop harassing him, I am going to call your superiors at your home office and lodge a complaint. You can't steal something that has no owner, and when my brother procured those French fries, they were sitting in a state entirely devoid of ownership. I understand that you think you are just doing your job, but I have a feeling that if I sought clarification about what that job was, verbally beating up on elementary schoolers would *not* be a part of it."

This is not how he's expecting a grimy high schooler in a mangy, ridiculous ski hat to talk. He pulls back from the tray and pulls back from the table, but in a way that makes it seem like he's uncovered a contagion and wants to get away from it as quickly as possible.

"You are not welcome here," he says. Then, end of subject, he walks back behind the counter.

Jesse and Jarid, sensing victory, gleefully finish their fries, and I can see Jarid starting to scout other people's trays. I know I've put the manager in his place—but while that felt good for about one triumphant minute, I now put myself in his shoes, the manager of a Burger King getting paid not that much to do the King's bidding. Putting him in his place doesn't feel as much of a triumph. I know he won't call the police to have us kicked out, but his words did the trick—I feel unwelcome in a way I didn't before. I feel like we're being watched. I feel I've intruded. I feel like at any moment it's going to be exposed that we're the people who can't afford Burger King, who have infiltrated Burger King and taken some fries.

"Come on," I tell my brothers. "Jasmine should be home by now."

Reluctantly, they pack up and we leave. When we get back to the motel, we find Jasmine doing homework in a stairwell, her books spread out over the landing as if it were a desk.

"We had fries!" Jesse reports.

"Lucky you," Jasmine replies, without any sarcasm I can sense.

I find myself wishing I'd brought her back some fries, even though I never had any to bring.

"Here," she says, clearing off some of the landing. "It's work time."

The three of us sit down on the stairs and join her.

When we get back to our room, the sun is nearly setting. I'm surprised to see our father's gone—then I realize he works the night shift and sleeps during the day, which is why Mom didn't want me around. She returns with a bucket of KFC—there isn't a kitchen in our motel room—and a Walgreens bag with something called a Licefreee! Kit inside. I think the extra *e* and the exclamation point betray a suspicious amount of enthusiasm . . . but I keep that to myself.

The shampooing happens after dinner's done. I tell my mom I can shampoo myself, but she tells me to sit down on the toilet and let her do it. When she pulls off the hat, she does not sound pleased. Under her instruction, I dunk my head beneath the tepid shower, then let her knead the shampoo into my hair. A thorough combing comes next, followed by an exhaustive search-and-destroy mission with tweezers across my scalp.

"You're nitpicking," I tell her. "You're actually nitpicking."

I worry this is a gouda comment, but she laughs and says, "Yeah, I suppose I am."

Since we're alone in the bathroom—Jesse and Jarid have settled into the bed—there are questions I want to ask her. But I realize they're my questions, not Joe's, and of the two of us, he's the one who has the right to ask questions, not me.

When she's satisfied we're done, I rinse out my hair again and dry it. It feels better . . . but not all the way better.

"We'll get up a little early and do it again before you go to school," she tells me. "And I hope you're enjoying it—because being Licefreee ain't cheap."

140

"This is the best night I've had in years," I tell her.

It's a joke, but she sighs in response and mutters, "Don't I know it." Then, catching me catching her, she adds, "Two more months, hon. Everything will be different in two more months."

Before it's time for bed, I tell Joe's mother I need some air; she doesn't ask any questions and lets me head outside. I go back to the stairs, expecting to find Jasmine there. But she's not. I walk the rest of the corridors, and still I don't find her. I search Joe's memory to find which room she lives in—but I also discover that Joe knows to never knock on her door. She's never told me why. We're hallway friends, not room friends.

I'm sorry I'm not going to get to tell her goodbye. Even though, of course, I wouldn't be able to tell her goodbye at all.

It's only when I'm back on the floor of our room, trying to find the best position for sleep, that I think about Rhiannon and the fact that I still haven't answered her. It feels more complicated now. She wants me to say something, but what if the thing I have to say is *This is why I can't do this?* Life will always get in the way. Whether it's my own life or the lives of others—it doesn't really matter. It's just life, and it's rarely convenient, and if I have to choose between the person in front of me and the person who isn't here, it's the one who's here who will always be more important.

Say something?

Right now, all I feel I can say is *I can't.*

NATHAN

He could be anyone.

Any teacher in my school. Any student. I've only seen him as an adult, but that doesn't mean he can't be my age.

I have no idea what the rules are. Or if there are any rules.

Don't let it get to you, I tell myself. *That's what he wants. Don't give in to it.*

But he could be in any car that passes. He could be in any store I walk into.

He could take over my mother. My father.

It's not paranoia if the threat is real. But it feels more like paranoia when you're the only one who knows about the threat.

The emails have stopped. It's like he knows he doesn't have to bother.

He's gotten to me.

"You're a mess," Rhiannon tells me. "Why are you a mess?"

We're at a diner midway between her town and mine. Nobody we know is around. We want it this way.

I wonder what makes her think I'm a mess. I actually tried to dress well to see her. I am buttoned up. Laces tied. Khakis ironed flat. But some wrinkles are coming through.

"I'm not a mess," I say.

She takes a sip of her milkshake. Seriously considers me.

I give her my best smile.

"Nope," she says. "You're definitely a mess."

I am trying so hard not to be. I am trying hard not to think he's the old man two booths away. Or the waitress. Or the guy coming out of the bathroom, looking at Rhiannon as he walks by.

She reaches for one of my fries.

"It's okay," she says. "I'm a mess, too."

Before I can contradict this, she goes on.

"Why hasn't A given me some kind of sign? I mean— okay, I guess what I'm really asking is: What if A's already forgotten about me? Do you think that's possible? What if it was all in my mind—not that A was here, but that it meant what I thought it meant? I know A wanted me to move on. I *have* moved on—but I also haven't. But what if A has? What if I'm the only one who can't stop thinking about it?"

I know this is why I'm here, so she can say all these things out loud. Because who else can she tell? I am her only-case scenario.

And the joke is that I have no idea what to say to her. She's talking about love, and I know more about table tennis than I do about love.

"There's really no way to know, is there?" I say. "I mean, you're looking for the Wizard of Helpful, but I'm afraid I'm just another jester at your service. And I don't even know that many good jokes."

I'm serious, but she laughs. Not a big *ha ha*, but an appreciative *hmph*.

She checks her phone and puts it down again.

"I can't stand knowing A is out there and not knowing anything else. And I also can't stand the fact that if A *isn't* out there—if something's happened, if A has disappeared—then I will never know. Silence can mean way too many things."

143

I want to ask her why she doesn't think he could be with us right now, right in this room.

"Ugh," she groans. "I'm only messing you up more, aren't I? You're nice to listen to me. I know there aren't any answers. But to hold the questions inside all day, every day—it makes me feel like such a fraud, because what I'm thinking is so different from what I'm saying to everyone."

"You can tell me anything," I assure her. "I just won't have anything remotely intelligent to say about it. I've totally got your back, but I'm only armed with a water pistol."

"You're such a dork."

"Yeah, but I'm *your* dork, right?"

"Of course."

I wonder if Rhiannon and I are like strangers who were sitting next to each other during a bus crash. We both survived, and we can talk a lot about that, and about what it's like after. But the further the topic gets from bus crashes, the more it might feel like we're fellow survivors rather than friends.

She checks her phone again. Looks at it. Presses a few keys.

"What?" I ask. "What is it?"

Not that it's any of my business. But even if I'm no love expert or even a girl expert, I can tell something's happening.

"It's A," she says. "A wrote."

She's not thinking about how loud she is. But I am. I don't want anyone else to hear. Because anyone else could be anyone.

After about four minutes of her reading and, presumably, rereading, I ask, quieter, "What did A say?"

She doesn't answer. She just hands me her phone.

"See for yourself."

It's not a post on Facebook; it's an email from a gibberish address.

Dear Rhiannon,

I saw your post about saying something . . . but it's hard to know what to say. I genuinely thought the best thing would be for us to be separate, to have our own lives, without any overlap or communication. That still might be the best thing. But I am also feeling doubt. And confusion. And sadness.

I want you to be happy. I am unsure I can ever be happy or make anyone else happy. Not with the way my life works. Not for any sustained period of time. And if you are happy, then I can absolutely go away again. But if you are not happy, and if you truly still miss someone, and if you truly want me to say something . . . then at the very least we can have this. Words. Overlap. Connection. I doubt that it will be helpful to tell you that I miss you, but I'm not strong enough to stop myself from doing it. I'm sorry. This may only make it worse.

A

"Wow," I say.

The paranoid part of me is thinking: There's no way to know for sure that A wrote this. Maybe it's Poole. Maybe he found Rhiannon's address. Maybe it's just part of the game. There are no specifics here. It could easily be a trap.

The not-paranoid part of me is thinking: Don't be stupid. No one else could have written this. A is the only person who can know how this feels.

"Yeah," Rhiannon says. "Wow."

"I guess this answers your questions," I tell her.

"Some."

"But it also raises new ones."

"Lots."

I can't tell if she's happy. Mostly she seems stunned.

"How are you going to respond?" I ask.

She takes back the phone. "I'm not sure. I want to know where A is. And I want to know what this means. The first will be easy to answer. The second—I don't think A knows, either. And if neither of us knows what it means, how do we decide what it means?"

"But what *can* it mean?" I ask. "I don't want to sound harsh . . . but it's not like you can be together, right?"

And now the look she gives me—it's like we survived that bus crash and I'm asking, *Are you sure you want to go on another bus?*

"I know the limitations, Nathan. I know that I am likely to be screwing my life up yet again. I know he's probably right, and that the best thing is for us to be separate. But not silent. That's the worst. So while I know what can't happen, I do want to see what *can* happen—alright?"

"Hey," I say, throwing my hands up, "it's your life. Do what you want to do. Just please make sure he stays out of my body while you do it."

Okay, now I'm *really* hoping nobody is listening to us.

"You sound mad," Rhiannon says, sounding mad herself. "Why are you mad?"

"First I'm a mess, and now I'm mad. Thanks."

"Okay, if you're not either of those things, tell me what you are."

"I'm mad, okay? I'm mad because even though I know it's allegedly not his/her/their fault, what A does *bothers* me. In a way that it doesn't seem to bother you. You're so excited to have gotten an email from A, but while A was writing it, someone else—someone like you, someone like me—was completely blanked out."

"What do you mean, *allegedly*? None of this is A's fault. A didn't choose this."

"How do you know that?"

"Because if A could choose, A would be with me now."

The moment she says it, she can't believe she's said it.

She backtracks. "I'm sorry. I don't know that. At all. I don't know anything. This is a lot at once. At the very least, we can agree on that, right?"

I don't tell her that what she's said has scared me. *A would be with me now.* What can that even mean? *In whose body?* I'm too nice to ask. But the question is there. Just like Poole is there. Somewhere.

"It's okay," I say. "It's definitely a lot at once." I think about what A wrote. "Do you think you're happier now than you were before? I mean, compared to when we sat down in this booth and you hadn't heard from A—are you happier?"

"Can I give you the honest answer?"

"No, I'd prefer you to be dishonest."

There's a second when she thinks I'm serious. Then, when she realizes I'm not, she goes on.

"I think this is one of those situations when the word *happiness*—or even the concept of happiness—is pretty meaningless. Because I think when people want you to be happy, they mean you're not anything else—the happiness is so big, so bright, that all you are is happy. And there are definitely moments like that. I've definitely felt that way. But hearing from A—if I were to list the adjectives it makes me, *happy* wouldn't be in the top hundred. I'm sure it's in there, as part of some of the other words. Like, *happy* is definitely an ingredient of *relieved*, and I am definitely feeling relieved I'm

147

not crazy and making it all up in my head. But when A says *happy*, I think A really means *hopeful*. And that's much more complicated. While I'm relieved and excited and glad, I'm not sure that I'm hopeful. Which is probably what you're getting at. Or what you're afraid I'll be. But no—I'm not happy and I'm not hopeful. I just feel . . . better."

"Well, good. I don't want you to feel *worse*."

Her phone rings. Both of us are surprised. I'm guessing both of us instantly think it's A calling.

But, reality.

Rhiannon looks at the screen. "It's Alexander. I should probably get it. He never calls."

She answers, and even though I try not to listen, I can get the gist of it. Something about plans.

After she hangs up, she explains, "His parents aren't home. And he wants to make me dinner."

"That sounds nice," I say.

"I know."

"So the problem is . . . ?"

"There's no problem," she says. "Except for, you know, all the problems."

"I wish I could help you."

"Believe me, this helps. Just being able to talk about it."

"How fortunate that your body-changing ex found his way to me!" I joke.

"He's not an ex," she says, not joking.

"Then what is he? Besides, you know, not a *he*."

"I just don't think of A as an ex. It's never felt over."

She stops herself there. And I don't let her shift away from it by saying something else.

Right there. We both know it.

We've gotten to the heart of all the problems.

Someone:	So what do you mean, that you're in different bodies?
M:	I mean exactly that.
Someone:	Tell me more.
M:	You don't want to hear this.
Someone:	I do.
M:	Why?
Someone:	Because I know you're telling the truth, and I also know that I'm not understanding it. I want to. Hopefully that counts for something. And remember, I'm the person who can lapse into thinking that life isn't real. There's not much that can surprise me at this point, in terms of the way you can perceive the world, and how individualized our perceptions can get.
M:	Fine. If you really want to know . . .
Someone:	I do.
M:	You know what you were saying about it feeling like life is a video game? That you're this avatar and someone else is at the controls? Well, for me it's the opposite. I'm holding the controller. I'm making the moves. But my avatar keeps changing. Every single day, it changes. And it's

this avatar that everyone else reacts to. That's the game. And even though I'm always the same person at the controller, everyone else's responses entirely depend on the avatar that I'm playing. But—and this is where it gets tricky— the avatars are never actually mine. I am only borrowing them from other players in the game. Which means if I do something wrong, they get points taken off. And if I lose the game, they lose the game. They die. So I can't stop playing, even though I want to stop playing.

Someone: You don't like the game?

M: No. If I had any chance of winning, I might. But I don't get to keep any of the rewards. I'm an empty player.

Someone: That's how life can feel to me when I'm at my worst. Diversion can be fine for a while. Sights and sounds. Trippy. But I guess what I learned— and it wasn't easy—is that in order to live, you have to believe that life is real.

M: My real and your real are not the same.

Someone: I think they are. Even if our perceptions skew us, we all share the same real.

M: I'm not sure I can get there.

Someone: You can.

A

Day 6102

I should be crashing. It's been a long day in Joanie Kennedy's body. School. An intense chemistry lab. Skateboarding with her friends after school. Dinner with Mom and Dad and Brother.

And also, in the middle, the forty-five minutes in study hall when she wrote an email she'll never remember, never know about.

She has been checking her phone ever since. Between every period. During the chem lab, to the annoyance of her lab partner. She tried to take the phone along when she ran track during gym, but the coach spotted it from a kilometer away, and it went into the locker. But even when she took it out of the locker—nothing. At the skate park, she kept looking at her phone and looking out into the distance, mind elsewhere. Her friends noticed but didn't say anything. (They also didn't say anything about how bad her skating was when she did try.) Not before dinner or after dinner or when she went to the bathroom to check her phone during the middle of dinner.

Of course, Joanie wouldn't care.

But I can't think of anything else.

Certainty and doom are keeping close company in my mind. I am sure I said too much. I am sure I said the wrong things. I am sure I scared her away. I am sure I broke a promise. I am sure I made things worse.

But I won't be totally sure until I hear back from her.

If I hear back from her.

After dinner, I listlessly work on Joanie's history homework. It's already nine o'clock in Maryland. Ten o'clock. Eleven. Rhiannon must have checked her email.

Midnight.

I am more alone than I've ever been. My life has always been full of small abandonments. This is my first big one.

I'm not taking it well.

12:01 her time. If I were there, I'd be asleep. If I were there, I'd be nowhere. I'd be inside someone's sleep, unknown and unknowable until that person's body woke up.

10:08 here. I check the phone. There's an email from her.

A,

Now that I know how to reach you, I'm not sure what to say.

You didn't ask any questions in your email. So I am not sure which answers you want and which you don't.

Or maybe it's all one big question. Is it possible that's what we've always been for each other: a question? Never an answer. You have never been an answer for me. I have never been an answer for you. It felt like an answer, maybe. But when it came time to make it real, to say it out loud—we lost the ability to answer. The questions took control again.

You say you thought the best thing would be for us to be separate, to have our own lives. Maybe you found your own life. But you didn't leave me with my own life. You left me with a boyfriend who feels like he was found for me, which is a shitty way to start a relationship. You left me with

152

friends who will never in a million years understand what
I've been through, or what I'm thinking or feeling. And,
more than anything else, you left me with questions.

You say you want me to be happy. But you don't ask me
if I'm happy. Which makes me wonder if you really want
me to be happy or if you just want to feel less guilty about
leaving. If you want me to say it was all for the best . . .
Nope. Sorry. You made it worse. This whole time, you could
find me. And you knew I could never find you. Did you
honestly think that would make me happy?

Sometimes you're a memory that I'm not really sure
happened. There are hours when I forget I ever knew you.
But there are many more hours when I remember.

I guess what I'm trying to say is: I've missed you. But you
coming back only makes me realize how mad I am.

R

I don't have much time to respond. I don't know what
to say—I never thought it out this far, never planned how to
answer her understandable anger. All I can do it push right
into it.

Dear Rhiannon,

I am so sorry. I'm sorry I left you with so many questions.
I'm sorry I don't have any of the answers.

I can't pretend to know how to do this. Any of it.

I'm not like you. I've never been in love before. I've never
been in a relationship before. You've learned things I
haven't learned. I didn't want to break up with you, but I

153

knew I had to. I didn't want you chained to the impossible. I left the way I left because I believed it was the best way to leave you. I'm sorry if it wasn't. I didn't know how to do it, and the only person I could have talked to about it was you—but that seemed wrong. I should have talked it over more with you. Even if it meant having the same conversation over and over again until we hated each other's guts—at least it wouldn't have felt so sudden.

I don't want to ask you questions because I don't want you to feel obligated to give me answers. But I guess I will say that only to ignore it, because of course the biggest question I have is: What do you want to do now? I will do whatever you want me to do. I made the decision last time. You get to make the decision now.

A

A

Day 6103

A,

Sorry. Fell asleep last night. Have to get to school soon. So this will have to be quick.

I guess I understand that while this specific situation is (very) new to me, the whole relationship field is new to you. Welcome! It sucks! (Except when it's amazing.)

So, keeping in mind that you have no idea what you're doing, I'll educate you when I say: You can't make it my decision. I understand what you mean, but this isn't the kind of thing where we take turns. The point is that we should always be making the decisions together.

It feels wrong to type that. It feels wrong to say that there's a "we." There is no "we." You took apart that "we." And I'm not going to put it back together as easily as typing a sentence with that two-letter word in it.

I don't even know what our options are. All I know is that absolute silence is not the way to go. We tried that. It didn't work. At least not when it comes to moving on.

Gotta go now. Promised Preston a coffee run.

R

R,

I don't know what our options are. I'm frightened by how excited I am, just talking to you.

A

A,

There's a part of me that's like: This isn't happening. Not again. Don't do this again.

That's the smarter part.

But the other part of me is welcoming it. Even as the smarter part tells me to shut up, don't type that—well, I guess I just overruled any sense I have.

This doesn't mean that I'm over being mad at you. I am still mad at you. But I'm also on the cusp of finding out what the next part is.

Who are you today?

R

R,

I'm myself. I'm always myself.

But I know what you mean.

Today I'm Christopher Mowrer. He has a pug named Gertrude that sleeps in his bed. It was hard for me to leave this morning.

That said . . . if there were any way for me to walk over there right now, I would.

156

Which is probably why it's best I can't.

Who are you today?

A

A,

I'm a girl caught in her own confusion. I can't even tell if I'm its prisoner or if it's the only thing keeping me going.

Preston tried to help. He thinks I'm having problems with Alexander. He gave me the all-relationships-have-rough-patches speech, like he's been married for forty years instead of dating someone for two months. I played along, because I could tell he was enjoying how useful he was being, and because he was reminding me that I have a boyfriend who treats me well and who is, if I step outside of the confusion and see him for who he is, a pretty awesome guy. I wish I had met him another way.

But that's not what happened. And it's easy to pretend that he could have gotten my attention even when I was with Justin, and that he could have gotten me away from Justin. Except . . . that doesn't feel true. You were the one who did that. Because you were the only one who saw me and understood what I needed. At least at first.

What happened to us?

R

R,

What happened is that I started to not be myself. I started to see myself through your eyes instead of through my own.

And I imagined a judgment there that I couldn't escape. I'm not saying that you were judging—you weren't. But there are some people you want to kiss more than others. There are some people you can imagine being with and some you can't. That's human. It's not the way it should be, but it's the way it is. And I kept worrying each day when I woke up that I wouldn't be good enough for you. And, even worse, I couldn't get out from under the burden of knowing I would always be leaving you.

So I left for good. To stop leaving you day after day. And to preserve myself before I started taking my frustration and insecurity out on the bodies I was in. I see people harming their bodies all the time. I didn't want to become one of them.

Again: These are not things that you did to me. They are things that are part of what my life is. And there is no way to change them. No real way.

A

A,

But we didn't really try, did we?

(I can't believe I'm saying that.)

R

R,

What do you mean?

A

A,

I mean, we gave it a couple of weeks. YOU gave it a couple of weeks. You were never too far away. And even when you were too far away—if we had known that there'd be a next day, and a day after that, it wouldn't have mattered as much.

Here's the weird part (okay, there are lots of weird parts): The whole time, I thought we were talking to each other, being honest. But now I'm seeing there were all these things we weren't talking about—like how you were afraid of how I might see the body you were in. And how we needed to figure out that a relationship could work even if we weren't seeing each other every single day. But instead of having those conversations, we stopped having conversations altogether.

Until now.

R

R,

So are you saying you'd want to try again? It's still impossible.

A

A,

I don't know what I'm saying, to be honest. I'm not saying things in order to lead up to something. I'm saying things in order to find out where I'm going.

I was supposed to be hanging out with Alexander now. But I couldn't. I told him I wasn't feeling well. When what I meant was that I'm feeling uneasy. Uncertain. Calling everything into question and wanting to bend it into the answer I want. I don't think that in itself is love. But it can definitely be a side effect.

What the hell am I doing?

R

R,

I don't want you to have to lie to Alexander. Or anyone.

A

A,

What's the alternative, exactly? Telling the truth?

The only person I could possibly tell is Nathan. Remember Nathan? Basement party? Thought he was possessed by the devil? He found me. We talked. And even though he's about as romantically clueless as you are, it's incredible to be able to tell the truth out loud without setting off any alarms.

But I haven't texted Nathan to tell him about all of this. He listened when I missed you, but I'm not sure if he'll listen now that I've found you. I think he'd give me the same advice any friend would give if I could tell them what the story was. I can hear Rebecca's voice in my head (remember Rebecca?): You got what you wanted. You got your apology. You know A's alive. Don't push it.

But I'm going to push it.

Where are you?

R

A

Day 6104

R,

Denver.

Specifically, at a debate tournament at Littleton High School, a little south of Denver.

More specifically, competing as Bernardo Garrido. Luckily, his category is Extemporaneous Speech.

Good morning.

A

A,

Good afternoon.

Denver is far. Very far.

And I can't spend all day writing to you and thinking about what to write to you and wondering about what you're doing. I can't.

R

R,

What if I were closer?

A

A,

But you're not.

R

R,

But what if I were?

A

X

I haven't answered his phone. I haven't checked his mail. I haven't picked up his dry cleaning. I have been separating him as much as possible from his life.

But still, I've been careless.

I'm just back from a run, so I'm taking a shower. I don't hear anyone come into the place. I don't even sense something's not right as I'm toweling off. It's only after I'm out of the bathroom, heading to the bedroom in the guy's silk robe, that I see her sitting in the den, waiting for me.

"Will you look at that?" she says. "You're alive."

Ex-wife or sister? I ask myself—her tone is one or the other.

Sister, the response comes.

She goes on. "Showering in the middle of the day? What a life you lead, Pat."

"I was out for a run," I explain.

"So I heard. Ran away from your office. Ran away from your friends. Even ran away from your reading group."

"I have a reading group?"

"Yeah. You do. And just like Donna from your office, and Ralph and Jack and some other friends of yours, the woman in charge of your reading group—Elsa? Elisa?—called me to ask where you'd gotten to, and if you were okay. Said it wasn't like you to skip, especially for a month when you chose the book."

"What book did I choose?"

"That's not my point, Pat. My point is that I've tried to call you, and I've tried to email you, and finally I had to come over here to see if you died in your sleep."

"I didn't."

"A pity. If you were already dead, I wouldn't feel such a pressing need to kill you."

Her delivery's good, and I almost laugh. But I don't want to give her the satisfaction of a positive response.

"Now that you've seen proof that I'm alive, can you show yourself out?" I say instead. "I have things to do."

"Like what? Is there a support group for people like you who want to disappear? Is it called Anonymous Anonymous?"

I go into my bedroom and close the door. I take my time putting on clothes. I know I'm not getting rid of her easily, but I can sure as hell make her wait.

I also try to grab hold of some of the memories he has left. This is his only sibling. Their parents are dead. She lives alone. It's been a while since he's seen her.

I take fifteen minutes before I go back to the den. She continues talking like it was only fifteen seconds.

"So are you in trouble? Is that it? If you are, you covered your tracks well, because nobody's accusing you of anything besides disappearing. Although your friend from reading group did insinuate you may have skipped because you didn't read the book, after forcing them all to read it. Heathen."

Now I laugh, and she looks at me like she's scored a point.

"I did read the book," I say to her.

"And which book was it again?"

"The one with all the words."

"That must've been hard for you."

"Do you want me to get you something to drink?" I offer. "There's plenty of rat poison under the sink."

"Too much caffeine," she replies.

I don't want to be enjoying her company. I feel the urge to yank her out of the chair, dislocate her shoulder, push her down the front steps. I was just getting into my routine, and this is disrupting the routine. It is essential that I not have anyone else around.

She stands up. I notice she's had her keys in her hand this whole time.

"Look," she says, coming a little closer, "I don't know if this is a life crisis or a religious epiphany or if you just woke up one morning and said, *Fuck it, I want a new life.* If that's the case, hooray for you. But you still have to return the calls of the people who care about you. That's Human Being 101. And while you were never a great student in that particular class, you always managed to pass."

"It's easier without anybody," I tell her. "You don't know how easy it can be."

"You don't believe that."

I look her right in the eye and say, "I do."

She sees something then—something in her brother that scares her. She blinks it back, but I catch the moment before the blink, the slip of the composure.

"Let's get dinner," she says.

"I don't want dinner," I tell her.

"You've got to eat."

"Yeah. But I don't have to eat with you."

She tries to smile it off with a sarcastic reply. She says, "I forgot how much I love this side of you."

"It's called the front," I tell her.

She doesn't flinch. She keeps looking me in the eye. Searching for something she's not going to find.

"We don't have to go out," she presses. "I can get some groceries and we can have dinner here. I'll make you some Grumpy Food. Remember Grumpy Food?"

I don't go looking for the memory. Or at least I don't mean to. But somehow it pushes its way in, and I am seeing her much younger, making him dinner because their mom is working and their dad is angry. Mac and cheese, right from the box. String cheese peeled and placed on the top.

I try to shake off the memory. I don't care. I don't care about her, or him, or any of this.

I need to make her understand that.

I need to cut the tie. I've cut all the others.

"You're pathetic," I say to her. "Can you hear yourself? *Grumpy Food*? What kind of piece-of-shit baby says something like that?" I see my words are hitting. I hit some more. "You're the last person I want to see and the first person I want to get away from."

She's genuinely shocked now. "Pat, don't—"

"Don't what? Tell the truth about what a sad, weak woman you've become? It's like the worst of each of our parents, bundled up in one homely body. If I never see you again for the rest of my life, I will consider it a triumph." She's crying now. Good. "You're nothing but deadweight to me, Wil. You are complete dead—"

I don't get to finish the sentence, because before I can finish the sentence, there's a shooting pain across my chest, then another. It is unlike anything I've felt before, and is so monumental it feels like it could be unlike anything anyone's ever felt before. I grasp at my chest, gasp.

"Pat!" she screams. I spin a little, then lower myself into the chair where she'd been sitting.

"Pat! Are you okay?"

I can't even joke that no, I am not okay. It's the body—the body is doing this. The body is pushing back. That has to be what this is.

I fall in and out of consciousness. She's called an ambu-

lance. An ambulance is here. I understand what they are saying. They tell me to hold on. I am holding on. They have no
idea how I am holding on, to this body that wants to destroy
me, this body that wants me gone. I don't know for sure this
is it, that if the body dies, I die—but I'm not about to risk it.
I do everything they tell me to do. I let them do whatever they
have to do. His sister holds his hand. We get to the hospital.
He is hooked to machines. I am fighting this. The monitor
traces the heartbeats, and while I know they are his heartbeats, I pretend for a moment that they are mine, that I am
in total control, that I can survive this. They say he needs a
bypass. They say they need to put me under. *Under what?* I
think. I try to keep my eyes open. My eyes close. I am losing I
am lost I am nowhere but I am inside, I am inside, as the body
is opened and the body is closed, I am inside, and nobody
knows I am here, nobody will ever know I am here, and this
doesn't make me sad—it makes me angry. I am angry at him,
angry at this body, angry that it pushed back, landed me here,
like this. I am flickering and I am here. I sense movement. I
sense I am being moved. When I open my eyes, they tell me
to sleep. So I sleep. And then I wake up the next morning
somewhere else, good as new.

A

Day 6106

So what do I do?

I try to live the life in my head and the life of my body at the same time, and feel like it's an impossible balance.

I wake up in the body of Colton Sterling. He's fallen asleep in his clothes, and the clothes feel like they've been on for a few days. Or at least the jeans have. His room is a haphazard wreck. He's fallen asleep with a game on pause. The screen is asking me if I want to resume.

I access some of Colton's life and realize quickly that it's a solitary one. No real friends come to mind. Just a lot of games, and a lot of people he talks to during games, using his headset. Unreal real people. Voices that manifest in pixelated bodies as imaginary worlds are explored and imaginary enemies are pulverized.

He hasn't charged his phone overnight, so it sits as a shell version of itself on the floor. I plug it in, wait for there to be enough charge to get an email to Rhiannon. It would be so much easier to text her or call her, but that would leave a trace, and I don't want to leave any of the lives I take for a day with mysterious numbers on their phones.

I head to the bathroom and take off his clothes. There are bruises on the outsides of Colton's legs that I can't explain. There are half-picked scabs on his arms. I can't wash them off in the shower, but I try to rid myself of the musty rind that covers his skin. I wonder if it's something he's grown used to, doesn't care about. I wonder if tomorrow he'll feel vulnerable without it. Exposed.

I want Rhiannon to see me now. I want her to take a good look at me and tell me whether she really thinks she can love me no matter who I am.

Which isn't fair to Colton. I recognize this. And in recognizing this, I get back at least a little bit of the sympathy I used to feel for each body I was in. I remember to see him through my eyes, not anyone else's.

When I get back to the room, I have to dig a little to get to the clean clothes. There isn't much time before school.

I send Rhiannon a quick message.

R,

Good morning. Or afternoon, if you don't check this until lunch. I'm a boy named Colton today. I think he spends a lot of time playing games online—want to meet up in an Elf Parlor later this afternoon? I'll be the Orc with a rose in its teeth.

(If only it were that easy to meet in real life.)

A

There's more to say. And I imagine if I skipped school to laze around all day, Colton wouldn't mind. But my responsibility is to do right by him, not right by me or right by what he wants. So I head to school.

Once I'm there, I use Colton's memory to navigate. I think I may have been in this school a couple of weeks ago, but I've already forgotten who I might have been that day. Whoever it was, they couldn't have been as alone as Colton—that I'd remember. I wait for someone to come over to him, or even to

170

say hi in passing—but there's nothing. There isn't even a glare of disdain, or a pity look-away. He is just a part of the general population, without any specific encounters.

Is he used to this? Does he mind it? Is it enough to go home and plug in to other places? Maybe.

I go to class. I open his notebooks and find that he's continued his gaming there, drawing screens and scenarios and avatars, starting in the margins, then making his way across the pages. Sometimes there are speech bubbles—"Duck and cover!" "But where do I find a duck?!?"—and I wonder if these are the only conversations Colton has each day.

Even at lunch, his usual spot is the cafeteria equivalent of a quiet car on a train—everyone wears their own force field as they shovel down fries and sip Cokes. Few people look up. Most look at phones. I expect them to get in trouble for that, but the lunchroom supervisor leaves us all alone. I take out my phone and find a message from Rhiannon.

A,

I think an Orc with a rose in its teeth is called a d'Orc.

Meanwhile, my friends are mad at me, and I don't know why. Or maybe I do. Rebecca made a comment at lunch, wondering if there was such a thing as a local equivalent of a long-distance relationship. At first I thought she was talking about you, and then I realized she couldn't be talking about you, and was probably talking about me and Alexander. I haven't really hung out with him since this started. I know I have to. I'm just not sure how I'll act around him. And that scares me.

Now . . . time for English. More later. Good luck with Colton.

R

* * *

By gym class, I'm going a little crazy from not talking to anyone all day. When I get paired with a guy named Roy for badminton, I start chatting him up as if we're old friends. He's polite, but clearly would rather focus on the game than on getting to know me.

I wonder if that's what's getting to me about Colton. The fact that he's completely unknown, and doesn't know anyone else in return.

I don't linger around school once the last bell rings. I bolt for home, as I imagine Colton does at the end of each of his days there. I know as soon as I get back to his room, I should sit down and respond to Rhiannon. But it feels more important to establish some connection for Colton, so I load up *World of Guilds* and put on my headset. Immediately there are people greeting me by my screen name (ElfGunner17). A few of the voices have European accents. All conversation is concentrated on the mission at hand. So it's not like it's personal. But it's enough to have people talking to me and listening to me. I start to feel better, even as I'm slicing up attackers and plundering treasure for my guild.

Hours pass, but I don't recognize them as hours. The room grows dark, but I can't really tell, because my eyes are trained on the daylight of the screen. It's only when other people start to log off for dinner that I look at the clock and see it's almost seven.

Colton's dad is still at work and his mom isn't in the picture. So I'm alone in raiding the refrigerator and fashioning a dinner out of the random things that are inside. As I gnaw on a buffalo wing, I email Rhiannon back, smearing buffalo sauce on the phone screen no matter how carefully I try to avoid it.

172

R,

I'm sorry your friends are having issues. And that you
and Alexander are having issues. That was always my
worry when I thought about writing you, that I would only
complicate things. I don't feel as if there's any way to go
back now . . . but I'm trusting you to tell me if you need this
to stop. Because I'm never going to be your life there. And
you need to have your life there.

There's nothing to report here. I'm playing games, killing
things that aren't real.

A

I'm worried that I've already run out of things to say—
that once we get off the topic of us, there aren't any other interesting contributions for me to make. We are too young to
be having how-was-your-day-honey? conversations. But what
else is there to talk about, when we're so far apart?

I go back to Colton's room and consider cleaning it up. I
only have a few hours, but I could really do some undamage
here. The only problem is Colton seeing it when he wakes up.
There's no way he'd believe that he'd done it himself. He'd
probably get into a screaming fight with his father about coming in while he was asleep and messing everything up. And his
dad would, of course, not just deny it, but wonder about his
son's mental health for making the accusation.

So I leave it messy.

I do, however, gather some of the clothes strewn across
the floor and do a load of laundry. Then I go back to Colton's
room and throw the clothes around again. Let him think
they're dirty.

I keep checking for a new email from Rhiannon, but nothing comes. When I get to bed, I feel a childish need to hear

her voice before I fall asleep. I can barely play it in my ears anymore. I know I could just call her, could try to delete the record of the call from Colton's phone. But she's probably asleep already. And I feel that having already interrupted her life by popping up in different bodies out of nowhere, I should probably ask her permission before taking that voice-step closer.

I email her again.

R,

If you ever want to talk—like, actually talk—let me know and I'll figure out a way to call.

Good night,

A

Luckily, I remember to clear the sent item from Colton's history before I fall to sleep.

RHIANNON

If I try to avoid my friends, they know something is up. And if I see them, they know something is up. So basically, I'm caught.

After giving me all the love advice he had to offer, Preston's largely laid off. And by *laid off* I mean he's gone back to talking about himself a lot. But I can feel him studying my responses, trying to figure out what's going on with me and Alexander.

As usual, Rebecca's more direct.

"I'm worried about you," she'll say. Or, "When you get lost in thought like that, where is it you're going?"

The only person who seems oblivious is Alexander. Or maybe that's just the way he works—taking everything in stride, not really caring too deeply about anything enough to let it drag him down.

No. Unfair. I can't lie to Alexander and then be mad at him for not knowing I'm lying. That's not how it should work.

The thing that completely unnerves me happens when I'm walking to my locker and I see Justin and his new girlfriend, Sonata. I know they're going out—nobody's shown any hesitation in telling me this—but instead of trying to throw it in my face, Justin's been careful to make sure I haven't gotten anywhere near it. They're hanging out by Sonata's locker, and as soon as I round the corner and notice them, I expect him to sense me there, to pull back from her or maybe to look at me while he's kissing her, to try to make me jealous. But instead I'm like a ghost hovering unseen. He says something and they both laugh at the joke. They look like they're having a good time. And I wonder if that's what I looked like when I was with him.

I walk past. I'm still expecting him to see me, but he doesn't.

Even when I'm safe at my own locker, away from them, I'm wondering if they're happy, and if it's possible that Justin knows how to make things work when I so clearly don't.

Between art and math, Alexander texts and asks me to come over for homework later. I've been putting him off so often that I know I have to do it. But the fact that it feels like an obligation makes it also feel ominous.

I'm starting to think Alexander and I need to have a talk, and as soon as I start thinking it, it grows inside me, like the conversation has its own soul and it's crowding out everything else I could possibly be thinking about. I know Alexander is a good boyfriend, in the same way that Justin was a bad boyfriend and A isn't a boyfriend at all. But just because he's a good boyfriend, it doesn't mean he has to be *my* boyfriend. Which is pretty obvious, but the two things (good boyfriend, my boyfriend) haven't seemed separable until now, because I was living with them both at the same time.

After using being sick as an excuse, I'm feeling sick, thinking about what's about to happen. Even if I'm in control of it, it's feeling inevitable. I tell myself it doesn't even have to do with A. It would have happened anyway. A just made me see it sooner.

I'm not sure I believe any of this.

The minute I see Alexander after school, I expect him to recognize the warning signs, to sense what's coming. But instead he looks happy to see me, and kisses me hello like there will never be a goodbye.

His parents aren't home, unsurprisingly. With Justin, this would have meant a quick lunge into sex. But with Alexander, it means a stop in the kitchen to get a snack, and then an afternoon that can be unfolded as it happens.

"Grape?" he says, offering me a bowl.

I take a stem, give him back the bowl.

"Look," I say. "We need to talk."

He pops a grape in his mouth. "Cool. Let's talk."

It doesn't help that he's so agreeable.

"I mean a real talk. The kind that hurts."

He eats more grapes, then holds out the bowl to me again. I shake my head. I haven't even eaten the grapes I took.

"You can tell me anything," he says.

"No," I say. "That's not true. You know that's not true."

"Rhiannon. What do you want to tell me?"

"This isn't working."

"What isn't working?"

"*This.*" I gesture to the two of us.

He pops more grapes in his mouth. His calm is infuriating.

"Don't you have anything to say?" I ask him. "Anything at all."

"Here," he responds. He takes the remaining grapes out of the bowl and hands it to me. "Take a look."

I don't understand until I look at the bottom of the bowl. There, painted in red, it says:

Rhiannon, I like you for more reasons than there are grapes in this bowl.

"Oh," I say.

"It was supposed to be a surprise. So . . . surprise."

I hold up the bowl.

"You made this?"

"Pottery class. Sundays."

The decisive gesture would be to smash it on the floor. Then I'd release him. Then I'd never get him back.

I put it delicately on the kitchen counter.

"I don't deserve it," I tell him. "That's what I'm trying to say. I don't think it's working, and that's because my head is in one place and you're in another. I know you don't want to hear it—nobody does. But, Alexander—I need to stop being unfair to you."

He comes over and puts his arms around me.

"You're not being unfair to me," he says. "Unfair to yourself, sometimes. But not unfair to me. I never wanted us to be one of those you-are-my-everything couples. I want us to be able to pull away when we want to pull away, and come back close when we want to come back close. I promise, there are going to be times when my head is elsewhere, too. I get that."

"It's not just that," I argue. But then I can't go any further—because what can I really tell him?

"You want to define things," Alexander says. "We all do, to some extent. We want to know where we stand, where we're going—as if feelings can be reduced to geography. We become obsessed with one another's coordinates. But I don't want to be like that, Rhiannon. And I don't think you want to be like that, either. I don't want a relationship to be a restriction of freedom—I want a relationship to be an enhancement of freedom. Which I know is a lot to lay down right now. I understand we don't come close to knowing each other all the way yet. I know it's early days. And I also know I'm your first relationship after everything went down with Justin—I know I'm in the shadow of that, in some way. But I'm serious when I say there are dozens of reasons I like you. I enjoy my life more when you're in the room—and that's as good a reason as any to be dating. Right?"

But there's someone else—that's what I should say to him. That would shut it down. Only . . . he'll ask who it is.

I could lie. I could say it's Nathan. I could make someone else up.

But the way he's looking at me . . . it's almost the way A looked at me when A was in Alexander's body. There is something real there.

I'm starting to falter. I pull away from him. Face him squarely.

"I'm trying to break up with you!" I blurt out.

He laughs. "I noticed. Grape?"

"This is not how this conversation is supposed to go."

"How did you imagine it would go?"

"Tears. Anger. Understanding. Or maybe anger, then tears, then understanding."

"I guess I'm trying to jump to the understanding. Look, I know I'm a weird dude. The artiness hides some of it, but at heart—I'm pretty weird. But you've never seemed to mind that. And it may be presumptuous of me to say, but I'm not getting a sense that you think I'm bad for you. Correct?"

"Correct."

"So . . . what this means is there's something going on with you, something that's causing you to question your life—and I'm definitely a part of that. I'm not saying I can make it all better—I doubt I can. And I'm not saying that our dating should be top priority over everything else—hopefully that's never been a message you've gotten from me. What I'm saying is: How can I help you? If it's by going away, okay. If you really think that, sure. But if you're worried I'm going to be devastated if you're thinking of things besides me—sorry, but that's not going to happen. I want you to be thinking of plenty of things besides me."

"Everyone says that!" I counter. "But when push comes to shove—"

"What pushing?" Alexander interrupts. "What shoving? Look at me, Rhiannon. Look at the person in front of you."

I tell him, "The pressure isn't you. But you're part of the

179

pressure of everything. I know that's not fair to say, because there's nothing you can do about it, really. I'm just really confused right now. And trying to be a good girlfriend only adds to the noise. I'm not going to be a good girlfriend right now. You're right—I'm not thinking about you. Not as much as I should. And the things I'm thinking about instead—they get in the way of me being the person you like. I'm sure of it."

"And there's no way for me to help?"

I shake my head.

"I don't believe that," he says. "Or at least I don't want to believe that."

I am now completely unsure of what I am doing. I am running away from a person who cares about me—and I'm running toward someone who will never be able to be here in the way that Alexander is here.

I'm on the precipice of doing something stupid. And all it will take is one wrong move on Alexander's part for me to fall from the precipice, into the regret. I want him to push. I want him to shove. Because then I would have at least one answer.

But instead he says, "Let's go do some homework. Let's not say yes or no right now, because this is an essay question we're facing. And we're not even halfway through. The good news is that there's plenty of time left."

He puts the grapes back in the bowl, then picks it up from the counter.

"I'm serious," he says. "Let's do this."

This is the moment to exhale. The moment for the benefit, not the doubt.

But instead I whisper, "I'm so sorry—I can't." And then, before he can say anything else to make me want to stay, I leave him behind.

M: My real and your real are not the same.

Someone: I think they are. Even if our perceptions skew us, we all share the same real.

M: I'm not sure I can get there.

Someone: You can. Because we live in the same world. We all live in the same world. Over time we've tried to fragment ourselves away from understanding that, and at times it's very easy to privilege our own perceptions of reality over others', to ignore the fact that we're living in the same world. But unless you are writing to me from another dimension, you are as real as I am, and your life is as real as mine is. Even if it doesn't always feel that way.

M: But you don't change every day.

Someone: Neither do you.

M: How can you say that?

Someone: If I came on here tomorrow and started chatting with you, would you sound different?

M: No. But only because you can't see my body.

Someone: I am not talking about your body. I am talking about who you are.

M: Your body IS who you are.

Someone: But you always have a body, don't you? Even if it's not the same one.

M: You're saying that like it makes sense to you. It doesn't make any sense!

Someone: I am taking you at your word. Because I trust your word. The body has nothing to do with that.

X

Even though I wake up in the body of a young woman, I still feel the need to celebrate. It's the adrenaline rush of a close call. I could commemorate my survival with something major. Maybe tonight she can get pregnant. Or drive a car into a store window. Or one and then the other. The body is once more at my disposal. Especially since I'll only be staying in this one for a day. I have no use for anything under 140 pounds. I aim to be more than that.

I am tired of waiting.

I need to force the situation.

A

Day 6107

A,

I think I broke up with Alexander. I say I think I did because I left before it could be confirmed. It just wasn't fair to him to say we were together when a part of me is still clearly feeling something for you.

R

R,

Are you sure you want to do that?

A

A,

No. But how can you ask that?

R

R,

I knew I would make it worse.

A

A,

I don't want to keep going back and forth like this. Call me.

R

"Hello."

It's her voice. I cannot believe I am hearing her voice.

"Hey."

Of course, she's never heard this voice before. Kristen's voice. Calling from the house's landline, so hopefully this call will just blend in with the rest of the phone bill.

But still, there's recognition.

"Hey."

"It's wonderful to hear your voice," I say to her. Then I realize it's impossible for her to say it back to me.

"It's strange," she says. "Talking on the phone. We never talked on the phone."

"This is so 1985."

"Thank goodness you didn't get my answering machine."

It feels good to be joking, but then it feels awkward, because neither of us knows what to say next.

"I missed you," I tell her. "I just wanted you to hear it out loud."

"I missed you, too. I'm still missing you."

"I'm right here."

"I know. Exactly."

I have made an awful mistake. I have led us to the same spot we were at before.

"I want to be there," I say. As if that matters for anything.

"What are we doing?" Rhiannon asks. "Not to jump right to that, but every time I write to you, it's what I'm thinking.

And every time I get a response from you, it's what I'm thinking. And most of the time in between, I'm thinking it, too."

"I'm sorry," I say. Because what else can I say?

"Stop. At this point, I'm doing this to us as much as you're doing this to us. We could spend our whole lives saying sorry to each other and to everyone else around us. But I'd rather find something else for us to say."

Words fail me again. Because what else is there to say? *I'm sorry* is natural. *I love you* feels more like a challenge than a declaration.

"I want to see you again," Rhiannon tells me.

"And I want to see you."

She hesitates for a few seconds. Then says, "So get on a plane."

"It's not that easy," I say immediately, reflexively.

"I know." She sounds annoyed. "But you did it once. You can do it again."

"Yes, but the last time I did it, it involved a teenage girl waking up in a hotel room in Denver with no idea how she got there. I tried to get back in the morning, to come up with some story that she'd believe, and to help her catch her return flight. But by the time I got there, she was gone. Hopefully she saw the ticket I left her. Hopefully she wasn't too freaked out. But I have to live with the fact that she'd have *every right* to be freaked out. What I did was wrong, Rhiannon. I know I did it in order to get away, because I felt I had to get away. But that's not an excuse. And I don't plan to do it again."

"So do it a different way."

"What do you mean?"

"I'm not sure! But maybe you wake up in the body of someone who's traveling east. Or who has family in Maryland. Let's try to figure it out."

But will it really make a difference? I want to ask.

186

Only . . . I also feel that asking won't make a difference, either.

The course is already set. There's no way off of it. I tried to run. It didn't work.

Now I have to try to get back.

MONA, AGE 98

Today is the day. Dear Lord, I know today is the day.

I have traveled so far and seen through so many eyes. Now I can hear the final notes of the lifelong hymn. I know this body is the one that will bring me up to You.

I am sorry this woman is not here to witness this, to see the grateful pain in her daughter's eyes. She is holding my hand, Lord, and I feel You in that touch, just as I feel You in this body's undoing, my life's release.

I knew this day would come. There was no call for me to be an exception just because I have lived my life within the lives of others. Lately I have been feeling their pain more than their joy; as the bodies cultivate the pain, only the minds can offer the joy. I spend most of my time in hospitals or hospices or under the tender care of nurses whose fatigue nearly matches my own. (They have the decency to cover it better, most of the time.) It is a mercy to be leaving this Earth from the comfort of a home, in the bed where this woman has slept for decades, the mattress bending its springs to the memory of her shape. It is not my own home or my own bed—no such thing, Lord, no such thing—but I am still enfolded in the signs of life that a hospital room cannot offer. I am grateful to You for that.

Breathing is hard right now. Soon it will be too hard. I have been close to You before, but never this close. I hope that when my spirit rises, You will greet me with open arms and wisdom. Why have I lived like this? Were the choices I made the right ones? Was there something special I was supposed to see? Was there a special way I was supposed to help?

I have failed and I have triumphed and I have failed and failed and triumphed and failed again, but I have always kept going, even when the world gave me no encouragement, when the only voice I could hear was Yours, clear as glass and loud as thunder at some times, faint and unknowable at others.

For many, many years, I fought on the side of fairness, but that struggle took its toll. I could change people's minds when they were under my power—but the deeper challenge was changing their minds once they were on their own again. I have endured this life by seeing the unbelievable expanse of what others can endure. I have held on to my stories by understanding that each of us contains a multitude of stories, and none of these stories end up saying the exact same thing. Each of us holds at least one story within us that breaks our hearts to tell it. Each of us holds at least one story in which we are surprised by our own fortitude. Each of us holds at least one story that never came true, the story we most wanted to be able to tell. A lot of the time, it isn't our fault that this story never came to be; a lot of the time, we were stuck when we depended on the stories of others to match our own. All these stories—I have been honored and sorrowful and aghast and awestruck to know so many of them, in the short time You allowed me to know them.

As all of the senses are pulled back into this body, as vision and hearing and smell and taste and touch all retreat beyond, I struggle to play back the days I cherish the most. As this body shuts down, it's like someone's moving through and turning off the lights room by room. I am awestruck not by what I have experienced, but by my persistent desire for more. I am tired, Lord, and I am ready, Lord, but if You offered me another day, I would take it. Not to say any of the words I never got to say. Not to see someone I will no longer see. More than anything, I would like one last time to sit in the sun on an April afternoon, a good book in my lap, a song coming over the radio. To have one of those days when we get to feel the pulse of life underneath everything—that pulse a glory that reflects in every cell of our bodies, expressing itself in an inner splendor we are often too busy or hard on ourselves to acknowledge. You give us the simple pleasures because the rest of it is so hard. I understand this, Lord, because of all You have allowed me to see. It is an honor to You that I am ready and that I want more.

I hold the daughter's hand. I don't have the strength to find her name, and even less strength to say it. This woman will be missed in a way I will not be missed. This woman will be remembered in a way I will never be remembered. To love and be loved is to leave traces of permanence across an otherwise careless world. I must rely on You, Lord, to know what I have done, to give some worth to my devastated, hopeful heart. For ninety-eight years, You have been my sole constant, my companion, the only one who knows the things I've seen and sees the things I've known. I hope I have aided You in some way to understand the truth at the core of Your fallible, vulnerable, remarkable creations. I have liked to think of myself as Your eyes, Your ears, Your translator in the sum of our ways.

I have loved these people as best I could. I have tried my hardest to leave them better than they were before they met me. I have tried my hardest not to leave them worse. I have worked to remain open to every possible definition of who a person can be, even when society didn't agree with me. To do this—to understand the full extent to which people can define themselves beyond their bodies—I have had to learn

191

and learn and learn, and then learn some more. And by *learn* I mean *unlearn* . . . and then learn and unlearn and learn some more. I have made mistakes, but I have never been hateful. I have made faulty judgments, but I always sought remedy when I discovered my faults. I have asked for forgiveness, even though You are the only one who knew I needed to be forgiven. I have tried to lead a life of good, because it is the only way I know to lead a good life.

If I had a last wish, it would be to say to You: *Don't give up on them.* By which I would mean: *Don't let them give up on each other.*

I always wondered if, when my time came, all their lives would be shown to me again—if all those people I've been would somehow return to me, if I would see how all of these single days have added up to a single life. But now I understand: They all fall away. It is only me now. It is only me and You.

I hold on to that hand. I breathe for as long as I can breathe.

Every traveler returns home.

I am

M: I don't know why you'd trust me.

Someone: I was lost in my own life. To the extent that I didn't even recognize it as a valid life. The first step was understanding something was wrong. The second step was sharing that with someone else. The third step was giving it a name and trying to understand it as much as possible, as a way of getting power over it. The fourth step is living with it, and knowing there will be good days and bad days, and that sometimes I will lose control and other times I will regain control.

The fifth step is understanding that many of the people around me are going through some variation of what I'm going through.

I know this might sound obvious. But you have to understand that empathy is not something that comes naturally to me. It is something I have to remind myself about. Because if nothing in the world seems real, other people can also seem unreal. I must remind myself they are real. I must remind myself they are, at heart, like me.

Why do I trust you? Because you are, at heart, like me. You feel your life is wrong. You must discover it's not. You must live with that and work with that and share that with others. I trust you because I recognize you. I recognize your soul. And you have given me no reason not to trust you.

Let me say what I said above a little differently.

I know what it's like to be lost in your own life. I know you can get so lost that you want to end it. Or you can get so lost that you retreat into a carapace you've constructed in order to keep the rest of the world outside. I felt both of those impulses. But now I no longer want to be lost in my own life. I want to step outside of it. I want to know what other lives are like. I want to connect instead of retreat, even though there are days I think I will die in the attempt.

M: We can never meet.

Someone: Haven't we already met? Isn't this meeting?

We're told that the most powerful words in the world are "I love you." And while I think those are powerful, I think equally powerful is this phrase: I have started to know you, and I want to know more.

HELMUT, AGE 64

I have been in this body for almost forty years now. There is not a single day when I don't think of what I've done, and tell myself it was wrong. But there is nothing I can do now.

After more than twenty-five years of moving from body to body, I'd had enough. I felt cursed. I wanted to break the curse. I was living in the center of Berlin, and even in the larger anonymity of a large city, there was no way to make a constant life in such inconstant form.

It is not like I woke up as Helmut and knew he was the one. There was an emptiness in his life, for certain . . . but I had experienced greater emptiness in others. That day happened to be a good day for him—a minor success in the office, a going-away party at night for a friend that left me tipsy and longing. I may have even, in my drunken state, convinced myself that I led Helmut's life better than he ever had. When I looked into his memories, there were all these dark corners, all this trauma that made it hard for him to go forward. I understood that. But I also knew that it would never bother me, not in the way it gnawed at him. I could break him free of that. The only hitch was that he would stop existing as himself. I would become his better form. It seemed, in my twisted logic, the benevolent thing to do. So that night, it was like I made this bargain: I asked Helmut if I could stay, and even though I didn't receive an answer, I woke up the next morning still inside his body, still inside his life. I was not intending to stay for long. But days became weeks. Weeks became months. I started to worry about what would be left of him, if I vacated. And I also worried about what would be left of me, if I had to go back to the way life had been. So I stayed. I squatted. I wore out my welcome, and there was nothing Helmut could do about it.

I have now occupied his life for longer than he ever did. But I still make the distinction between us. I have not become him. I will never become him. I will always be the pretender, the borrower, the thief.

I did not want to be captive to fate. So I made myself my own captive. Which still made me captive to fate, and I have taken someone else down with me.

The only person who can absolve me is the person I cannot let free.

MORRIS, AGE 5

I told Mommy I wanted to go to the beach again today, and she asked me when did I go to the beach, and I told her I went yesterday when she had brown hair, and she told me she didn't know what I meant, so I stopped talking about the beach and asked her if we could get ice cream, and later when she asked me what flavor I wanted, I got that right.

X

What do I remember?

Not very much.

I have expunged the insecure sentimentality that causes people to cling to their memories, to set some measure of their own worth in the unreliable miasma of recollection. Memories—particularly ones that can be called *fond*—are pointless distractions, the act of putting your life into rerun when you should be focusing on the matters at hand.

You do not bring your house along with you when you travel. There's no reason your mind should be any different.

Also:

The fewer attachments you have to other people, the more you have to yourself. This has served me well. Undistracted, I can take hold when I need to. I can erase the people whose bodies I am in, because as they reach out, I can spend all of my strength grabbing the memories away.

I keep a few touchstones. Or, perhaps, the touchstones are too heavy for me to throw over the side, so I don't have much choice. Whatever the case, it's not like there is a blank space where my memory should be.

My strongest memory from childhood makes sense to me. I haven't kept it because it matters, but it has stayed because it was at the time, and is still, *instructive*. I must have been eight or nine. Still in elementary school. Still going out at lunchtime for recess. Still not understanding why I was different from all the other boys and girls. What my name was that day is unimportant. I was a boy, and I was at the top of the slide. There was this girl trying to cut in front of me, saying it was her turn. Possibly there was an order to it that I was breaking, since I had not been there the day before. Whatever the case, she was pushy, and I pushed her back. I can still feel the force in my arms, and the contact of my hands on her shoulders. I wasn't thinking of the direction. I pushed her back the way she came. Which meant I watched as she fell past the ladder and landed on the ground.

There were wood chips. I remember the area around the slide was covered with wood chips. I remember the cedar smell of them, even though I couldn't possibly have smelled them from my perch, which seemed to my young self like skyscraper height. I remember other kids screaming. Everyone screaming. Except the girl, who lay there, her leg an unnatural angle beneath her. There wasn't any blood, but she wouldn't open her eyes. Adults ran over. I had no idea who they were, since I hadn't been there yesterday. I just stood at the top of the slide, watching as some kids pointed at me, as one of the adults yelled at me to come down, come down right this minute. Someone said the girl was breathing; no one knew whether to move her. I knew I was in trouble. I knew it wouldn't be right to slide my way to the ground, so I lowered myself down the ladder at a funereal pace. No one grabbed me when I got to the bottom. I could have gotten away. But I stayed there as the girl started to stir and then, awake, howl like an animal. Teachers began to collect the other students, herd them back into the school. But I stayed. I punished myself with that girl's pain. The woman who'd yelled at me to come down finally pulled me into the principal's office. The ambulance came while I was walking inside.

The rest of the day was a series of adults yelling at me.

Asking me why. Saying, *This isn't like you*, but showing in their eyes that now this was exactly who I was to them. They knew what I was capable of; if they hadn't noticed it before, it had been lying in wait, unleashed on this poor girl with the broken back, whose name I cannot remember. But I do remember that phrase, *broken back*. Also *broken legs*, but I had heard of broken legs before. I hadn't known a back could break.

I cried. I said I was sorry. I knew I was terrible. If I could have broken my own back to save that girl from falling, I would have. I was sure of it.

I remember going to sleep that night, knowing I was just as bad as all the adults suspected.

Then I remember waking up in a different house, in a different body, in a different life.

This had always been the case, of course. But young me somehow thought I would be punished if I did something really bad. The privilege of escape would be taken away.

I remember realizing: The pain and the punishment were no longer mine. I was free of them. I had achieved what all people want at various junctures of their days. I had found the reset button.

I have been divorced from consequence ever since. I have no idea what happened to that girl. It would make a better story if she'd died, because then I would have gotten away with more. For all I know, she recovered valiantly and then got into Harvard ten years later with her stirring essay about the time a boy shoved her off a slide, and how she walked the road to recovery. *My back may have been broken, but my spirit never was*, she may have written.

And the boy? They probably put him on meds. If he hadn't been the kind of boy to push a girl off a slide, he probably is one now. Most men are. I know I am.

It's not that I drive around thinking about this. It's not like when I'm in the shower, I slip into reveries for the damage I've caused. There are no crimes dying to be confessed. There is only the secondary crime of forgetting. Insult to injury. I hurt you, and then I hurt you more by not remembering it.

The past means nothing to me.

I erase it wherever I go.

AEMON, AGE 18

I met Liam at the Melbourne Writers Festival. I was Peter at the time.

This was two years ago, when I was sixteen. I was in my lazy stage . . . which, okay, hasn't entirely gone away. But I was especially not paying attention that morning. I arrived at school to find I was the only boy not wearing the school's blazer-jumper-tie combo, which was apparently required for field trips. They almost didn't let me go, but an English teacher intervened, saying I of all kids would benefit from being exposed to so many authors. Suddenly I was paying attention, because I've always been a reader, but the odds were slender of me landing in the life of someone as die-hard about books as I was.

Sure enough, there were three different novels in Peter's bag for me to read on the bus ride into the city. I always faced a dilemma in situations like this: Go back to the start or pick up reading where Peter left off? If it was a book I'd already read, I'd pick up in the middle. But if it was new, I'd keep the bookmark in place and start at chapter one. Sometimes our tastes would match, and I'd learn about a new author. Other times . . . it felt like homework.

Peter's taste was pretty good—some Larbalestier (*Razorhurst*), some Lanagan (*Yellowcake*), and a copy of *Jasper Jones* for class. Even though we were going to a book festival, I was the only one on the bus reading. Peter's friend Edward sat next to him, but I think Edward was used to Peter reading, because he just loaded some comedy videos on his phone and watched those.

As a group, our school was signed up to see some Very Worthy Authors talking about some Very Worthy Topics. Mr. Williams, the teacher who'd defended my wardrobe, pulled me aside to say that he trusted me to make my own choices, but that I absolutely had to check in with him at lunchtime, and absolutely absolutely had to be back on the bus at the predetermined departure time.

"Don't get me fired for losing you," he requested.

I assured him I would do as he said, and with a nod to Edward plunged into the crowd at Federation Square. All these different schools were there, each with its own blazered plumage. It was funny to me how much you could tell about a school by the way the students wore those blazers—some like it was their posh, God-given right, and others like they'd been dressed by their mothers for a church they didn't want to attend.

I checked out the schedule and found there was a panel on queer lit. Since I've identified as queer ever since the first time I read the words *gender nonbinary*, I figured that's where I'd go. It was in a small black box of a space, and clearly none of the schools had chosen to attend this panel en masse. That meant a profound lack of blazers, and a surfeit of university students with dyed hair, some of whom (I could tell) were gender nonbinary as well.

I walked in. I could've sat anywhere. I ended up sitting next to Liam.

First thing I noticed: He'd taken off his blazer.

Second thing I noticed: A copy of Margo Lanagan's *Black Juice* in the blazer pocket. Not *Yellowcake*, but close.

Third thing I noticed: Elvis Costello glasses.

Fourth thing I noticed: Him looking at me looking at him.

"You've gone rogue, I see," I said, pointing to his blazer.

"I like to think of myself as more a rebel than a rogue," he replied, his self-deprecating tone making it clear he thought of himself as neither of these things. Which was endearing.

He introduced himself as Liam. I introduced myself as Patrick. Because I didn't want to introduce myself as Peter, and in that moment, my mind couldn't get that far away from it.

The moderator came on to tell us where the exits were, and the panel began. Even though it was very interesting, I was paying as much attention to the space next to me as I was to the authors in front of me—and I thought I sensed Liam doing the same thing. This thought was confirmed as soon as the panel ended, because we resumed talking as if there hadn't just been a fifty-minute pause.

Take two queer, bookish teenagers and give them the run of a literary festival—we might as well have been strolling on the Left Bank in Paris, for all the enraptured thoughts that rose into our queer, bookish hearts. Liam was from Melbourne proper; his mum managed a card shop in Fitzroy and his father was an ophthalmologist. I told him I was from Adelaide, in town for the festival with my dad, who worked for a festival there and wanted to scout out the authors. None of this was true, but I also told him the things I felt were the most true about me—about seeing myself as a person, not as a boy or a girl; about feeling like an outsider; about using books as a way to get inside something larger than my immediate life.

I pretended Mr. Williams was my father when I checked in at lunch. Then I went right back to Liam, who told me he wasn't going to check in with his teachers, even though he was supposed to. We spent the afternoon dipping in and out of panels, jumping from science fiction to environmental essays to debut authors not that many years older than ourselves. At some point, I told Liam my name was Peter, not Patrick. He didn't seem fazed. I asked him if he wrote, and in a quiet corner of the AMCI building, he pulled out a notebook and nervously debuted some poems to me, saying he'd just written them that morning. He asked me if I wrote, and I told him the truth—that I was still observing, and hadn't yet found the words.

The afternoon was quickly counting down. His hand brushed mine as we went to see four authors discuss Margaret Atwood. We both noticed, and we made sure to brush them again. Then we were holding them, neither rebel nor rogue, just romantic.

I knew it wasn't true, but I could believe that the hundreds of people who'd planned the festival had done it just so Liam and I could meet. They thought they were festival planners, but really they were scenic designers. We had stumbled into starring in the production.

Then it was time to go. I gave him my email address, Aemon808. He said *Aemon* was a cool word. There was no way for me to tell him that it was what I thought of as my real name. Until I found myself saying it was what I thought of as my real name.

He liked it. He liked that I'd chosen it.

We hugged goodbye. And we held that hug for as long as it could go. Our bodies recognizing the thing our minds and hearts already had.

I didn't want to let go.

The mistake would be to think it would have been better if it had ended there. Just one perfect day.

It still would have hurt. Any ending hurts.

For months, we wrote to each other, about anything and everything. I told him about school, about thoughts I had, about things I read. The weird part for me was that it felt like I was telling the whole truth—the bodies I was in didn't matter to me, so they didn't matter to the story, either. We shared secret Instagrams with each other. When he wanted photos of me, I went onto Peter's social media and borrowed some. When he wanted photos of Adelaide, I made my way there—and, because of the way my life worked, I stayed.

The photos I could take from Peter started to become limited—he'd found a girlfriend, and so many of the photos he posted were with her. I had come to feel this strange kinship with him, as if he was what I really looked like, because that was how Liam was seeing me. I knew it was wrong, but when you're different from everyone else, you can start to believe you get a pass on certain aspects of right and wrong.

Then I got a message on my Instagram: *Who are you and why are you using my photos?* Somehow Peter had found me. Right and wrong reasserted themselves. I told him I was sorry and wouldn't do it again. Which meant I couldn't do it again.

I told Liam I'd sneaked out to see his favorite band when they'd played in Adelaide, and had been caught by my parents on the way back in. I told him they'd found the Instagram, had taken my laptop and told me I needed to focus on my studies. I made it sound like their fault. I made them sound awful. But I told him I could still email. He went along with everything.

We went on for more than a year, in that strange space that was romantic but not dating, essential but not best friends, tied to each other but not tied to any physical space. We thrived there, and both felt we should want more.

I wasn't even thinking when the next Adelaide Festival came along. Although I'd kept up the story about my father working there, I wasn't paying attention. Then, a month before, Liam surprised me by saying he was going to come. So many of our favorite authors were going to be there—and he wanted to see me again. Finally.

I had to tell him not to come. I had to find a way to tell him that didn't tear down everything we'd built. I had to be as true as I could.

So I told him I wanted to stay in our space. I wanted to be romantic but not dating, essential but not best friends, tied to each other but not tied to any physical space. He was a writer and I wanted to know him through his words, and his words alone. And I wanted him to know me the same way.

Okay, he wrote back. *Let's keep it pure.*

I was so relieved. And, paradoxically, so disappointed. But we resumed writing as if there'd never been any chance of being in the same place. He didn't ask me about the Instagram or any other photos.

I still tell him everything-with-an-asterisk.

He is easily the most important person in my life. So every day, I am afraid of losing him.

A

Day 6132

R,

Today's the day. Do you think you can make it to New York City?

A

A,

Yes.

R

"Hello."

It's her voice. I still cannot believe I am hearing her voice.

"Hey."

"Oh! Hey."

I tell her the plan. I tell her why it has to be today.

It has taken weeks to find the right person. I could not forget Katie, the girl whose body I had taken in order to get here.

I could not ignore the word for what I was planning to do: *kidnapping*. I could not take someone from their home and strand them in an unfamiliar place. Before, I didn't know better. Now I did, which would make a repeat action inexcusable.

So I waited. I wrote to Rhiannon. I gave her updates. I tried not to think I was leading her to an impossible place.

Rita had a boyfriend who would've flown to the East Coast with her . . . but they both would have been grounded for life when they returned. Simon's mother didn't care and his father didn't exist, as far as his life was concerned, so if he'd disappeared, nobody would have noticed—but there also wouldn't have been anybody to help guide him home. Ana had a friend who'd moved to DC—but her parents had been relieved when this friend had left, and would never have allowed a visit. I didn't want anyone to get into trouble. I didn't want anyone to miss school. Or their jobs. Or even a date that had been planned the week before. Who was I to detour them from anything?

Then, one Saturday, I wake up as Tyana Jenkins.

She lives with her mother and stepfather in a nice house in Lakewood.

Her father lives in New York City.

I check and double-check: They appear to have a good relationship. She spends most holidays there. Even though this isn't a holiday, it *is* a weekend. She doesn't really have any plans.

I go to a last-minute-bargain website. Since it's not vacation season, there are cheap flights to New York. There's credit card information already loaded onto the computer.

I buy a ticket.

Then I text Tyana's best friend, Maddie, and tell her I need her to cover for me. I say I'm missing my dad and I really want to see him and New York. I tell her I'll explain it to my mother later, but that I need Maddie to say I'm sleeping over if she's asked. She writes back, *Patty will never know.* I figure Patty is my mother.

My family makes it easy for me. My mother has to take two of my stepsisters to what she calls a "dance intensive" while my stepfather has to take one of my stepbrothers to football. They say they'll see me tonight. I tell them I'm sleeping over at Maddie's. It's settled.

I go back to my room. I book a hotel room near JFK Airport. I email Rhiannon. Then I call her.

"So you'll meet me at the airport?" I say after I've explained everything.

"It will take me at least four hours to get there. Maybe five. I've never driven in a city before."

"It looks like JFK is outside the city. You won't have to go through Manhattan."

"It's all the city to me. And I've never driven five hours to anywhere before. So let me be nervous, okay?"

"Okay."

"Right. So . . . this is really happening?"

"Yes," I promise. "I'm already on my way."

I make it to the airport with plenty of time. I debate when to text Tyana's father to let him know I'm coming—too soon and he might call her mother, too late and he might be out at midnight when I need him to be home. I decide it would be best to wait until I'm actually in New York, irretrievably.

I have spent a lifetime avoiding planes, knowing the dislocation that would happen because of such travel. But this time, I allow myself to be comfortable. Even though Tyana's ticket is round-trip, mine is one-way, and for once, I am okay with that. If anything, it feels like the second leg of a round-trip.

It's only as the plane is landing that Tyana's hands start to shake. I stare at them, wondering how it is that the body knows what I'm feeling, how a body that isn't mine can still reveal me.

As we wait for the plane to get to the gate, I text Tyana's father.

I want to see you, so I'm on my way to New York. Just for the night.

He texts back right away.

Are you kidding me?

I tell him I'm not. I tell him I wanted it to be a surprise, and that I'll take a cab from the airport and meet him at his apartment around eleven.

It's already seven o'clock.

We shuffle off the plane. I expect to see people waiting with signs by the gate, but the only people waiting are the ones who are getting on the next flight. I realize that if Rhiannon's here, it'll be outside the security gates. I realize this means she's near. So near.

This is happening. This is real.

There.

Searching the crowds even though she doesn't know what I look like.

Confident she'll be able to find me.

Holding a sign that says, simply, A.
She turns in my direction.
She sees me.
I smile.
She knows.

Love may change forms, but it never goes away. Love allows you to pick up where you left off. Absence borrows time, but love owns it.

"Hey."
"Hey."
I drop my bag to the floor. I kiss her and she kisses me. We become, for a few short seconds, our own time zone. Everyone else can pass through. We hold tight.

Yes, there are people watching. Only when we pull apart do I see the reactions. Some people are smiling. Some are annoyed. Most don't pay attention.
We don't pay attention, either. We don't care.

I'd thought I remembered her perfectly. But it is much better to see her imperfectly, to see something new every time she moves.

She's parked at the airport hotel, but we don't have time to stop there. I'll have to get Tyana to her father's on time, so we have to get to Manhattan on time.

212

"I've never been here before," I tell Rhiannon as we get on the AirTrain.

"I've never been here without my family," she says.

"It's exciting."

"That's one word for it."

I can tell she's nervous. I'm not sure if it's about me or the city or both.

I take her hand. "We've got this. I promise."

She nods.

I want to tell her not to worry about the future. What matters is now. But I also know that thinking like this got us to the wrong place last time.

I knew I'd be excited to see her. But now, with her actually next to me, I also feel the need to be careful.

We catch up on the long subway ride. I hear about her friends. She hears about my last few lives.

At first she doesn't mention Alexander. I worry about this. Then, when the omission is too intrusive, I ask her about him directly.

"He's great . . . I think. I haven't seen him that much. Actually, I think the word for it is *avoiding*. I've been avoiding him."

"Because of this?" I have to ask.

"Yes and no. I mean, obviously it's related. But it's not the only reason."

We are coming dangerously close to talking about us, and I don't want to talk about us yet, not until we've had a little time to feel this out.

Rhiannon goes on. "I need you to know, even though there was some warning, I am far from feeling like life is normal right now."

"Just think of it as a date," I tell her. "You've come up to New York City for a date. That's pretty romantic. Wild, even. And it might only be for the weekend, but you will definitely make the most of it. That's perfectly normal. I'm your long-distance girlfriend who's flown into town to see you."

She leans her head against mine. "Lucky me."

"And lucky me."

I feel her there. Next to me. Even if the trip ended now, it would be worth it. To have her presence overlap my presence, and to feel the comfort of that overlap so palpably.

The city amazes us.

We get off the subway at Times Square and are blinded upon our emergence. It feels like we've entered an artificial world—day in the middle of night, a rush of people that seem randomly selected from the global population. Rhiannon takes out her phone and starts to take pictures. I assume she won't want me to be in them, because I won't be like this tomorrow. But when I try to duck out of the frame, she tells me to get back in.

"I want to remember you," she says, and it's clear which *you* she means. She won't remember Tyana, because as far as she is concerned, Tyana isn't here. There's only me.

That becomes the most amazing thing about the moment. Not the neon. Not the fact that we are at the center of the universe. No—it's the fact that she is going to remember me. I have found a way to exist like that.

We're both hungry, so we go to a restaurant that serves a soft pretzel with every meal. We talk about whatever comes into our minds, sharing our favorite New York movies and TV shows, then comparing them to what we see out the window. I don't want to look at the time, because it feels like the only thing right now that isn't entirely controllable. We are edging closer and closer to eleven o'clock, and Tyana's father's is a decent cab ride away.

"You need to go," Rhiannon says, looking at her phone.

"I don't want to."

"Don't worry. We have tomorrow."

We both smile at the sound of that.

I offer Rhiannon cab fare to get back to the hotel. She promises me she'll be fine.

I lift an arm to flag down my own cab, just like they do on TV. I'm spotted immediately, giving us only a short time for a goodbye.

"I'll let you know where I am as soon as I wake up," I promise. "We'll have the best city date ever."

She kisses me. "Sounds amazing."

I can't help but watch her from the back seat as the cab pulls away. She doesn't stop looking in my direction until I'm out of sight.

"I have a sinking feeling your mother doesn't know about this," Tyana's father says once I've walked into his apartment and we've hugged hello.

I can tell he's happy to see Tyana, but he's worried, too.

"Not exactly," I tell him.

"What does she know?"

"That I'm at Maddie's tonight?"

"So by *not exactly* you mean *not at all*."

"That's about right. . . ."

"And your flight home is tomorrow?"

"I get back in at six. Believe me, it doesn't matter if I'm at Maddie's or here. She'll never know the difference."

"Well, let's just hope you're right about that," he says. Then he shakes his head and laughs. "When your mother ran off during high school to visit her boyfriend, she got caught. But you didn't hear that from me!"

He says he went out and got us some ice cream. While we eat it, I ask him lots of questions, each of which he happily answers. But then when the conversation turns to my life, I let out the yawn I've been holding in for hours.

"Can we talk more in the morning?" I ask him. "I'm exhausted."

It's 11:35. I don't have much time.

"Sure thing. But if I only have you for less than twenty-four hours, you better not plan on sleeping late. We have at least two museums to visit, and frozen hot chocolate to consume."

"Agreed!" I say, then yawn again.

I hope Tyana will remember this agreement in the morning. I hope she won't mind being here. I am guessing she'll be happy—but I recognize that my guess may be tinted by what I want to be true.

Before I go to sleep, I text Rhiannon good night. I wait a couple of minutes, but midnight is coming too soon, so before I can get a reply, I text her again to tell her not to text back. Then I delete the whole chain and any record of Rhiannon from Tyana's phone.

I close my eyes at 11:52 and fall right asleep.

RHIANNON

I don't want to get in a cab, because if I do, I'll have to talk to the driver—or at least that's the way I think it goes. Plus, cabs are expensive, and even though the girl A was tonight clearly has money, I still feel weird taking money from someone who has no idea they're giving it to me.

I want to be alone in my thoughts, and strangely, the only way to do that is to get on a crowded subway. It's amazing to me how many people are up at this hour—I think all the people in my town who are out at midnight on a Saturday night could probably fit in this subway car. But I think it's safe to say that none of these people are thinking the same things I'm thinking, wondering what kind of person is going to show up for my "date" tomorrow.

This is weird. I knew it would be weird, and it is weird, and I'm telling myself that of course it's weird, but soon it will go back to being something less weird. I know I spent tonight with a girl I'd never met before. But despite that, I still felt like I knew her instantly. Because A was A. It may have been a different body, a different voice, a different size and height. But when she looked at me, it was A. When she talked to me, it was A. How I felt—it was A.

I don't remember the subway trip taking nearly as long earlier. Maybe because I wasn't alone. Or maybe it's making more stops at this hour. It's just taking a long time, and I don't have anything to read or do. And I'm afraid to stare at anyone for too long, because then they might pull a knife on me or try to talk to me. I'm not sure which would be worse.

My phone's running low on battery, and I don't want to risk running out completely, so even though there's service every now and then, I shut it off. I'm cut off from my friends, who are probably asleep by now, or out partying and not on their phones. Excuses, excuses. Truth? I wouldn't know what to say to them even if I did get in touch. Rebecca thinks I'm up here visiting colleges. So I'm sure that's what my other friends think, too. That's what I'll tell them on Monday. Rebecca will give me a little shit because she wanted to come, too.

It's almost one in the morning by the time we get to the JFK stop. Then I realize the stop isn't all that near the hotel, and while I could go to the airport itself and see if there's still a hotel shuttle, I'm not sure there will be one at this time of night. So I end up getting in a cab anyway.

The driver's a woman, so I don't mind when she starts talking to me. The questions she's asking aren't difficult ones. Is this my first time in the city? What am I doing out at this hour? Is the hotel any good? I could be talking to my parents' friends.

The hotel lobby is dead. I guess an airport hotel isn't really where New York City gets its kicks at this hour on a Saturday night. My room smells like cigarettes even though it's a non-smoking room. The bed feels damp. Not in one spot, but all over. I wonder if I'd be better off sleeping in my car.

The bathroom isn't that bad. The light's harsh, though, and before I brush my teeth, I look at myself in the mirror and it's like I'm being bleached out. I ask myself the question then, out loud: "What am I doing here?" Once it's in my head, I can't get it out. *WhatamIdoinghere?WhatamIdoinghere? WhatamIdoinghere?* Not just in this crappy hotel, where the only things you can see outside the window are a highway and other hotels. But here in New York, chasing after someone I will never be able to be with. It's not the same at all, but I can't help but think about the way it was with Justin, how there were so many times I thought it was over, and then I would convince myself that, no, we should be together. So we'd stay together. And then it would happen again. But we'd stay together. And it would happen again. Until finally there was too much evidence to be ignored. I know A is not Justin, and the reasons it won't work with A are completely different from the reasons it didn't work with Justin. But even if the person is different, maybe the pattern is the same. That childish belief that if you want something badly enough, you'll get it. So what if A is good for me and Justin was bad for me. What doesn't work doesn't work.

Stop. I have to tell myself to stop. Brush my teeth, then grit them in order to get into the damp bed. The sheets aren't as bad as the comforter. But the heater's making noise. I remember my phone and turn it on to find goodnight texts from A, then one before midnight telling me not to text back—as if I'd forget that part. Or maybe I *would* forget that part. Maybe I need to stop underestimating my own power of delusion.

I get back in bed. The heater doesn't get any quieter. The bed doesn't get any more comfortable. There's light coming in around the window shades. I can hear the cars on the highway. Why are there so many cars on the highway? I am alone. I am here to be with A, and I am alone.

But you knew you would be, I tell myself.

I just didn't know it would feel like this, I answer.

WhatamIdoinghere?WhatamIdoinghere?

I know it's too late and I'm too tired to drive home, but for a few minutes, I actually think about getting in my car and doing it. Telling A, *It's your turn to follow.*

Which is not something you should be thinking about telling someone who wished you a sincere good night.

I try to quiet myself down, even though everything around me feels loud. The only way to sleep in this place is through pure exhaustion, and eventually I get there. But once I get up, way too early, there's no going back to sleep. I email A to say I'm awake, but don't get a response.

I can't wait here. I pack up the few things I unpacked, check out of my room, and head to my car. I don't know where I'm going, but I know this hotel isn't the answer. I map out Manhattan and figure I'll go to Central Park, which is the thing in Manhattan that's easiest to find. It's dead early on a Sunday morning, so there isn't really traffic. I'm grateful for that. It's strange enough to be driving toward that skyline, to enter into it. I have no place here. I have no sense of anything.

I find a space right against the park, and have to check the street signs three separate times to make sure I'm allowed to park there on a Sunday.

Then I get out and walk. Only the pines are offering green against the sky at this time of year, but the bare branches speak to me more. I find a path where they meet overhead, crowning the space I'm in. Most of the people around me are walking dogs, although at this hour it looks more like the dogs are walking the people. I never stop being aware I'm in the middle of one of the biggest cities in the world, but at the same time, I like that the park is big enough to put the city to the side. I'm hungry and I probably need coffee, but all the vendors are still asleep. I walk twisted paths where the people and dogs disappear, and I wonder if I'm safe. I walk back to a more open space, a gigantic expanse dotted with empty baseball fields. I walk until my feet hurt, and my phone buzzes, and I find out my next place to be.

A

Day 6133

Rhiannon and I sit on a bench overlooking a particularly
steep hill on the east side of Central Park. I've brought her
coffee. As she sips it, I look at her lips and the way they touch
the lid. I've missed this.

I am telling her about this morning. The *telling-her* is something I've missed, too. The feeling that something I've experienced isn't complete until it's shared with one particular
person.

"So Arwyn's apartment is only about a block and a half
away from Tyana's father's. Which sort of proves something
I always thought—that the more people there are around, the
less distance I have to travel from body to body. Just think
about it—if I lived here, I could live in the same neighborhood
for months. Maybe years. I might never leave Manhattan."

"That would make life easier," Rhiannon says. "But not
really. You'd still be changing."

"I know, I know."

I hadn't been saying it as an argument for what we should
do. Not this time.

Rhiannon gestures at my body. "So tell me about Arywn."

"Honestly? There's a lot I'm not sure of, since they're not
sure. So let's just call them questioning, about pretty much
everything."

"You're saying *they* and *them*."

221

"I kinda want to do that now. If I don't know for sure how they identify. Makes sense to me that way."

"It didn't before?"

"I didn't have to talk about them before. You know, to anyone else."

"Then I came along," she says, cozying in.

"Yeah," I say, cozying back. "Then you came along."

I think that Central Park must be one of the only places in Manhattan that doesn't feel like it's owned by anyone or named after anyone or making anyone a profit. It's this oasis of pure existence in a realm of sustenance and maintenance. Because of this, I've already decided it might just be my favorite part of the city. Not that I've seen much of the rest of it yet.

I'm lost for a second, looking at the park, imagining it within the city. Rhiannon's gone quiet, too. And I think that's okay. No, that's good. Even after being apart for so long, we don't feel we have to rush our lives together.

We are acting as if we have time. Plenty of time.

RHIANNON

I ask myself, *What if this were our bench?*

I imagine it. Every morning, we meet here. Some days, A might be walking a dog. Other days, A might be on the way to work. I would probably be on my way to work—at a coffee shop, or a bookstore, or at a coffee shop in a bookstore. It won't open until ten—no, eleven. I'll have time to spend on the bench, sipping a latte with A, talking about our yesterdays, our todays, and maybe a tomorrow or two, at least for me. Sometimes I'll get to the bench second, and I'll have to wonder if the person sitting there is actually A, or if some interloper has . . . interloped. But I'll know as soon as they look up at me. I'll know as soon as they say good morning.

We'll grow old together on this bench. All the dog walkers, all the joggers who pass by this particular bench—they'll know it as our bench. Or at least my bench. Because I'll be the one who doesn't change. When it rains, I'll have a polkadot umbrella. When it snows, A will bring a blanket for us to sit under. In the autumn, we'll dress like the leaves. We won't realize we're aging. But we'll age on this bench. And always be the same two people at heart.

We won't live together. We'll rarely get to see each other at night. But every morning, we'll have the bench.

It's a nice fantasy. But it doesn't sound like anything real.

A

Day 6133 (continued)

Arwyn had to break plans with their friends to go see a movie downtown, and since I don't want to accidentally run into any of them, I suggest we stay uptown—whatever that means. I look on the city map for a divider, but I don't see any.

"Want to go to a museum?" I ask Rhiannon. There seem to be plenty of museums on the map.

"Let's go to the Metropolitan Museum," she says. "It's right over there."

She points to a building that looks like a mansion at the edge of the park. Then, the closer we get, the bigger it becomes, more like a castle than a mansion.

I've seen the massive stairway leading up to the Met in so many movies and TV shows that I feel I already know it; seeing it presents a thrill of recognition, not a thrill of discovery. Once we're inside, I get a map, and it's like we're suddenly time travelers, able to walk to any spot in history to see what it will end up leaving behind. I don't know much about art, so I have no idea where to begin. I also don't know which periods Rhiannon likes best, or if she doesn't have a preference, like me. The museum will help me find out more about her, too.

"So where should we start?" I ask.

She yawns, and then blushes in embarrassment at her

yawn. "Sorry! I didn't sleep much last night. Let's start with the impressionists. Those rooms are always my favorite."

I consult the map. "Upstairs!"

"You are way too cheery."

"I guess I always get some sleep."

"You wouldn't have, in that hotel."

"That bad?"

"No—it was fine. I'm just not used to sleeping alone in hotel rooms."

"I wish I could've been there with you."

"I know. Me too."

Our wishes hang there between us. There is a spellbinding quality to having them expressed, in knowing this is what we both want. But there's a sorrow, too, because this kind of choice will never be ours.

We're walking through a corridor lined with sketches and old photographs, each in its own alcove, public yet requiring some effort to be seen. "I like that one," Rhiannon says, moving closer to a black-and-white scene from the 1940s, where four girls—three small, one bigger—are watching six soap bubbles rise in the air over an empty city street. There's a certain symmetry between the girls and the bubbles, as if there is some meaningful relationship between them. The photographer's name is Helen Levitt, and she's left no trace of where the bubbles have come from or who the girls are. The title of the photo—*Children with Soap Bubbles, New York City*—tells us nothing.

Rhiannon yawns again, then apologizes again. We walk from black and white to color, then from print to canvas. We're greeted by ballet dancers caught in their poses. Rhiannon walks over to observe them, and I stand a little bit back, to see her lean into them as they lean toward the barre.

"Degas might be my favorite impressionist," Rhiannon says to me when I get closer. "Though Monet's close behind."

"Why are they called impressionists?" I ask. "I mean, aren't all paintings impressions?"

Rhiannon takes her eyes away from the Degas dancers to look at me. "Agreed. But there's something different with the impressionists. They recognize that their subjects are constantly changing, and that they're only capturing one moment. It's not even a *definitive* moment. Like, they're not saying this is the best possible way to show this scene or this person. They're saying this is just one of the ways you could see it. This is the way I saw it . . . and then it was over. Only I caught some of it. I managed to get some of it down, before I, too, was gone."

Other people are trying to see the dancers, so we step to the side, head to new rooms, to Monet's haystacks and Van Gogh's straw hat. No color is a single color. No solid is completely solid. Everything looks different when we look closer. I think about what Rhiannon said, about how these are singular moments, flashes of impressions. At the same time, they feel like composites, built from many different moments and observations to achieve something nearly impossible: a timeless immediacy.

I want to tell Rhiannon this, but she is already three paintings away from me. She drifts down the wall until she sees something that merits her attention; then she goes in, gives the painting at least a minute before moving on.

I look through a frame of my own devising. We museumgoers are a part of the paintings for as long as they remain in our view. We separate from the room in order to peer through the poplars. Two of us stare at the same woman from over a century ago, and we know nothing about her and yet know something about her at the same time. We look for the clues in her expression.

We are strangers here. We assemble to look at art, and in our way, for the smallest amounts of time, we bring the art back to life.

RHIANNON

We are strangers here. We look at different things, see different things. If I didn't know Arwyn was A, I would walk right
past them. Even now, I don't know what to say. We are surrounded by some of the most famous paintings in the world,
and I can't think of anything to say that I wouldn't say to
someone else.

If anything, I think about how much Alexander would
love it. Alexander would want to dip his fingers in the brush-
strokes. He would want to find a landscape and wade inside.

DAWN, AGE 45

We are strangers here. I've talked to Irene, the guard in Gallery 964, so many times over the years. I know the names of her nieces and nephews. I know where she's vacationed. I know that she likes Monet more than Manet. I know she likes Vermeer the best, but doesn't get rotated to his room nearly as much. Her boss thinks that when she's in Gallery 630, she pays more attention to A Maid Asleep than she does to the potential thieves and vandals who step inside. She admits this is probably true. Why work as a museum guard if you're not going to look at the paintings?

I know all this about her, but still, we're strangers. Because every time Irene meets me, I'm someone else.

I sit in front of the same painting each time. I've spent hours studying it. If I was the same person each time, it might cause suspicion. Or at least Irene would know me to say hello to. But since I come in a different body each time, I haven't been pegged as a scholar plotting a thesis or a thief planning a heist.

The Monet Family in Their Garden at Argenteuil. Painted by Manet, when the Monets were living across the Seine for the summer. I like that they were friends. I like how comfortable Monet's son Jean is in the painting, while his mother takes the time to pose and his father, the one who should know the most about posing, stands to the side, gardening.

Why do I love this painting so much, when there are so

many other great paintings around it? I've never been to Argenteuil, or out of the United States. It could be that I simply like it. But to come day after day (when I can), it also has to speak to me, and I must return to it again and again to try to understand what it's saying. In my heart, I think it's about family. It's about how that boy leans on his mother, perfectly drowsy with contentment. I must have felt that way about someone, sometime. I know I must have had a mother—even if it was just for that first day, I must have had a mother. She must have liked certain kinds of paintings. Maybe she would have loved this one. Maybe that's why I love it so much. Maybe that's what I want it to say to me. I want to believe that I come from somewhere, that there are pieces of that somewhere embedded in my thoughts. It is not like being adopted or raised apart from biological parents—those children can at least look in the mirror and see some traces of where they came from. I must rely on the things that feel like they come from somewhere deeper than mere memory. Songs speak to me. People glimpsed in shopwindows speak to me. Certain names speak to me more than others. And this painting speaks to me.

Irene comes over and asks me if I knew that Renoir was standing right next to Manet, making his own portrait of the Monets. I tell her I did know that. I don't tell her that she was the person who told me, many years ago, and that she's told me many, many times since.

A

Day 6133 (continued)

Rhiannon yawns again. This time she doesn't turn to me to apologize. She might not even remember I'm here.

RHIANNON

I'm already thinking of the drive home. I shouldn't be. We still have plenty of time.

A

Day 6133 (continued)

Another yawn.

I'm starting to panic. Not because she's yawning—I know that's from a lack of sleep, and I know that in a way the lack of sleep was my fault. I'm more worried that we're not talking to each other, that we're not learning anything more about each other.

Then I tell myself to stop. Calm down. I am putting too much pressure on a single day. I have to believe that, like all other couples, we'll have plenty more days after this.

I follow her from room to room, circling around the centuries and the continents. Rhiannon pauses in front of a woman named Madame X. She is a very white matron in a very black gown, painted by John Singer Sargent as she looks to the right. I get a sense that she isn't looking at anything in particular; she's looking off to the right so she can be painted looking off to the right. That is how we will remember her.

"Have you ever looked like that?" Rhiannon asks me.

"What do you mean?"

"Have you ever had a day when you looked like that?"

There are people nearby. They might hear us.

Rhiannon must see my alarm; she laughs and says, "Don't worry—this is New York. I'm sure you can say anything and nobody will care."

I study the painting. I think of really white skin, of being afraid of sunburn. I try to remember a dress, any dress. . . .

"I'm not sure. I don't really remember what I look like. It's not that important."

"That's weird," Rhiannon says. "I see a painting like this, I wonder what it must be like to have that face, that skin, that much sophistication. But I also know I'm never going to look like that, or live that kind of life. But you might."

"I love that you're thinking that way," I tell her. "But that's not the way I think. Maybe I should—I don't know. I guess I could look in the mirror more. I just don't really see myself when I'm other people, if that makes any sense."

"Let me ask you—what do you look like right now?"

I tell her the truth. "I have no idea. I know I have short hair, because I can feel it's short."

"But what color is it?"

"Brown?"

"Ish. I'd go with auburn. What about your eyes?"

"I have two."

"But what color?"

"I have no idea. Why would I pay attention to that?"

"Are you pretty?"

"I would never think that. I mean, if other people were reacting to it, I'd notice, I guess. But I never look in the mirror and go, *Oh, hey, how pretty am I today?*"

"God, that must be nice."

"Do *you?*"

"I mean, those aren't the exact words I'd use—but I definitely notice whether it's a good day or a bad day."

"You couldn't possibly have a bad day!"

"Thank you. But no. I definitely have bad days."

"Then what's today, on the good-to-bad scale?"

"I had two hours of sleep and took the fastest shower I could. I think that escorts me straight to the bad-day category."

"Well, that just proves it. You have no objectivity. Because your bad day is pretty great."

"I never claimed objectivity. And neither should you."

"It was a compliment!"

"I'm aware of that. But I'm still stuck on the fact that you don't know what you look like."

"I'll never know what I look like."

"You know what I mean. The body you're in."

"But that's what I'm saying—it's not me. I don't remember what they look like because they're not me."

A man walking through the gallery gives me a long, strange look. So much for Rhiannon's theory about saying crazy things in New York. A guard walks in on her rounds, and the man tells her, "Have a good day, Irene!" He keeps walking, and she calls out, "You have a good day, too, sir!" Then, under her breath, she asks, "Do I know you?"

"So when you picture yourself, what do you picture?" Rhiannon asks.

"I don't picture anything. I don't have a shape."

"Everything has a shape."

"Then I don't have a *discernible* shape."

I know these are all obvious questions she's asking. I know they mean she's thought about me, and what it must be like to be me. But they're still questions nobody has ever asked me before. And I worry that she's not satisfied with my answers.

"How do *you* picture me?" I ask.

"I just remember you as you were, whichever day. I'm sure

that will change once there are more days. But right now, I remember you that way, and know I'm both right and wrong each time."

"So how do you know it's me?"

"Because your reaction to me isn't what Arwyn's would be. There's a kindness there I can recognize. An affinity. A way of seeing the world, and of seeing me, Rhiannon, in it. From that very first day."

"So it doesn't matter that I don't have a shape?"

"What I'm saying is that you *do* have a shape. It just isn't made of skin and hair and eyes and cells and blood. It's made of other things."

I think about this as we wander into the surrealist galleries and I look at the works and the names of their makers. Am I shaped like a Giacometti sculpture, a person worn down into the thinnest of lines? Am I a Miró, a floating circus of whatever shapes appear? Dalí paints lions of varying degrees of facelessness coming out of eggshell-colored rocks and calls it *The Accommodations of Desire*. Picasso reduces us to geometric noise. Magritte divides a woman's body into frames and calls it *The Eternally Obvious*. This—all of this—is more like who I am. But not exactly.

Rhiannon stands next to me as I stare at Picasso's *Nude Standing by the Sea*.

"Maybe that's me," I say, nodding in its direction. "More a contortion than a person."

"I don't think so," Rhiannon says quietly. "That's not the A I know."

I know my sudden despair is ridiculous. But I look at her and I think about me and I think, *How?*

I don't want her to think I'm so serious—not this soon, not this early in us being back together. So I say it like this:

"How can you expect surrealism and impressionism to have that much in common?"

I think it's an unanswerable question. But Rhiannon has an answer. She doesn't even stop to find it.

"Because," she says, pointing to her head, "they both come from up here."

RHIANNON

I think we need to get some food. I check my phone to see what time it is, and find a couple of texts from Alexander, asking me what I'm up to. Ever since our non-breakup, I've kept him at a distance without entirely pushing him away. Even though I feel the impulse to text back and tell him I was just looking at the Van Gogh he has in postcard form on the wall over his bed, I don't. I don't text him back at all.

A catches me checking and asks if everything's okay.

"It was just Alexander," I say. "No emergency."

"And how's Alexander?"

I don't know why this question annoys me, but it does. "Please don't ask me that."

"Oh. Okay. I won't."

"He just wanted to see what I was up to. It's nothing. The much more pressing question is: Where are we going for lunch?"

"I actually know the answer to that one. Or I will, once I map it out."

It ends up that A did some research on vegetarian restaurants on my behalf, and we end up at a place called Candle Cafe. It's more elaborate than any vegetarian restaurant I've ever seen, serving things like southern-fried seitan and tempeh empanadas. It's also the most expensive vegetarian restaurant I've ever been to, though it's probably not all that expensive for New York City.

I come right out and say to A, "I can't afford this."

"My treat," A says.

"We've been through this. It's not your treat. It's *Arwyn's* treat."

If I'm slightly exasperated at A, A's slightly exasperated right back at me.

"If Arywn were out with their friends, they'd be spending this much on lunch, too. I'm not costing them any more than if I weren't here. Believe me, it's something I've given some thought to."

"One of your rules."

"Sure."

I remind myself that we all have rules, not just A. Things that aren't universally right or wrong—just personally right or wrong.

I give in, and when the food comes, I'm thankful, though I'm not really sure whether to be thankful to A or to Arwyn or to both of them. Probably both of them.

A asks me about all of the things we haven't really talked about in our emails—school and friends and parents and other things that aren't us. For someone who forgets so many days, A has remembered a whole lot about the time spent in my town; we talk for a long time about Steve and Stephanie and their ons and offs—because A's met them, A knows what I'm talking about, but because A doesn't really have a side in the fight, I'm able to observe things that maybe I couldn't observe with Rebecca or Preston.

I have to take out my phone and look up tempeh so I can explain what it is. A tries it, likes it—and suddenly we're eating off each other's plates, laughing and talking. We've shifted back to normal, and neither one of us had to steer. We could be any couple in the world having lunch, and at the same time we are distinctly the two of us having lunch. We are a couple

239

like any other couple, and we are us. I don't say anything because I don't want to jinx it. This is what we've been trying to return to. Not effortless—we still need to engage, we still need to care. But the effort doesn't feel like something extra. It feels like normal effort.

I know I should probably be aiming higher. But I'd rather aim on target.

"Look!" A says, pointing over my shoulder.

I turn around and see it's started to snow.

A
Day 6133 (continued)

We walk outside, and outside has changed. We are standing on the sidewalk, showered with cloudpiece snowflakes that layer us as they fall. We are smiling at this offering of magic, brushing it out of our hair and then letting it stay there. We know there are places that will take us in, for a small admission fee—places full of medieval masterpieces and ancient riddles, reconstructed dinosaurs and priceless gems. But we resist the indoors and retrace our steps, even though our steps are covered now, blanked out by everything that's happened since. We marvel to one another at what we are seeing. We say it aloud so we can share it. We dance along to the snowfall, and in doing so, we lift. We return to the park, which has fallen eternally quiet. We can hear our own steps. We can see our breath. We watch as all the paths turn white, and take them anyway.

RHIANNON

The skyscrapers disappear. Daylight filters gray. The trees bow and the streetlamps beacon blindly. The wind swirls, contradictory patterns spelled out for the eye to see. The dog walkers retreat to their kennels and the squirrels retreat to their secret city. The sounds of stillness emerge as the cars no longer touch the ground. We can hear the shape of our footsteps.

For all we know, we are the only two people in New York.

A
Day 6133 (continued)

We are missing all the winter vestments—scarves and hats and coats to keep out the wind and its claws.

She shivers and I pull her close.

I shiver and she kisses me.

I rest my forehead on her forehead. Both our foreheads are cold.

The snow gathers around us. Our breath is still warm. We are alive to wonders, and we are recognizing them.

Not a word needs to be said. But we say them anyway.

RHIANNON

It is a small miracle that we find my car.

The snow has transformed the parked cars into statuary, with only an occasional headlight peering out. I go to wipe off my windshield with my sleeve, but A stops me, says we should just get inside, since we're not driving anywhere right now. There isn't enough snow to block the door or the exhaust pipe, so I make my way carefully inside, then turn on the heat and unlock the passenger door. A slips inside, and lets out a loud "BRRRRRR" until the temperature rises to accommodate us.

With the windows covered, it's like we're in our own co-coon. The snow melts into us as we lean back in our seats, let the heater do its job. The cars that pass on the street are slow and rare. Our car shudders when a plow passes, scraping its way south.

A's hand drifts into the space between us, and I take it. I can feel my phone vibrate in my pocket—another message.

"Do you need to get that?" A asks.

"No. All that can wait."

I am too comfortable. I can feel my eyelids starting to flut-ter themselves closed.

"Don't leave me yet," A jokes.

"I'm trying."

"I know."

A's voice is so gentle, it ushers my eyes closed. But I am still holding on to A's hand. I am still here.

"I can't believe I have to drive back tonight," I say.

"There's no way you're driving back in this."

"I have to. I have school tomorrow."

"It's a snow day."

"Says who?"

"Says me."

A's thumb is running up and down my wrist. Time slows to the rhythm of this movement.

Soothed. I am soothed.

The radio stays off. The phone stays in my pocket. A's hand still touches mine. The snow continues to fall.

I slip so seamlessly into dreaming.

A
Day 6133 (continued)

As she drifts off, I close my eyes, too.

This is what I've wanted: to slow down the frequency of expectation and doubt, to find the nameless peace of following each other and following the day.

I can sense when the snow stops falling. There are more people walking by, and the sound of shoveling. I don't disturb Rhiannon. I turn off the car and hope our own heat will hold us until she wakes.

RHIANNON

It's only when we're walking to dinner that I take out my phone. I have to call my mother and explain to her that the snow has prolonged my college visit, that I'm crashing another night on the dorm room floor of a fictional girl who used to go to my high school. I figure at least some of the messages have to be from Mom—and maybe there will be a couple from Alexander as well. I'm surprised to see that while both Mom and Alexander are represented, most of the messages are from Nathan.

"Wait a second," I tell A.

Something's going on.

X

The pain should be gone. I do not understand why it's not gone. That body has already been forgotten. Yet even in this new body, I will feel a twinge in my chest. Instinctively I will feel the crash about to come, the explosion about to rise.

But nothing happens. Because I am in a healthy body. I am fine.

You hear the phrase all the time: *a brush with death*. What they don't tell you is that the brush has paint on it. And once it touches you, you can't get it off. Not even if you change bodies. Because it's not the body that's been brushed—it's the mind.

I must get over this. Otherwise, things will slip.

Case in point:

Three mornings ago, I woke up in a new body.

I did not choose to leave the body I was in. But I could feel its resistance. I could feel him kicking at the door. And maybe I thought the kicking was other things, another attack coming on. Whatever the case, when I went to sleep that night, I didn't tamp him down hard enough. Or maybe I didn't want to stay badly enough. Maybe worry—stupid, persistent worry—did that.

The result? I woke up as a woman who needed a cane to walk.

Unacceptable.

The next day: a man scheduled for surgery in a week.

I thought, *Are you kidding me?*

Yesterday: an eighteen-year-old wrestler.

Much better.

Even so, I rooted around his medical history, to make sure all was well. Or at least all was well as far as he knew. Beyond a broken arm in fifth grade and a case of mono in eighth, I was in the clear. He liked his life, so I knew it would be a bit of a fight to stay. But I needed his life, so I could fight harder than he could comprehend.

I dug in. I'm still here.

But even in this body, I am struck by a wavering, an uncertainty. As if his heart knows what the other heart went through. As if the mind is turning itself so the brush marks show.

And with this reminder of pain comes a nearly subconscious call for urgency. If I had children, I suppose I'd feel I should spend more time with them. If I were searching for a cure for cancer, I'd step it up. If I were building an ark, I'd tell my wife to gather the animals.

But I don't have any people like that in my life. Or projects. I only have the person I'm trying to find.

I sigh, pack up the wrestler's gear, and throw in a knife for good measure.

NATHAN

After getting caught having sex-not-really in the bathroom, I've had to find a new library to study in. I know I'm probably exaggerating the importance and memorability of the moment for anyone besides myself, but I can only guess what would happen if the connection was made—I don't think my parents would ground me so much as they would bury me in the ground and build a new house on top of me, to keep me from getting another stamp on my Sinner Card.

I'm only a couple of towns over from mine, but I don't recognize anyone, which is great. Of course, in the back of my mind, I can't help but worry that one of these new faces is actually a mask hiding Poole. And if someone's paying extra attention to me—well, it starts to move to the front of my mind.

Like this girl. She keeps looking over. And when I look up, suddenly she finds the book in front of her interesting again.

It's a slow Sunday at the library. Mostly it's parents and kids gearing up for story time at two o'clock. Then there's me. And there's this girl, with a sports duffel next to her and a book with a title I can't make out. When I try to see what it is, it's her turn to catch me, and I imagine both of our glances shoot away.

I try to ignore it. I tell myself if I stay in public, everything will be fine. No bathroom breaks. And OF COURSE the minute I start to think that, my bladder starts raising its hand, desperate for me to call on it.

Not. Helpful.

At least the bathrooms in this place aren't single-user. So I wait until I see a dad bringing his three sons into the men's room. Safety in numbers. Then I bolt for it, keeping my eye on the girl the whole time.

The peeing goes fine. I might break a speed record. When I get back, the girl isn't in her seat—she's wandering past my carrel, looking at my stuff. Not, like, pawing through it or anything. But definitely scoping it out. Then she disappears into the stacks, so I get a chance to look at the book *she's* reading—something called *Memoirs of an Invisible Man.*

Subtle. Very subtle.

Part of me is like, fine, I'll pack up my things and go. But the other part of me is thinking that if it keeps going like this, I'm not going to have any libraries left. And I am *not* about to stay home all the time.

Plus, it's like, why are you stalking me? What do you want me to do? I've been given exactly one order, *find A,* which is impossible.

I can't let this creep haunt me like this. He needs to get it in his thick skull that *I can't help him.* Or her. Whichever form he/she decides to menace me with.

The girl sees me standing by her stuff. I can tell she has no idea what to do.

"Hey," I say. "You."

She's far enough away that my voice carries and a couple of other people look. I don't care. She looks mortified. But she comes over.

"Look—" she starts, reaching for something in her back pocket.

But I'm not in the mood for her threats.

"No, you look," I say. "You have to stop it. I can't help you. I can't do anything. And you driving me crazy is only

251

going to . . . well, drive me crazy. How does that help you? What good does that do? Just leave me alone, okay?"

She's got her phone in her hand. I don't know why.

"What are you talking about?" she says.

"I saw you looking at me," I tell her. "I saw you looking, and I saw you going through my stuff. I mean, not physically, but with your eyes. When I went to pee. So I know it's you. I know what you're doing."

She actually reaches up her hand and pulls at her hair a little. Her face is getting red.

"Oh God, this is so embarrassing. I am so, so sorry. You totally caught me."

This is not the reaction I was expecting from a body-swapping demon.

I sputter, "I mean, I just—"

She waves off the sputtering. "No, no. I'm an idiot. It's just—I've never seen you here before. I'm here every Sunday, and I've never seen you. So I was curious. And, fuck it, you're cute. So there was that, too. Now, naturally, I've made a complete fool of myself and you will conclude that I'm this crazy, foulmouthed library stalker girl who undresses you with her eyes."

"I didn't say you undressed me with your eyes. I said you were going through my stuff with your eyes."

"Oh Jesus. That's of course what I meant."

"Who the heck are you?"

"I was about to ask the same question. Only I wasn't going to use the word *heck*."

Okay, so either Poole is an incredible actor or I was 100 percent wrong about this girl.

"Now I'm starting to feel a little idiotic," I admit.

"I should've warned you—it's contagious."

"Well, I guess we both have it now."

She holds out her hand. "I'm Jaiden. But you can call me Library Stalker Girl for short."

I take her hand and we shake like we're in business school. "I'm Nathan. But you can call me Massively Overreacting Library Boy for short."

"Initial unpleasantness aside, it's nice to meet you, Massively Overreacting Library Boy."

"A pleasure, Library Stalker Girl."

She moves her duffel off the seat next to hers and gestures to the chair like it's a game show prize. "Care to join me?"

"Beam me up."

She snorts. "Did you really just say *beam me up?*"

"Don't judge."

"Not judging!"

Since I've never been on a date before, I have no idea what exactly counts as a date. Is it goofing around at a library for three hours on a Sunday afternoon? Shooting jokes back and forth, then being the oldest nonparent attendees of story time? If a girl leans against you while a volunteer reads aloud from *Last Stop on Market Street*, is that as much of a come-on as, say, kissing in an alleyway? If she insists on getting some crayons to do the activity sheet, and then colors in everything you outline, is that a good sign? When, at the end of the three hours, she says, "We have to do this again," does she intend that to be as specific as it sounds—i.e., *We have to hang out at story time at the public library again*—or is there some leeway? If you propose going for lunch or dinner or coffee or something else that doesn't involve young children, are you asking her on a first date or a second? If she says yes, does it even matter?

* * *

253

So I'm happy when I get home. The kind of happiness that I'm a little worried my parents will smell on me. Like, if I told them I met a girl, they'd say, *We can't wait to meet her.* But what they'd really mean is *We can't wait to wire her to a lie detector and see what horrible things she's done in her past, because surely they must be bad if she's willing to be seen with you.*

I take a moment in the car to compose myself, then get out and head to the garage door. I don't even sense the movement, I'm so in my own head. I don't know anything's wrong until I feel the sharp tip of a knife pressing into my back, and hear an angry voice in my ear saying, "From now on, you're going to do *exactly* what I tell you to do."

A

Day 6133 (continued)

I need to talk to you.

Please. Call me.

It's Poole. He's here.

Nathan's messages to Rhiannon aren't long—but they make their point.

"And you're sure he doesn't know you came up here to meet me?" I ask.

"Positive. He knows I was looking for you. He knows I found you. But he doesn't know you're here."

The waitress must wonder what's going on. We are two teenagers sitting in front of a pizza without taking a bite. This must never happen.

"I have to call him," Rhiannon says after we look at each other for long enough to realize that looking at each other isn't going to answer anything. "I can't just leave him hanging."

"You have to assume he's with Poole, even if he says he's not."

"I know."

"I know you know. I just had to say it. I'm nervous."

"So am I. And I'm not even sure why."

Before I can explain further about who Poole is and what I think he does, she raises her hand to quiet me. She's already dialed, and Nathan's phone is ringing.

"Hi—Nathan? It's Rhiannon. I got your texts. What's

happening? . . . Are you okay? . . . Is he there now? Where are you? . . . I'm out for pizza with some friends. . . . No, no. . . . I don't know where A is. . . . Really. . . . What's the message? . . . I know you're supposed to insist on speaking to A, but I have no idea where A is or how to speak to A, so I'm your best bet. . . . Okay, okay, Nathan—calm down. . . . Yes, I understand. . . . When? . . . Oh. . . . I see. . . . So what does he look like now? . . . Okay. And he's *not* there now. But you have to get back to him tomorrow? . . . Got it. So here's what I need you to do. . . . No, listen. I need you to try not to worry right now. I know that's hard—but it's out of your hands now. It's in my hands, okay? There's nothing you can do. Nothing. I promise I will get back to you tomorrow morning—maybe even tonight. Okay? . . . That's right. And, Nathan? . . . Thank you. You didn't do anything to deserve this. Nothing. And I promise, we'll get out of it. We'll figure something out. . . . I know. I can't believe it, either. At all. . . . Exactly. I will. . . . Night, Nathan."

She hangs up and gives me a nearly helpless look. "You have no idea how badly I wanted to pass the phone to you. Because, honestly, it was like he was going into season-seven details of a show I'd never seen. But let me try to recap: The reverend is back, and he wants to see you. Only he's not the reverend anymore. He's been a few women and a few men in the interim, and some of them have been stalking Nathan. Now he's a strong jock near our age, and he promised to make Nathan's life really miserable if he doesn't deliver you up. Like, the violent kind of miserable. Nathan said he isn't there now—it sounded like Nathan is safe at home with his parents—but he's going to contact Nathan tomorrow and is going to expect a meeting with you to have been set up. If Nathan doesn't do it, he'll be hurt badly. Nathan believes this. He's very, very scared. More scared, he says, than when you left him where you left him."

"So the message was that I have to meet Poole?"

"Oh yeah—that. It was more specific. It was: *Listen to me. Listen to all you can do.* That's not ominous *at all.*"

"It does have a whiff of cult leader, doesn't it?"

"Or guidance counselor. Same thing."

I can't believe I'm laughing. "Why are we joking about this?"

"Because we don't know what else to do?"

I sit back and sigh. "Oh yeah. That."

"Nathan sounded really scared."

"You were good at talking him down."

"I'm not sure it worked."

"Want to try it on me?"

"Tell me what you're feeling."

I look at her for a second. I don't think she realizes fully how strange it is—*still*—to be asked a question like that, and to know that she wants my answer, not Arwyn's answer.

I don't hold anything back.

"I'm feeling confused and angry and sad and then confused some more."

"Okay. Let's take them one at a time. Why confused?"

"Because I gave Poole an answer. Because I thought we were done. Because it's like he senses I'm here, even though there's no way for him to know I'm here."

"Why angry?"

"Because I just found you again and that's all I want to be thinking about."

"Okay. That—I didn't think it would be that. But yes. Alright. Sad?"

"Sad because I know there's no way to get out of dealing with it."

"There are plenty of ways. You're just not going to choose them. And confused again?"

"Because I have no idea how to deal with it."

"Why?"

"Because what are the choices here, really? You weren't there the first time. You didn't see his eyes. I don't know if I can explain it—it was like I could see the pain the body was in, and at the same time I could see his triumph in the middle of that pain. He does all the things I won't let myself do, and I have to believe one hundred percent in the reasons I don't let myself do them. So there can be no conversation. No listening, if listening is really what he wants . . . which it isn't. He wants me on his path. And I don't want to be on his path."

"Staying in the same body?"

"Well, obviously he can change them at will, too. I can't help but wonder what happened to Reverend Poole after. Is he walking around with this months-long hole in his life? Or is it worse? And what kills me is that this guy—who I still have to call Poole, because what else can I call him?—knows the answers. He could tell me. All of these questions I've been dealing with on my own, all these years—he's the first person who can actually give me a second opinion. But his opinion is destructive, Rhiannon. I know it is. Look at the way he's bullying Nathan! And what's so stupid is that if he had just tried to talk to me as one person who goes through this to another, I would have talked to him. I would have . . . compared notes, I guess. But now—what do I do? If he's gotten to Nathan, what's to stop him from getting to you? What would I do then?"

"Whoa—one thing at a time. The only thing we have to figure out right now is how to respond."

I shake my head. "But can't you see? One thing leads to the next thing leads to the next thing. And if you don't try to measure the chain reaction, if you don't think about the next thing and the next thing, people get hurt. I've gotten so many people hurt, Rhiannon, without meaning to. Because there was something I missed. Something I didn't see."

"Like what?"

I tell her about Moses, about what happened there.

"I messed up," I conclude. "And because I messed up, his life could be messed up forever."

"You can't attack yourself for that. What you're asked to do every day is impossible to do perfectly, A. You do realize that, right? To immediately navigate someone else's life for them— I'm sorry, all of us would mess up in that situation. No matter how many consequences we tried to consider. You could spend your whole life considering consequences. And the only consequence would be that you would have no life whatsoever."

We're not arguing, exactly, but it doesn't feel like we're agreeing, either.

"I'm just saying, the minute we respond to Nathan, it's *on*. We've engaged. And then we'll have to see it through."

"It's already on, A. We're already at the seeing-it-through part."

The waitress has returned. "Is something wrong?" she asks, gesturing to the pizza.

"No," Rhiannon tells her. "We just like to talk before we eat. It's a syndrome."

"Just checking. Jesus," the waitress murmurs, walking away.

"We better eat," Rhiannon says. We help ourselves to slices. We're not really hungry, but it's pizza, and the moment we start eating it, it's guaranteed we'll keep going at least two slices past where we should.

Rhiannon continues. "So, putting the considerable logistics aside, if you meet up with Poole, what do you think will happen?"

"The same thing as last time. He'll want me to be his

259

partner in this thing that we do. He'll want to teach me how to abuse it."

"And if you say no?"

"That's the thing. I'm worried he will create a situation that won't allow me to say no. Before, I would have been fine. I would have just disappeared."

"But now?"

"You know exactly why I can't now."

She pushes her pizza around a little. "Okay. Let's look at it a different way. What does he get from having you 'partner' with him?"

"Someone to talk to, I guess."

"Exactly."

"Exactly?"

"I'm just trying to think this through, okay?"

"Go ahead."

"I'm just thinking—Poole has to be lonely. Like you were lonely. I think you're right—he wants someone to talk to. He's been looking for someone like him for a while. Then he found you. And lost you. Now he wants you back. So he won't be alone."

"But even if that's true, how does it help? He still won't take no for an answer."

"It helps because it means you have leverage."

"How?"

"Because he wants more from you than you want from him. That means you have the leverage. That's how relationships work."

"That's cynical."

"It isn't. Because most of the time, the balance is always shifting, and the difference isn't that significant. But in this case . . . you definitely have the upper hand."

"But he's willing to hurt people!"

"Don't mistake evil for power. That's a bad mistake we all make. Thinking that it takes more strength to break the rules of human decency than to follow them, and therefore if we follow them, we have to be the weaker ones. Bullshit. Yes, he's scary. But the fact that he wants you to listen means he's dying to talk to someone who understands what he's talking about. It makes sense. We seek out the people who understand us. We are scared and suspicious of the people who understand us, but we also need them in our lives."

"How do you figure out these things?"

"Bad relationships. Good relationships. Being with people who don't understand you. Finding people who do."

"Is that what happened with us? How can we understand each other when our lives are so different?"

"Because we want to see the world the same way, I think. I'm not sure. Honestly, I've never been sure."

"I don't understand how anything works. I don't understand how you can randomly fall into my life one day and now here we are, in New York City, telling the truth in a way that I never, ever thought I'd tell the truth."

"If I ever get a tattoo, that might have to be it: *I don't understand how anything works.* I just have faith that it would be much worse to think you actually knew how anything worked."

"He can't give me any answers, can he?"

"I have no idea. But I'm pretty sure that he can't give you many answers you can actually use."

"But still . . ."

"But still, we're going to have to find a way to deal with him. Because we owe that to Nathan, who never did anything to deserve getting caught up in all this."

* * *

We eat more pizza. We don't come up with a plan.

Arwyn is going to need to go home soon. And Rhiannon is going to need to go—

I'm not exactly sure where.

"Do you want to come back with me? To their apartment? I'm sure we can come up with a story. . . ."

"And what if they wake up in the middle of the night and wonder who the girl sleeping on their floor is?"

"You wouldn't be sleeping on the floor."

"Stop. You know what I mean." She looks out the window. "The roads actually look pretty clear. I should try."

Now I actually feel the despair widening within me. "No. Please. Stay."

"A. I'm going to have to go back home."

"Then I have to go back with you."

"Oh, great—do you want me to drive? I think there's a word for driving someone somewhere else without them knowing about it. *Kidnapping*, I think?"

"What if I drive?"

"Arwyn is from New York City. Don't think for a second they have a license."

"I'm serious. I should come with you."

RHIANNON

I don't understand how I can be this far in, and still not know what I want.

I want to stay like this. In the city. The two of us.

It feels like a believable now.

But back in my regular life. With my friends. My family. Where we used to be—

I can't imagine it. It doesn't feel like a believable future.

Which feels like a cop-out. Because who wants to end up with a future that was always believable?

"We have time," I tell A, because I want that to be both believable and true. "The only pressing thing right now is Nathan. We have to get back to Nathan. I vote for giving Poole some of what he wants, but not all of it. Tell him you're considering meeting with him, but aren't sure. Make him want it more. Then we wait for the opportunity for you to get down to Maryland in the same way that you made it to New York. Or we get everyone up here. Let's just see how it plays out a little."

"Okay."

"That's it? *Okay?*"

"I'll do whatever you tell me to do."

"No. That sounds like something someone would want to hear, but it's not actually something I want to hear, and you wouldn't want to be with me if it was."

A nods, gets it. "Fair. But in this case, what you're saying makes sense. There's just one change I want to make."

"Which is?"

"At least stay 'til midnight."

"Okay."

Someone:	I would walk around, and I would think, *I am lost.*

I would know exactly where I was, and I would think, *I am lost.*

I would look at my own body, and I would think, *I am lost.*

You have to believe that the opposites reach for each other. I had to understand that when I was thinking *I am lost,* I was actually *finding* that I was lost. The two opposite things were true at the same time: found and lost.

What was it with you?

M:	I'm not sure. I would look in the mirror in the morning and I'd think, *That isn't me.* Which was true. It wasn't me. And that's how I'd start the day. Knowing I wasn't me. And I guess what changed was that after a while, I realized that most people who look in the mirror don't think, *That is me. That is me exactly.* Most of them think, *That isn't me.* And I guess it made me feel a little better, to know they thought that, too.

NATHAN

Rhiannon texts me on Sunday night to say she'll call me on Monday morning.

I'm not sure Rhiannon fully appreciates what it's like to have a body-shifting madman threatening to kill you and the people you love, because by the time second period comes around, I still haven't heard from her, and I'm worried I may seriously compromise the learning atmosphere of third period with the loudness of my palpitations, so I slip into the restroom to shoot off a few texts, and then finally call her, even though I think it's just wrong to make a call from a toilet, even if you're not using it. I'm worried that somehow she'll *know*. But I'm more worried that she'll never call.

She picks up after the fourth ring. It's 9:34 and it sounds like I've woken her up.

"Hello? Nathan? What time is it?"

I tell her.

"Oh, shit! I got in so late and was going to just nap for an hour. . . . I guess it lasted longer than that. I gotta get to school. The whole point was for me to not miss school."

"Rhiannon?"

"Nathan?"

"What am I supposed to tell our malevolent friend?"

"Tell him A's thinking about it."

"*Thinking about it.* That's not going to go over very well."

"Point out that it's not a no."

"I believe in anger management terms, what you're doing is called *poking the bear*. Which is very easy for you and A to do, because you won't be in the room. But I'm the one who's left holding the bear."

"Well, while you're poking, poke around as well. Find out anything you can about him. Anything that can help us."

"Anything that can help us *do what?*"

"Stop him."

I don't like the sound of that.

"Please. Hold right there. Because anything you tell me after that is going to be completely written on my face when I see him, and he may very well knock my face off in order to have a transcript."

"Okay. I've gotta go anyway. Let us know how it goes."

"Is there anything else you'd like me to do for you? Get you a latte? Jump off a bridge?"

Rhiannon sighs in frustration—but at least I can tell she's frustrated with herself, not me.

"Sorry. Thank you, Nathan. Honestly, I'm just waking up."

"Is A there with you?"

"No. A's somewhere else."

"Where?"

"I don't want it written on your face. Just know it's nowhere near here."

"What a coincidence—that's exactly where I wish I were!"

"Nathan. Really. Thank you. You're one of the good guys."

"At least until proven otherwise!"

We say goodbye and I flush the toilet, as if I need to provide a bathroom alibi for some unknown audience.

Okay, I half expect New Poole to come out of the stall next to mine, to say he's heard everything.

But instead there's just some freshman at the sink. From the way he's looking at me like I'm totally unhinged, I can tell he's not New Poole.

He hasn't given me a phone number or anything—just in case, I guess, he wants to try on a new life while he's waiting for my call. But he wanted an answer today, so I'm sure he'll find me one way or another.

It's for this reason that I avoid going to the library after school. Of course I'm curious about whether Jaiden's there, or whether she's a strictly weekend Library Stalker Girl. But the presence of Poole 2.0 would definitely be a dating downer.

I drive to the mall instead. I have as much use for the mall as I do for a lobotomy or a condom (meaning I'm not having sex, not that I'm having sex without condoms). As I'm driving there, I see a car following me, and after a few turns, I'm pretty sure I know the driver. At a stoplight, I type the license plate into my phone, although what I will actually do with this information, I have no idea. Rhiannon wanted me to pay attention, poke around. I think a license plate should count for that.

There's a spot right by the mall entrance, and there are lots of moms with strollers in the vicinity, so I figure this is about as safe as a mall parking lot gets. I go inside and head to the food court, figuring it highly unlikely that Mr. Poole Party is going to brain me in view of the Sbarro staff.

I'm only alone at my table for about thirty-seven seconds before Poole's frat-boy version sits down across from me.

"I hope you have something for me," he says.

I don't know if it's out of nervousness, or out of the fact that my answer to his question is *not really*, but for whatever reason, the next words out of my mouth are, "Do you want coffee? I want coffee."

Before he can react, I'm out of my seat and headed to the Starbucks. There's a short line, but I put him off by studying the menu. I order a mocha Frappuccino—with whipped cream, because, hey, it's a special occasion—and pay with a credit card, slowly putting it into the chip slot. The power of suggestion is very strong, because instead of pushing me along, Poole Boy orders his own Frappuccino (no whipped cream—whatever) and pays with his own card. And that's when I get to see the name on the card—Wyatt Giddings.

License plate: check. Name: check.

You're welcome, Rhiannon.

It is, admittedly, awkward as we wait for our drink orders. He's pretending not to know me, but at the same time not letting me out of his sight.

Once I get my drink, I head back to our table. He joins me a minute later.

"Why wouldn't you get the extra calories and the joy of whipped cream? It's not like it's your waistline."

It appears my don't-let-him-see-how-full-on-frightened-you-are gambit is working, because he's actually at a loss for words for a second. I guess he's not used to sitting at the food court, shooting the breeze about his body-hopping.

"Do you have a message for me?" he finally asks.

"Yeah. Rhiannon has been in touch with A. And A is thinking about it."

"*Thinking about it?*"

"Those were her exact words. I don't know anything more than that."

Poole looks like he's about to crush his Frappuccino in his hand.

"That's not good enough," he growls.

"That's all I got. At least for now."

"I said . . . that's not good enough."

"I heard you the first time. Don't shoot the messenger."

"You have no idea what I will do to the messenger if he keeps delivering answers like this."

"Here? In the food court? That can't possibly be allowed. Plus . . ."

I stop there, to see what will happen. After about three impatient seconds, he says, "Plus?"

"Plus, you can't hurt me right now."

"And why is that?"

"Because I'm the only link to A you've got."

He starts to get up. "I'll give you twenty-four more hours. I will meet you back here tomorrow, and if you don't have a meeting set up, I will do whatever I want to you."

"Can I ask you a question?"

He's standing now, but doesn't leave.

"What?"

"What's your name? I keep thinking of you as Reverend Poole, though obviously that name reached its expiration date. Who are you now?"

"Why does it matter?"

"What a person's name is? I happen to think it matters a lot. I want to know what to call you when I talk about you."

"My name right now is Wyatt."

"Well, hello, Wyatt. I'm guessing you don't hang out at the mall very much. Did you when you were a teenager?"

"How do you know I'm not still a teenager? Or maybe I never was a teenager. You've seen me at all kinds of ages."

"I guess I just assumed. Silly me."

Poke around. Don't poke.

"Is it weird that I'm talking to you, knowing that Wyatt

isn't you? Does that happen to you a lot, when people actually know the deal going into the interaction?"

"No," he says. I'm not sure which question he's answering.

I'm trying to think of a follow-up, but he takes his drink and leaves.

I text Rhiannon: *We have 24 more hrs.* She doesn't respond right away. I go into a few stores, delay delay delay, and then finally head back out to my car. I wouldn't be surprised to find the windows smashed, a dead animal thrown inside. But it's as I left it. And there isn't any car following me as I head home—at least not as far as I can tell.

As soon as I get in the door, my mother yells at me, asking me where I was. I tell her the mall, and she says, "You know I don't like you to go there," which (a) is not something I know, and (b) is kind of a weird epicenter for her concern at this point. I wonder if she, too, was ever a teenager.

But I'm not about to ask her about it. I have more important things to do.

There's a web search that needs to be done on Mr. Wyatt Giddings.

X

"Are you eating with us tonight?" Wyatt's mother asks me when I get back home.

"Yes," I say, and head straight to his room.

I am trying to be strategic here. If I have been getting pushback from my body hosts, it might be good to not push so hard against this one's life. I feel this is the right body for right now—strong, imposing, virile. But also, I am hoping, relatable to A. Perhaps my mistake last time was approaching as an authority figure. Perhaps I am better off approaching as a peer.

I miss the freedom of having a space of my own larger than a room. And I am not exactly about to go back to *school*— we'll see how long it takes the attendance office to catch on. But otherwise, it's good to visit what you've left behind every now and then, to remember why you left it behind.

Like all perfectly nice people, the members of the Giddings family are defined mostly by their capacity to be boring. Mrs. Giddings is a good cook, though, so that keeps dinner moderately interesting. Wyatt's younger brother, North, is a chatterbox—and, luckily, is still in eighth grade, so he isn't chattering about Wyatt's newfound absenteeism.

People live their whole lives doing this every night. I have no comprehension of how that's bearable. It sets all the borders way too close.

If A still believes in things like this, I need to set her right.

I know the pause here is just to make me wait, make me think they're calling the shots.

But they have no idea.

In the meantime, I pass the salt. I watch hockey with Dad. I watch the porn on Wyatt's computer and do the same things along to it that he does.

He has no reason to resist. And because of that, he'll be mine for as long as I need him.

A

Day 6134

I think it was easier for her to leave than it was for me to stay.

Watching her drive off, I felt myself pulled behind the car. But I didn't feel the car pulled back to me.

I know I need to be patient. I know we are in a better place than we were a couple of days ago. I know I need to give it some time.

But the power of missing her is stronger than any of this knowledge, at least when I wake up without her.

Again, I haven't gone far—just three blocks north this time. Today I'm in the body of Rosa Thien. Her alarm has gone off at 5:32 a.m.

At first I assume this is because she has practice of some kind. But no. It's because she takes the subway downtown for school, and has to leave plenty of time to get ready.

I stumble to the bathroom and find that even though the radiator is blasting a temperature roughly the same as that on the surface of Mercury, there's no hot water in the shower. I let it run, thinking maybe it'll warm up, but after a minute there's a sharp knock on the door and a man calling, "Four minutes! No dawdling!"

I grit my teeth and bear as much of it as I can. As I'm stepping out, the showerhead burps and a little warmth comes out.

There's another knock at the door.

"One second!" I call.

I put on a robe and wrap my hair in a towel. I barely get out of the bathroom before someone—an older brother, I figure out—pushes past me and closes the door. Another brother pokes his head out of a bedroom and asks, "Did he just go in there?" I nod. The bedroom door slams back closed.

Rosa's desk is covered with makeup, and her mirror is lined with photos that give me a sense of what I need to do before I head to the subway. I'm sure Rosa can put on her face in fifteen minutes; maybe she even does the finishing touches while she's riding the subway—I'm not sure I could pull that off. I take more time and, I'm sure, cut more corners. So many mothers have taught me how to do this, and it's still not second nature to me.

I zone out easily and think about Rhiannon. And when I'm not thinking about Rhiannon, I think about Poole, and about what I'm going to do. Around me, the apartment gets louder and louder as more people get up—Rosa has four older brothers, it seems. All of them still live at home.

I access Rosa's memory enough to know I have to get moving. I have to concentrate on which way to swipe the subway card and which direction to take the train and which train to take. I don't expect to have much time to think on the subway, but it ends up that it's at least fifteen stops to get to my school. At each of the fifteen stops, more people get on, until we're pressed about as tight as clothed people ever get.

I don't know how I feel about this.

It's overwhelming, actually. Not because of who I am or what I am. But on a basic human level, it's overwhelming. To press against so many strangers. To have so many faces to look into. To have so many eyes looking back or looking away.

My mind returns to the fact that I'm waking up so near to where I went to sleep. Does that mean there are more people like me around? Or is there no correlation? Is it just that there are more people?

But if there are more people . . . wouldn't that mean there are more people like me?

I never think about it. I did for a time, but then I stopped. Now I'm thinking about it again. And that's Poole's fault.

I think Rhiannon's right that he wants to see me more than I want to see him. But I'm also afraid that once we start talking, that will flip. I will want to know more and more and more. And from there, will it be enough to know just one person like me? Will I want there to be more and more and more of us? Would my life change if suddenly everyone knew we existed?

Yes. Because they would never accept us.

Yes. Because we would be blamed for everything that goes wrong.

Yes. Because we would only inspire fear, not understanding.

They would never see us as human beings. And history is clear about what happens when someone is seen as less than human.

So what's the point? I ask myself.

And then the answer: *The point is that you don't want to be alone.*

What if Poole's the same way?

"Rosa?"

I look up and find a girl who hasn't spent nearly as much time on her makeup this morning as I spent on mine. After a beat, Rosa's memory offers up a name: *Kendall.*

"Hi, Kendall."

"Wow, you were really focused there—it was practically yoga. Subway yoga. That should totally be a thing."

We spend the rest of the ride with Kendall telling me about her weekend and me being vague about mine. She says she went to a warehouse party, and I picture teenagers drinking around boxes that are about to be shipped to Walmart. I know that can't be right.

I am lucky to have Kendall as an unknowing guide, because there have to be thousands of kids going to this school. It takes all of my attention to navigate the halls, and all of my agility to make it through the other students to get to class on time. There are moments when I think I've accidentally walked into a college, because there are classes with names like Memoir Writing and Beginning Thermodynamics. It ends up that Rosa is near the top of her class in a school where there's a whole lot of grappling to be at the top. Every grade counts. Every day counts. I try my best.

At lunch, I email briefly with Rhiannon, who tells me she talked to Nathan. We go back and forth a couple of times, and it's clear we've switched over from catching-up to making-new. I try to remind myself that it doesn't make much of a difference if I'm in New York or Maryland—I'd still be in school, not seeing her.

After school, Rosa has debate practice. When it's over, a couple of her friends are going for coffee, but I tell them I need to get home. They don't question it.

I should go back on the subway . . . but I'm in New York. For all I know, I may never be in New York again. Even though it's over a hundred blocks north, I decide I'm going to walk home.

The sidewalks are crowded, but because it's cold, nobody is lingering. They are bundled into their own worlds, and the street is just a passageway from one point in the city to another. I don't spot many tourist glances; even though there are hundreds of people around me, I might be the only curious one in sight. They want to bypass the details while I want to notice them.

Rosa's shoes are very cute and not suited for walking more than twenty blocks at a time. I did not plan this well—but, really, I didn't plan this at all. I end up in a park across from the Flatiron Building; if people look at me at all as I sit on my bench, it's to wonder why I'm sitting on a bench in the cold. I know they're probably right—I don't want Rosa to get pneumonia from staying outside or a back injury from walking much more in her heels. The body is making up my mind for me. Which is as it should be . . . but I find myself wishing that it weren't.

There's always tomorrow, I tell myself. Which sounds less possible than *someday,* and much more possible than *never.*

I stop off at a French café and get a hot chocolate that tastes like they've taken a slice off a chocolate cloud and placed it in a mug. If I cannot have a greater peace, I can slide into smaller satisfactions. I am alive. I am tasting this. I have a warm jacket on a cold day. There's a girl out there who knows me. I will go home and sleep well. I will try not to think about all the things I cannot control.

RHIANNON

When people ask me about my weekend, I don't know what to tell them. I only know I can't tell them the truth.

When Rebecca asks me how my weekend was, I tell her I'm not sure I could ever go to NYU. I tell her the streets are very loud at night. She asks me if I got to go to any parties, and I tell her I was boring and went to sleep when everyone was going out.

When Preston asks me how my weekend was, I tell him, no, I didn't see any celebrities on the street, and no, I didn't get to go see anything on Broadway, but yes, I did get to see Central Park, and while no, I didn't go ice-skating, I still felt I was in the center of the world.

When Alexander asks me how my weekend was, I'm as shy answering as he is asking. He tells me he missed me, especially when it started to snow. He says he was about to call me to go sledding; he'd even had the hill picked out. Then he remembered I was away. "You didn't go sledding in the city, did you?" he asks. And I say no, I didn't. I make it sound like I didn't have any fun. I make it sound like I was lonely. I tell him it would have been fun to go sledding, just the two of us. It's not a lie, and doesn't feel like a lie. But I still feel shy saying it.

When my mother asks me how my weekend was, I tell her I liked being in the city, but I'm not sure it's where I'm going to end up. "You can go to school wherever you want," she says to me, kissing my forehead. "Just as long as it's not that far."

When I ask myself how my weekend was, I'm shy again. Because I don't know what I want to hear.

A

Day 6135

I rise from sleep on a tide of sickness, and the moment I wake up, I open my mouth and the sickness comes pouring out. Luckily, someone's left a garbage pail by the side of the bed. I retch and heave until it feels like there's nothing left to release but the lining of my stomach.

This is not a good start to Anil's day. Or mine.

Anil's mother comes in soon after, cleans up, takes my temperature, and gives me some ginger ale. The bubbles feel like warfare in my mouth. The ginger ale comes back up.

I find myself apologizing. Anil's mother just shakes her head, says, "No no no," and tells me to lie back down again. She says she'll call my school. While she goes into the other room, I fade out. When I come back, I see she's left my phone, my laptop, and the remote control for the TV next to my bed. A note says to call her at work if I need anything.

I have the whole day to myself, but I can't make it very far. The body is operating under its own gravity, and that gravity pulls it straight to bed. I used to look forward to days like this, when I had a solid excuse to avoid trying to act out someone else's day. I could laze around and just be me. Read a book. Watch some TV. Play some video games. Happy in my own company. No need for anything else.

I look back on those days and realize the only way I could live them was to believe myself completely separable from any other story line. I had my own plot, but it didn't link to anything greater.

Now I lie in bed and feel all of these connections. To Rhiannon. To Poole. To anyone else who's like me.

I can't retreat into myself anymore.

I sit up in bed and pull Anil's laptop over. There's a message from Rhiannon—Poole's been in touch with Nathan again, and is demanding a meeting.

It's time.

I know it's time. I keep scrolling and see all of these posts about a march on Washington the coming weekend. A bunch of Anil's friends are going. Their school is chartering a bus.

I know I won't still be in Anil's body . . . but I hope that whoever I am will be in a position to go.

X

I am aware of how destructive my impatience can be.

I am tired of Wyatt's routine, so I step away from it. I load some clothes and a baseball bat into his car and drive away. Easy as that.

I find Nathan on his way home from school. I pull over, don't say a word. He starts to talk to me, but I still don't say a word. He sees the bat in my hand but is not quick enough to get out of its way. I bash his knee, then take a threatening swing at his shoulder after he falls to the ground, stopping just short of a decisive shatter. I don't have to say a word. He gets the message.

I leave him Wyatt's phone number, which will be mine now. I get back in the car. Drive away.

I imagine Wyatt's revulsion. Or thrill. Unleash a boy and he often revels in being a dog.

I know I will not be returning to his boring parents and his boring home. He may never return there. I have not made any determination, beyond the fact that his life is now inalterably mine. The body does not protest when I think this. Wyatt has no idea.

The fact that his body is now mine is the only thing stopping me from doing more damage. I must not call attention. Not yet.

I wait.

RHIANNON

All my friends are excited about the Equality March on Saturday. We're gathering Thursday night at Rebecca's house to make posters. I plan to drive with them to DC; what they don't know is that, if everything goes as planned, I'll also be going the night before, to see A.

Thursday afternoon, I head over to Nathan's house. During the school day, he sent me a text: *I need you to take me to the library*. I didn't ask him why he needed me to drive; I just said yes.

Now, as he opens his front door, I see what the problem is. His leg is in a brace.

"What happened?" I ask.

"There are a few things I forgot to mention in my role as courier," he says, limping out the door. "You drive, I'll talk."

I help him into my car, putting the passenger seat all the way back.

"He could have at least had the decency to smash my non-driving leg," he says when I've settled into the driver's seat. "I guess it's wrong to expect base consideration from a psychopath."

"Back up a second and tell me what happened," I say. "Also, which library are we going to?"

He fills me in, explaining how Poole ambushed him, then left a phone number. Which is the reason he texted me to say

Poole was growing impatient, leading us to arrange a meeting for Saturday.

"Why didn't you tell us what he'd done?"

"Honestly? Because I was embarrassed. It was hard enough to explain to my parents that I'd been jumped by some random assailant on my way home from school. They think I'm being bullied and am stoically refusing to name names. They have no idea!"

"I'm so, so sorry."

"There's also that. You have no reason to be sorry. You didn't get me into this mess. The mess just kind of formed around us, didn't it?"

"Still—"

"He has to be stopped. That's the bottom line, right? Because your boygirlfriend isn't going to, like, talk Poole out of being evil. He might be lonely, but he's also, like, an überasshole, and reason tends not to work with überassholes. They make their own reason and get all pissy when people don't agree with them that the world is flat."

"I don't know if we're going to stop him. First we need to see what he wants."

"Apparently Wyatt's disappeared."

"Wyatt?"

"The teenager whose body Poole's in. Wyatt. I've been monitoring all his social media, and it's taken a turn. A lot of *Hey, buddy, where are you?* and *Call your parents, okay?* Timed with him using my body for batting practice. That doesn't bode well for Wyatt."

"Has he posted anything back?"

"Nope. He hasn't posted anything for days. I guess Poole doesn't like social media. Which is weird, since so many modern megalomaniacs do."

"Poor Wyatt."

"Yeah. I have to tell you, I wasn't thrilled about losing a day of my life. But at least A had the decency to leave when the day was up."

"I guess in a way we got lucky."

"*In a way.* I like that. How many of them do you think are out there? Dozens? Thousands? Just the two?"

"I have no idea."

"Neither do I. It's like there's this whole other layer to existence. The dark matter of humanity."

"Is that why you're going to the library? To research?"

Nathan smiles, shakes his head. "Nah. I'm going to the library hoping to see a girl."

"Any particular girl? Or just, like, a girl in general?"

"A very particular girl."

He tells me a little about Jaiden—a little because that's all he knows.

"It sounds like a promising start," I tell him.

"Well, we'll see how she feels once she sees what a rough-and-tumble crowd I hang with."

"Tell her you were rescuing a kitten."

"From Satan. That's my story—I was rescuing a kitten from Satan."

"How could she possibly resist?"

"Easily?"

He looks out the window, and we fall silent. Finally he says, "I also wanted to talk to you. Before this weekend."

"About?"

"About whether the Caps have a chance at the Stanley Cup this year."

"Really?"

"*No.* About the mess we've gotten ourselves into. I know I fell into it, while you're more like a volunteer. Because you love A. I get that. And I know you have plenty of friends who probably give you plenty of unsolicited advice—but I'm guessing that in this case, they have no idea what you're up to, or what might happen to you. So I'm going to step into the breach. You've known A as a lone wolf—and from all accounts, A's been a good wolf companion. But A's about to meet the leader of the wolf pack. And, as discussed, he's not a good dude. Even if A doesn't join the pack, A's going to get more of a sense of what can be gotten away with. And I have to believe that's dangerous. Not just to you and me, but to everyone. Which is why I said what I said before: Poole needs to be stopped. And if A isn't prepared to stop him, you're going to have to get the hell out of there. Not just away from Poole, but from A as well. Even if it breaks your heart."

"Where is this coming from?"

"It's what keeps me up at night, Rhiannon. You and I—we're getting to glimpse something very few people see. But we have to remember that we're only glimpsing it, not living it. We have no idea how the people who are living it will react to an invitation to the pack."

"A will react like any other decent human being. That's who A is."

"I want to believe that. *You* want to believe that. But how are we ever going to know it for sure?"

"You can't know it about anybody, Nathan. Belief is all we have."

Nathan nods. "Fair. And, for the record, I believe in you. Which is why I can say these things."

"And I believe in you. Which is why I'm glad you're saying them."

"We have reached an understanding. And whatever happens this weekend—I'm only a text or a call away."

"I will definitely keep you posted."

When we get to the library, I start to get out of the car, to help him out.

"No, no—I've got it," he tells me.

"Do you need a ride back?"

"Probably. I'll text you. I'm not even sure if she'll be here."

"Well . . . good luck."

"Thanks. I'll need it!"

He gets out of the car and hobbles into the library. I know I should drive away, but I park instead. I just want to make sure he's alright.

I don't have to walk that far into the library to see I'm no longer needed. He's made his way to a carrel in the center; a girl is standing up, gesturing for him to sit down. His hand gestures imply that he's telling her how he rescued a kitten from Satan. She's laughing, praising his bravery.

I sneak back out before he sees me. I've only driven for ten minutes before I stop at a light and see I've gotten a text from him.

Jaiden will give me a ride home. ☺

The simplicity of this makes me happy.

And jealous.

But mostly happy.

That night at Rebecca's, I try not to be distracted. Rebecca is always nervous when people are over at her house—her dad likes to interrupt every five minutes with a joke he's heard, and her mom, who worries about everything, worries even more than usual that her valuables will be stolen or broken. She moves them all into her bedroom and keeps watch . . . only there are always valuables she's forgotten, so every few minutes, while Rebecca's dad is throwing around pope jokes as if they're still things that high schoolers tell their friends, her mom will sneak behind him in her nightgown and robe, take a Hummel figurine off a shelf, and run back to their room.

Rebecca's parents like me more than they like most of her other friends, so as soon as I get there, I stop in her parents' room to say hello. Her mom's in bed, polishing her silver. When I say hi, she acts like this is a perfectly normal thing to do on a Thursday night.

"It's good that you kids are going to the march," she tells me. "It's important."

"It is," I tell her. "We're all really excited."

A big group from our school is going to the Equality March. The premise is very straightforward: We're protesting any law, any action, that doesn't treat people as equal. Whether it's about gender, race, LGBTQIA+ identity, physical ability—anybody who wants us all to be treated equally is being encouraged to march, to send a message to a government that often feels like the final fortress of straight cis white men.

In the kitchen, there are art supplies everywhere. Alexander is in heaven. As I watch over his shoulder, he sews a row of silhouettes onto a banner. They are people of all shapes and sizes. Underneath, he's sketched out a caption: WE ARE ALL DIFFERENT. BUT UNDER A JUST LAW, WE ARE ALL THE SAME.

When Alexander's in an act of creation, he fully immerses himself. It's actually visible from the outside, like I can see all of the possibilities swirling around him, and then the flash of focus as he reaches for one of them and brings it down into his illustration. Preston and Will are having what can only be called a biodegradable-glitter fight over the kitchen sink; Rebecca is asking Ben to double-check her spelling of *disenfranchised*; Stephanie is in the corner, sobbing and whispering into her phone. Alexander doesn't notice this. But after a few minutes, he surfaces and notices me behind him. He turns and smiles.

"What do you think?"

"It works," I tell him. "It really works."

He nods, ties a last knot, and puts down his thread.

"I think we're going to have five posters for each person who's marching," he tells me, gesturing to a stack on the floor. On the top, LOVE THE RIGHT TO LOVE is written in rainbow glitter.

"Preston and Will's creation?" I ask.

"Rebecca's, actually. Theirs is underneath."

I lift the rainbow proclamation and unveil a fierce glitter dragon.

YOUR FEAR DOES NOT GET TO DICTATE MY LIFE, it reads.

"Do you like it?" Preston says.

"I love it," I tell him.

"We're just trying to find different ways to state the obvious," Will says. "Because, let's face it, it's really messed up that we have to march for something that's so damn obvious."

"What do you mean, I'm not hearing you?" Stephanie cries into the phone.

Rebecca jumps toward her. "Oh no. Hang up, Stephanie. Just hang up the phone."

"I can't!"

Rebecca grabs it out of her hand; she doesn't put up much of a fight.

"Steve, not now," Rebecca says. "We're in a no-fuckery

zone. And you are bringing fuckery into it." She hangs up. Stephanie sobs some more.

Rebecca pulls her to her feet. "C'mon," she says. "Bedroom time."

As soon as she leaves, as if he's been waiting, Rebecca's father steps in.

"Hey, guys," he says, sounding like the boy who's been picked last for kickball trying to charm his way into being picked third-last next time.

"Hello, Mr. Palmer," Preston and Will say.

"You got everything you need?"

"Everything but equality, sir!" Will answers, all golly-gee. Preston elbows him.

"Speaking of equality . . . did I ever tell you the one about the Frenchman, the Dutchman, and the Brit in the POW camp?"

"I think you have, sir," Ben says. "It's certainly memorable."

"Well, here's a new one. The pope decides he wants to have his own website, so he calls IT, and IT sends him a priest, a rabbi, and a woodpecker. You following so far?"

"I think I left some of my paints in my car," Alexander says to me. "Want to help me get them?"

"Definitely."

We escape the room before Mr. Palmer gets to the rabbi.

Outside, Alexander gestures to the front steps, and we sit down there.

"I've missed you," he says, reaching for my hand. "Where've you been this week?"

His hand is covered with dots of marker and specks of glue and glitter. There's also glitter in his hair, on his cheek.

"You look like an art project," I say.

"I *am* an art project," he replies. "I mean, on my best days."

"And on your worst days?"

"On my worst days, I feel the frustration of being separated from the things I was born to do."

"Born to do?"

"Don't you feel that way about some things? Even though they're a choice—it's all a choice—they're also part of your mission. I will never be a consumer, in the sense that I would consume something to destroy it. Instead, I'm a cycler—I'll take something in, but then I want to put it back into the world in a different form. In an ideal world, I get to take the inspiration I receive and put it back out as inspiration for someone else. I want to make things. Not in a selfish vacuum, but as part of the world. And I want to love. I want to love indiscriminately—people, places, and things. But not just those. I want to love verbs. Adjectives. I want to love beyond category. Because, in my heart, I know that's what I was born to do. And life? Life is just the time I have to figure out how to do it well." He laughs, shakes his head. "I'm sorry—I must sound so full of shit. It's just what I've been thinking about while I've been making all these posters, with all these friends I basically know because of you."

"You don't sound full of shit," I tell him. "You sound full of the opposite."

"Thank you."

"There's no need to thank me."

"There are hundreds of things to thank you for."

"Stop."

"Why?"

It's a good question. Why, if he's sincere, do I want him to stop? Why can't I let him thank me, if he's happy? Why can't I thank him back, for having made me happy?

I think about his banner. I think about all those silhouettes. I want to ask him: If they were all the same person inside, only in different bodies on different days, would they
still be equal to us?

He'd say yes. I know he'd say yes.

But he'd also think it was a crazy hypothetical.

"Rhiannon."

"Yes?"

"How was your week?"

I think about snow in New York City. I think about Nathan's leg in a brace. I think about Poole, who I can picture
even though I've never seen him. I think about the drive I will
take tomorrow. I think about glitter and glue and skin.

"My week has not been under my control," I tell him.

"And how do you feel about that?"

"I think I want it to be more under my control. But I don't
know how I can get it there."

"How can I help?"

I lean into him. "I wish you could. But you can't."

I know I shouldn't kiss him. But I also know I shouldn't
turn away when he kisses me. I cannot slight him like that. I
cannot send that message, that he means nothing. He means
much more than nothing.

After the kiss is done, I lean back on the steps.

"I have no idea what I was born to do," I confess.

"Then you'll figure it out," he says. "I have faith."

I don't deserve you, I think. But I already know what his
answer to that would be:

Love should never be thought of in terms of deserving.

"We should probably get back in," I tell him. "You don't
really have paint in the car, do you?"

"No. It was sitting on the floor next to your feet."

"The joke has to be finished by now, right?"

"Let's hope the woodpecker has had its say."

He stands, then holds out a hand to help me up. For a second, I look at him, and I remember the day I met him, when A was inside.

I find myself asking, "What if you weren't you on the day we met?"

He doesn't think about it for more than a second.

"I guess I'd ask you to judge me based on all the days after that."

His hand doesn't go down to his side. He doesn't tell me it's a strange question, a strange thought. He's still here for me.

I take his hand and head back inside.

That night, when I get home, I write to A.

A,

More thinking. Much more thinking.

I am looking forward to seeing you tomorrow. I am. But it's still strange to be in a room with all my friends and not be able to tell them about it. To know they will never meet you. To know that you will never be a part of the rest of my life.

I mean, we could tell them. But could I guarantee the secret would be safe? No.

I want you to understand: I want to rewrite the world to make this possible. I do.

But since I can't rewrite the world . . . something else needs to be rewritten. Whatever we're going to be—we have to write it ourselves. And it's not going to fall into any category we've ever seen before.

We need a new category that allows us to be us.

Maybe that's what we're meant to do.

I'll see you tomorrow.

R

A

Day 6138

Friday morning, I get very lucky.

Eboni's family is already planning to go to the march with a group from their church. The bus leaves right after school.

I pack quickly and let Rhiannon know where I'll be staying. I've read her message and tell her we'll talk about it then. Mostly because I have no idea what to say to it now.

I know she's right. I know we need a new category, a new word for what we are.

I just don't know what it is.

I figure I'll have time to think about it on the bus ride down—but the bus ride has other ideas. The pastor hasn't brought a radio—he wants his congregation to be the radio. So even before the bus hits a bridge or a tunnel, the songs are under way. I'm sure Eboni, like everyone else on the bus, knows the tunes by heart. So every time a new song begins, I dive in and try to find it. She has a lovely voice, but her performance today might not be as assured as usual.

We pass many other buses on our way down. We hold signs up to each other, cheer each other on, sing louder, sing until our bodies feel the strain, and then sing anyway.

There is a fervent joy in taking action. There is a nonabstract importance in what we are doing. The balance between right and wrong is always in question, and the only way to ensure we tip toward justice is to make sure our weight is firmly planted on the side of right. We are driving down to add our weight to the scale. We are singing because voices add as much weight as bodies do.

I know I am a pretender. I know I am here for other reasons, and will take part in other plans. But I have to believe that I, too, am trying to strike on the right side of the balance. I have to believe I am doing my part, even if that part is obscured from the people who surround me.

Around Delaware, people quiet down, retreat into their own conversations, their own naps. I feel the nervousness in the pit of my gut, and wonder if it's about Rhiannon or Poole or both. Probably both. It's the nervousness that comes from knowing that beginnings and endings are the same exact thing, and not knowing where that knowledge leads.

The hotel lobby is alive with energy—a reunion for people who've never met before. Now comes the hard part, since I have to peel Eboni away from the group without raising much suspicion.

I can see Rhiannon waiting for me. She's looking around, but I'm too far away to signal her. I'm just one person in a big check-in crowd.

I want to go over and say something. But I don't want to have to answer if anyone asks who I was just talking to.

It's only when we're heading to the elevator that I get close enough for eye contact. That's all it takes. I see her recognize me. Without saying a word, I tell her I'll be there as soon as I can. Without saying a word, she shows me she understands.

In the room, Eboni's mom asks her if she's going to go to the vigil at Third Baptist or if she's going to the youth activity at the hotel. I see my opportunity and tell her I'll go to the youth activity. She hands me a schedule, and I see there's poster-making and fellowship in the Tubman Ballroom. It goes until ten, and it's eight o'clock now. I have to hurry.

I'm worried that someone will see me leaving with Rhiannon, so instead of going over to talk to her, I send her another look, willing her to follow me outside. I even walk an extra block before I turn around and find her there, smiling.

"We'd make very good spies," she says.

"The best," I tell her. "I probably need to be back by ten, so we have . . . not much time."

"That's okay—I have to drive back tonight anyway. So I can, you know, drive in tomorrow morning."

"I'm sorry you can't stay over."

"Yeah, I'm not really sure how I'd explain that one. My parents think I'm at Rebecca's. Rebecca thinks I'm home, getting some sleep before the big day. If Rebecca and my parents ever start texting, we're in big, big trouble."

"Never introduce them."

"It's a little late for that."

"Then I guess we'll just have to be risky."

"The best spies are."

"Now, where to?"

"The Mall? It's a few blocks that way. And, honestly, DC isn't exactly the safest two-teen-girls-wandering-around-alone city. Let's stick to the well-lit paths."

"Lead the way."

The sidewalks are busy even though the buildings are not. Most people seem to be in town for tomorrow . . . or maybe DC is just a city where everyone out on a Friday night seems like a tourist.

"So Nathan confirmed with Poole—he'll meet you at the

National Gallery food court at noon. You know it's going to be crowded tomorrow, right?"

"The more crowded, the better, as far as I'm concerned."

"Nathan also sent this."

She holds out her phone so I can see Wyatt Giddings's Facebook profile.

"That's what he looks like. So you know who to look for."

"Got it."

"Assuming he doesn't change first."

"Yeah, assuming that."

Rhiannon doesn't look at me when she says, "I know this isn't a normal conversation. It doesn't have to be a normal conversation. I'm not expecting it to be."

"But don't you wish it were?"

"No. I think I'm realizing it won't be. Or no. That's not right. I'm realizing it won't ever be normal for anyone who isn't us. But if it becomes normal for us—that's good. That's all we can ask for."

We're at the Mall now. I turn left and see the Capitol, presiding like a bald man over his domain. I turn right and see the Washington Monument, a rocket too heavy to launch.

We sit down and it's a little strange because I'm shorter than Rhiannon. I'm not used to that. Not that it matters—it's just another minor adjustment.

"So what's your name today?" she asks.

"Eboni."

"Tell me about Eboni."

I describe the bus ride down.

"Okay, but what about her? Have you gotten to know her at all?"

"Not really. I guess my mind's been on other things."

I can tell this isn't the right answer.

"What's wrong?" I ask.

"Nothing. I just think of you as always knowing them, at least a little."

"That makes it better?"

"I think it does."

"You're probably right. I'm just distracted by . . . myself."

"Believe me, that's easy enough to do. For all of us."

I know this part is hard for everyone, not just us. The hot excitement of first meeting has to cool into the warm satisfaction of being together. I have visited all stages of relationships; I've just never been in one myself before. I feel like I've seen the map, but now I'm living in the actual landscape.

"Do you want to talk about your message last night?" I ask.

"Sure. I'm not even sure if it made any sense."

"It did. I just—I don't know what the answer is."

"Neither do I. I only know we have to find it together. You tried to find it for both of us last time. That didn't work. And you can't try to find it for both of us tomorrow. Poole can't offer you anything that will give us an answer. He may try. He may try to use it as leverage. But you can't let him. I don't want to be your weak spot."

"And I don't want to be your weak spot."

"Then I guess we're clear. About everything we're unclear about."

I push her hair over her ear. Look her in the eye. Feel so much love for her then that it feels like the love I have for life itself.

"Whatever we are," I say, "whatever we do, I will always be grateful for whatever together we have. I know you have plenty of togethers in your life. But you're the only one I have. And as hard as it is sometimes, and as much as it may hurt, it matters to me more than you can understand."

She wraps me in a hug then. Really holds on to me. And whispers, "I understand."

We stay like that for a few minutes, holding on and letting the city walk past us. Then we gather ourselves and reenter the world.

"Let's talk about tomorrow," she says.

Together, we go through the plan.

A

Day 6139

I wake up in a different room in the same hotel.

I should have known the risk—I am at a tourist hotel in a tourist destination. But it's still a surprise to wake up in the body of a teenager visiting from the Philippines, to find so many thoughts in a language I don't understand. Rudy also knows English, so at least I can translate the thoughts. I learn that his family is in America for a week; they've come from New York and are headed to Orlando tomorrow. They had no idea their trip would coincide with the Equality March.

I don't need to access Rudy's memories to know this. His parents are in the room, loudly agitated, peering out the window and arguing about what to do. I understand everything on a three-second delay, since I need to use Rudy's memory to translate as best as I can.

Even though nobody's asked my opinion, I say, "We're here. We should see things."

I've taken my father's side, and he swells with satisfaction. Rudy's mother argues some more, but it's a losing battle. I feel bad, because her argument is that it's dangerous, and that we could easily lose each other. Which is exactly what I am planning will happen.

As we take turns going into the bathroom to get ready and dressed, Rudy's father turns on the TV. Traffic cameras are showing buses flooding into the city. The crowds are already growing around and across the Mall. They are predicting as many as a million people are going to march, possibly more. Security is on high alert. The president says he is "monitoring the situation" from a golf course in Florida.

Whenever they show cars coming into the city, I keep an eye out for Rhiannon's. I know she's out there somewhere with her friends. We're supposed to meet at eleven.

I also know Poole is out there somewhere, getting closer and closer. We'll meet at noon.

These people mean nothing to Rudy. And at the end of the day, he will hopefully forget them.

But for the next few hours, I am going to have to make them more important than his parents. Not more important than him—no matter what happens, Rudy *must* remain the most important. I must not allow myself to forget that.

It feels worse, to be borrowing the life of someone who is so far away from home, so far away from friends. But I have no choice.

I think I'll have plenty of time to get to the Mall . . . but then we stop at the hotel restaurant for breakfast. I power through the buffet, but Rudy's mother eats like she's staging her own protest, taking her cereal one cornflake at a time, her grapefruit with a minute between each segment.

"We'd better go before it's too crazy," I say.

Then, five minutes later, "If we're not quick, the Air and Space Museum will be blocked off."

Then, as 10:15 approaches, "I'm sure you could take that croissant with you if you wanted. Do you want me to ask if they have a bag?"

"The buildings aren't going anywhere," Rudy's mother replies, breaking off a piece of croissant so small that even a bird would ignore it.

Rudy's father just checks his phone.

*　*　*

It's 10:37 when we leave the hotel. It only takes a step for us to hit the crowd. It's astonishing to see so many people—a slow flood of protestors carrying signs and wearing rainbow hats and cheering whenever someone decides to lead a cheer. I can sense that Rudy's mother is about to return inside—so I turn around, say, "I'll meet you back here later," and plunge right in. Apologizing to Rudy for the trouble he will no doubt be in, I bob and weave through the crowd. Nobody seems to mind when I slide past. Nobody's in a rush; everybody is here to be here. After I'm satisfied that I've put enough distance between myself and Rudy's parents, I take a look around, see all the people in the crowd, really see them. And the thing that strikes me—the thing that really amazes me—is that I see *everyone*. It's not the usual American crowd where the majority group is easy to pin down. No—this crowd is actually America, all different races and genders and ages and clothing styles and love inclinations on one street together, making their steady march to the destination. I have been so many of them, and I haven't been nearly enough of them. I could live to be a million years old and never get to be everyone, not like this. But even with what little experience I've had, what's happening makes sense to me—the thing that can make us most equal is our belief in and desire for equality. I have felt that in so many hearts, and now all the other concerns can be set aside so we can let that feeling rise to the top.

I don't know what Rudy would make of this. I don't know very much about his life in Manila. But I have to believe that he would feel at home, that he would add his voice. We are all invested in this trajectory; we all share the want to be seen as seriously as anyone else.

I keep going forward, keep passing the families and the

304

friends and the church groups and the GSAs and the high school basketball teams marching in their jerseys. I see faces that look familiar, faces that I may have once seen in a mirror—but I don't have the time to stop and remember, or the memory to stop and find. I tell myself I am a part of this, that my body is being counted even though it is not my body. I tell myself I am adding weight to the right side of the balance. I tell myself this even though I know I have to leave.

The National Gallery comes into view. I am already a half hour late, and I'm not even there yet. Rudy's phone isn't picking up any wifi, and doesn't work in the US without it. There's no way for me to get in touch with Rhiannon. I must trust she'll find me when I get there.

There are police officers all along the Mall, keeping watch. In other circumstances, it might seem sinister—but the officers are smiling, chatting, returning the salutes of the children who salute them. When I pull off Constitution Avenue, separating myself from the union of cheer and protest, an officer approaches and asks me if I need anything. Suddenly I'm worried he'll tell me the museum has been closed, even though I checked the website repeatedly over the week to make sure it wouldn't be. When I tell him my destination, he nods and points me to an entrance on the side of the building.

I know my one body won't be missed, but I will miss being part of the whole. I'm sure the protest will still be happening when I leave the museum; hopefully Rhiannon and I will be able to experience it together.

I am supposed to meet Rhiannon in front of Monet's *Bazille and Camille*, but when I get to Gallery 85, I find that Bazille and Camille are there, but Rhiannon is not. For a Saturday, the museum is very quiet . . . but you can hear the sound of the crowd outside, the waves of congregation and hoots of proclamation. I am guessing that Rhiannon is caught

305

in the crowd. With all the traffic, she may not have even made it downtown yet.

It is 11:45. I am going to have to meet Poole on my own.

I head down to the basement connecting the museum's two buildings, where the food court is located. As I walk through the gift shop, Rudy's heart starts to pound, and I wonder yet again how his body can be so attuned to the pulse of my thoughts. It is more crowded down here than it was in the galleries—mostly tourists taking refuge from the protest, along with a few protestors taking a break to get some food. I am glad I'm not alone, even if all of these people are strangers. They will not let anything happen to me.

I am a few minutes early, but he is already there. I spot him right away, the only teenager with a table to himself. It's hard not to think of him for a moment as Wyatt, since it is clearly Wyatt I am seeing.

This is the moment when I can still walk away, and I walk forward instead.

He sees me approaching and stands up. I am surprised by the politeness of this, and by the smile on his face that looks almost grateful that I've shown up. He extends his hand and I shake it. We are friends from the summer who are meeting in the winter. We are Internet acquaintances finally face to face. We are two boys who've been set up for a job interview or a date. What we must look like is nothing like what we really are.

"Do you want something to eat?" he asks. "Or just coffee?" He points to his own cup. "I'm happy to wait here if you want to get something."

"I'm fine," I tell him. "I had a big breakfast."

"Well, then—shall we?"

He extends his hand to offer the chair across from him. I take off my coat and put it on the back before sitting down.

"I really appreciate you coming," he says. "And before

306

anything else, I want to apologize for the last time we met. I handled it badly, and I know I hardly deserve a second chance. The only way I can explain it is that I was overwhelmed when I finally found you, someone else like me. It was something I'd never attempted to do before, to talk over . . . what we are. And I can't say this enough times: I completely botched it. I was so worried that you were going to leave that I of course overdid it and forced you to leave. What's the opposite of beginner's luck—beginner's misfortune? Beginner's stupidity? I'm hoping we can chalk it up to that. Although I would certainly understand if you couldn't."

When I imagined this conversation, it did not start like this. I am looking in his eyes, and instead of seeing something imprisoned, I am seeing a vulnerability that appears to be his own. I have spent days as boys like Wyatt before—popular, insecure, his good-heartedness sometimes roughly conveyed. I have to remind myself that I'm not really talking to him, just as the person across from me isn't really talking to Rudy.

"Thank you for saying that," I tell him. "You're right—you scared the hell out of me. But I have to warn you: It wasn't just the way you were saying it, it was what you were saying. So if you're planning to say the same things . . . we're just wasting time."

"I'm not going to try to convince you of anything. I'm not going to try to make you do anything. I just want to talk. And I'm guessing you want to talk, too. Because I imagine this is as astonishing to you as it is to me—the possibility of talking to someone who actually knows what it's like to be us. To be so transient, and yet so grounded in the lives of others. To have to navigate every single day as both ourselves and as someone else. Who else knows what that's like? I have so many things to ask you. I have so many things I've tried to figure out on my own."

"I think you've figured out more than I have."

"Why? Because I've managed to stay in bodies for longer than a day? That's true—there are a few things I've figured out, which I'd love to share with you. But there's still plenty where all I have is speculation."

"Like what?"

He smiles. "Where do I possibly begin? On the grand scale, why are we the way we are? Or on the small scale, when we hurt ourselves in someone else's body, does the memory of the pain stay with them, or does it travel with us?"

"It doesn't come with us. But the shame and regret at hurting someone else—that does."

He leans back, looks at me. "That," he says, "is a very interesting answer."

The strangest thing about this is how unstrange it feels. I immediately know I can tell him things that I couldn't expect Rhiannon to understand. Because even if we're different, we've been through so many of the same things.

Remember, he beat Nathan up, I remind myself. But then I wonder if I pushed him to do that, by playing games with him. Not that it's an excuse. But it could be an explanation. I think he understood even more than I did what this would feel like, to finally find someone who understands the way our lives work.

"You must have questions, too," he says. "Don't let me dominate the conversation—because I will, if given a chance. I've had all these thoughts and questions locked away and now, ta-da, here comes the key that opens the door to seeing how everything works outside of my own experience."

"Okay," I say. "Let's start on a basic level. What's your name?"

"This is Wyatt."

"I don't mean his name. What's your name? I keep thinking of you as Reverend Poole. But you're not Reverend Poole."

"Huh. You do realize, nobody's asked me that before?"

I smile, remembering when Rhiannon asked me the first time. "It's crazy, isn't it? To go your whole life without anyone asking your name."

"You can't laugh if I tell you."

"My name is A. I have no grounds for laughing."

"Because you chose it when you were young?"

"Yeah."

"Me too. Maybe not as young as you. But still . . . young."

"So what is it?"

"Xenon."

I laugh. Not out of ridicule. Out of surprise.

"You said you wouldn't laugh!" But he's laughing, too.

"Sorry, sorry . . ."

"It's alright."

"Why Xenon?"

"I liked the X. Later, I found out what it means, and it fit. But even if it hadn't fit, I would have kept it."

"How old were you when you picked it?"

"I'm not sure—doesn't it all blur after a while? Seven, maybe? Eight? You?"

"Probably five or six. It *does* blur. Years. Weeks. Days."

"That's one of the reasons I decided to stay longer than a day. To have more of a sense of periods of time. Other people can say, *Oh, that's when I lived in that house. Or Oh, that was when I was dating her. Or My parents were alive then.* I wanted to have that. Some measure that was longer than a single day. Because a single day is too hard to hold on to."

It's like a punch to my brain, hearing these words come from someone who isn't me.

I have to ask, "But don't you feel that's unfair to the people whose lives you're taking? Don't you feel you're stealing that time from them?"

Wyatt leans in, as if this is the first time he's saying something he doesn't want anyone else to hear. "The thing is—if they didn't want me to take over for them, I wouldn't be able to do it. There's a beautiful complicity to it. I can only take the places of the people who don't want to be there. I know you could easily say it's a self-serving justification—believe me, I've interrogated myself *in depth* about it over the years. But I've done it enough to know that nobody gives over their life force unless it's willingly. Does that mean I'm preying on the weak? Possibly. But does it also mean I am giving the weak a break? Also possible. There's no certainty in any of this, is there?"

"No," I tell him. "There's not."

"Exactly."

"So what about Wyatt?" I ask. I'm not sure I'm being told the truth, but I don't want to cut him off. I want to hear what he has to say.

"Wyatt's lost. Everyone thinks he's got it together, but he doesn't. To be honest, I don't think I'll be able to stay here much longer—eventually he will want his life back, and I will wake up as someone else. But, as you've seen, almost anyone can spare a day. Most can spare a week, Wyatt included. Who are you today?"

I tell him about Rudy.

"You see, it would be harder with him. You have the strong combination of being excited to be on vacation, and also missing home acutely. You would think someone away from home would be more vulnerable, but I think the opposite is true. Plus, of course, I'm sure he wants to see Disney World for himself."

310

"So you're saying I shouldn't try to stay here for more than a day?" I ask.

"No. Why would I do that?"

When I met him as Poole, he seemed dead set on getting me to be like him, as soon as possible. But maybe he's learned something since then. Again, I want to see how this plays out.

"No reason," I say. "I'm still trying to find the right footing here."

"Me too."

We've both discovered new territory. We both want to explore.

"Look," I tell him, "I lied to you before. I *am* hungry. Wanna get lunch?"

He smiles again, waves toward the cafeteria.

"I have all the time in the world," he says.

I know I don't. But for now, I feel like I do.

We go and get some pizza. He offers to pay, and on the way back to our table, I ask him about that, about how it feels to always be using someone else's money.

"I consider it wages," he says, sitting down. "For a day's work."

I've never thought of it that way.

I ask him to tell me more.

RHIANNON

It takes forever to get into DC, and even longer to get down to the Mall. We have to abandon our cars in a suburb and take the train in, along with hundreds of thousands of other people. At first it's a party atmosphere, but as it gets busier and busier, it becomes an overcrowded party atmosphere, which isn't nearly as fun. Or at least not on me—Preston is loving it, and is getting a lot of compliments on his outfit, which looks like Waldo from *Where's Waldo?* mated with a rainbow. Alexander's posters are also getting a lot of compliments. Alexander, being Alexander, is always sure to compliment back, finding some button that the person is wearing, or even the bright pink shoelaces they're proud of.

I'd probably be enjoying it, too, if I weren't so late.

I've tried emailing A. I've even texted Nathan, putting him on standby. But there's no word. By the time I get out of the Metro station, it's past noon. A is already with Poole. I am the backup that hasn't arrived.

I hope he's okay.

I think the hardest part is going to be losing my friends—but that proves to be the easiest part, because the crowd is so crowded, and because it's hard for groups to stay together in all the shifting currents. I made sure we had a plan for meeting up after if we got separated—I just didn't tell them I was already aiming to use it. When I slip free of them, I hear Alexander and Rebecca call after me. But then one of the speakers starts to talk, and the crowd surges forward, and I duck around a taller group, so visual contact is broken.

I've also made sure my phone is off. I'll tell them I thought it was on.

When I get to the National Gallery, I ask the guard where the food court is, and he points to a staircase heading down. I have to take a moving walkway covered in lights and mirrors, like something that would have seemed like science fiction in the 1950s, and then I'm at the food court, almost an hour late. I have no idea what A looks like today—but I know what Wyatt looks like. The trick is to find him without being seen. A was adamant about that: Under no circumstances should Poole see me. We must remain separate. That is the only way to make sure I remain safe.

I stay on the periphery, where parents are trying to herd their children and older protestors are taking a rest from their marching. My eyes pass over Wyatt and A at least twice before I find them . . . because their body language is so comfortable, so coupled, that I mistook them for family members or friends. They are fully engaged in one another, talking animatedly, completely oblivious to anything that's going on around them.

I can't help it: I think it looks like a date that's going really, really well.

Then I feel stupid for thinking that. A knows what needs to be done. A is playing along. A is learning as much as there is to be learned.

That is the plan.

I know the whole point is that Poole's not supposed to know I'm here. I understand this means that A can't look for me, and even if A senses my presence, it can't be acknowledged. Still, I'm surprised by how outside of it I feel. I want to get closer to hear what they're saying, even though I know it would be dangerous. I want A's eyes to flicker my way, to give me a sense of what's going on. I want to make sure A's okay.

But . . . it's plain to see A is okay.

A looks happy.

At home.

I am sure if I pulled out my phone and turned it on, I would find my friends are looking for me. They are probably concerned. I will have to answer their messages. And the temptation is to run back outside, to find them, to pretend I never made it here.

But no. I promised A I would be here after, to figure out the next step.

So I sit down. I try to make myself invisible while keeping my own vision clear.

I watch. I wait.

I wonder.

A
Day 6139 (continued)

"So how old are you?" I ask him.

"I'm not sure, really. Once I untied myself from the regularity of changing every day, it didn't seem as important. Twenty-two? Twenty-three? Not that much older than you. I used to count. You still count, don't you?"

"Yes."

"Let me guess. You started on Day 3653."

"Yes! My 'tenth birthday'—or at least the first tenth birthday my body had."

"A nice, round number."

"Exactly. Plus three leap days."

"But why do you still do it? Why bother?"

"Because without it, I'd be a watch with just a second hand. I need to keep track of the larger measure."

"That larger measure being your life."

"Exactly."

We both sit back. Look at each other for a second.

This is the most incredible conversation I've ever had.

And I think he feels that way, too.

"How many of us do you think there are, Xenon?"

He groans. "Please. Call me X. If you're A, I'll be X. Xenon wasn't meant to be used anywhere besides my own head. It sounds silly when you say it."

"But it's your name!"

"X. Please."

"Okay, X . . . how many of us do you think there are? And do you think we're all related in some way?"

"Like, some poor woman keeps giving birth, and the result is us?"

"That might be a little more related than I thought. But possible, I guess."

"I think there are more of us than that. And I think there have been people like us for a while, secret for the same reasons we've kept ourselves secret. Both our power and our survival depend on it."

"And do you think we've always been like this? From the very first day?"

"There's no way to know, of course. But what I think? I think we were born just like everyone else, and then on our second day, we woke up in another newborn's body. That first baby lost the first day of his life—but how will he ever know? We leave long before any memories are formed." He looks at me. "You're smiling. Why are you smiling?"

I tell him the truth. "Because I've asked myself this question thousands of times over the years. And at a certain point, I gave up on ever hearing anyone else's answer. So to be talking to you about this . . . it's not what I was expecting."

"You thought I was going to hit you over the head, spirit you away in my white van, and suck out your soul to put inside a monster I'd built."

"Something along those lines," I say. His mention of my wariness has reminded me of it. Just because he's joking about the white van doesn't mean there's not one parked outside, the keys in his pocket.

He seems alarmed by my alarm. "I really made quite a first impression. It's been over an hour—will you allow me to apologize again?"

"It's okay," I tell him. "The hour has changed things." Because before, I would have assumed the worst. Now I'm trying not to assume anything. Because I want us to keep talking.

"For me too."

"So what else?"

"You said you don't think of yourself as a *he* or a *she?*"

"No. You do?"

"I'm definitely a *he.*"

"That's so weird to me. You still wake up female sometimes, right?"

"I wake up in women's bodies. But I never wake up female."

"But why would you choose?"

"Because every human being has to be one or the other."

"That's not even remotely true."

"Okay, okay—I concede that point. But for me, it's important to have a concrete identity, even when you are changing your physical form so much. Perhaps even more so. It's important to know who you are. What you look like—"

I can't believe he's saying this. "You know what you look like?" I interrupt.

"I know what I *should* look like. It's very clear to me."

I gesture to Wyatt. "Is this it?"

He looks down at Wyatt's hands, then back up at me. "This is close enough."

"So you chose it."

"In some senses, yes. I took the do-overs until I got it right. Or right enough. You'll be able to do that, too."

"But I don't want that."

"Why not?"

"Because once you have preferences, once you start thinking of people in terms of better or worse—then suddenly there will be bad ones and good ones. And I'll treat the bad ones badly, just because I have preferences. I don't believe in that. I don't believe any body is inherently better or worse than any other. The outside world makes its judgments. And I'm sure the people themselves make their own judgments from the inside. But when I'm in there, I am not there to judge. I felt it happen a couple of months ago, when I was starting to see myself as I thought the outside world saw me. I could feel myself tilting into feeling I wasn't the right size or the right gender. And that, more than anything else, made me know I was going down the wrong path. So I left. I tried not to see myself through the outside world's eyes."

"Through *her* eyes."

"Her?"

"The girl you love. You haven't told me about her yet. But I have to imagine the two are related."

"How do you know about Rhiannon?" I ask, even though I know the answer.

"Nathan, remember? Don't worry—he wouldn't tell me much. I just knew she was his conduit to you. But I inferred. You must love her."

It seems pointless to deny it. "I do."

"And, naturally, that makes you feel seen. By the 'outside world,' as you say."

"It does. Have you ever been in love like that?"

"Absolutely. It's hard for us, isn't it? Almost impossible. But not entirely impossible. That gap between *almost* and *entirely*—that's what we're always trying to squeeze through, isn't it?"

"Yes."

"But listen to yourself. How is she supposed to love you if you don't give yourself any true form? What is she supposed to love—a name? A? How can you give her something that you don't have?"

"We're figuring it out."

"Which is what you need to do. And I want to help. I know I don't have much standing to do so. But I've been through this, A. I know exactly what you're talking about. And because of my own experience, I can see all of the barriers that are currently invisible to you. I can see the core problem that builds all the barriers."

"And what's that?"

"Are you sure you want to hear it?"

"I want to hear it."

"I think you have spent your entire life making yourself subservient to the people whose bodies you occupy. Instead of treating yourself as a full human being—and we *are* full human beings—you treat yourself as if you're a parasite, an infection, a twenty-four-hour virus that has some choice about the damage it does. So you hold back. You deny yourself your own humanity in order to perpetuate theirs. But I ask you this—and it is something I have asked myself many, many times: Why are their lives worth more than yours, just because of who you are?"

"I don't think of them as worth more than me."

"Really? Who have you taken more energy to care for over the years? What pattern did falling in love with Rhiannon disrupt?"

"But what choice do we have?" I ask.

"The first choice you have is to define yourself." He pushes back his chair and stands up, and for an outlandish moment I think this is the end of our conversation, that he's so disappointed in me that he's going to walk away. But instead he says, "Let's take a field trip. I hear there's an art museum nearby?"

"Okay," I say, gathering my coat and picking up my tray.

"There have to be thousands of images of people in these

galleries. I have to believe that, deep down, you have some sense of who you are. Let's walk through the museum until we find one that connects."

"It's like you're asking my type. And I'll telling you, I have no type."

"And I'm saying, I think we all have a type. It's just a question of whether we admit it to ourselves or not."

"Fine," I say. "Let's try." It's not too different from what Rhiannon asked me to do at the Met. I don't think the results will be any different this time.

I am only now seeing how crowded it's become. The speeches are still happening on the Mall, but more people are coming inside, resting their feet surrounded by art.

"That's good," X says. "Museums are for people-watching as much as anything else. You may find yourself in one of them, too."

I want to tell him that I find myself in all of them. But I haven't even given it a shot. So I ask myself what I look like. Not what I want to look like—I can knock on that door, but there's no room behind it.

There's a photography exhibit on the ground floor, images from across the stretch of the twenty-first century we've traveled so far. I look into the eyes of peasants and publicists, Anglicans and Africans, suburban families and soldiers half a world from home. I don't look at where they are, but try to look into their faces instead, their eyes. But while I feel I could wake up as any of them, I don't feel that any of them are more me than any other. Certainly, some speak more to my experience. But not to who I am.

We move to paintings. Jazz Age flappers, and migrants working in sepia fields.

"Nothing?" X asks me.

I shake my head. "You? Do you see yourself anywhere here?"

"In this gallery, I guess that's the closest." He points to a sculpture—*Torso of a Young Man*. Typical Greek shape for a torso of a young man. Strong. Somewhat blank. "Only I have all my limbs."

"I'm guessing you're not bronze, either."

"Depends on the day."

I am trying to reconcile this person talking to me with the Reverend Poole I met. I tell myself I didn't really meet X that day; I ran before I could. And it seems he's learned a few things since then.

"Let's try upstairs," I say.

I lead us into a gallery of black lines on white canvases.

"Not me," I joke.

Then I walk into the next gallery and am taken aback. We are suddenly surrounded by all of these strange fields of color floating into each other. Some look like horizons, others like stacks. Some colors go together. Others clash and complement at the same time. They are clouds, but they are solid. They are quiet, but they speak. They make no sense, and they make perfect sense.

"This?" X asks.

"Yes," I say.

"Rothko. Interesting."

I don't want my shape to be a shape. I want it to be colors. Every color. Each day a different combination.

I know this isn't me. I know I'm not an abstraction. This is not the answer. But it's the best answer, much better than picking a kind of body and saying, *This is me.*

"I don't want to disappoint you," I admit. "I don't want you to think I'm not trying."

"No! You can't disappoint me. Anything you say is meaningful to me. We're discovering, aren't we? That's the whole point of us getting together. To discover. Don't you think there are so many things to discover?"

"Absolutely."

We stand next to each other, looking at a rectangle of gray hovering over a rectangle of red. Although the more I look, the more the gray becomes many colors, like there are waves of green and purple and blue underneath.

I hear footsteps behind us and am surprised, because I know it's Rhiannon who's come into the room. Rhiannon, looking for me. I was supposed to meet her so many hours ago. I hope she's seen what's been happening. I am sure she'll understand.

It would be easy enough to turn, to tell her to join us, to introduce them. But at least some caution remains from my first encounter with X, because I decide against this. Instead I step back, and while X is still looking forward, I put my hands behind my back. I make a heart with my fingers, then flash five fingers three times, hoping she'll know I mean I'll go to our meeting spot in fifteen minutes. I hear the footsteps move away.

"I don't suppose a visit to the Renaissance galleries would make any difference, field-trip-wise," X says.

"I don't think so."

"Well, then. What now?"

"I'm afraid I'm supposed to go meet someone."

"Rhiannon?"

"No. Rudy's parents. They must be petrified by now about where he is."

"Again, I will mildly but forcefully point out that Rudy's life is not more important than your own. Rudy is missing a bout of DC tourism that staring at a few postcards will cure.

322

Have you been to these monuments? There's nothing memorable about them beyond their size. Whereas what you are doing today—that, I daresay, has more importance."

"I know, but I guess I'm assuming we can continue it tomorrow."

"That's not in doubt. We're only just starting. You'll just have to pardon me—I'm impatient! This has been a massive afternoon for me."

"Me too."

"Good. Then we'll continue tomorrow. I've gotten a suite at the Fairport. You can come by and we can go from there. If you give me your email address, I can send you the details and my phone number."

It seems ridiculous to use Nathan as a go-between at this point. So I give him the information and he types it into his phone.

I mean, Wyatt's phone.

"What about Wyatt?" I ask. "Doesn't he have to go home?"

"He will, eventually. I'm telling you, I wouldn't be able to stay in here if he didn't want me to be here. And it's the weekend. His parents will think he's stayed an extra day after the protest."

"They don't know where he is. They're worried."

"Why do you say that?"

"Nathan sent me his Facebook page. So I would know what you looked like."

"Crafty Nathan. I'll be honest—I haven't checked Wyatt's Facebook page myself. Do you post as them when you're in their bodies?"

"I try not to."

"Me as well. It seems wrong to contribute to something that counts as permanent—or at least as permanent as modern technology can offer. So no, I haven't been posting.

And yes, I'm sure that's freaking some people out, because heaven forbid someone goes off-line for a week. How dare he! But I assure you, that's the only place Wyatt's considered missing. And he'll go back soon enough."

"Okay. So I'll see you both tomorrow."

"I'm sorry you have to go now."

"Me too."

"I'll send you the information right away, so if you end up having free time later this evening, let me know."

"I doubt Rudy's parents will let him out of their sight."

"So don't go back!"

"Stop."

"Sorry. I get it. Truly, I do. I'm just being selfish. I want to talk to you more. We haven't even scratched the surface. Which, come to think of it, is a very poor metaphor to use vis-à-vis you and me. But you know what I mean."

I can't help but smile. "I do."

"Good. Now go be the catalyst for a family reunion. I hope they don't ship you back to Manila this evening as punishment."

"Don't even joke about that."

"Yes, please don't make me fly for eighteen hours for part two of this conversation."

"I'll make sure not to."

The only way to pull myself out of the room is to remember that Rhiannon is back with the impressionists, waiting for me.

"I may stay here a little bit longer, to try to see what you see. Good luck."

"You too."

I start to leave. Then X says, "And, A?"

I turn back to him.

"Yes?"

"It's great to meet you."

"You too."

My mind is barely in my body as I walk from the East Building of the museum to the West. It was almost ridiculous to be searching the walls for something similar to me, when the most similar person to ever come into my life was standing right next to me.

The museum is kind enough to provide plenty of reflecting surfaces, so I can check to make sure X is staying true to his word and remaining in the Rothko gallery rather than following me. It's only as I get farther from him that the reality of the day returns. I think about Rudy, and about his parents. And I think about Rhiannon, who I find waiting exactly where we were supposed to meet a few hours ago.

"I'm so sorry I'm late," I say immediately.

"And I'm sorry I was late. We underestimated the traffic by about two hours. How'd it go?"

"It was incredible, Rhiannon. I don't even know how to describe it. He knew exactly what I was talking about. From the inside. He's been asking himself all the same questions I've been asking myself."

I tell her more about it—exactly what we talked about. I don't want to hold anything back from her.

I don't expect any particular reaction from her—I know this is as new to her as it is to me. Still, I'm a little surprised by how concerned she is.

"You're talking about him like he's a really good guy," she points out. "But that's not really the sense of him that we've been getting. He beat the hell out of Nathan, A. Not once—twice. Did you ask him about that?"

"No. It didn't come up," I say, knowing how lame it sounds.

325

"Well, I wasn't expecting him to bring it up. But you might have mentioned it. Just out of curiosity."

"I'll ask him tomorrow. I thought about it—I did. But it wasn't the right time. I was learning so much from him. I didn't want to shut that down."

Rhiannon sighs. "Did you make sure he didn't follow us here?"

"He was staying behind to look at those paintings some more."

"He's still in the building? Seriously?" She looks around quickly. "Let's go. Now. I am going to walk ahead and go out on the Mall side, because it will be more crowded. Stay behind me, but not too close. And if you run into him again, I just want you to know—I'm going to keep walking. Then I'll email you."

"I don't have phone service without wifi."

"There's free wifi in every one of these museums, A. I swear to God."

There's no goodbye. She just heads out. I wait half a minute and follow.

I don't see X dodging away, or hiding behind any sculptures. I don't think we need to act like spies right now. But there's no way to call her back.

So I push ahead, the crowds getting thicker and thicker. When I'm outside on the steps of the museum, I've lost her completely . . . until she's at my arm, saying, "Come on."

It feels like there are indeed millions of people on the lawn. Over the loudspeakers, we can hear someone singing "Imagine," with a large part of the crowd singing along. I try to add my voice as we push toward the National Museum of American History. "Wait," I say, holding Rhiannon back for a second. "Look at this."

Millions of people adding to the harmony, imagining the world at peace.

"It is pretty inspiring," Rhiannon says.

I tell her my theory about the balance between right and wrong, and how we're adding our weight to the right side.

"I like that," she says. Then, for the final verse, we both sing along.

When it's over, there's more cheering.

"Let's go in there. We'll find a quiet spot."

We head inside the American history museum, and find an alcove where there's a display of adding machines that isn't getting much foot traffic. When Rhiannon says she has to run to the restroom, I ask if I can use her phone. She doesn't ask me why, just unlocks it and hands it over. I call the hotel where Rudy's family is staying and leave a message for his parents, saying everything's fine, and that I'll be back by dinnertime.

"Are you sure you don't want me to patch you through to the room?" the hotel operator asks.

"Nooooo," I tell her. "This is fine." Then I hang up.

The phone buzzes almost immediately—I'm expecting it's hotel security, tracking me down for my parents. But instead it's a text from Alexander: *Hope you're feeling better. We want to come and find you.*

When Rhiannon returns, I hand over the phone and tell her why I needed it.

"You also got a text," I say.

She reads it, looks back up at me.

"I texted them that the crowds were getting to me and that I needed to separate myself and sit down. But I do have to meet up with them again. I don't want to miss it entirely. I mean, I want to be in some of their stories, you know. But I was thinking—you could come with me."

"You think so?"

"Sure—why not? We can say we met in the museum, both taking a break. What's your name?"

"Rudy."

"And where are you from, Rudy?"

"Manila."

"As in—?"

"The Philippines."

"I hope you're not flying back tonight."

"Why does everyone keep saying that?"

She looks at me strangely. "How many people have you been talking to?"

"Two. But we're two for two now, as far as that comment's concerned."

"Can I ask you something?"

"Anything."

"You didn't notice me following you, because I was never really that close. So I couldn't really hear what you were saying. But in that last room, the one with all of the Rothko paintings, something happened. What was it?"

"I saw them, and I also saw myself. X—Poole—asked me to find someone in a photo or a painting who looked like me. What I imagine me to be. But nothing clicked until I saw those paintings. I know it sounds weird. . . ."

"No, it doesn't sound weird at all."

"It doesn't?"

"No. I feel the same way. That's my favorite room in the whole museum. We have this whole landscape that's our physical self, and other artists paint that. But when it comes to our inner landscape, our thoughts and our emotions—I think that's where we get Rothko and Picasso and even O'Keeffe, who can paint a flower and make you feel like it's the one that's blooming in your rib cage. So I guess what I'm trying to say is: When you feel that way about the Rothkos, don't think it's because you're different. It's something we all can feel."

"Okay," I say. "That's good to know."

"Guess he's not the only one who can teach you something today."

I smile. "No, he's not."

She kisses me. "Alrighty, then. Should we find my friends?"

"I don't know."

"You don't know?"

"Correct."

"Why don't you know?"

"Because I'm not sure I can treat you like a stranger I just met. Your friends will see through that. I'll slip. And you're going to be on guard, too, if I'm there. Completely on guard. Especially with Alexander there. You're not going to be comfortable with me, and I'm not going to be comfortable with you. I get it—I know if there's ever going to be a good opportunity to hang out with you and your friends, it's an event like this, where everyone is mixing together so naturally. I love that you think we're ready for that. But I'm not sure we're ready for that."

"I guess it seemed like a good idea when it was just in my head," Rhiannon concedes. "I just have to get back to them, but I want to be with you, too. Especially since we haven't really talked about all the implications of you being so friendly with someone who could easily be dangerous—did you call him X?"

"It's short for Xenon."

"Was he named after his home planet?"

"That's not nice."

Rhiannon sighs. "No. I don't suppose it is."

"I probably shouldn't have told you in the first place. Him telling me was a really big deal. I'm the first person he's ever told. Just like you were the first person I ever told."

"Just like."

"You know I'm not saying it's the same."

"Okay. I do. I'm just worried by how well you're saying you got along. I wish you'd seen Nathan all banged up."

"I know. We'll see how it plays out. I said I'll ask him tomorrow."

"When are you seeing him tomorrow? Is he going to call Nathan to set it up? If so, I better let him know."

"No. I gave him an email address. We'll figure it out directly."

"Great."

"It's an email address, not a tracking device."

"I want you to see him during the day. Then I want to see you after, for dinner. I can drive back."

"Sounds like a plan."

"Okay, then."

"Wait," I say. "One more thing."

"What?"

I kiss her. Once. Twice. Three times.

"Oh, that," she says.

"Yeah, that."

Her phone buzzes again. "I better go find them."

"Good luck. There are a few people out there."

"If I run into Rudy's parents, should I let them know where you are?"

"Very funny. Only . . . not." I quickly translate something inside Rudy's mind, and say, *"Tayo nagkakaintindihan sa ganito eh."*

"What's that mean?"

"'We understand each other so well.'"

We say goodbye about a dozen more times. Then finally she leaves me to the adding machines.

I am sad to see her go. But glad I only have to wait until tomorrow to see her again.

I check Rudy's phone and see that there is indeed wifi available.

I don't even have to check to know that X has emailed me. I could be in contact right now. I could spend the rest of the day continuing the conversation.

But no. I remember Rudy. I remember his parents.

I start to head back to the hotel.

I know I'm doing the right thing, facing the consequences of Rudy's departure myself. But I can't help but think that, in some way, X was right: This day has meant more to me than a day in DC would ever mean to Rudy. Even if his parents were worried, even if he gets into some trouble . . . it will still have been worth it, just for today.

NATHAN

I feel bad about missing the protest, because of the whole can't-really-walk-much-in-this-brace thing. Jaiden suggests she come over and cheer at the television with me. I say that sounds great, except I'd have to come to her. At my house, if we cheered at the television, my parents would jeer back.

My knee is feeling okay enough to get in the car—whatever it takes to get out of my house.

Jaiden doesn't exactly warn me that her family has four dogs and what feels like sixteen cats—maneuvering is a task, but Jaiden swoops in to help me out, giving us plenty of excuses for excessive physical contact. We watch the march on TV, cheering along as promised, eating far too many nachos, and then switching over to make ourselves a marathon of this show about the British royal family acting Very Important and Very Messed Up.

It isn't until Jaiden is in the kitchen, making us more nachos, that I think about Rhiannon and A. I text her, *How did it go?*

They talked, she texts back.

And did A figure out how to destroy him?

Not quite.

What do you mean, not quite?

I think it was friendlier than that.

I can't believe I'm seeing this. I call out to Jaiden that I'm hobbling to the bathroom, then call Rhiannon from there.

"Not acceptable!" I say. "Totally not acceptable!"

"They need to talk more. It means a lot to A, to find some-one in the same situation."

"It's not the same situation. A is nice! Poole is NOT."

"I know that. You know that. And A needs to learn it. Which A will."

"I don't like this."

"I know. Neither do I."

"So they're meeting again. Is Poole sending me the when and where?"

"No. They're in direct contact now."

"Shit, Rhiannon. I mean it. *Shit*."

"Don't worry—"

"What about Wyatt? Doesn't he get a say in this?"

"I genuinely don't know what to tell you."

"Sorry. I know it's not you." I hear what sounds like an ocean of voices behind her. "Are you still there?"

"Yeah. We're going for some Thai food in Dupont before heading back. It's too crowded now. It's going to be a late night."

"Okay. Keep me posted."

"I will."

"Have fun."

"You too. Are you home?"

"I'm at Jaiden's. The girl from the library."

"Well, then definitely have fun."

I feel myself blushing. "Okay, yeah, whatever."

"Bye, Nathan."

"Bye, Rhiannon."

I return, and Jaiden and I eat more nachos and suck up more of the queen's problems. It's fun. Totally fun. I don't want to go, but I'm tired and my leg is starting to feel sore. I'm about to tell her this, but then she says I have nacho cheese on the corner of my lip, and somehow her wiping it away becomes our first kiss, and I don't think of my leg or anything else for a while.

I plan on driving right home. But then something pulls at me, and I find myself punching Wyatt's address into my phone and heading there.

I don't know what I'm expecting to see. Police cars, maybe? Detectives scouring the lawn for clues about his disappearance?

Instead, there's a guy shooting hoops in the driveway. In the darkness, I can't make out his features. Is it Wyatt? Has he come home? I step out of the car to get a closer look. I figure I'll just pretend I'm out for a rehabilitative walk. But I must be a pretty bad actor, because the guy stops shooting the ball, looks at me, and says, "Can I help you?"

It's not Wyatt. It's someone younger than him, a little younger than me. His brother, who I feel I know from his Instagram photos.

"I'm looking for Wyatt," I find myself saying.

"We're all looking for Wyatt," he replies.

"I guess I knew that."

He looks me over. "Did he do that to you?"

"No, he didn't," I say. Because it's true. "Does this seem like the kind of thing he'd do?"

"Nah. It's just, he was so weird this week. Didn't go to school. Totally not himself, you know. And then—*poof*. This is a guy who'd text to say he was moving from one room to another, just in case we were looking for him. So I'll believe anything at this point."

For a second, I think about telling him the truth. But then I think: *What would he do with it?* I also can imagine him ask-

334

ing my name, then going back inside and putting it in a search engine and finding all of my history. I guess at least I'd be consistent. But not in a way I can expect him to believe.

So all I say is, "I wish I could help."

"What did you want him for?"

"I'm just his bio partner at school. We have this project? And since he hasn't been answering my texts, I figured I'd just drop by."

"Well, I'll tell him you stopped by. If, you know, he ever comes back."

Another chance to tell him the truth. But instead I say thanks and walk back to my car.

It doesn't feel good to be driving away.

X

I can feel Wyatt pushing against me. I can feel him wanting life.

I tamp him down. Shut him out.

This means too much to me now.

I have felt power before, but it has always been the power of one. Now I am grasping something beyond that, understanding what can happen when the power of one grows to include others like you. I know my own force. But with A, I can at least understand that force more, if not increase it.

Because, deep down, I think A wants the same thing.

It is not enough to live in isolation.

If you want true power, you must unite with your kind and undermine the rest.

A

Day 6140

I wake up in the same hotel, until I realize it's a different hotel. I don't remember the room enough to see the difference. But when I look into Andy's memories to see where I am, I'm three blocks over from where I was before. I also have two roommates, Shane and Vaughn. I guess at first we're here for the protest, but it ends up that we're actually here for a Junior State convention, and came down a night early for the march.

I am relieved we're not checking out at eleven.

I am up before Shane and Vaughn. There's a third bed in the room, a foldout, but Shane and Vaughn are snuggled into one another on the bed that's a twin to my own. That tells me just about all I need to know.

I tiptoe to the bathroom and bring Andy's laptop with me. The first thing I see when I open it is an hour-by-hour schedule he's made for the whole convention. Today he has debate prep with Shane and Vaughn until noon. Then there's the opening ceremony and the first day's worth of panels and events. Andy has marked his choices, but none of them are mandatory. Their team doesn't compete until tomorrow.

Next I check my email and find X's contact info. I tell him I'll meet him at 12:30 in his lobby. We can go from there.

I also message Rhiannon and tell her I can meet her at six, and ask her to pick a place.

I hear some stirring from the bedroom and call out a loud "Good morning!" so the stirring doesn't escalate too far. Then I close the laptop, hop in the shower, and try to get ready for the day. My mind is crowded with all the things X and I could talk about. But I have to give myself a little space to lead Andy's life for a couple of hours before that.

You don't have to do anything, I imagine X telling me.

When I emerge from the bathroom, Shane and Vaughn both smile sleepily at me. Vaughn pulls himself out of bed and takes the next shower. Shane continues to smile, stretching out on the bed.

"I am awash in contentment," he says.

On the other side of his bed, three posters lean against the wall, one for each of us. I AM INTERSEX AND EQUAL. I AM ACE AND EQUAL. I AM QUEER AND EQUAL. Accessing memories of yesterday, I discover the first poster is Shane's, the second is mine, and the third is Vaughn's.

After Shane takes his shower, we go down for breakfast, then retreat back to our room to fine-tune our debate. The topic is that water is humanity's most important resource, and it is the government's duty to provide it freely to all. We are meant to argue that this is the case, and the three of us have spent months researching the history of governments and water supply. In this particular prep, I am far behind my partners—but I'm not the one who's actually going to be debating tomorrow, so I can be a temporarily weak link.

Shane can tell I'm distracted. "Still buzzing from yesterday?" he asks me.

I tell him yes, and it's not a lie.

When it's time to head to the opening ceremony, I tell Shane and Vaughn that I want to skip out and explore the city some more. I ask them to cover for me, and point out that I'll be away from the room for at least the next few hours. I tell them I'll text updates. They call me a slacker, a rebel, an offense to all things Junior and Statesmanlike. But when I leave, they give no indication that they will vacate the room in the near future.

I am a few minutes early getting to X's hotel, but he's already waiting, his leg bobbing up and down with either excitement or impatience. He doesn't know what I look like today, but when he sees me coming, he springs up and smiles.

"A, I presume?" he says when I get close.

"At your service."

He asks me if I'm up for lunch, and I willingly follow as he takes us to a Capital Grille around the corner. Along the way, he asks me about the rest of my day yesterday, as if there aren't so many other things to talk about. I tell him about the trouble I got into when I returned to the hotel, and how Rudy's parents threatened to take away his trip to Disney World.

X laughs. "They have tickets to Orlando. They'll go to Disney World. And if his punishment is that he only gets to Wizarding World, then he actually comes out ahead."

"Have you been?"

"Yes."

"Have you been all over?"

"More than most people, I would guess." He looks at me and shakes his head. "You really have no idea how much freedom you have, do you?"

"I just haven't made it far."

"Why?"

"What do you mean, *why*?"

"Why haven't you gone far?"

"Well, because you can only go where the people you're

339

inside are going. And I get used to an area, which makes it not that easy to leave it."

"I can understand that before you were driving age—then just about everyone is subject to a certain limitation of travel. But after? You could go anywhere."

"Until midnight."

"NOT until midnight. You can stay. I've told you that. Or, if you insist on vacating the premises at midnight, then simply take them as far as they can go."

"And strand them? I've done that. It feels awful."

"It feels awful because you're letting it feel awful. And you probably leave behind that awful feeling in them, too. That's not how to do it. You have to think of it as an adventure—and make them think that way, too. Yes, it's disorienting for people who aren't used to it to wake up in a new place, not entirely remembering how they got there. But how much better if they wake up thinking they did something wild and crazy the night before, and spontaneously pushed themselves somewhere new. You can leave that thought behind. You can make them believe that."

"But what if you're harming them?"

"I think you must be careful not to mistake inconvenience for harm. They are two very different things. You are clearly petrified of doing harm. Fair enough. But I would guess, ninety-nine percent of the time, what you think is harming them is actually only inconveniencing them."

We get to the restaurant, and are seated at a window. We pause to order, then continue.

"What's the farthest you've ever been?" he asks me.

"Denver."

"When?"

"Until a week ago."

"Ah, so that's where you were hiding."

340

"I wasn't hiding. Why bother to hide when you're hidden every single day?"

"Because you found someone who saw you. Rhiannon. And you weren't hidden every day. You had to go back to being hidden every day."

"How do you know that?"

"You're not the only one who's had a Rhiannon. Mine was Sara. I'll tell you about her another time—it's a long story, and there are other things to discuss."

I want to discuss Sara. But I wonder if it's too painful. And I respect that we're not close enough to go to those places yet.

I ask him more about the parts of the world he's been, and then ask him about some of the people he's been. It's so strange to me that he's been so many different ages; when I tell him this, he says, "You could experience life that way, too."

"Whatever happened to Reverend Poole?" I ask.

"A direct question, and I will give you a direct answer: He's dead."

"When?"

"Shortly after I left him. Natural causes."

"What does that mean?"

"In this case, it means that the reason I could stay inside his body for so long was because the part of him that I replaced— it was already dying. Maybe already dead. My presence kept him alive much longer than he would have lived otherwise. Then, when I moved on, he moved on as well."

"And do you think if his body had died while you were still inside it—"

"—then I would have died as well. I don't think we are immortal, A. I don't think a life can exist without a body. So if the body we're in dies, then I imagine we die. I would love to be wrong—but it's not the kind of thing one tests, is it?"

"No, it's not," I say. Then I think again about Reverend

341

Poole, and about X's current body. "What about Wyatt? If you stay in him long enough, will the same thing happen?"

"I suspect that when I leave, he'll be fine. There will be a week missing from his life, but I'll try to fill it in as best I can."

"But you said yesterday that he's allowing you to be in there?"

"Yes. If he didn't in some way want me here, I don't think I could do this. Which is why I think you should do it, too. Or at least try. What's the name of the person you're in today?"

"Andy."

"Okay. So if Andy misses tomorrow as well as today, is it really such a loss? If he really wants to live for himself tomorrow, then you won't wake up as him. As simple as that. But if in some way he'd be relieved to have someone else take the wheel . . . then you get another day. And you'll be amazed when you see how much you can accomplish when you're the same person for a few days."

If this were a debate, I would lose, because the best argument I have is *That's not the way it's supposed to work.* Which makes no sense, because the same thing could be said about waking up every day in a different body. We left *supposed to* behind as soon as we were born.

So I don't debate. Instead I ask him to tell me some of the people he's been. And he says he will, as long as I tell him some of the people I've been.

Most of my stories involve situations in school, or families I particularly remember. I don't tell him any of the ones involving Rhiannon, because those belong to her and me. In turn, he tells me about flights on corporate jets and nights in Paris. Almost all of the people he remembers being are men, and I remind myself that's just who he feels he is, which is as legitimate a choice for him as my own vagueness (or is it openness?) is for me.

We stay so long talking that the waiters change shifts. At the end, X insists on paying again. I don't put up a fight.

"Should we take a walk?" he asks. "Keep talking?"

I excuse myself to the bathroom so I can check Andy's phone. I text Shane and Vaughn to tell them I'm running around museums. They tell me I'm not missing much, and that our advisor is probably doing the same, since she can't be found.

I check my email and find a message from Rhiannon, telling me to meet her at a bookstore, Politics and Prose, at six. I'll need to take the Metro or a cab, but she promises me it'll be worth it.

When I get back to the table, the check is settled and X is ready to go.

"Anything in particular that you want to see?" he asks.

I think about everything I've heard about and experienced in DC over the years.

"The pandas?" I say. I actually remember going to the National Zoo many years ago with my mom.

"That's not close, and it's pretty cold out. But we could, if you want."

"Nah, I have to be back at my hotel by five."

"You don't *have to.*"

"I'm *going to.*"

He smiles. "Understood. How about we just go back to my suite? There's a sitting area where we can make ourselves at home."

If you'd told me two days ago I'd be following Poole to his lair, I would have called my two-days-later self an idiot. But now it doesn't feel crazy or risky at all. What did I think he'd do to me? He could chain me to a radiator and insist I do his bidding—but all it would take is the approach of midnight for me to escape.

As we walk over, he says, "You've been very polite to me."

I'm not sure if this is meant as a compliment or a complaint. "How so?" I ask.

"You haven't brought up what I did to your friend Nathan. I owe you both an apology, which isn't complicated at all: I am very sorry I did what I did. And I also owe you an explanation, which is more complicated, because I don't fully understand it myself. I don't want you to think I'm blaming him at all—I'm not. It is all my fault.

"For reasons that I'm guessing are clearer now, I was desperate to find you. To have gotten so close to having these conversations, this *recognition*, and then to have you disappear—it was devastating. The only time I'd been seen in that way was with Sara . . . and that wasn't the same. Even though I let her know me, she couldn't truly understand what I was going through. Again, not her fault. In this case, nobody's fault. But with you—there was the possibility of a true exchange, a true understanding. Which I lost. Because, as already established, I handled it very badly.

"I realized Nathan was the only connection to you I had left. And I knew a straightforward plea was not going to work. What did he owe me? So I decided to spook him. And it worked. It worked well. Until we became stuck again, and the way I thought to unstick it was to spook him some more. But, again, what I did was inexcusable, no matter what desperation I was feeling. I just want to acknowledge that so we can move on."

I'm surprised he's brought it up. And relieved.

"It's really Nathan you should be apologizing to," I say. "Not me."

"I know. But I can't imagine he wants to be in a room with me right now. So can you at least pass it on?"

I nod. "I will."

I feel there are other things I should be saying, but I don't know what they are. That violence is wrong? He seems to know that. That desperation is no excuse? He seems to know that also. I think of some of the mistakes I've made, particularly the way I kidnapped Katie to Denver. It's not like I'm blameless when it comes to harmful decisions made in the heat of wanting something.

"I remember Nathan right after your experience with him," X goes on. "How scared he was. You must have left him abruptly. Because usually I feel there's a transition when we leave. Don't you?"

I remember talking to Rhiannon about this, after I had seen life through her eyes for a day. Her reaction wasn't the same as Nathan's at all.

"I like to think there's a way to make it easier for them," I say.

"There has to be. Otherwise, people would catch on. They would talk about it more. They'd figure it out—and that would be devastating to us. And to them. Our private power would become their public crisis. Can you imagine how many more minds would be further destabilized, in this already destabilizing age? Bad enough to have to grapple with your own biology, your own chemistry. But then to think that one day you might wake up with someone else in charge? What's already fragile would break."

"So you're saying our secrecy serves them, too?"

"Absolutely. It serves us all."

We've gotten to his hotel, and he takes me up to the top floor. When he said he was staying in a suite, I pictured something like a Residence Inn—a regular hotel room, only with two beds and maybe a kitchenette.

This room is much grander than that.

It actually feels like we're in a rich person's apartment.

There's a living room. A dining room. A kitchen. And, presumably, a bedroom and bathroom (two bathrooms!) beyond.

X gestures to one of the two couches. "Make yourself at home. Do you want something to drink?"

"Water's fine."

"There's a full bar here. Go crazy."

"Okay, then—ginger ale."

He shakes his head, amused. "Suit yourself."

I don't think X knows how funny it is to see Wyatt being the lord of this particular manor. Wyatt looks like he might have a job driving deliveries for a pizza place. He does not look like he should have the keys to a suite.

X hands me what I'm sure is the most expensive can of Canada Dry I've ever held. He's gotten a Coke for himself.

I know it's not one of the questions you're usually encouraged to ask, but since we're in far from usual circumstances, I ask, "How can you afford this?"

"Wise investments."

"With whose money?"

"I'll explain."

And explain he does—something about offshore accounts, shifting assets, and "choice liquidation." I only understand about half of it, but the half I understand is this: He takes money from some of the people he occupies and he puts it in his own bank accounts.

"Isn't that, like, stealing?" I ask.

"Yes and no. Yes, in that what was once theirs becomes mine, and it is not a gift that is freely given. And no, because I am very careful to only take from the people who have plenty to spare. All you need to do is dip into that top income bracket three or four times a year and you're set. I'm not going to take money from a family of seven living in a two-bedroom apartment. If anything, I may dip into my own accounts and leave them something for their troubles. It is one of our great abilities, to be able to redistribute wealth."

"But you're taking advantage."

"Yes! And you need to take advantage as well, A. We need every possible advantage we can get in order to survive. You believe that freedom is essential, correct? That every man deserves his own independence?"

"Of course."

"Well, how else are we going to have our own freedom, if we don't have our own means? How are we going to have our own independence, if we don't get to make our own choices? You may have noticed—our society revolves around money. You may also have noticed that our temporal bodily state does not give us any direct way to earn money. So we must 'take advantage.' If we see any advantage whatsoever, we must grab it."

"What other advantages are there?" I ask him, both curious and afraid.

"We have the advantage of being able to walk away from anything, A—anything short of death. We don't have to live with consequences like other people. Nor do we have to be anchored to bodies that we hate, which is the truth for so many of them. We have the advantage of being able to see from angles they can't imagine. And when we take on positions of power, we assume that power as our own, for as long as we'd like it—just by virtue of waking up in the right place."

"There are still consequences of what we do."

"Of course there are. I'm just saying we have a different relationship to them."

"*You* might."

"If you don't, you will. But I suspect you do already, even if you don't acknowledge it."

"What do you mean?"

"I mean, you can't possibly live with all of the consequences of your actions, for all these people. The capacity of memory does not stretch that wide. They live with what you've done to them. You do not. Which is as it should be."

"I can't see the world like that. I can't deliberately take advantage."

"You can. You have. And you will."

"You don't know that."

"Of course I know that! You're young, A. And this is a very early stop on your learning curve. I can tell you've already grown restless. You've already been disrupting the rules you set down. You're already looking beyond what you are. That's good. Are some of the things I've done breaking the law? Yes. But you and I, we were breaking nature's law from the day we were born. You can say right now that you want to follow the rules, not take advantage, keep going through life without anyone knowing you've ever been there. But if it hasn't worn you down already, it will wear you down soon. Day after day of not living your own life. Year after year of never being yourself. It would be one thing if you actually believed you were these people. But you know you're not. You know you're pretending. And a person can only pretend for so long before he faces a choice: compromise himself or compromise the rules. The only way to live is to compromise the rules. Find a way to support yourself as yourself. If it means other people must suffer for you to get what you want—well, A, that's the way of the world. And making yourself the one perpetually suffering doesn't make you a better person. It only makes you miserable."

"So you don't think about them at all?"

"Are you listening to me? I think about them all the time! If I wanted, I could ruin every single one of their lives. Just for fun. The very first day I was Wyatt, I could have found a gun and had him kill his whole family. If I wake up tomorrow as a girl at your debate convention, I could get trashed at the hotel bar and hook up with an insurance salesman from Colorado, without any protection. I am aware, in a way you are not aware, of all of the consequences our actions can have. It takes a great restraint not to take more advantage."

It's like he's asking me to praise him for avoiding things I've never even thought of in the first place.

"By staying in there longer, aren't you hurting them more?" I ask. "I know you say they're letting you do it—but even if that's true, aren't you still taking advantage, by giving them that option? And when you leave, aren't they worse off?"

"There's no way for us to know, is there?"

"What about Wyatt? How long has it been now? Wyatt, what's going to be left of you?"

I'm looking in his eyes as I say it—and as I ask my question, there's the flicker I saw the first time I met X, back when he was Poole. For a moment, I see another set of eyes beneath. Pleading. Entreating.

Then X blinks, and Wyatt is gone.

"What?" X asks, taking in my expression. "What did you see?"

"I might have seen Wyatt. I don't know."

X smiles. "Amazing. To be able to ask that question and get an answer. What did it look like?"

I describe it.

"Okay. Remind me your name today."

"Andy."

He leans forward, looks into my eyes. "Okay, Andy. Are you in there? Show me where you are."

He stares for a few seconds. Then a few seconds more. I try not to blink.

"Nothing. Did you feel Andy at all, trying to rise to the surface?"

"No. Did you feel Wyatt?"

"Possibly."

"Doesn't that mean he wants to get back?"

"I don't know what it means."

He drinks a gulp of his Coke, finishes it.

"I think that might have to be it for today. I'm suddenly very tired. But, again, this has been extraordinary. Don't you think so? To get to talk about these things—extraordinary."

I've only taken a sip of my ginger ale, but I also feel it might be time to go.

"Tomorrow?" I say.

"Of course. Tomorrow. I'll be in touch. Let me know who you are when you wake up."

"You too," I say.

"Oh, I expect I'll be Wyatt. But I suppose we'll see."

I'm hoping he's not Wyatt. But I keep my mouth shut. For all our honesty, I still sense there are things I can't say.

And yet . . . X is right. Even if I don't always agree with him, having these conversations is extraordinary. I can't see any way I can let them go.

RHIANNON

I'm starting to feel like a commuter, driving back and forth to DC three days in a row.

The drive this afternoon is different from the one home last night. Then the car was full of singing—Preston playing iPhone DJ, and me, Alexander, and Will singing along with whatever he threw our way, whether or not we actually knew the songs. Every now and then, we'd pass Rebecca's car, and there, in the middle of the night in the middle of the highway, we'd roll down our windows and have a sing-off. I wasn't thinking about A at all. Not until I dropped Preston and Will off at Will's house, and then it was just me and Alexander in the car—me and Alexander and the invisible presence of A sitting between us, preventing me from saying some of the things I wanted to say, because I didn't want A to overhear me tell Alexander what a great night I'd had.

He kissed me good night, and I know it could have been a much longer good night. But when I let go of it, he didn't insist I pick it back up. He just smiled, told me I was the best protest driver a boy could ask for, and went up to his room, to create more things from the day.

Now he's the invisible one in the car. I guess they're all invisibly in the car. A, Alexander, Rebecca. Nathan, too. Nathan, who's been texting me nonstop, telling me I can't let A back out of getting rid of Poole.

I've seen Wyatt's brother, he told me. *It's bad.*

I know it's bad. This whole thing is bad.

But what can I do?

I get to Politics and Prose early, so I check out their recommendations table and find a few books that sound interesting. Now all I need is for them to sell gift certificates for time to read them all. That would be a good trick.

When I'm done browsing, I get a coffee for myself and a table for us both, and wait for A to show up. I think about sitting and waiting for A at the bookstore near my house, back before I knew A was A. I was expecting Nathan to walk in, and a girl walked in instead.

It feels like a long time ago. Not in a bad way. Although I can recognize the girl I was then, I see nothing more than a resemblance to the girl I am now. Life before A seems even emptier than life without A did.

At the same time, I wonder if this is another one of those days. What if the conversation at this bookstore has the same effect as that other conversation? Is that even possible?

My eyes were opened. I don't want to close them. I want them to open more.

I see A walk in. I see A finding me. The smile.

I think: *Don't underestimate the gift of someone who smiles every time they see you.*

A tells me about Andy, about X. I listen. A asks about my day, about the rest of the protest. I give a short version of the story. I want to get back to X.

"Nathan went to Wyatt's house," I tell A. "They have no

idea what's happened to him. Can you imagine what it must be like for them? We have to figure out a way to save him."

"It's not that easy. It's not like I can just say a spell and set him free."

"But won't X listen to you?"

"I'm not sure he will."

"Then why are you still talking to him?"

"Because he knows things! I'm having conversations with him I can't have with anyone else. And if that stops—I don't know what I'd do."

"So you're willing to let Wyatt's parents worry he's dead so you can have someone to talk things over with?"

"Don't make it sound like that."

"But that's the way it is, isn't it?"

"I'm not the one in control! He's the one in control."

"Because you're letting him be in control."

"Because he knows more than I do."

"I'm not convinced that what he knows is worth knowing. Teaching you to take advantage? That's the big advice?"

"Again, you're making it sound—"

"I'm making it sound the way I'm hearing it!"

A presses their palms against the table, sits up. Then takes a deep breath and looks at me.

"We're fighting," A says. "Why are we fighting?"

Once upon a time, I was the girl who would have answered, *I don't know.* I was the girl who would have leaned so our knees pressed together, and said, *I don't want to fight.* I would have stopped, because even if it wasn't what the other person needed, it's what they wanted.

Not anymore.

"We're fighting because love isn't just the times when you're getting along perfectly, when everything is effortless," I say. "We're fighting because these are not trivial things we're

353

talking about—they are about as meaningful as it gets, and because I love you and you love me, we have an obligation to engage with the meaningful rather than giving it a pass just because we don't want to raise our voices. We know we're on the same side. I just need you to see how troubling X's influence is. Just like you helped me see how dangerous Justin was. Just like I imagine you'd help me see how dangerous X is, if the roles were reversed."

"The roles will never be reversed."

"I know that. My point is that I am helping you in the same way you'd help me. That's part of love, too. Remember what you said yesterday about the protest, that there's a constant balance between right and wrong, and that what we were doing was trying to add our weight to make the world tilt to rightness? Well, guess what. That battle is fought inside of us as well. You decide which way the balance will tip at any given moment. And if you're lucky, if you're very lucky, then you will have people in your life who will throw their own weight into your balance, to help you even when the force of wrong seems to have the heavier influence. That's what I'm doing right now. I am trying to help you keep things weighted the right way. But I can only make it tilt so much. You ultimately control the scale."

A stares at me a second, then tells me, "You're right."

"I know I'm right," I reply. "Still, it's nice to hear you say it."

"So what do we do?"

"At the very least, we tell Wyatt's parents where he is. Maybe that will chase him out."

"Maybe. But it might also put Wyatt's parents at risk."

"Why do you say that?"

"Nothing. I mean, a hypothetical X used. Which I'm sure was a hypothetical. But still."

"What other option is there?"

"The only one I can think of is if there's some way to get Wyatt to push X out. But . . . I'm not sure that would work. And the only person I can ask about it is X."

"Or maybe you deliver an ultimatum: If he doesn't free Wyatt, you'll never talk to him again. You'll disappear."

"I don't know if that will work."

"Or you just ask him to do it because it's the right thing to do."

"I'm really not sure that would work."

"So we go for the nuclear option."

"Which is?"

"Getting Wyatt to push him out."

"Okay. But let me give X one more chance. See if I can talk him into it. I really think he's getting as much out of these conversations as I am. Can I have one more day?"

"One. That's it. And even that's unfair to Wyatt."

"I understand. And thank you."

"I'm not giving you permission here."

"No. Thank you for fighting with me. I appreciate it."

I smile. "Any time."

"So that's a part of our nameless whatever-this-is?"

"Yup."

"And are we going to figure out what we are?"

"Not tonight. Tonight let's just run around a bookstore, reading things to one another."

"Sounds perfect."

"No such thing. But I'll settle for close to perfect."

For our next span of time together, we don't talk about X or Wyatt or Alexander or Nathan or anyone else. It's just us, a bookstore, and thousands upon thousands of books. We dip from poetry to gardening, politics to prose. We seal ourselves into our own world, and in there, we are all the company we need.

A
Day 6141

Victoria has only one roommate, Lara. Their third debate partner, Lionel, is in the room next door. Lara wakes me up at seven-thirty on the dot and tells me I have exactly a half hour before final prep. The debate itself is at ten.

I message the situation to X and say I'll be there when I can. He messages back, telling me to ditch the debate. I tell him I can't do that to Victoria, Lara, or Lionel. *You don't even know them,* he responds. Then, a few seconds later, he adds, *Which is very noble of you. I will see you this afternoon. You know where to find me.*

When I get out of the shower, I find Lara's set up all of our notes on the hotel desk. She must signal to Lionel as soon as I'm dressed, because the knock comes at the door less than a minute later. I sit down at the desk, open the folder, and find the same debate question that Andy had yesterday.

Only we're the other side.

"You've got to be kidding me," I say.

"Excuse me?" Lara says.

"You prepared, right?" Lionel sounds anxious.

"Maybe too much," I mutter.

It feels even worse when we get to the conference room where the debate's being held, and there are Andy, Shane, and Vaughn, already sitting up on the stage. Shane looks energized, Vaughn looks nerve-ridden, and Andy looks . . . tired.

Really tired. I know for a fact that he was in bed by midnight. But I have no idea what time he got up, or how much catch-up he felt he needed to get before the debate.

I wish I could unlearn everything I saw in their notes. But since I can't, the dilemma becomes: Who do I owe more, Victoria or Andy?

In some way, Lara saves me, because she speaks whenever she gets a chance. And when she's not speaking, she's busy writing Victoria and Lionel notes about what to say. So I follow her lead. I don't head off the points that I know Andy's about to make. It remains about as fair as it can be, with me here.

I have no idea if we did well or not. When the judges come back and say that Andy's team has won, I am neither surprised nor unsurprised.

Lara, though, goes berserk.

"Are you kidding me?" she says, loud enough for the whole room to hear. Our advisor tries to hush her, and that only makes her angrier.

"You can't win them all," Lionel mumbles.

"Speak for yourself!" Lara shouts back. Then she gathers up her things, says, "I have to go prepare for my next event," and storms off.

"If you need half my bed tonight, it's all yours," Lionel says. He's not coming on to me; he's just afraid of what Lara might do.

"It'll be fine. I think."

Our advisor suggests we go to lunch. I start to make an excuse, but then Lionel looks at me with pleading eyes, and I relent.

It's after two by the time I hit X's suite.

"Couldn't pull yourself away from the oral hijinks?" X says as soon as he sees me. I think for a moment that he and Lara might make a great couple.

357

"It actually played out in a really weird way. Remember Andy from yesterday?"

I tell him about what happened, and the dilemma I felt. He gets me a ginger ale without asking me if I want one. He's drinking either water or vodka.

"So what would you have done?" I ask.

"I would have used the information I had."

"But isn't that unfair to Andy?"

"Maybe—but how do you know Victoria wouldn't have anticipated Andy's arguments even without the inside information? You can't. And if you happened to wake up as her after spending a day as her opponent—that's hardly her fault. If I were you, I would've gone for the kill."

"Why doesn't that surprise me?" I say.

I think he might be offended, but instead he smiles. "I'm glad we're starting to understand one another."

I know I should ask about Wyatt again . . . but I also remember how that shut down yesterday's conversation. And there are other things I want to know first.

"How do you think it works?" I ask X. "How do I get to be Andy one day and Victoria the next? And why are we never the same person twice? Do you think there's some overall pattern? Do you think any of it is supposed to make sense, or is it all just random?"

"Starting with the easy questions, I see." X takes a sip of his vodka-or-water. "But I understand. Those were the ones that I kept going back to as well."

I feel a rush of excitement—is it possible he actually has answers? Then the rush slows when he says, "I can tell you my theories, but they're just theories. We need to gather more evidence. With you here, at least we've doubled the pool."

"What are your theories?"

"Let's first tackle the question of why there are no repeat

performances. My theory is that the body develops an immunity once we leave. A spiritual immunity, as it were. The door we enter can only be entered once. After we leave, the body knows how to lock it behind us."

"And what about how we end up where we end up?"

"I think it's in relation to each other. I think when there are more of us near, we stay closer. Spread apart, we travel farther. But, again, that's speculation."

"I've thought that, too."

"The only way to test it would be to have a much larger sample. I suspect that's not going to happen in the near future."

"Okay, stepping back: Do you ever wonder what's behind it?"

"The big question. And the answer is: We'll never know. Is it God? An algorithm? Are we all just a part of some twenty-fourth-century high schooler's science project? That's beyond my expertise. The important thing, I've found, is not to care one way or the other."

We talk more about this, and then about living life in secret.

"You let Nathan think I was the devil," I say.

"It's the language he was going to listen to the most. And it was better than telling him the truth."

"Did you tell Sara the truth?" I ask.

"Somehow I knew you were going to bring her up. And the answer is no, I didn't tell her the truth."

"But how did you explain your changes?"

"You can guess the answer to that one."

Of course. "You stopped changing."

"Exactly. It really improves a relationship, having the same body every day."

"But it wasn't enough."

"Why do you say that?"

"Because you've been talking about her in the past tense."

"Oh, that. Yes. It's certainly over. But that doesn't mean it wasn't enough. It was enough, until I'd had enough. Then I realized—we are meant to be solo travelers. Or, I see now, meant to travel with our own kind. Love with someone quote-normal-unquote . . . it's not for us."

"Not for you, maybe."

"Awww. You look so sad. I'm sure Rhiannon is a lovely girl. I'm sure she's worth all your affections. You're not ready for the long view, and that's fine. But the long view, A? She will always want different things than you want, because she will always have different things available to her. I'm sure she's understanding, but I'm also positive that in the three days we've been talking, I've shown more insight into your life than she ever could. This is not a slight to her. Nobody who isn't like us could possibly understand what it is to be us. I know you're a fan of empathy, but it only goes so far."

"I don't think *fan* is really the right word for—"

He waves his hand dismissively. "I know. Poor choice of words. But surely you understand what I'm saying."

"You don't know Rhiannon. Or what it's like with Rhiannon."

"Then introduce me! I'd love to meet her."

I don't want to. In the pit of my stomach, I don't want to. And I know that's a bad sign.

I say, "First I'd love to stop meeting Wyatt. Can you please let him go back to his parents? It'll make it much easier to talk to you if I'm not thinking about them or him."

"Another limit of empathy!" X sees this doesn't land well with me. "I feel you're getting hung up on Wyatt. And if you're hung up on Wyatt, you haven't really been hearing a thing I've been saying. Wyatt has no more or less right to live than I do. Ultimately, it is the victor who gets the spoils—in this case, I get the body because I want the body more. You will, I assure you, learn to make your needs as important as theirs."

"What if I say I won't come back here unless you switch to someone else?"

"I don't think you'd be able to handle the guilt if something were to happen to that someone else. Are you sure you want to take that on?"

"What do you mean?"

"You know exactly what I mean." He sighs. "Look at us, ignoring common ground again, and getting caught in these petty squabbles. We are certainly better than that."

"I want you to let Wyatt go."

"And I am not subject to your or anyone else's wants."

I stand up. "Then I guess I'll be going."

"Oh, don't ruin this, A. Your bleeding heart is getting blood in your ears. You're not listening when you should be listening the most."

"You don't know me."

"I do. So I know you'll be back tomorrow. I would think less of you if you weren't resisting. But I do think the resistance is just a show you're putting on for yourself. Eventually the show will be over, and I'll really be able to teach you things."

When I get to the door, I turn around and say to him, "One last time, I'm going to ask you to not be Wyatt when I see you tomorrow."

He laughs and shakes his head. Then he returns to his drink, as if I've already gone.

I go.

A

Day 6142

I need to buy time, so I tell X I have Junior State activities all day because the convention is wrapping up that night. Which is true enough, though Marlon's friends notice that he's a little distracted from the activities at hand. They give him a particularly hard time when one of their debate opponents flirts madly with him afterward, and he barely registers it.

"Where's your mind?" one of the friends asks.

I have no way of telling him that my mind is on a last conversation I'm about to have. Because no matter how the plan goes, I am sure that I'm never going to speak to X again.

It should feel like a relief, but it doesn't. I have to keep reminding myself of Wyatt. If it's a contest between having more questions answered and a person getting his life back—it shouldn't be a contest at all. The priority is clear.

It's just after five when I get to X's hotel. I message Rhiannon and let her know that I'm going in, and that I won't be able to check the phone again in X's presence. She says to put Marlon's phone on vibrate; she'll call when it's time.

I have about twenty minutes, maybe thirty, to have any last questions answered.

There's only one thing that could call it off: if I knock on X's door and it's answered by someone other than Wyatt. I find myself hoping for this as I stand and wait.

But it's Wyatt who opens the door.

"At last," X says.

I can't look him in the eye. Not yet. "Sorry. Debates ran late."

"Did you win?"

I honestly can't remember. But I tell him yes.

"Well, then. At least there's that."

He walks ahead of me and I make sure the door is left open a crack, unlocked. Then I follow him to the sitting area. He's left a ginger ale out for me.

We settle in and talk a little bit about our days—he says he went back to the National Gallery to look at the Rothkos again, but I don't totally believe him. I think he's only telling me what he thinks I want to hear.

Maybe he's been doing that all along.

I'm telling him I'm lucky that Marlon's school isn't leaving DC until tomorrow when he interrupts me.

"I notice," he says, "that you've yet to ask me how I manage to stay in other people's bodies for so long."

"Are there magic words I need to know?" I say, trying to keep the tone light.

"No. But as with all things, there *are* strategies."

I'm curious. Of course I'm curious. But I remind myself that staying too long in someone's body can only lead to damage. So it's better not to know.

I need to ask something else. What comes out is, "Have you ever killed someone?"

X laughs. "Where did that come from? Are you still thinking of Reverend Poole?"

And from that, I know: He killed Reverend Poole.

"No, I'm just . . ."

"It's okay. I never thought I'd be asked that question so directly—it just reinforces the bond we have. And I'll answer you truthfully: It depends on your definition of *killed*. Have people ended up dead because of my actions? Certainly. Do I know the total number? Not at all. But have I deliberately killed someone? Murdered them in cold blood, knowing I could get away with it simply by waking up the next morning? No, I have not. But I have definitely enjoyed the notion that I could. It is the extreme manifestation of our condition, the ultimate advantage. You will see this soon enough."

The glee with which he says this—it feels like he's speaking from knowledge, not the speculation of the hypothetical.

"Have you hurt people?" I ask.

"Yes. But never more than they deserve. I need to be provoked. Humans, alas, are accidental experts at provocation. Especially when they drink."

"And you've never met anyone else like us?"

"I see you've been compiling your list, A. But I'm up for your cross-examination. The answer is no, I have not. I have heard from people who claim to live as we do, but either they're hoaxes or they disappear before I can properly follow up. You are the only one who left enough of a trail to follow. And I am grateful that it led us here."

"But why? What do you think we'll do together?"

"Since this is DC, I should probably answer 'world domination' and then laugh maniacally. I wish my goals were so lofty. And maybe someday they will be, with enough of us. The way I see it, doubling our power doubles the opportunity. If I could amass what I have from my life, we could amass twice as much together."

"By stealing?"

"By *living*. By being at the right place at the right time. Whether that's New York or Tokyo or Paris. Would you like to go to Paris?"

"I've never even thought about it." Because I didn't imagine it was possible, without having to stay there forever.

"We can go there next. Bring Rhiannon. It's very romantic."

For a moment, I picture it—running through the cinematic avenues, holding her hand as we gaze at the Eiffel Tower in twilight.

Only . . . who am I in this picture?

Whose body have I taken?

"Will you still be Wyatt?" I ask.

"I imagine it would be more advantageous for me to be older," X answers. "You too. We'll work on that."

"How do you get to move between ages when I can't?"

X shrugs. "You'd have to ask God or the algorithm or the twenty-fourth-century boy with the science project. Once I started staying for longer than a day, I fell out of the pattern. Much to my great regret, I still can't direct who I'm going to be next—but that, I believe, is the next step. Once we conquer that, can you imagine what we can do?"

"What you might do and what I might do are, I think, different things," I venture.

X laughs. "For now. You haven't gotten a taste of it yet. Once you do, you'll never stop being hungry for more."

The phone starts to vibrate in my pocket. It might as well be ringing, it's so loud.

"Do you have to get that?" X asks.

"Nah," I say, trying to sound casual. "I'm sure it's someone from his school, looking for him."

"Best not to answer, then."

I have time for one more question.

I can't think of any.

Instead I say, "I want there to be more of us."

X looks at me strangely, then says, "Me too."

There's a knock on the door.

X stands, confused, and calls out a hello.

I stand as well. Between X and the bedroom door.

The door opens. Nathan comes limping in.

"Well, hello, *Xenon*," he says.

Wyatt's parents and brother are behind him.

"Wyatt," I say, "you are trapped in your own body. You have to fight against that right now. You have to take control."

"What are you doing?" X turns to me and says.

He tries to bolt into the bedroom, but I block him. I wrap my arms around him.

"Wyatt!" Mrs. Giddings cries.

Mr. Giddings looks stunned.

Wyatt's brother, North, runs over and puts his arms around Wyatt, too. X is struggling, raging.

"Wyatt!" North yells. "Wyatt, we need you to fight."

Mr. and Mrs. Giddings join us.

We hold on.

"His name is Xenon," I tell Wyatt. "Get him out of there."

WYATT

"Wyatt, can

"You

                              "Wyatt

        "in there"

                    "We love you. Come back to

        "Wyatt, it's

                                    "Find your

"Wyatt!"

North?

                              "right here"

Mom?

"We need you back. He's hurting you. You need to come

          Who is that?
                                   "Oh, Wyatt"
Don't cry, Mom.

                         "fight"
What?
                         "know you're in there. We
can see you. Can you see us?"

          "WYATT."
                                             Tired.

"We need you, Wyatt. We need you here. Tell
Xenon to go away. You are our son. He is not our son.
You are the one who needs us. He'll hurt us, Wyatt. We
need you, Wyatt."

I'm here.

Right?

Am I here?

                                    "We love you, Wyatt.
We love you so much."

I know, Mom.

"We do, Wyatt. We love you and need you here."

Dad?

Wow, Dad.

"Come on, Wyatt. We need you. The team needs you. I need you."

                                    "Wyatt, don't be such a dork."

You're the dork, North.

"We can't hold on much longer. We need you, Wyatt. We need you back. We need you

                                said, do you want to be here?"

Who are you?

"Wyatt, do you want to be here?"

Yes.

"Do you miss them?"

Yes.

"Do you want to be here with your mom and your dad and North and all of your friends?"

Yes.

"They need you."

I'm here.

"Show us you're in there, Wyatt. Show us

I'm here.

It hurts.

"WYATT!"

Mom.

"WYATT!"

It really hurts. It really hurts.

I want

to breathe.

"What's happening?"

It's okay, North.

It's okay.

A

Day 6142 (continued)

"Is he alive?" Nathan asks.

"He's breathing," North says.

I am standing there over them, standing as if he's still in my arms. I don't think I've ever felt anything scarier than the moment he went from struggling to completely slack, like a rope that had just been cut from the ceiling.

Wyatt's mother cries out.

He's opened his eyes.

She says his name over and over again.

He coughs. "Mom?"

He is covered with sweat. Shaky. Breathing hard.

"It's like he had a heart attack," Nathan says.

"Only his heart returned," I say.

"Let's hope."

I see the look in his eyes as his family hovers over him, crying.

I see the look in his eyes, and know it can't be X.

"I think he's gone," I tell Nathan. "X is gone."

"Or did he just jump into another body?"

I shake my head and tell Nathan, "I don't think a person can live without a body. Not even for a second."

I really think he's gone.

Nathan sends a text, and a minute later there's a knock on the door.

"Is it okay for me to come in?" Rhiannon asks.

"Yeah," I tell her. "It's safe now."

Wyatt has no idea where he is, or why. His family asks me to explain.

I try.

I'm sure it took a lot of convincing from Nathan and Rhiannon to get them here. I imagine that they didn't really believe it, but were willing to do whatever it took to get them back to their son. Now they're in a different kind of state of disbelief, one in which they know what they now know, even if it doesn't make sense with the rest of their world.

Wyatt is still stunned and disoriented, so I'm not sure how much of what I say sinks in. He doesn't remember anything from the past week—doesn't remember talking to me, doesn't remember beating up Nathan. (Both he and his parents wince when that's brought up—but I bring it up because I hope it was the most visceral, memorable act that X did while he was in Wyatt's body.)

I entreat Wyatt and his family not to tell anyone about this. Mr. Giddings actually laughs at that, and assures me that the secret is safe. As he says this, I start to see the shame creep into Wyatt's consciousness. Nathan and Rhiannon must see it, too, because they jump in and say they'll be happy to talk more to him about it, and about what it's like.

"You're going to think nobody understands," Nathan tells him. "But that's not true. We understand."

Wyatt nods at that, but I think he's still trying to figure out who we are.

"How did he pay for this room?" North asks, looking around.

"It wasn't him. X, inside him, had his own means."

"Looks like he was loaded."

"Maybe."

For a second, I wonder if there's a way to get the billing information from the front desk. To track down X's accounts. Then I think: *No. You do not want that.*

I look at the table next to the couch where Wyatt's lying down, and I see the ginger ale just sitting there. My mind starts to feel like it's being pulled to a dark place. As evil as X may have been, he was always nice to me. And now I've made him disappear. I've killed him.

"Maybe we should leave you alone for a little bit," I say to Wyatt and his family.

"Yeah," Rhiannon says.

Mrs. Giddings protests, but not too vehemently. I think they all need to catch their breath a little.

"Okay, then," Nathan chirps.

I'm not sure where we'll go; I just want to get out of that room.

While we're waiting for the elevator, Nathan says, "That was *awesome.*"

And I lose it.

"No!" I yell at him. "That was not awesome. That was us erasing someone from the face of the earth. That was us saving someone, but it was also us making someone else vanish. I know it was the right thing to do, but it's *not* a cause for celebration."

Nathan's backed up, and it takes a moment for me to realize I've grabbed his shirt in my fist. I let it go.

"Sorry," I say.

"No, no—I get it," he replies. "But maybe, you know, I'll stay here and get a ride home with them, okay? I'm sure you two have a lot to catch up on anyway."

I'm about to apologize again, but Rhiannon interrupts and says, "Yeah, sounds like a good plan."

The elevator arrives. Only two of us get on it.

We're quiet for a few blocks, as if we both know we need some time in our own heads. Then I start to tell Rhiannon what it was like, all of us with our arms wrapped around Wyatt so fiercely, telling him what was going on and urging him to help us, even as X screamed and howled and resisted. North, smart, had gone for his legs, so even when X lashed his arms free for a moment, he didn't have anywhere to go.

We find a bench in the National Gallery's sculpture garden and sit across from a tall metallic tree.

"You didn't know it would work, did you?" Rhiannon asks.

"No. Not at all."

"And it must feel weird that it did work."

"It's not weird," I tell her. "It's terrifying."

"Why?"

"Why do you think?"

Rhiannon shakes her head. "No. Don't think that way. That could never happen to you. Because you don't do what he did. You care about the lives that you're borrowing. They don't need to push you out."

"But if they wanted to, they could."

"Only if they know you're there."

"But you're talking to me as me—how does Marlon not know?"

"Because I'm not talking to him. I'm talking to you."

374

Her phone rings. She takes it out, looks at the screen, and says, "Nathan." After talking to him for a minute, she turns to me and says, "They're getting ready to go home—they want to say thank you. Nathan's going to ride back with them." She passes over the phone, and I talk awkwardly to each of the Giddingses. They are very grateful. I don't know whether or not they realize the only reason X was anywhere near Wyatt was so he could get close to me.

Once she hangs up, Rhiannon tells me she brought her own car just in case things went wrong.

"I didn't want to ride home with them if we failed to bring Wyatt back," she admits.

"Makes sense."

Now it's Marlon's phone that vibrates. His friends are wondering why he missed dinner, and where he is.

"We'd better come up with a pretty good alibi," I say. "What do you think Marlon likes?"

"*Hamilton?*"

"Why do you say that?"

Rhiannon gestures to Marlon's phone case. Which is, indeed, a *Hamilton* phone case.

"The touring company is here in DC right now. Let's send him there."

"How will we get a ticket to that?"

Rhiannon smiles. "He doesn't need to attend. He just needs to think he did. Come on."

We get to the theater just as people are filing in. Rhiannon takes a picture of Marlon in front of the marquee with his thumbs up. He sends it to all his friends. They respond immediately.

No way!

How did U—

We'll cover for ya!

Rhiannon and I head to dinner then, earbuds shared, blasting the cast album.

We end up at a pizza place a few doors down from Politics and Prose. We're both excited for food, and exhausted from the day. I am enjoying my time with her, but about once every five minutes, I think, X *is gone. He's really gone.*

And I don't feel relief. I feel regret.

I know I can't keep this inside. So I tell Rhiannon.

She has no idea, X's voice says in my head. Not really his voice, of course. But now a part of me will use his voice to get its points across.

It doesn't matter. I want to tell her, I say back.

"There have to be others," she assures me. "If there were two of you, there are likely three, if not three thousand. You'll find them. You can have the same conversations with them. Without the evil streak."

I'll never know how evil.

Nor will I ever know if I could have somehow convinced him to go the other way.

I doubt it. But I'll always wonder.

"So what's your plan?" Rhiannon asks. Then, seeing my expression, she clarifies, "For tonight, I mean."

"I'm going to go back to *Hamilton* when it lets out, and get someone to give me a ticket stub. Then I'm going to head to a residential area, because if I keep going to sleep in a hotel, I'm going to end up flying to Paris before I know it. And I want to stay here. Near you."

"Do you want me to stay with you?"

"No. You need to get back. You have school tomorrow."

"I know. But I'll stay if you need me."

"If that's the condition for you staying, then you'll never get to leave."

"You don't need me."

"I absolutely need you. And our whatever-this-is."

"The love that can't find the right word."

"Yes. That's what we have."

"It's weird."

"It definitely is."

"No—something else. I was going to say that it's weird the way I always thought our big question was whether we'd manage to be together. But it's like the question's shifted, and now it's not *whether* we can be together but *in what way* we'll be together."

"And what's the answer to that question?"

"It's the word we haven't found yet. But it's there. I can feel it there."

So can I. And I don't know what to call it, either.

I am just grateful it exists. I am grateful that after everything that's happened, it holds.

An older couple is nice enough to give me one of their ticket stubs. Then I listen to the cast album some more as I walk up to Dupont Circle, writing Marlon's evening inside his head and hoping the memories I'm creating will feel real.

A little before midnight, I use Marlon's phone to order a Lyft. The driver knows to take him back to his hotel.

Very quickly, I fall asleep in the back seat.

RHIANNON

I return to my life. The fact that A is near is definitely a part of it. But it doesn't define it. It can't.

That night, I take my time walking back to my car. I can't get the sight of Wyatt and his family out of my head, or the thought that if we hadn't done something, he might have been lost forever.

This, I realize, it what it feels like to be part of something much bigger than yourself. Not just with friends, but with strangers.

It allows me to understand the strength it takes not just for A to be human, but for all of us to be human, if we want to be important not just to friends, but to strangers.

Months ago, back when I was with Justin, I never would have even approached such thoughts. I was too busy staring down to look out. I can see this now.

It's not that I feel that everything's shifted.

It's that the shifting, once started, is continuous.

That's what it feels like.

When I get to school the next morning, it feels like any other Wednesday. The excitement from the protest has given way to the usual mix.

At lunch, I say to Rebecca, "Do you think that every single

thing that happens in high school can be categorized as either gossip or stress?"

She thinks about it for a second, then says, "That sounds right to me."

Every conversation I hear wears its label instantly. Gossip. Stress. Stress. Stress. Gossip. Stress. Even my own conversations. But not my thoughts. Those are much more complicated. And when I am messaging with A, finding out where A is, what A is up to, it feels like more than gossip and less than stress.

After school, I hang out with Alexander, and I find that our exchanges also resist the labels. When I explained to him that I'd sought shelter in the National Gallery during the protest, he asked me what I'd seen. I told him about the room of Rothkos, and how I was still trying to figure them out. Now, when we get to his room, I see he's hooked a projector up to his laptop.

"Before we hit the books, how about we take a walk through Mr. Rothko's universe?" he asks.

I turn off the lights, and for the next hour, we slip from one painting to the next, the room reflecting the colors off the walls. Alexander plays some music and we don't say too much—only the things that we don't want to keep in, the observations meant to be shared.

I have found someone lighthearted who takes me seriously.

I really like you, I think. Not relative to anything else. Not based on the day we met. On its own terms.

This becomes one of the observations meant to be said out loud.

I tell A about this. I want to be able to tell A about everything. I tell that to A, too.

A responds immediately, saying this is exactly the way it should be. Whatever I feel for Alexander or anyone else doesn't affect our whatever-it-is-we-have.

Together, we are in a separate place, looking at everything else.

After school that Friday, I drive back to DC.

A is waiting for me by the cherry trees, which are looking like any other trees in the months before they bloom. We decide to walk along the Potomac until sunset. The paths are winding and tourist-quiet. The weather is holding back its coldest gusts.

Even though we've written to each other about our weeks, it's not the same as talking about them. So now we get to talk about them, see how the events form themselves into stories.

"There's been no sign of X?" I ask.

"No." I see the burden in A's face, and want to know how to lift it.

"Nathan's been going over to Wyatt's every day," I say. "He's bounced back well, considering. He's certain that he wouldn't have lasted much longer."

"I'm happy for him."

"You don't sound happy."

A looks at me mournfully. "I'm happy and sad at the same time. They don't cancel each other out. They coexist."

"We had to do it," I remind him.

"No, it's not that. It's . . . it's the way he's just *gone.* I keep thinking about how Nathan and I are the only people in the world who will remember him, and Nathan only barely. Because he was hidden, nobody knew he was there. And I know he did awful things—I probably have no idea of the depth of what he did, and how many other people's lives he took away or ruined. But I guess I'm not really thinking of him as much as I'm thinking of myself, and of how easy it would be to disappear without a trace. For sixteen years, if that had happened to me, it would have been like I'd never existed. I knew I could die—we all can die. But having never existed—that feels so much worse."

"But that's not going to happen to you. Not anymore."

"When Wyatt pushed X out—what happened to his body was like a fever was breaking. The body didn't want him there."

"Because X was harming it. That's not you."

"I hope not. But how can I know? How can I possibly judge what harm I do? Nobody should ever be assigned to be their own judge."

"That's why you have me. And you'll find other people. To talk to. To make sure everything is right."

"But why would you want to do that? Why would you want to shackle yourself to a person like me? I can't understand it."

"And I don't understand why you'd want to shackle yourself to a person like *me*," I say. "Don't you think I need your help as much as you need mine? Don't you think I need someone to help me make my judgments, make sure my actions don't cause harm? Yes, our situations are different. But we're both human, and that means we both have the nearly infinite potential to mess things up, and need a nearly infinite amount of patience and grace in order to be the people we should be."

"You are not as messed up as I am."

"I can tell this is going to be a very fun contest."

A stops walking. "Seriously. I wonder if you'd be better off without me. I only make things worse."

Now I'm mad.

"Haven't you learned *anything*? Are you really telling me you want to run again?"

"No. Not at all. But—"

"There's no *but*. We've been through that once, and we are not going to turn it into a cycle. Are you listening to me now?"

"Yes."

"Good. Because I'm only going to say this once. The whole point of love isn't to have fun times without any hard times, to have someone who is fine with who you are and doesn't challenge you to be even better than that. The whole point of love isn't to be the other person's solution or answer or cure. The whole point of love is to help them find what they need, in any way you can. What we have—it's definitely not normal. But the whole point of love is to write your own version of normal, and that is exactly what we're going to do. I am never going to be your girlfriend. We are never going to see each other every single day and introduce each other to all our friends. We are *not* going to the prom. We are not going to worry if we're going to break up after high school. We are not going to worry if we're going to break up after college. We are not going to worry about getting married or not getting married. What we're going to do is be there for each other. We are going to be honest and we are going to share our lives and we are going to mess up together and help fix it together and we are going to make mistakes, often with each other's feelings. But we are going to be there. Day in, day out. Because I don't want you to be my date, A. I don't want you to be in my life and back out of it. I want you to be my constant. That, to me, is the whole point of love."

The minute I say it, I realize: I've found it.
I've found our word.
"Your constant," A says. "My constant."
"Do you understand?"
A smiles. "Yes. I completely understand."

LIAM, AGE 18

You are a coward. You are a coward. You are a coward.

I spent two years telling myself this.

Okay, maybe there was a grace period of two or three weeks—the two or three weeks after I met Peter at the Melbourne Writers Festival.

It was too entirely good to be true. Two bookish, anti-blazer genderqueer kids meeting at a book festival. Like, if you'd asked me, *When you find your true love, where will it be?* I would've said, *At a bookstore or a book festival, duh.*

But I didn't believe it was actually possible.

Until I was right there, in the moment, looking at Peter and thinking, *I must have conjured you. There's no other explanation.*

I didn't usually allow myself to have such thoughts.

No, strike that.

Amend to:

I never, ever allowed myself to have such thoughts.

My best relationships were always with my notebooks, or with the scraps of paper I'd subjugate to my whims each and every day, typing up the words that were worthy of typing each nightfall. I was pretty sure I was going to spend much more time writing about life than actually having a real one.

Enter: Peter.

Of course he had to live in another town.

Of course he had to live way too far away.

Of course, I thought this was a mere formality. What mattered was words.

And words—well, we shared our words every day.

But I was a coward. I took the easy route. I didn't try to see him, hid behind the Internet. Because it wasn't like he was inviting me over. I suspected something was going on with him. I suspected he thought there was something going on with me. He had no idea. I was such a coward.

Then, finally, after two years of trying to get up the courage to see him again, come what may, I saw that a bunch of our favorite authors were going to be at the Adelaide Festival.

I got tickets for the festival.

I saved up money for a last-minute plane ticket.

I told him I was coming.

And in the hour it took for him to respond, I thought, *This is it. The next level. The truth.*

Then he wrote back and said he didn't want to change things. He said words were our thing. We should live and die and love by words.

I was like, *Oh, that's so cool. We're so pure. Blah blah blah.*

But what I was thinking was: *Now you're the coward.*

And I thought: *What are you hiding?*

And I thought: *Was that question directed to him or you, Liam?*

And then I thought: *I have to see this through. Because words are great, but they aren't everything.*

And: *If he's not going to love me in person, then it's not really love.*

So the day came, and I bought that plane ticket.

I didn't message him until I landed.

You can't be here, he wrote.

Oh, I definitely am, I wrote back.

I can't, he wrote.

And I wrote back:

Whatever you're afraid of, I'm afraid of it, too. Whatever you think you're risking, I assure you I'm risking more. I want to see you, whoever you are. And I want you to see me, whoever I am. All or nothing. Now or never.

And he wrote back:

All.

Then:

Now.

By the time I got to the festival, it was in the middle of its opening night party. Revelry in every corner, fireworks in the air. He said he would meet me at the main stage, which would be empty for the night as everyone drank and embraced their merry. He told me he'd be holding a copy of *Black Juice*, the book I'd been reading the day we met. I assured him I'd recognize him, even though I hadn't been sent a photo in a while. He said not to be so sure.

I told him I'd picked up a copy of *Yellowcake*. So he'd recognize me.

I walk into the empty amphitheater, the chairs all waiting for the next morning's first speaker. Behind me, there's music and disco lights and what sounds like a thousand conversations blooming at once. I see a figure in the shadows, can see it's holding a book.

"Peter?" I call out, my voice giving everything about me away.

He steps out of the shadows and I drop my book in surprise. Because he is not a he. He is not Peter at all—he is a girl nowhere near Peter's height.

And she—she is looking at me in surprise as well. Because I am also a girl; not quite as short, but certainly not the height he met me at, either. (I am, however, wearing the same glasses. For some continuity.)

Suddenly it all makes sense. All of it.

"It appears," I say, "we are much more alike than we ever could have imagined."

"And now look," he says. "We've found each other for real."

A: Hello. You don't know me, but I saw your post from a few weeks ago and was hoping I could talk to you.

M: I was a mess then. I'm feeling much better now. But I appreciate your concern.

A: It's not that. (Although I'm very happy to hear you're feeling much better.) It's about what you were describing.

M: The depression?

A: Not that. The other part. About changing every day. I know exactly what you mean. Exactly.

M: Oh.

A: Can we talk?

M: Sure.

NATHAN

I keep going back to it: the one day that altered the course of my life.

But the more I live with it, and the more I live in general, the more I realize: We all have days that alter the course of our lives. Not each and every day, maybe. But a lot of them. Most of them.

Jaiden and I talk about this some, and Wyatt and I talk about it a lot. Sometimes we'll drive up to DC with Rhiannon and Alexander and meet up with A, and we'll all talk about it.

There's no real conclusion to be made. We all agree: There are some days you know ahead of time are going to be important, but most of the important ones end up catching you by surprise. The best thing to do is to treat all your days well.

Then see what happens.

RHIANNON

What I'm learning is that the heart has the capacity to love so many people. I used to think I had to give that capacity to just one person, and never hold back any love for myself. But how wrong I was. I can love A and Alexander and my old friends and my new friends and all of the people A is for one day and all of the people around me who are also trying to throw their weight on the better side of the balance. And I can still have enough love left over for myself, to give me the strength to love all of these other people, to take on some of their burden as they take on some of mine.

Some days I'm up for the challenge.

Some days I need to catch my breath.

But it's a long story we're writing.

Even on the days when it's hard, I know that someday it will be better.

A

Day 6359

The important thing to remember is that I am not alone.
On days when it's hard, I remember I am not alone.
On days when it's easy, I remember I am not alone.
That is what gets me through.
Every day, it gets me through.

ACKNOWLEDGMENTS

Thank you to my parents, who make all my days brighter. And a special thank you to my mother for titling this book.

Love to all of my family and friends.

Thanks to all of the authors I work with, for their patience.

Same to my co-workers at Scholastic.

Special thanks to all of the friends who shared writing space and/or travels with me as I attempted to pin down this book, including but not limited to Billy Merrell, Nick Eliopulos, Zack Clark, Nico Medina, Derek McCormack, Mike Ross, Libba Bray, Justin Weinberger, Chris Van Etten, Alex Kahler, Kurt Hellerich, Caleb Huett, and Lawrence Uhling.

When I heard that a movie was being made of *Every Day*, I thought, *Oh, I have to finish writing the sequel before I see it so it won't have any influence on how I envision the story.* That did not happen. In fact, they made an entire movie in the time it took me to write a hundred pages. Happily, they made a movie I love, and any influence it had was entirely positive. So I would like to thank my friend Jesse Andrews (aka screen-writer extraordinaire), ace director Michael Sucsy (who saw the heart of the story so clearly), all of the movie's producers and crew members, the kickass Orion team, and the remarkable actors who brought A to life, especially Angourie Rice, Justice Smith, Lucas Jade Zumann, and Owen Teague.

Very big thanks to Bill Clegg, Simon Toop, David Kambhu, Marion Duvert, and everyone else at The Clegg Agency.

As always, I must acknowledge the graciousness and enthusiasm of everyone at Random House Children's Books, including (but in no way limited to) Jenny Brown, Barbara Marcus, Mary McCue, Sylvia Al-Mateen, Judith Haut, Adrienne Waintraub, Lisa Nadel, and everyone in the sales, marketing, and production teams. And I'd love to thank everyone at Egmont in the UK, Text in Australia, and all of this book's other foreign publishers for giving it such a wonderful life outside the US.

Thank you to all the readers who've taken these characters to heart.

And to Nancy—all the promises of eternity still hold. May the velvet curtain never be taken down.